LOVE, MAGIC
&
MISFORTUNE

KARLA NIKOLE PUBLISHING

LOVE,
MAGIC
&
MISFORTUNE

KARLA NIKOLE

KARLA NIKOLE PUBLISHING

First Karla Nikole Publishing Edition, July 2021

Copyright © 2021 by Karla Nikole Publishing

ISBN: 978-1-7355898-4-8 (paperback)

ISBN: 978-1-7355898-6-2 (ebook)

Library of Congress Control Number: 2021902846

Cover illustration by Lily Uivel

Contact@LoreAndLust.com

Printed in the United States of America

10 9 8 7 6 5 4 3 2 1

This book is dedicated to anyone and everyone who's striving to live their own authentic and colorful life.

1

THEN

*V*iolet's foot slipped against the tree trunk, but she quickly caught herself, scraping her knee and probably her stockings in the process. She winced at the unmistakable sting. That wouldn't do. Gram would fuss about that later, no question. Although, Violet despised stockings—the scratchy, static-laden material always hung awkwardly low at her crotch —and she'd be glad for one less pair, quite frankly.

Her small fingers gripping the rough crevices of the bark, she steadied herself before lifting an arm to pull up higher. Then a little more, and a little more still. Violet had climbed bigger trees than this. The ones within the wood behind her grandmother's house were much larger—like the beanstalk giants or great kings in the fairy tales from her bedtime stories. This scraggly little apple tree was nothing. A side character. A measly peasant.

Finally, she reached her target: a split where a branch stretched out over the stone gate behind Laurent House. She'd never climbed this particular tree before. Never had to. Usually when she rang the doorbell to the very grand, old home, Mr. or Mrs. Laurent welcomed her inside, smiling and polite. They *were* a little odd. Maybe even eccentric (as old families with old money often were), but always kind. That was just the way of the Laurent family. Everyone thought so.

But something had changed. The adults were being difficult and not telling her anything. When she rang the doorbell now, she was turned away. Sometimes there was no answer at all, even though she distinctly saw smoke rising from the tall chimney above the study.

It was time to take matters into her own hands.

Lifting her head, she scanned the small, cluttered yard, soaked in dreary gray colors despite the morning sunlight. The subtle edges of winter had already frayed the garden, leaving the rose bushes lining the paths thin and brittle. Hollowed. A few short months ago, they were thick and green, dancing with vivid color—singing with the hum of fuzzy bees and the whispered beat of butterfly wings.

Violet's breath puffed in the frosty air. To her amazement, he was there. Her best friend in the world with his big gray eyes— too large for his face, if she was honest about it. Like giant full moons on a stormy night. He was sitting on the ground just beside the stone birdbath, whose covering of twisted ivy leaves had also dried and withered around the basin.

Leaning forward, Violet laid her palm flat against the outstretched branch, cautiously settling her weight. It was a bit wobblier than she would have liked, but no problem, peasant tree that it was. She scooted her body along, just an inch at a time, and leaned a little further forward before taking a deep breath. *"Jasper."*

Her friend looked up with a snap. Moon eyes on hers, his dark eyebrows furrowed. "Vi? What the heck are you doing?"

"Why haven't you come to school?" Violet demanded. "It's been *four weeks*. Are you still itchy all over?"

The silly branch shook underneath her weight. She resettled herself, gripping it tighter and noticing the flakes of bark

2

latching onto the wool of her powder-blue coat sleeves. She'd make sure to pluck those off before returning home—ripped stockings were bad enough.

Jasper paused, blinking at her for a moment. "Yeah... I'm sick."

"You don't look sick."

"Well, I am. Not all sick people *look* sick."

"What's sick about you—" The branch wobbled and Violet gripped it harder. Stupid thing. "When will you be better?"

This time he looked down, staring at whatever strange object was cupped within his small hands. Knowing him, it could be anything—a mathematics puzzle or brain teaser, a dried-up beetle husk or rock that he would swear was remarkable in some way.

"I won't," he said. "Never."

Surprised, Violet jerked against the branch. "What? How can you *never* get better? I don't understand!"

It hadn't been very long. It couldn't have been. Well, in truth, Violet hadn't kept track of the last time they'd met and played together. She never remembered the exact days. Time was just this fuzzy, invisible thing that only seemed to move because the adults around her had told her so. But she knew school had resumed on the fifteenth. *That* had been highlighted on Gram's kitchen calendar: circled in bright red with the thick marker she kept in a jar on the counter.

It had been warm the last time she and Jasper were together —in the clearing of Pont du Coquelicot. Their favorite place. She remembered that much, because he had taken her by the hand and they'd walked together through the tall, swaying grass and late-afternoon sunlight. It had felt like a ride at the fair, the way her heart raced. Jasper had taken her among the trees and shown her the place where he'd found a caterpillar cocooning a nest around itself in preparation for winter. She remembered it because it had all been so exciting. But he'd also been acting a little strange. Afraid, even.

Something inside her felt all wrong now. She couldn't breathe very well, like an elephant was sitting on her chest. "Jas, just—please come to Gram's with me, okay? She's making lemon tarts and—"

"I *can't*, Violet," he said. "I can't... I'm—"

Nothing. She waited, just staring at her friend behind the cold stone wall, sitting in his dreary garden surrounded by dead things. Her dearest friend, so curious and full of life and energy. She couldn't understand.

He lifted his head, meeting her eyes once more. "Listen. I know... Well, Freddie Martin always teases you about your hair when we're at school. But he's an *idiot*, alright? You—your hair is great. It looks happy."

"Happy?" Violet blinked, reaching up and gripping the wild, curly dark mass in her fingers. Dad always told her that it floated about her head like a halo. Whatever that meant. "Happy hair?" she asked.

"Yeah." He smiled, staring with his giant moon eyes. "It-It's pretty. Don't listen to him, okay? Ever."

"Jas—" A distinct cracking sound made Violet's breath hitch, then something like a *womp* made her stomach jump up into her throat. The next sensation was very hard and cold. There was pain in her leg and arm, and she felt dizzy—spinning, although there was no way she could have been.

And then nothing. There was nothing at all after that.

NOW

*G*ram looked tired and ancient. Technically, she'd seemed old ever since Violet was a little girl. That's what a grandmother was to a child: a lovely elderly person (for the lucky children, anyway).

Even so, the woman had always radiated life, tenacity and love. It overflowed from her like the buttery, sugary goodness of a cake spilling over and out of its Bundt pan.

"The cottage is yours," she whispered to Violet, stretching her withered hand up and placing it on Violet's cheek. "Everything. And my secret recipe for the cannelés."

The sterile white hospital room felt like a dim cave. A highly advanced one, with its monotonous hum of machines, echoing beeps and chilly atmosphere. Violet shook her head, tears pouring down her face. "Gram, that stuff isn't important right now."

"You've been pestering me about that recipe for years. I thought you'd be pleased? Just... promise me you won't make them for any of those selfish boneheads you date—"

"*Gram.*" Violet laughed. They both did.

"Save my cannelés for someone special. You haven't mentioned anyone in a long while."

"Because there isn't anyone," Violet assured her. "There won't be for a long time, I don't think. I'm over it—dating and trying to find 'the one.' What does that even mean?"

"Well, I could tell you that there are many fish in the sea, but I don't blame you. I've found that the world is chock-full of interesting things for a woman to do."

Gloria was a woman who'd done many things. She lived freely, dabbling and creating, giving and supporting herself and others. All the while, she exuded an aura of joy—a soul truly living in their own freedom and choices.

Gram took a deep breath, her fragile state apparent once more. The signs of her fatigue had almost disappeared for a second. Just a glorious moment, as if she'd hop up out of the bed, pull Violet toward the door and insist on showing her the secret, prized canelé recipe step-by-step.

But it wasn't so. Gram closed her eyes, her chest slowly rising and falling in the silence. When she spoke again, her eyelids seemed heavy as they opened. "I want you to do something for me."

"Anything." Violet smiled. Gram would have all manner of unfinished business to address: money to be raised, cakes to be baked and townspeople to be helped. The local schoolhouse might require a new roof, or a bridge tournament would need to be organized at the local community center. Gloria ran the village like a queen, and her loyal subjects had filled her hospital room with flowers, potted plants, balloons and well-wishes from the moment she'd fallen ill. It was only calm like this in the evenings. During the day, Violet directed streams of people coming in and out like an air traffic controller.

Soon, the queen would pass her torch. Of course there were things that needed to be done.

"I'll do whatever you want," Violet whispered, lifting and

kissing the back of her grandmother's hand. "I'll take care of it. Bake sales, church bazaars, whatever. You don't need to worry." It wasn't all just cookie-cutter grandma stereotypes. There were more eccentric things, too, but Violet wasn't sure how she'd handle all that. She would, but it would take a more delicate hand. A little bit of research and study.

Gloria Marie shook her head. "No, sweet pea, nothing like that. The town will take care of itself…"

"Okay, then, what is it?"

Gloria opened her eyes wider, her gaze soft. "Jasper. Just, check on him sometimes. Don't… Don't leave him all alone."

Violet's stomach did a twisty thing as she sat straighter. "Wh-What? Why?"

Another gasp. A gentle rise and fall of the sheets covering Gloria Marie's frail body. "That boy was dealt a very bad hand. I left instructions. Please, sweet pea?"

Gram closed her eyes again, her lips parted—then nothing. The weighted silence was only broken by the rhythmic beeping of the machines around them. Violet rested her head at Gloria Marie's side, clasping her wrinkled, frail hand in both of hers as if to hold onto her and keep her in the land of the living. Willing it with all her might.

But her effort was useless. The next day, Gloria went quietly —peacefully encircled by her granddaughters and cherished friends within the community. They wept together, holding each other against the loss of a great anchor that had stabilized them in countless ways.

Violet had been given specific instructions. Her grandmother's dying words. Not "I love you," of which Violet had no doubt was true. No insecurities there.

No regrets or lamentations of missed opportunities in life. No deep, dark secrets confessed. Nothing one might expect of a person lying on their deathbed. Instead, a sincere request: Please check on Jasper. Go and see about the boy with big moon eyes. But he wouldn't be a boy anymore. He'd be a man now—nearly twenty-five, the same as Violet.

What in the world for?

~

VIOLET DABBED the cotton handkerchief at her eyes, wiping away the tears there. It wasn't fair. She'd known it was inevitable: these moments were one of the few, absolute certainties of life. Inescapable. But still, she found herself unprepared. Perhaps, a person could never be prepared enough to lose someone they love. Not ever.

Rose, Violet's older sister, snaked an arm around her shoulder, holding her tight. Of course Rose wasn't crying. She was always the sensible one, with everything in perfect order: her character akin to a solid, immovable boulder while Violet floated through life with the whimsy of a bird's stray feather.

Lifting her head, Violet focused on the puffy white clouds overhead, drifting silent across the perfect blue sky. At least the weather was nice for Gram's funeral. Crisp with a light breeze. It was chilly for so early in October, but the day proved to be a lovely send-off, nonetheless.

When the Bishop recited the last prayers, Violet turned into her sister's embrace and wept, letting all the sorrow and hurt pour out. She'd received the call about Gram taking ill a week ago. Had it been a week? Time felt fuzzy even as an adult. But now, its movement was rampant and utterly beyond her control: much too fast in some moments and excruciatingly slow in others.

Eventually, she pulled her head from her sister's embrace as they stood in the graveyard washed in overcast sunshine.

"I'll head over to the community center first to greet everyone. You two take your time." Jillian leaned in, giving Rose a quick peck on the lips before affectionately rubbing Violet's shoulder.

"Thanks, Jill." Rose sighed. She reached down, taking Violet's hand as her partner walked away. "Are we alright?"

"More or less," Violet shrugged. The crowd dispersed, moving across the dried lawn and toward the long row of parked cars on the gravel road. The view from the hill of the cemetery was majestic despite the dour setting—shadowed purple mountains framed the horizon, enclosing the charming country village she'd grown up in. Violet inhaled deeply, filling her lungs with the cool earthiness of the air as if it would cleanse her.

"Who is that?" Rose asked.

Violet looked up, following her sister's gaze. Past the row of cars and atop the gentle slope of another hill, a lanky man stood in a hooded coat. As if knowing he was being watched, he turned and descended the other side of the slope, disappearing from sight.

"One of the newer townies?" Rose guessed. "I thought everyone we grew up with was here."

"Maybe..." Violet said, skeptical. "Let's head to the hall and get this over with. I'm tired of being around all these people."

SEVERAL HOURS LATER, Violet sank deep into the couch in her grandmother's sitting room, a hot cup of spiced tea cradled in her palms. A profound weight sat heavily in her heart... But somehow, the house felt like a loving embrace. Gloria's embrace. The vibrant smell of Roman chamomile and mint blooming on the covered back patio, the fire burning low just before her and a soft knitted blanket across her lap. Gram might be gone, but in many ways, she was still very much present.

"A couple years ago, she told me she was leaving the house to you." Rose walked into the sitting room holding her own mug, taking a seat just beside Violet on the couch. "I think she didn't want me to be upset. As if I would be."

"You never liked it here," Violet acknowledged, bringing her own cup to her lips. "Your daily, teenaged lamentation of 'I miss my friends in LA' made it very clear… I'm surprised it's not tattooed somewhere on you—"

"I couldn't wait to get the hell out of this boring little town and start my real life, but Gram had to push *you* out of the nest. I couldn't believe you almost turned down that job."

A sudden clang in the kitchen made both Violet and Rose sit straighter and turn their heads.

"Sorry, I'm fine, I swear," Jillian called out.

Violet looked at her sister, her voice low. "*Is* she fine? She always seems scatterbrained to me."

Rose shrugged. "It's because her work is so crazy and demanding. There was some big buyer's meeting she was prepping for, but it got cancelled at the last minute. She said it was with a famous company, too. Huge upset for her team."

"What famous company?"

"Oh, I have no idea. She insists the details are confidential, *and* mind-numbing, so she spares me."

"Hm," Violet sighed, laying her head back against the couch. "I still don't quite understand what she does. Whatever it is, is her company hiring? I hate my job, Rosie. My bosses are—Do you know what it's like to have to keep track of everything you do, because at any given moment, you might be accused of *not* doing something? I literally have a folder on my desktop called 'Proof,' where I screenshot every single task I complete—a spreadsheet of every action I take because I always need to cover myself. What kind of work environment is that?"

"A steady one. A profitable one."

"It's hostile."

"You make excellent money—"

"Is money everything?" Violet asked. "Is it worth my sanity? That's how they get you stuck in the hamster wheel. You make money so you can survive and buy things, and then you need more things so you have to keep making even more money. Gram wasn't stuck in a hamster wheel. She lived by her own rules. And Ambrose Marcello says—"

"Oh no, here we go—"

"*He* says, 'Chasing money yields money, but chasing life yields riches beyond measure.' What am I chasing, Rosie? Being a drone and always covering my tracks."

Rose turned and stared at her. Awkwardly.

"What?" Violet asked, frowning.

"You. Quoting that goofy writer. And Gram was a total hippy."

"She wasn't. She was free. And Ambrose is *not* goofy."

"He's hot." Rose smirked. "I'll give him that. That's seventy-five percent of his appeal."

"Well, it certainly doesn't hurt him, does it?"

They were both silent, but Rose's expression shifted into what Violet recognized as her serious 'big sister' face. "Keep your excellent job. Stay the course. If you move back here, what are you going to do in this sleepy Mary Poppins town, huh? Piddle around Gram's creaky old-lady hippy cottage—"

"Charming cottage. It's charming—"

"Read through her weird herbalist books and daydream about how much fun you had living here when we were kids? Hoping to catch a glimpse of that creepy boy in Laurent House."

"Don't—No. That's *not* it, Jasper has nothing to do with my decision. Don't talk about him that way."

"You haven't seen him since you were nine. Nobody has. He's allegedly 'sick' but his parents moved away ages ago and left him up there alone in that rundown manor. Who knows what the hell is going on? And I don't like the idea of you back here and fixated on that situation, *again*." Rose set her mug on the table in front of them, then twisted to fully face her sister. "You finally left here and started building a good life outside this boring village. Please don't use Gram's passing as an excuse to saddle yourself back here."

Violet considered her sister and the sincerity in her eyes. Rose always wore her brown hair straightened, and it framed her pale, slim face like a very dark and heavy curtain. "*Rose is so lovely, she should model.*" People had said as much over and over when they were both young. Within the ethnic spectrum between their parents' genes, Violet had gotten *all* of the curls, and *all* of the curves. Every last bit of them.

And she was glad for it. Growing up, she'd thought of herself as odd compared to her peers. Different. But now, she felt unique—embracing her brown, sun-kissed skin and the smattering of dark freckles across her nose.

Turning her head, Violet stared into the fireplace. She understood her sister's perspective, but they were different people with different lives. Violet had tried the "young woman moves away from home for a fancy job in the big city" bit. She'd been doing it now for three years. She hated it.

"You just don't get it. I love this house and this town. I'm staying."

"Ugh." Rose fell back into the couch, slouching.

"What's the problem?" Jillian said, pulling her blonde, straight hair into a ponytail as she walked into the room. She plopped down in a nearby armchair. "You trying to boss your baby sis around and failing miserably?"

Violet lifted her mug to her lips. "As per usual..."

"This house is beautiful," Jillian said. "There's so much interesting stuff here. I don't blame you for wanting to stay."

"*I* do," Rose whined. "You're too young and headstrong to be stuck in a sleepy place like this. You could do and be so much more. I just feel like you're wasting your potential."

"First, that's insulting," Violet said, frowning, "I'm enough.

Right now, as I am. Screw 'potential.' I had an ex-boyfriend that used to say that to me and I really disliked it. Second, it's *my* life. Stop making me feel bad about my choices. You're being a jerk."

Rose whipped her head toward Violet, her lip stuck out in a full pout. "I'm a jerk for wanting to protect you? For keeping you from chasing unrealistic hippy-dippy fantasies when you've already got something solid? And I know Gram used to take your weird little friend groceries every week. She asked you to take over, didn't she? *That's* what this is about."

"Stop calling him weird and creepy—and he's not 'little' anymore. He'll be twenty-five on Christmas Eve."

Silence. Both women stared at Violet, accusation written all over their faces. Violet shrunk. "This is not about a man. I'm still going to work my terrible job remotely, alright? They know I'm here managing Gram's estate. Surprisingly, as long as I'm accessible online, they've told me to take my time. I just want to be here and mourn right now. Can you stop being so pushy about it?"

"Yeah, stop being so pushy," Jillian chimed in, smiling. "Pushy woman—like you're always in a bloody courtroom. Vi never listens to you anyway."

"Exactly." Violet smiled at her sister. "So give it a rest. Your lawyer is showing. Might want to cover that up."

Rose lifted her chin. "Oh shut up, both of you. Why shouldn't you listen to me? I have a career that I love, stability, a wonderful partner—"

"Aw, cheers, babe," Jillian gushed.

"And I want these things for you, too," Rose continued. "I don't see how that makes me a jerk."

"So, Vi," Jillian said, sitting straight and narrowing her green eyes at Violet. "What are you going to do with all your gram's stuff? Are you just going to keep everything as is?"

There was so much stuff, in the typical way that people who lived long lives ceaselessly gathered worldly possessions across time: trinkets placed in corners, books stuffed in shelves, boxes stacked in closets. Violet sighed. "I have no idea."

"Well, let us know when you decide," Rose said, folding her arms and smirking. "I'll try to stifle my inner *jerk lawyer* when we come help you."

Violet grinned. "You're feeling pretty salty about that comment, huh?"

"I am."

"Good," Violet said. "That'll teach you."

3

NOW

Notes for my sweet pea:

#1. Jasper needs groceries once a week.
Only visit between 2pm—5pm. Otherwise
he won't answer.
#2. Be patient with him.
#3. Contact Simone Bisset about the
pantry herbs. She'll help.
#4. Take all the Bingo stuff in the
garage over to Old Sal.

"*W*hy are there specific visiting hours? Isn't he in the house all the time?" Violet flipped the little notepaper over in her hand. It was two-sided and filled with Gloria Marie's unmistakable handwriting. Gram had also organized her will, land deed and all remaining documents into a neat folder in a bedroom dresser drawer.

Violet leaned her head back and closed her eyes, exhaling and listening to the rain pitter-pattering against the car. She missed her grandmother's voice and the very soul and essence of her being. Her physical presence. But the absence of Gloria Marie's voice—that self-assured and bright tone singing over her, always encouraging her, comforting her—created an unexpected chasm in the center of Violet's chest. A hole that might never again be filled.

She took another breath in the rainy silence, opening her eyes and staring at the note in her hands just as a ray of gray sunlight caused the surrounding slick pavement of the parking lot to glow. On the backside of the handwritten note, her grandmother had written two sentences: *Live the life you really want, sweet pea. I love you.*

"The life I want..." What did she want, exactly? Violet glanced around, taking in the mundane view of the local grocery store with its faded green scalloped awning. The line of bright red grocery carts neatly arranged out front and dripping with water. Today was particularly gray, with raindrops pelting against the windshield before racing down in long streams. Quiet tears from the sky to match her melancholy.

After several days of crying and staying huddled within the loving comfort of Gram's cottage, Violet finally mustered the energy to go out. Unfortunately, the weather wasn't in agreement with her decision. Autumn was officially settling in and having its way.

Violet knew that she wanted to be here, in this village. It was her home and she loved it. The wild, grassy fields swaying in the summertime, all stretched out around Gram's cottage and framed by thick woods. The flowers blooming in spring like fireworks, and the way the snow flattened everything down in winter—a heavy, fluffy comforter. All around, the jagged bluish-purple mountains acted as a loving fortress, protecting the town's inhabitants. She wanted to be here, but she wanted to be free, too.

What does that mean? What does it look like?

Her phone buzzed and she pursed her lips. This. This long leash was *not* freedom. Reaching inside her bag, she groaned and pulled her mobile out to glance at the screen.

[Janet: Did you send me the estimates for the T-shirt order?]

Violet switched over to her email to verify, then typed out a text before hitting send.

[Yes. I sent it in an email on Monday at 2:47 p.m.]

Three days ago, mind you. Not that they were in a time-crunch to get the T-shirts ordered. Except they *were*, as had been emphasized by her bosses in earlier meetings.

[Janet: Well, I don't see it.]

"Did you even look?" Rolling her eyes, Violet quickly flipped back to her email, found the correspondence in question and re-forwarded it to her boss. Yes, she could have just texted the info, but... Proof.

[I just re-sent it to your email. Please let me know you received it.]

Dropping her hands and the phone in her lap, Violet contemplated. She needed something hearty and warm to eat tonight. Some kind of baked casserole with molten cheese. Lasagna? After a moment, her phone buzzed in her grip.

[Janet: Got it. Thanks. Let's place the order.]

[Will do.]

Violet punched the necessary information into the website and placed the order. When finished, she twisted around for her umbrella in the back seat, drew up the hood of her raincoat and grabbed the door handle. Her phone buzzed again—over and over.

[Karen: What's happening with the T-shirts?]
[Karen: Don't order them yet!]
[Karen: They're way too expensive!!]
[Karen: Should we look into a cheaper alternative??]
[Karen: My cousin might be able to print T-shirts for us.]
[Karen: He has a thing in his garage.]

Violet exhaled a heavy sigh, threw her phone into the passenger seat and took her chances with the rain.

◊

"DIDN'T GET to talk with you at Gloria's funeral last weekend." Freddie Martin scanned her groceries (at an excruciatingly slow pace), smirking like he knew something she didn't. Whatever it was, Violet would rather not know. Anything he knew probably wasn't worth knowing.

"Didn't think there was anything to talk about," Violet said, avoiding his gaze and digging in her purse.

18

"You moving back here?"

"Not sure yet."

"You got that fancy-pants job in the city... you're a fancy-pants girl now."

"I don't know what that means. Please don't talk about my pants."

"No boyfriend up there? Girlfriend?"

"That is *unquestionably* none of your business."

Freddie swiped the peanut butter across the scanner, then paused, holding the jar up and looking at it in great detail. She'd never seen anyone ring groceries so slowly. It was a wonder how he stayed in business.

"Can you move with a little more urgency, please?" she asked, shifting toward the end of the lane and pulling her reusable bags from her purse to pack the groceries herself.

"Are you taking over *all* your Gram's business affairs?" he wiggled his dark golden eyebrows. "I know she's got some fun stuff in that greenhouse out back. And is all of this going up to Jasper?"

"Again, none of that is any of your business." She rearranged the items, frowning. Strawberries, fresh salad greens, almond milk and a bar of dark chocolate. Packing grocery bags was a bit like playing Tetris. Violet enjoyed the humdrum task, but she needed to concentrate. Good spatial reasoning took focus.

"He comes out once in a blue moon—was down here the other day since Gloria passed and nobody can take food up to him anymore. He's like the Boogeyman."

"You're the only Boogeyman around here that I've ever encountered."

"I offered to help him... said I'd take the groceries up to him, but he didn't want me to, of course..."

"Sounds like his intelligence is still firmly intact." Finally, the last item, a large bag of sunflower seeds, made its way down the conveyor belt and Violet placed it on top.

Freddie cocked his eyebrow. "Sassy Violet Ainsworth—you grew up pretty. The city's been feeding you well. Your hips match your hair."

"And your mouth still matches your butthole. Ring up my groceries and spare me your observations." Violet dug into her bag and pulled her wallet out with a little more force than was needed.

He chuckled again, totaling her order. "Relax, darling, I meant it as a compliment. Fancy-pants women don't like compliments?"

"We don't like idiots." Her transaction complete, Violet put her debit card away, dropped her wallet into her purse and grabbed the grocery bags, moving as far away from Freddie as quickly as possible.

THE BOOGEYMAN...

Laurent House was one of the oldest manors in the village. It sat a little farther off than the other homes, but was still easily accessible. The perimeter was lined with a stone wall. Oddly, it had seemed much higher when Violet was little, the enormity of it exaggerated in her capricious child's mind. Dry ivy crawled up the front face of the home like spider limbs, reaching and creeping along the dusty beige stucco—even stretching over the dirty white window shutters.

Juxtaposed with the skeletal apple orchard, it wasn't spooky, exactly. It simply... needed some love. A little affection. From whom, Violet didn't know. But she'd played in the gardens here as a child. Had run amidst the apple blossoms in spring. It had been wonderful and not scary at all. She held those memories like warm candlelight at the forefront of her heart as she climbed out of the car, grocery bag in hand, and made her way toward the wrought iron gate. Thankfully the rain had subsided, leaving the air heavy and chilly with damp. It made her feel like a mist-breathing dragon.

Jasper was sick, but with what? No one knew for certain. There were speculations, of course. The adults had rationalized possibilities of a more serious nature—leukemia, lupus or some other autoimmune disease. But the children were, of course, ridiculous in their guesses: he was a vampire or rife with cooties. Overflowing with them to the point where contact with another person was detrimental. Violet hadn't known any better than the rest despite being his best friend, but she'd always defended him fiercely.

She never saw him after that day in the garden when she fell from the apple tree. The situation had been a mess: a broken arm and wrist, coupled with a strict mandate from Gloria that she was forbidden from climbing another tree ever again. Her wrist still ached on rainy days like this.

The iron gate squeaked loudly as she pulled it open. Walking down the cobbled path, she glanced around at the wide, open yard. The grass was overgrown and dry where once it had been luscious and green.

As she approached the wooden door, she lifted her wrist to check her watch: 4:22 p.m. Well within the apparent 2:00 p.m. to 5:00 p.m. visitation range. Shouldering the single grocery bag, she took hold of the brass knocker and struck it against the faded olive-green surface.

A rustling immediately to her right made her jump in surprise. When she looked down, a black cat with white paws came hobbling out of the bushes underneath the window.

"Hey kitty." She looked closer, finding that one of its front paws was wrapped in a bandage. The cat meowed in response, but then walked away, turning a corner and disappearing around the side of the house.

Violet waited. No sound. No movement. She stepped back from the porch, glancing around at the five rectangular windows: three on the second floor, two on either side of the door on the first. No lights were on despite the dark, overcast gloom of the weather.

Stepping forward, she tried again. Knocked. Waited. Nothing.

"Is he here?" Truthfully, she wanted to see him. Perhaps deep down, and in a place she'd never speak of (especially not to her bossy sister), she desperately wanted to see him. A small part of her ached with it. She wasn't proud. Surely, she should have moved on by now. Should be the uncaring, flippant and mature woman she presented to everyone. The one that said, "Jasper? Who? Oh, the eccentric boy from my childhood? I never think of him."

It would be a lie. She thought of him often. For five years of her life, he'd been a staple—an integral part of her existence, not unlike water or sunlight. After her mother had died, Violet, her father and Rose had moved here to live with Gram. She'd been five years old then, and in complete misery. It had been so empty and lonely: the world suddenly a scary, sinister place that had snatched someone precious away from her.

But then Jasper was there. Her very first friend in this new, terrifying world. A kind and gentle guide in an unfamiliar landscape.

After a third knock with no response, Violet set the grocery bag down, tucking it as closely to the pale, paint-chipped door as possible. She walked back down the lane, looking over her shoulder once. Then a second time. As she walked back through the gate and toward her car, she repeated to herself the second instruction of her Gram's note. The quick but elegant handwriting practically floated to the forefront of her mind.

Be patient with him.

4

THEN

"Iguess the colors are pretty..." Violet tilted her head, examining the bug. She frowned, then shifted her head the other way for a different perspective. *Still creepy.*

Jasper moved in closer. Uncomfortably so. No person's face should ever be that close to such a large insect. He placed his palm against the dark tree trunk, careful to avoid the creeping beetle. "This one is a Rosalia longicorn. It's my favorite because of all the little designs on its back and antennae. Can you see?"

"Yeah, I can see."

Violet watched him shift along the tree trunk, squatting down in a kind of duckwalk as he moved.

"Bugs and animals... They have their own completely separate world from ours. I think it's amazing. We act so important, but they don't mind us at all. We just get in their way."

"Well..." Violet considered. "This one is definitely better than that other one you showed me before. That yellow 'musky' one."

Jasper laughed. "The Capricorne musqué. Yeah, that one's a stinker." Jasper adjusted his hands to carefully scoop the slow insect into his palms. When he stood straight, he turned to Violet. "Do you want to try?"

"Hm, okay." Violet held her palms flat as Jasper stepped in front of her. His fingers brushed her palms, delicate in placing the large, colorful insect against her skin. Violet bristled but stood her ground. The bug sat still in her hands. "It's so light." She squinted, examining the detailed markings on its back and legs. "It's like he has art all over his body."

"*She*, maybe?" Jasper smiled. "It's cool, huh? It hangs out here because of all the flowers. This species likes pollen." Jasper placed his palms underneath hers, cupping her hands. "I'll put it back. You can open your palms."

Violet did as instructed and Jasper placed the artsy bug back against the tree. While he did so, Violet turned away, the spring breeze flittering her sundress as she hopped, then hopped again like a bunny toward the open field. The grass swayed all around her, the birdsong especially noisy, as if they were having a concert just for the two of them. She spun around.

"Jas?"

"Yeah?"

"Do you want to study bugs and animals when you grow up?"

"Maybe. There are so many different kinds. It would be fun to see them in different places."

"Oh, in other countries?"

"Sure." Jasper stood, wiping his palms against his pleated trousers. "Forests, jungles, deserts... A traveling bug scientist of some sort. What about you?"

Violet paused. He was staring at her with those great big eyes and her heart was beating way too fast. She flipped around, looking toward the field. "I don't know. I haven't got a clue."

He moved toward her, his feet shuffling through the grass. "Well, you can decide any time. Don't worry about it."

Glancing from the corners of her eyes, she spotted him

standing beside her. "Let's try lots of different things together. Maybe we'll find something you really like?"

Hesitating, she reached down and took hold of his hand. When she gripped his palm, he squeezed. Her heart was still beating much too quickly to be considered normal, but when he met her gaze, she smiled. "Okay."

"Do you think your gram is finished with the tarts?" he asked, a bashful little smile on his mouth.

Violet stepped forward, pulling Jasper as she moved toward the cottage. "Let's find out!"

5

NOW

*J*anet fumed through the phone. "We don't have enough T-shirts. I sent you emails with updates for the order. Did you not get them?"

Violet had made a shared spreadsheet with 'names,' 'dates' and 'number of requested shirts per family,' asking both of her bosses to update the data as they saw fit and as they received direct requests. Perfect organization and meticulous planning—a wonderful system to keep things in order.

Utterly ignored. What Violet had received instead was a barrage of carelessly forwarded email chains across four weeks with any number of correspondences that she was expected to manually decipher and count. It had been a complete mess.

"I received them," Violet explained. "But the number of participants in your correspondences weren't always clear and there were multiple emails. I tried my best to keep track of your numbers. I'll have more T-shirts delivered as soon as possible—"

"Do you know how expensive expedited shipping is?" Janet exclaimed. "Just forget it. I might have some T-shirts from last year's event in my basement. I'll pull those out and count them.

This is one of the most important marketing events of the year, Violet. I expect things to be flawless."

Violet sighed. Things *would* be flawless if she weren't always being set up for failure. Should she mention that she ran the final T-shirt count by her bosses twice? Probably not.

"I understand, and I apologize sincerely for this mishap." Should she mention that they were only missing three T-shirts, and that two people had already cancelled attending the event (and that they had ordered one for her, too, and she could always give hers up)?

Nope.

"We'll talk more about this in our meeting next week. This is *your* job, Violet. The expectation is for these things to be taken care of. I know we're letting you work remote because of your grandmother but... if I have to step in and do things like this, maybe we should reevaluate your role here."

Gosh, over three T-shirts. Mind you, because of Violet's marketing efforts, this event had already raised more funds than any of their past events, and would have the highest attendance.

"Understood," Violet said.

When she hung up the phone, she looked at her wristwatch: 12:46 p.m. She logged off her computer. It had been a week since she'd dropped the first bag off at Laurent House, so according to Gram's schedule, she was due for another trip. She grabbed her coat and purse, deciding to make the hour-long drive into the city for her grocery haul. An uncomfortable encounter with Freddie Martin was the absolute last thing she needed right now.

When she reached the front door to the cottage, her work phone buzzed. Pulling it out of her bag, she glanced at the screen.

[Karen: Shoot I missed the call.]
[Karen: What are we doing about the T-shirts we're missing?]

Karen: How many is it?]

[Karen: OMG this is so stressful!!!]

[Karen: Should I ask my cousin about the thing in his garage?!]

Violet set the phone down on the foyer table and left.

THE DAY WAS sunny and bright after a week of dreary rain. It made the drive into the city all the more pleasant and Violet had even cracked her windows for some fresh air despite the chill.

Pulling up to Laurent House, it looked slightly less homely because of the sunshine. It was still in desperate need of some care, but its derelict nature wasn't as severe juxtaposed against a lovely blue sky.

She pulled her wool coat a little tighter against her body, then grabbed the heavy grocery bag and headed toward the door. She'd bought a little extra for Jasper since she knew she'd have to travel into the city next week for the work event. She'd do the shopping again the day after, but she wanted to be certain.

Standing on the porch, the yard and house were silent again. Nothing stirred as she used the heavy knocker. She waited.

Quiet. Only the rustling of dry leaves in the apple orchard.

"Well, last week's bag is gone, at least..."

Sighing, she placed the new grocery bag against the door. But she lost her breath when it whipped open as she bent down, scaring her half to death.

"Oh *good God.*" Her heart in her throat, she lurched upright. Violet blinked, palm flat against her chest as she stared at the man peeking through the cracked door.

It was Jasper, for certain. He was the same, but different. Not Jasper as a boy, but Jasper as a man. Taller, with squared features rather than soft, rounded ones. And those big gray eyes. He'd grown into them a little. But not entirely.

"You *scared* me," Violet breathed, her heart pounding.

"Sorry... Hello."

"Hi..."

Time—that fuzzy, indiscernible thing—stood still. She took him in. His cheeks were shallow, pale, but he wasn't a Boogeyman like Freddie had said. He did look a bit... something. Not akin to a monster. Perhaps a human that lived his life among the dust bunnies underneath a bookshelf. Like maybe before running to the door, he'd set his book down, rolled out from under the shelf and hastily fluffed out his hair—the color of it dark but warm, like black coffee or chocolate.

He looked like that.

Violet swallowed. "I... You—"

"Listen, you don't need to keep doing this."

She blinked, drawing back a little. His voice had changed, too. A smooth, warm tone. Assured. Not the animated squeak of a little boy or the breathy rasp of a sick person. "Wh-What?"

"Gloria put you up to this, I know. But you don't need to do it. I can manage, so please don't feel obligated to take this on?"

He stared, awaiting her response. Violet swallowed and settled her shoulders to knock herself out of whatever had come over her. "Jasper Oliver Laurent."

He winced as if she'd cursed him. "Yes?"

"We haven't seen each other in almost *fifteen years.*" She paused, wide-eyed, letting that truth sink in.

Taking a breath, he reached his hand up, mussing his hair. She half expected a puff of dust to swirl up as a result of his action. "It-It's been a long while."

"Would it be okay if we had tea together? Maybe caught up a little?"

Jasper bit the inside of his bottom lip, a subtle movement,

but Violet noticed it nonetheless. It was at least one trait he'd carried forward from his boyish days. "I... Hm..."

"Yes?"

He'd looked away, but his anxious gray eyes flicked back to her. He inhaled another deep breath. "Well, okay. Alright. Just for a short time... I'm sick, Violet."

"Are you contagious?"

"In some intrinsic ways. Potentially."

"What does that mean?"

He shrugged. Nothing.

Violet shook her head. "Are you tired? Will I get sick if I come in and have tea with you?"

"Well, no... and no."

"Okay..." The nervousness Violet felt in this moment slowly morphed into something else. She repressed a laugh, marveling at the awkwardness between them. Life was interesting in this way. The same two people who were once so close—sharing significant time, space and affection together—could later transform into complete strangers.

He took a deep breath, dropping his shoulders as he leaned down to grab the grocery bag from in between them. "Sorry. Okay, please come in."

"You don't need to be sorry," Violet said, stepping over the threshold. "Thank you for having me."

The light inside was dim, the curtains drawn closed in the adjacent great room. Even still, it was easily apparent that the house was a mess. Jasper didn't need to live underneath a book-shelf to be among the dust bunnies. The house itself was filled with them.

Newspapers, magazines and books were stacked on and around the foyer table, all frosted with a thin layer of dust. A tall oak coatrack stood beside a large gilded mirror hanging on the wall. The ornamental rug was the same one from when they were kids, and it too had seen better days—now faded to a pale burgundy, the pattern worn in the center and the edges frayed. She looked up. The light fixture overhead was also covered in wispy, floating cobwebs.

Why on earth is he living like this?

"Um, this way…" Jasper said, gesturing with his free hand. "The house is a mess but the study is a little better. We can sit in there."

He walked forward, down the dim corridor, and Violet followed. The house even smelled timeworn. Not bad, but of dusty things—old furniture and paper, the air dry and cool. Opening a few windows would be an easy fix. Old family portraits on the walls showed Jasper as a boy, grinning ear-to-ear as a happy and healthy child. Other photographs revealed his parents smiling and posed close together—one of his father and mother gazing romantically into each other's eyes and another of the three of them, hugging and laughing. The images were like stills from a movie reel of a blissful family.

"You can sit on the couch," Jasper said when they reached the wide entrance to the study. "I'll put the groceries away and make tea." He stalked off, his long legs carrying him toward the kitchen.

Violet stepped inside. Here too, the curtains were shut. Only a single beam of sunlight streamed in, hitting the creaky hardwood floor. The rest of the room was primarily lit by warm firelight dancing in the hearth, casting shadows over the adjacent wall of bookcases and the desk in a nearby corner. She settled on the brown leather couch. It was soft, and not dusty like everything else she'd seen thus far. Clearly, this room was where Jasper spent most of his time.

Glancing around, Violet observed the details of the space. A laptop on the desk. Beside it, black-rimmed glasses, a coffee mug and… nuts? Trail mix, just sitting atop some papers. A different coffee mug on the low table in front of her along with lots of books. She immediately recognized some titles. Violet leaned forward and picked one up, turning it over in her hands in amazement.

She flipped through the pages, skimming one of her favorite passages as Jasper returned with a tray of cups and a teakettle. She narrowed her eyes. Something about the tea set was very familiar as he placed it down on the table (and atop a stack of books, inevitably).

"Is this Gram's?" she asked. She hadn't seen this particular set since she was a teenager.

He nodded. "Yes. She gave it to me a long time ago for when she came over—you can take it with you today if you—"

"No, that's not what I meant. I'm just surprised. So, she would sit with you?"

Violet knew that Gram had been dropping off Jasper's groceries for many years now. At least since he'd turned eighteen. But she was under the impression that it was a simple "drop and run" delivery arrangement. She hadn't known that Gloria regularly spoke with him, let alone sat and had tea with him. Why wouldn't she have mentioned that?

Jasper stepped around the table, sitting in the armchair adjacent to the couch. The fireplace flickered and popped behind him. "Yes," he said, rubbing his palms across his faded charcoal trousers. "She'd come inside and visit when she dropped off the groceries." There was a moment of hesitation, but then he looked up at Violet, meeting her eyes. "I'm so sorry about her passing. She—Gloria was truly a wonderful person."

Smiling, Violet took a breath to soothe the permanent ache in her chest. "She was. And pretty fond of *you*, it seems."

Jasper waved a hand. "She pitied me. There's a difference." He leaned forward, gripping the kettle handle and pouring hot water into her cup. "I only have chamomile, but there's lemon or honey, if you'd like."

Pitied him? Violet didn't say so, but she disagreed. Gloria Marie wasn't the type of person to do things out of pity. She gave her time and energy to people she found deeply valuable in some way. She'd been a very intentional woman.

The silence was awkward as they arranged their tea. Eventually, Violet asked, "Are you doing okay?"

His tea in hand, he shrugged. "I'm fine. How are you? Are you still working in the city?"

"How do you know I work in the city?"

"I—well, I hear things from time to time. And where else would you be working? How's it going?"

"I've had the same job for about three years, but I'm working remotely now. I'm thinking of moving back and staying in Gram's house for good."

"Really? There's nothing here. Everything is the same as it was when you left."

Violet smiled. "Yeah. Freddie is still working in the grocery store—ringing up groceries like when we were teens."

"Well, he's the owner now. He's still an idiot, though."

"I noticed. Did he take over for his father?"

Jasper nodded. "His father died maybe five years ago? I'm surprised he hasn't run it into the ground, but I suppose it's what he knows."

"Probably the only thing he knows." Violet grinned. Jasper smiled with a huff, a little breath of a laugh, before pulling his tea to his mouth and glancing away from her.

"You read Ambrose Marcello?" she asked.

He paused, lowering his cup. "I read a lot of things. Why?"

"I saw the books on the table, but I've never seen these editions before. I love his writing so much—it's expressive and vivid. Reading his books makes me feel like I'm traveling the world. My absolute favorite is *The Moroccan Butterfly.*"

"That was his third book," Jasper said.

"Yes. The first two books were a little bumpy, but in book three, he really hit his stride with the mystery and intrigue. And the descriptions of Morocco... gosh. I've always wanted to go there because of Mom."

"I remember. Chefchaouen, right?"

"Yes. There were even scenes written in Mom's hometown. Just reading the book, it was like I could smell the air and feel the humidity. Practically transcendent. And Marcello—I went to one of his speaking engagements when he came to the city. Wonderful."

Jasper furrowed his brow. "He's a little too 'mystical guru' for me."

"Really? I think he's insightful. He teaches all these lessons with beautiful subtlety in his books, so it's nice to have him say things directly when he gives talks."

"I prefer subtlety. Not everything needs to be beaten over a person's head."

"Rosie would agree with you. She enjoys the books, but doesn't like his personal ramblings."

"How is Rose?" he asked. "Is she doing okay?"

"She's fine. In love with Jillian, her partner. They've been together... two years, now? They met on the patio of a coffee shop because the waiter accidentally switched their orders. It's a really cute story—well, except that Rosie's wallet ended up getting stolen that same day. But even with that, Jill helped her out, and they hit it off instantly. Rosie is working as a family lawyer in the city. She loves her job, has a fab apartment. She's doing great."

"Sounds like she has the perfect life," Jasper observed.

"Well, almost. She's weirdly had her identity stolen a few times. It's annoying, but she doesn't let it get her down. You know Rosie. Unshakable."

"She is. And that kind of thing happens a lot these days."

"Yeah, unfortunately," Violet said. "She wants to introduce Jill to Dad because they're talking about getting married, so they're planning to visit Los Angeles in the spring. Dad's being wishy-washy about it, as usual. He couldn't even make it here for Gram's funeral."

Violet paused, blinking as if waking up from a trance. She was sitting and talking to Jasper like no time had passed between them. As if it hadn't been fifteen years since they'd seen each other—as if he hadn't abruptly disappeared from her life because of some mysterious illness.

She focused on him, her brows drawn tight. "Jasper, are *you* doing okay?"

"I'm fine. I told you—"

"Why—In what way are you sick? Why are you living like this?"

It wasn't her place to demand an explanation, but she needed one. *Something* to help rationalize what had happened back then.

He straightened in the chair. "I'm perfectly fine with the way I'm living, Violet. And I... I don't like to talk about my sickness."

"Alright, I don't mean to pry. I'm sorry."

"It's okay."

"You just... *disappeared* when we were kids."

"I had to," he said.

She shook her head, taking a deep breath. "I guess I don't understand. I was worried about you. It's not like you were in the hospital for visits, and *no one* would tell me what happened or what was wrong. It was awful and I really missed you." The confession was a bit naked, but true. Lately, Violet felt as if her emotions were constantly running at level-ten intensity (or zero, once she finally wore herself out and fell asleep).

Jasper glanced down into his cup, avoiding her eyes as his skin flushed a rosy shade. "It was awful for me, too. I—" He inhaled softly, but nothing followed except another quiet moment. A brief space in time for them to mutually acknowledge the hurt within their past. To mourn together.

Violet tilted her head. "But you're okay? You're still sick, but..."

"I'll always be sick, but yes, I'm fine."

"Earlier, you said that Gram used to visit with you. What if—"

"*No*, Violet," he said, serious gray eyes on hers.

"But you don't even know what I was about to say."

"You were about to ask if you could visit when you drop off groceries. But you don't need to do that, alright? You... You are a vibrant, exciting young woman—full of life. You shouldn't be sitting around in a dusty house with an invalid. *Please* don't."

Despite herself, Violet grinned. "You think I'm exciting?"

"Is that the only thing you heard?"

"No, I heard the rest." She snickered, reveling in the growing ease of their banter. It was similar to when they were little, but different somehow. Enthralling in a way she didn't quite yet understand. "If you think these things about me, why wouldn't you want to have tea together?"

"Because bad things might happen."

Violet's expression dropped, the dark nuance of his statement utterly sobering her. "What... what kinds of bad things?'

A loud *snap* made them both jump in their seats. They turned, looking over at the hearth and watching the fire whip and lash the log like a clawed monster devouring its prey. Jasper laughed, standing and grabbing a poker to move the logs. "Bad things like that."

"That's not so bad." Violet adjusted against the sofa, calming herself from the shock of the unexpected sound. "I was thinking more like a gang of debt collectors banging down your door and threatening to break my knees, or a house falling out of the sky and onto my head."

He turned, his eyes full of amusement. "I don't have any debt. The other option also feels improbable, but I can't promise you anything."

"It happened in the movie *The Wizard of Oz*—the house thing, not the knee-breaking debt collectors." They both snickered as Jasper returned to his seat. He exhaled, his expression softened and relaxed from their moment of laughter. He looked up, only briefly meeting her gaze before glancing away again.

"About having tea, Violet, I... Well..." He rubbed his palm against his face.

She leaned forward slightly at the waist, catching his downcast stare and making him meet her eyes. "Just tea. Sometimes?" she prodded, smiling. "Once a week when I drop off the groceries. I don't pity you, and it's not just because Gram asked me. I'm enjoying this—seeing you again. Is that alright?"

Dropping his hand, he shifted his head to look at her from beneath dark lashes. The innocent movement caught the narrow stream of light from the window, making his haunting eyes shine like silver. He nodded. "Once a week. Okay."

Violet nodded too, grinning and feeling whimsical, as if she'd invoked her preadolescent self. The version of herself that spun around in floaty dresses and was overjoyed at the sight of a Monarch butterfly drifting across a field of radiant flowers.

She bit back her silly smile, then took a breath to calm her racing pulse.

6

NOW

THE HERBALIST'S ALMANAC
MAGIC ALL AROUND US: A PRACTICAL GUIDE TO HEALING HERBS
THE WIND IN THE TREES AND THE POWER IN YOU
HOLISTIC HERBALISM: HARNESSING YOUR OWN MAGICAL GARDEN

A few days later, Violet set all four books on the floor beside her, then pulled a small bag filled with dried herbs from the large chest. This chest—painted with the most vivid, gaudy pattern of oversized red poppies—had originally belonged to her great-grandmother. The bright crimson petals and little black centers were like beady eyes looking out in every direction. On the porch, it came across as charming and eccentric. Anywhere else it might have been an eyesore.

The artist responsible for the flamboyant illustration was Violet herself: the ten-year-old version who'd been experimenting with art styles and colors. Before that, the chest had been a warm brown color. Completely unimaginative.

With a little encouragement from her gram—likely an effort

to help cheer Violet up and distract her from asking about her missing best friend—the chest had been reimagined. Transformed so that the outside justly represented the eccentricities therein.

Raising the herb bag to her nose, Violet inhaled. The contents were not something she could easily recognize. She flipped the package and read the small sticker in the bottom-right corner. "Saint John's wort. What on earth?" She set it aside, reached into the chest and grabbed another. She didn't smell this one but instead turned it over. She drew back. "*Valerian*, oh no... Don't killers always use this in cozy murder mysteries? Wait, maybe I'm confusing this with hemlock." Violet's knowledge of herbs and flowers was basic. She was by no means the gardening aficionado and forager that Gloria had been, and could only remember a few arbitrary tidbits from her childhood: ripened blackberries only lasted a day after being picked —so eating and using those was always a high priority under Gram's watch—and that mint is a 'garden bully' and should always be grown in its own pot.

Violet's phone rang on the floor beside her. Thankfully, it was her personal mobile. "Hey, sis."

"Happy Saturday. What are you up to in Mary Poppinsville?"

"Going through Gram's chest."

"Ooooh, where she keeps her mother's creepy witchy things—"

"I think they prefer Wiccan. And Gram wasn't an actual Wiccan. I feel like she was Wiccan-curious. Bi-Wiccan."

"I might be offended by that. Find anything good in there? A monkey's paw, or maybe a spell to permanently eliminate morning breath?"

Violet laughed. "No severed animal limbs just yet. I found great-grandmother's journal, though."

"Yikes. Ginger Ainsworth was a for-*real* for-real witch. Remember Gram told us about it once and Dad got mad at her?

She never mentioned it again, but I couldn't forget that image—Gram as a little girl and Ginger doing weird things in the woods behind the house. She made me think that magic was real."

Violet had only flipped through the withered pages of the leather-bound journal. There were all kinds of intricate drawings, mathematical equations and words in Latin and other languages she couldn't identify. She hadn't looked at it for very long. It all felt foreign, like words and symbols from another time and place. "I think Gram just liked the idea of healing and treating people with remedies from the natural earth. She was more of a naturopath vigilante."

"She was an herbalist, Vi."

"Hm, I'd rather have 'Naturopath Vigilante' on a resume."

"What are you going to do with all that illegal marijuana in the greenhouse?"

Violet sighed, rolling her eyes. "Oh, who knows. I don't want to think about it."

"You can quit the job you hate and become a full-time dealer. Turn the village into Mary Jane Poppinsville."

"Stupid. Are you being funny right now? You didn't even want me to move here, now you're encouraging me to become a drug lord?"

"I don't think selling sandwich bags of weed makes you a 'drug lord.' If you want to quit your stable job and live out some crazy fantasy life, might as well go full throttle."

Violet frowned, holding the phone up to her ear with her shoulder hunched and using both hands to shuffle herb bags and books around in the chest. "Yeah, no. Anyway, I wonder if the local police know about this? They *have* to. How could they not? I'm going to ignore it for as long as possible. Nobody's been knocking down the door about it so far—except Freddie Martin made a lewd reference to it last week at the grocery store."

"Ugh, Freddie Martin. Objectively, and aside from being a

dimwitted bully, he's tall and quite good-looking. I swear he had a crush on you. That's why he was such a jerk to you all the time. Misdirected schoolboy angst and all that."

"Whatever." Violet picked up another small, unlabeled bag that appeared to be filled with tiny tan-colored seeds. She held the bag to her nose, then cringed. It reminded her of sulfur. "This bag is like fart seeds."

"*What?*"

"Nothing. Sorry. I'm still going through the chest."

"Did Freddie ever try anything with you?"

Violet frowned. "Why are you still talking about him?"

"Because I'm convinced you're special to him, somehow."

Tossing the bag into the chest, Violet stood, rubbing a palm across her jeans to rid herself of dust and stinky herb debris. "Listen, between these fart seeds and you talking about Freddie, I'm going to throw up."

"Ha. Alright, alright..." Rose paused for a moment before asking, "So did you go to Jasper's again?"

Not wanting to talk about this, Violet pursed her lips, frowning. She knew very well how Rose felt about the entire Jasper situation, and it was a delicate thing for Violet, always. Especially right now, after years of nothing, suddenly having him around again. She took a breath. "Yes."

"And?"

"Nothing. I delivered his groceries."

After a distinct and awkward silence, Rose laughed. "Oh wow, she's being tight-lipped about this. Ms. Outspoken is keeping this one close to the chest."

Violet didn't respond.

"Vi, c'mon. Am I that bad about this topic?"

"Yes. Yes, you are."

"Okay, baby sis, I'm sorry. Did you see him this time? You've been wanting to see him since you were *nine*. May I ask if he opened the door?"

Violet rolled her shoulders, trying to ease the tension there. "He did."

"How was he? Did he look sickly? Was he Jasper the Friendly Ghost?"

Violet snorted. "He said he's fine. He looked alright. A little ghost-like but solid. Not frail at all." She decided to keep the part about him appearing unkempt and living among the dust bunnies to herself.

"Do you finally feel a little better?" Rose asked, calm. "You stopped talking with me about it a long time ago, but I know that had been bothering you—not knowing anything about what happened to him."

In truth, she still didn't know what had happened. He'd shut down her questioning so fast that there was no space for any meaningful revelation or closure. But seeing him and verifying his well-being in person, at the very least had been satisfying. "I do, actually. I'm relieved."

"Good. Maybe we can move forward now?"

Violet drew back. "Ah, see there? You ruined it. Move forward where, Rosie? Where am I going, exactly?"

"Don't play dumb," Rose chided. "It's like Jasper is this *standard* in your head. This nine-year-old boy that captivated you with all his whimsy and curious wonder, dragging you around in the enchanted forest behind Gram's house. You've been comparing every man you meet to that image ever since."

Shaking her head, Violet smirked. "Wow, whimsy and 'enchanted forests'? That's some pretty bold conjecture. You should consider being a psychiatrist. I bet life is *super great* for Jillian existing under that kind of scrutiny—"

"Am I wrong?"

Violet turned to face the windows of the patio, basking in the warm light. She bent forward toward the luscious planter filled with mint and Roman chamomile. The puffy yellow centers of the small flowers seemed to glow in the bright stream of sunshine pouring through the glass. She loved this smell. On the opposite side of the porch, there was another solitary pot of chamomile. Jasper had served her chamomile tea. She suddenly wondered if Gram had dried it for him.

"It's good to have standards." Violet stood straight, staring out at the autumnal foliage framing the landscape. Gram's greenhouse was set just before the thick grove of trees covered in red and golden leaves.

Rosie laughed. "Sure, but he was nine. Actually, I think this is good. You *should* spend time with him. Maybe he'll say something really offensive to you and the whole thing will come crumbling down."

"That's... a terrible thing to hope for, Rosie."

"Well, not *morally* offensive. Something light but important to you, like that he hates cake and thinks it's gross."

Violet scrunched her face in horror. "What monster doesn't like cake?"

"See?"

"I'm hanging up."

Violet ended the call in the middle of her sister's loud cackle. She was deciding whether or not she should continue going through the poppy chest when there was a loud knock on the front door of the cottage. She wasn't expecting anyone, so she kept her footfalls quiet while sneaking to the front room. She looked out the peephole. To her great disgust, Freddie Martin was on the other side.

She stood still. There was no way she was opening the door for him. Violet jumped when he knocked again, harder.

"Violet Ainsworth," he called. "I know you're here. Gloria's dang car is in the drive. I just want to talk a little."

Nope. Violet leaned with her back to the door and folded her arms. He knocked again.

"C'mon fancy-pants! I gotta open the store in twenty

minutes. Why didn't you come in to get groceries this week? I was lookin' for you."

Such a creep. Do not ever look for me.

Freddie mumbled to himself. "Maybe she's in the bathroom or something." He stomped away, down the gravel path and back toward his car. When she was sure he'd gone, she stood straight and walked back toward the sun porch.

Freddie had bullied her when they were younger: from the time she'd moved to Libellule Commune in first grade, and in every subsequent grade up until she'd finally left for college. He'd make rude comments about her curly, coily hair, or the peppery freckles across her nose. In high school he'd taken to calling her "turds for eyes" because he said the deep brown of her irises had reminded him of poop. Who said that kind of thing about someone with brown eyes? Statistically speaking, *most* people in the world had brown eyes.

The summer before she'd left for college, the whole town threw a big party for all the graduates at the local community center. It was there that Freddie had caught her off guard and grabbed her shoulder, declaring he wanted to talk. But the minute she'd felt his hand, she'd turned and shoved him, screaming. It had been quite the scene, but that was the absolute last straw. Words were bad enough, but when he'd physically accosted her, she swore she'd stab him if he ever did it again. She didn't carry a knife, per se, but there were plenty of sharp objects lying around.

On the back porch, Violet's brow furrowed with inherent worry. She sincerely hoped this wouldn't be a problem with her moving back here. Having regular conflicts again with Freddie would be a nightmare.

Shaking her head, she looked back down into the large antique chest. There was another book stashed underneath a pile of herb pouches. She reached down, pushing the small bags aside and wrapping her fingers around the book's thick binding.

It was heavy and dark with a hard, worn cover—an unmistakable symbol etched in silver within the center. The pages were dusty and discolored along the edges, with frayed ribbons, tags and folded corners marking specific places.

She read the title, frowning as a certain discontent washed over her.

SALEM WITCHCRAFT AND SABBATH SPELLS

7

THEN

$\mathcal{V}$iolet dug her fingers into the grass at her sides, her mind distraught and swarming with adolescent fury when she heard a familiar voice overhead.

"What are you doing back here?"

Jasper was standing there, his dark hair neatly parted and combed and his face filled with worry.

"Nothing," Violet mumbled. She pulled at the grass, gripping it in her fist and tearing it from the earth. When she didn't say anything else, Jasper sat down beside her with his back pressed against the brick wall of the schoolhouse. He shifted, reaching into his pocket to remove a square, complicated-looking puzzle. Focusing on it, he manipulated the toy with his fingers. Unspeaking.

"What's that?" she asked.

"A brain teaser. I'm supposed to get all the parts to line up so that it makes a symmetrical shape. I think this one is some kind of flower? If I do, Dad says he'll buy a Jean Claude Constantin lock for me."

"Who is Jean Claude Constantin?"

"He's a master puzzle maker—maybe the best."

Despite her inner turmoil, Violet smiled. "You always like things I've never heard of... maybe things most kids have never heard of."

Jasper shrugged. "I'm weird. Violet, why are you back here?"

She sighed. "I'm sick of Freddie being mean to me. Why is he always picking on me? I haven't done anything to him."

Jasper's fingers paused as if something had struck him but then he thought better of it. His fingers moved once more, his eyes focused on his puzzle. "Freddie is stupid, you know?"

"I know—"

"No, Vi. I mean *really* stupid. He puts carrots in his nose at lunch to make people laugh. And then he eats them. That's not funny."

"No, it isn't," Violet said, but she laughed, more so at Jasper's declaration and disgust than Freddie's weird sense of comedy.

"One time—it was before you moved here—the teacher left the room for a second to talk to the principal just outside the door. Freddie got on the teacher's desk and started dancing. But then his pants dropped because he never wears a belt with his uniform. When he went to grab them, he lost his balance and fell off the desk. He broke his arm."

This time, Violet laughed at Freddie. A piece of the puzzle in Jasper's hands clicked into place and he smiled, satisfied. He looked over at Violet. "Then he made a big stink about everyone signing his dumb cast. Freddie always wants attention. You moved to this town, and you and Rosie are so different from anyone we've ever met. Freddie can't handle that. It's like he doesn't know what to do with himself. Plus, he's really stupid."

Violet nodded, a quiet question bubbling to the surface. "Is different so bad?"

"Different is great! How boring would it be if everyone was the same all the time? Freddie probably thinks so, too. But the way he shows it is all wrong."

Grinning, Violet scooted a little closer to Jasper so that she could lay her head on his shoulder. She sighed. "Talking to you is like talking to an adult sometimes."

He tinkered with his puzzle. "I'm just weird."

"No," Violet said. "You're different. Different is great, remember? Someone really smart told me that."

8

NOW

*O*n her third visit to Laurent House, Jasper opened the door as Violet made her way up the narrow cobblestone path. He met her with his gentle smile. "Hello."

"Good afternoon. Grocery delivery at your service." Violet beamed, crossing over the threshold.

He took the bag from her hand. "Thank you for doing this. Really." He turned, walking down the hallway. Violet quickly shut the door and followed as he went on. "If you get tired of helping, just tell me. I can—"

"I know, you told me already." She shook her head, smiling as she stepped into the kitchen. The room was at the back of Laurent House, awash with overcast light and overlooking the decaying garden and orchard through a neat row of square windows positioned over the sink. The cabinets were antique white: distinctly characteristic of a charming country home. Although this room was less dusty than the others Violet had seen, it would still benefit from a deep clean.

Jasper placed the grocery bag on the island in the center of the kitchen, then diligently removed its contents. Violet paused, taking the moment in. She was in the same room with Jasper.

She'd known nothing about him for almost two decades, but suddenly here he was, standing before her. It didn't seem real.

The permanent hole in Violet's chest still ached with the loss of Gloria Marie. But this unexpected turn—being reunited with her childhood friend after so long—stirred an entirely new feeling inside her. Something warm and gentle that helped to distract her from the hollow loneliness.

As he dug through the reusable bag, she smiled. "Your grocery list makes me feel a little like I'm shopping for a squirrel."

His hands froze. When his large eyes flickered up to meet hers, she drew back at the startled expression there. He didn't say anything, but slowly removed a jar of almond butter from the bag and set it on the counter.

Violet stepped forward. "I'm sorry, I didn't mean anything malicious by that. Mostly I meant you eat very healthy, which is a good thing." She pulled two pouches out of her purse. "I brought these, too. Gram has a lot of dried chamomile in her pantry for tea, and peppermint, too—"

"I can't have peppermint." Jasper snapped his head up. "At all. I—I'm very allergic."

"Okay, sorry..." Violet placed the small bags back inside her purse, then sighed. "I'm off to a terrible start here, aren't I?"

"No, no you aren't." He shook his head. Walking toward the fridge, he opened it to transfer the items. "I'm... just being uptight. Would you mind starting the tea?"

"Sure." Violet turned and stepped toward the gas stove, glad to have an assigned task. Maybe it would help keep her mouth under control? The kettle was already there and filled with water. She turned the dial, *tick-tick-tick* until the blue-yellow flame puffed out with intense heat. She lowered the flame just a little.

"The chamomile tea bags you brought... Gloria always made two separate batches."

"Ah, the planter that shares the mint versus the isolated pot," Violet realized. "I don't know her pantry and herb system yet, so let's just use yours, if you have any left? I'll be sure to dry a new batch myself, next time."

"I do. And thank you, that's very kind. The tea is in the white container on your left. How was your work thing yesterday? The event with the T-shirts."

"It went perfectly fine. A complete success."

"So, a lot of fuss for no reason?" Jasper said, tearing his requested bag of pumpkin seeds open as he stood at the island.

"That's my job, really. I have three key responsibilities—one, fielding my bosses' crazy requests. Two, talking them down when they freak out and three, being showered in accolades when everything turns out great."

"Exhausting but rewarding?" he asked, munching a mouthful of seeds.

"Much more so the former."

"So why subject yourself to it?"

Violet shrugged. "Money."

"Mm, the great motivator."

"What about you, Jas? How do you sustain your lifestyle? How is it you can hand me a bank card and tell me to do whatever I want?"

He chuckled with a warm, airy sound while digging his hand into the bag for another round of seeds. "I didn't say 'do whatever you want.' I said buy yourself groceries and gas."

"That's sweet of you, but you don't need to pay for my groceries. I did buy myself a nice bottle of wine though."

"You could have gotten more... if you wanted."

Violet lifted her chin. "How do you know I won't? Maybe later I'll hit up Tiffany's and buy those earrings I've always wanted. A new candy-apple-red Mercedes."

He laughed again and it was such a nice sound. It seemed to fill the chilly, shadowy space. "You wouldn't have gotten that far. If anything, you would probably be in jail for fraud. Is that what the twenty-five-year-old version of Violet Ainsworth likes? Expensive cars and fine jewelry? Should I have Jeeves prepare the caviar?"

"No." She turned toward the stove behind her at the whistle of the teakettle, then threw a feisty look over her shoulder. "But *you* don't know that."

He shifted his stance, lifting his bag of seeds toward her. "True... You want some?"

"No thanks. Cups?"

"Top cabinet on your left."

Lifting to her tiptoes, Violet pulled the handle of the chipped cabinet door open and grabbed two cups from the shelves. "I'd like to meet this Jeeves and learn about what other luxuries he can offer. And you didn't answer my question."

"He's off today. What question?"

"How do you spend your time every day? Do you work?"

"I do things. I keep busy."

"That's not vague at all." Violet grinned, setting the kettle and teacups on a tray, then lifting and carrying them toward her friend. The island in the center also functioned as a table. Jasper pulled a tall stool out from underneath and made himself comfortable as Violet placed the items down in between them. She sat on the opposite side.

"My work is just my work," Jasper said. Violet chuckled at the second very vague statement and Jasper added, "I'm not living off of an inheritance, if that's what you're thinking. There wasn't anything like that when Dad died—and if there was, Mom is probably living off of it now. This house and the land around it are a family heirloom, for better or worse." Jasper reached for the kettle and filled her cup before his own.

"Gram told me when your father died. I was so upset. I sent flowers here, to the house. When we were little, I always thought he was a wonderful person. He ran around in the orchard with us sometimes, and he always had those funny little brain teasers and games for you. He was one of the few adults that actually played *with* us instead of just sending us off on our own. It stuck with me."

Jasper nodded, his eyes downcast. "Dad was really great. And I got your flowers. Thank you for that."

"Of course. Where is your mother?"

"She went back to Lisbon since her brother and sister are still there. But she and Dad lived an hour away in the city together for the past almost... six years? When they were planning to leave, I overheard her telling Dad that she wanted to go back to Portugal, but he didn't want to be that far away from here. From me, probably."

Violet considered, doing the math. "So they left here when you were eighteen?"

"Yes."

"Isn't it supposed to be the other way around?"

Jasper nodded, bringing his tea to his lips but pausing. "Typically. Yes."

"Why did they leave you here alone?"

He turned his head, looking off into the distance. "My mother had a very difficult time with my sickness. If she could have left earlier, she would have. But Dad encouraged her to stay until I was eighteen. So..." Jasper finally met her eyes and shrugged.

"I'm sorry that happened."

"It's fine. I don't blame her at all."

A lull fell over the space, emphasizing the melancholy coolness of the kitchen. She glanced past Jasper's shoulder and through the window. The wind whipped the bare branches of the orchard's trees—the cloudy sky was the color of steel. She held her warm cup between her palms, the comforting heat flowing up her arms.

What kind of parents abandoned their sick eighteen-year-old son? It didn't make any sense. Yes, he was legally an adult at that age. But emotionally, mentally... Was he capable of running an estate on his own? By the looks of things, the answer was no.

The memory of Jasper's father was easy for Violet to recall: his tall, wiry frame, bright, happy smile, unruly sandy-brown hair and golden-rimmed spectacles. Something about his warmth and kindness, the gangly quirkiness of him had been cemented within her psyche.

But when Violet thought of his wife, the memories were blurry and scattered. Violet had to dredge them up from somewhere deep within.

She'd been an innocuous woman: dark hair, fair skin and with a simply stated beauty. A little too stiff, uppity and outwardly pleased with the Laurents' social standing within the village. The family had done well for themselves with the orchard. They'd been big fish in a little pond.

It was strange to imagine her being so unsupportive of her only son, considering his sickness. She'd fawned over Jasper when he was young—always making sure he was clean and smartly presented. That he exhibited excellent manners and intelligence. What could have happened to make her abandon him? Was his sickness so terrible?

"Has Freddie been bothering you when you go to the grocery store?" Jasper asked, his expression serene. He'd inherited his light eyes and coffee-colored hair from his mother, but he'd unquestionably been saddled with his father's awkward and gangly (but charming) demeanor.

Violet sighed. "I haven't been back since he told me my hips match my hair."

Jasper choked on his tea. "Ex-Excuse me?"

"That's what he said."

"Dear God, what an idiot. What does that even mean? Your hips are—"

Violet straightened, her eyes wide. Jasper adjusted in his

seat, too, and the tension in the room thickened despite the cool ambiance. But then he shrunk, looking away and bringing his tea to his mouth with his dark brows scrunched together. Violet chuckled.

"How the heck were you going to finish that sentence?"

"I *wasn't* going to finish the sentence," Jasper said, still avoiding her gaze. "There is literally no appropriate way for that sentence to have ended."

She laughed again, and this time Jasper laughed, too. He lifted his palm to his forehead and shook his head, his face changing to an increasingly familiar rosy shade of red.

Violet raised her chin. "Enough talk about my hips, sir."

"We are *not* talking about that."

"Being back here, it's making me think a lot about when you and I were kids. Little things, you know? Like when we'd go exploring in the woods all day on the weekends and you'd show me creepy bugs."

"Was I the stereotype of a boy?" Jasper smirked. "Did I have toy trucks and baseball cards in my pockets, too?"

Violet chuckled. "No. Not at all. You picked the bugs up but never chased after me with them or anything. You were alright."

"I'm glad." Jasper smiled, his face returned to its normal shade. "Our weekends together were really great, weren't they? Gloria would test all of her new dessert recipes and teas on us. The blueberry lemon bars were my favorite."

"And the lavender tea she concocted that one summer?"

"With fresh honey," Jasper added. "I remember that one— and the raspberry hot cocoa in fall. Brilliant woman. We asked her to make it so much that she eventually cut us off."

"She spoiled us... I was so anxious and sad when Rosie, Dad and I moved here. But between Gram and you, it ended up being pretty darn wonderful." He'd played a big part in her acclimating to a new environment—in finding a sense of joy and wonder again amidst the sorrow and drastic changes. She wondered if he understood the significance of the role he had played. If she'd ever had the chance to properly express her gratitude.

She was working up the courage to tell him, but he looked away and cleared his throat. "So... have you decided what you're going to do?" he asked. "About Gloria's cottage?"

Leaning on her elbow, she cradled her chin in her palm. "I'm staying. I haven't officially announced it to my job yet, but it's been three weeks and... I love that house. It makes me feel close to her and honestly, I feel calmer and more content here than I ever have in the city."

"It seems like it would be boring here for you," he reasoned. "There's so much more variety in the city—more people your age and you have easy access to the airport to travel anywhere you want."

"*Our* age. And after almost four years of living there, I hardly took advantage of any of those things."

"But you've done well, Vi. You have your own place, a high-paying job, and you've traveled to Spain and Greece. Those things are all remarkable—"

"Jasper, how do you know I've traveled to Spain and Greece? Did you and Gram talk about me?"

"Sh-She mentioned things. Just sometimes." He reached for the kettle, busying himself with refilling his cup.

That felt unfair. Gram had been keeping Jasper updated with her life, but she'd never mentioned sitting with Jasper. Never once revealed that she talked to him—had sat inside his house and brought him handmade chamomile tea from a special flower pot she kept separate just for him because he was allergic to mint. Gifted him one of her favorite tea sets.

Why? Why had Jasper let Gloria so close to him when he'd spent years hiding himself away? It didn't make any sense.

"Do you have any plans to travel to Morocco?" Jasper asked. "Since you've always wanted to go there."

Violet sat back, sighing. "No. Not yet."

"May I ask why?"

"Well, I want it to be a special trip, and I don't want to go alone. Rosie isn't interested and doesn't care—even though she was *literally* named for El Kelaa M'gouna and the Rose festival. You would think that she'd want to see the place her namesake is derived from. It's like... growing up in Los Angeles brainwashed her. I barely remember living there because we left when I was still so young. But she tells me she used to be teased for looking different, and it was worse when she spoke in Darija. She doesn't remember *any* of Mom's language because she just refused to speak it after a while—even with Mom. That makes me mad. I would give my left arm to speak Arabic fluently."

"Have you considered taking classes?" Jasper asked. "It's not too late. And you don't need to sacrifice your limbs."

"I've thought about it time and time again, but work was insane back in the city. And when you're paid a good salary, you're *always* on call. I'm a corporate modern-day slave and it doesn't leave a lot of time for personal endeavors. Maybe with moving back here, I can achieve more balance."

"You only get one life, Violet. You should do the things you really want to do."

Violet blinked, then clapped her hands together and bowed from the waist. "Thank you, O wise and great teacher."

"I-It's just an observation."

"No, I know you're right." Violet grinned, lifting her mug. "I'm going to do better. What about you? What do *you* really want to do?"

He shook his head, his face blank. "Nothing."

"I don't believe that for a second."

"I can't do much because of my sickness, so I don't think about anything. What I'm doing now is fine. Being here..." Jasper lifted a hand, then raked his fingers through his thick, unruly dark hair. "Sitting with you like this, it's nice. I never expected this, so it's enough for me."

What's wrong with you? Why couldn't he just explain it? Whatever *it* was. Why was it a secret? It was nagging her, but she wouldn't ask again. He'd made it clear that he didn't want to talk about it.

Still, as she stared at the man across from her—his calm demeanor, linty blue sweater and pale gray eyes that almost constantly avoided her direct gaze—she wished that he would just tell her. Or perhaps that she could read his mind.

9

NOW

"*I*t happened again."

"Oh no," Violet moaned. "Seriously? I'm so sorry, Rosie. How much this time?"

"Five thousand. My bank is so accustomed to it now, they actually called *me* first, preemptively suspecting the charge was fraudulent."

"Yikes. This is the third time this year."

Rose exhaled a heavy sigh into the phone. "It is—but it's fine. We caught it right away, and when Jilly gets back from her work thing in Paris, we're going to start planning wedding stuff. Life is good."

"Oh very exciting. Have you talked her into letting you meet her parents yet?"

"Nope," Rose said. "She's still insisting they're terrible people and we shouldn't bother. I think I have to leave it alone. Anyway, what's happening in Sleepyville? Entertain me with colorful stories of charming local yokels."

"Hm, let's see… Oh, Art was here last weekend. He was visiting his grandfather's grave along with his grandmother."

"Art? Who the heck is Art?"

"Arthur Malle. You dated him for two years in high school? You told me he was your first."

"He was *not* my first."

"Um, 'kay?"

"I think I just said that to make it seem like I waited. I didn't want to corrupt your young, impressionable mind."

"Great."

"What about him?"

"Nothing, really." Violet shrugged. "We bumped into each other in town, so we had coffee. It felt weird though. I think he was being flirty."

"Don't have coffee with my ex-boyfriend."

"It wasn't like that, and you didn't even *remember* him a second ago, Rosie."

"Still. It's a sister code. Did he ask about me?"

"Yeah."

"What did you say?"

"I told him you're happy and living in the city with your charming girlfriend."

"Ha! Did he freak out?"

"He didn't do a spit-take or anything, but yes, his eyes went wide and he repeated, '*girlfriend?*' It wasn't subtle."

"Good. I hope he tossed and turned in bed all night, questioning his masculinity."

"I assured him that you're bisexual."

"You didn't."

"Of course I didn't. But I don't understand why you're suddenly hoping to upset the psyche of an ex-boyfriend you barely remember."

"Meh," Rose spat. "I'm a hundred percent certain it's divine retribution—probably on behalf of some other woman he's wronged during the never-ending maturation process of the male ego."

Boom-boom-boom. A heavy knock at the front door made Violet bolt upright on the couch, her heart pounding in her chest. She whispered into her phone. "Someone is at the door."

Rose whispered back. "Okay... So go answer it."

"No way—it's after nine o'clock and I'm not expecting anyone."

"Vi, if you have the lights on, it's obvious you're home. The cottage has all those picture windows."

Violet stood, then tightened the belt of her robe before moving around the couch and silently stalking toward the front door. "So what? They don't know what I'm doing in here," she said, her voice low. "I could be on the toilet."

"Now *there's* a lovely image."

"Shut up." When she reached the door, she lifted to her toes, pressing her palm against the cold wood as she leaned into the peephole. "It's Freddie."

"Ah, Jean-Pierre Frédéric Martin strikes again. Why is he stalking you? Isn't this the second time he's come to Gram's house? Sheesh, you've only been living there a month. Just answer the door and see what he wants. Get it over with."

Staying silent, Violet shook her head as she watched. He was looking all around: over at the large living room window, then back at the door, over his shoulder at the front garden. Every movement appeared nervous and suspicious.

"Violet?"

"I'm here," she whispered, just a breath. After a long minute, Freddie grumbled, turned, and made his way back through the yard to his shiny red pick-up.

She sighed. "I really just want him to go away. What's his problem? We're not kids anymore and I am *not* interested."

"Go to the grocery store where there are lots of witnesses and ask him directly," Rosie urged. "Take control of the situation. You ignoring and avoiding him obviously isn't working."

"You're right. I'll go sometime this week—ugh, what a pain."

~

AFTER A NIGHT OF HEAVY SLEEP, Violet awoke to a frosty late October morning. It was the coldest it had been since she'd moved back home. Sitting upright, she shivered. Her mind was cloudy with exhaustion and her mouth tasted like sleep. Usually she left the fireplace in the living room burning when she went to bed, making sure all drapes were shut and windows closed to help insulate the house. The back-patio door off the kitchen was essential in keeping the warmth inside. The sun porch was wonderful, but more exposed to the natural elements, which made the temperature fluctuate in tandem with the day's weather.

She got out of bed, stepping into her wooly house slippers and wrapping herself in her robe. She walked up to the large window overlooking the area behind the cottage, taking in the view of the dried meadow backed by the imposing silence of the woods. The sky was overcast again today, giving the scene an air of barrenness.

When she looked toward the greenhouse, something felt off. She tilted her head, trying to identify the subtle difference. The glass of the front door was cracked and broken—littered across the walkway in jagged shards.

She swept out of the room and into the hall. Immediately, the cold intensified as she moved through the living room, past the darkened hearth and into the kitchen. She flicked the bolt-lock mechanism and opened the door to the sun porch. The frigid wind rushed against her flesh, making her gasp from the shock of it. Here, too, the glass of the outer door had been broken in, the remains of it messily scattered across the wooden beams of the porch.

"What in the world? Why—" She looked over to her grandmother's poppy chest—the massive trunk was askew, set in the center of the floor with the rug beneath it bunched up and wrinkled. But it was still closed. Locked and intact. Whoever did this had tried to take the trunk, but had clearly given up. Violet bent down and examined the surface. She could see a barrage of deep scratch marks around the padlock securing the chest. It had been tampered with but held strong.

Shivering from both cold and unease, Violet stepped over the glass, opened the porch door and walked down the stone steps toward the greenhouse. The wind whipped around her, making her robe flap no matter how tightly she held it against herself. Her dark hair bounced and swayed in its low ponytail, striking her cheeks like tiny whips. She smoothed it away from her face and restrained the curly mass as she peeked through the broken door. The floor of the greenhouse was a mess of leaves, dirt and other plant debris.

Timid, she grasped the cold brass knob, her fingers trembling as she pulled the door open. Nothing like this had ever happened to her before. Especially not in this village—her sleepy, charming hometown. This place where everyone knew everyone else. Except new people were slowly moving in. The town had expanded over the years after Violet had left for the city.

Hesitating, she walked down the narrow path, the greenhouse and its plants eerily still around her despite the rushing, howling wind outside. The structure creaked and moaned from the pressure, and Violet jumped when the door behind her creaked open and banged shut again from the suction. Another section of glass fell, loudly smashing against the cement floor.

As she approached the end of the row, an entire section of the long planter was cleared out: hastily, sloppily, because Violet could still see roots and stems sticking out of the soil. Messy footprints and squished leaves lay scattered across the floor.

In the silence, Violet stood straight. She deliberated only for a moment, then huffed out a laugh. "Well, that's one thing that's been taken off my plate." That, as well as her potential career as a drug lord within her small commune.

The marijuana was gone.

10

THEN

*V*iolet picked up each empty cup and counted, *one-two-three*, then placed them in front of her new friend. At least, she was hoping they were friends, because he always sat with her when they had math lessons on the carpet, and almost always played with her at recess.

Everyone else stayed away from him and said he was weird. That his family was weird, too. And rich. But as far as Violet could see, he was really nice. She liked him.

"Okay, here are yours." She pointed to the cups she'd placed in front of him. "These are mine. I have three and you have three."

Her new friend frowned, pursing his small mouth. "You kept all the pretty colors."

"I didn't."

"You *did*," he said, then pointed. "Can I have purple? I'll trade you for green."

"But purple is a girl's color."

"It's not. It's just a color. Can we trade?"

"Yeah, okay." She shrugged. "I like green." She picked up her purple cup and switched it out for his green. "Better?"

He grinned, nodding his head as if there was music in there that Violet couldn't hear. "Mmhm."

"Okay, now we fill each cup with sand," she explained. "And we turn them over and try to stack them on top of each other. Let's see who can make the tallest castle."

Violet's eyes widened with excitement. But her friend... his nose only crinkled up again. "What is it now?" she asked.

"If we make a castle together, it'll be much better. We should see how high we can make it with *all* the cups."

Violet tilted her head. She liked that idea very much. When she and her sister did this back in California, it was always a competition. But working together... That might be fun, too.

"Okay, let's do it—"

"Violet, *watch out!*"

In a flash, Jasper rose from his seated position in the sand, leaned forward and reached for her. He grabbed hold of her wrist and yanked her forward, causing her to flop onto her belly in the dusty dirt beside him and knocking the wind out of her. She climbed onto hands and knees, turning her head to look back. Jasper now had sand all over his dark head—in his hair, trickling down to his shoulders and over his face. Freddie Martin stood over him with a large blue bucket in his hands, his eyes wide.

Jasper coughed, causing the sand to slink and pour down underneath the collar of his shirt. He hunched his shoulders, shuddering. Violet scrambled upright, dusting out Jasper's hair as he kept his eyes clenched shut. She looked up at Freddie standing over them. He had a strange look on his face. Violet scowled. "You big mean *dummy*."

As if her words had shocked him into action, he dropped the bucket and ran away. When Jasper's hair was mostly clear, she brushed his face with her palms before grabbing his hand. She pulled him up to stand. "Let's go inside to get help. Don't open your eyes, okay?"

11

NOW

hen's the last time I painted something...
Sitting back and relaxing against the couch, Violet's body felt at ease for the first time in weeks. As a result, her mind wandered. Not strictly focused on the past: her heart aching as memories of her Gram flashed like vibrant moving images from a photo album—in full color, because Gloria Marie's life was not that of a black-and-white or sepia-toned album. Absolutely not.

Today, and in this quiet moment within Jasper's study, Violet thought of the future, as if cautiously peeking one eye open toward hope and possibility. She thought of a blank canvas, or a sketch pad, and how the potential there had always excited her. It represented infinite opportunity. What could she create? How could she forever alter the canvas with her own imagination? Opening herself to inspiration—letting it sweep her away as it had when she was a child, when her mind was unburdened by adult responsibilities, fears and hesitations—what could she produce? It had been forever since she'd given herself the space to try.

Four weeks had passed since her first official visit with

Jasper (not including that time when he hadn't opened the door). The air in the study was cool in an increasingly familiar way—laced with the scent of chamomile tea and crammed bookshelves. Jasper sat at his desk, his long fingers clicking and clacking away on his keyboard and his eyes focused behind his brown-framed glasses. She didn't know what he was doing, but he was utterly absorbed. Studious, even.

When she stood to stretch her legs, he paused, hands frozen as he glanced in her direction such that their eyes met. Taking in his slim face and bright eyes—the undeniable, tangible realness of him—her smile broadened. He smiled, too, a little quirk at the corner of his mouth before hastily shifting his focus back to his laptop. The light was dim so she wasn't certain, but it seemed as if a flush of color was slowly creeping up his neck and to his cheeks as he resumed typing.

Violet strolled toward the wall of bookshelves, stopping at random and running her fingers across the textured spines. To her surprise, they weren't dusty at all. "Have you actually read these?" she asked.

He nodded. "Yes. Some multiple times."

"You read books more than once?"

"You don't?" Jasper faced her, his dark eyebrow cocked in disbelief.

The fire crackled in the hearth beside her as she scanned title after title. "Nope. Sometimes, if I really like a book, I might skim my favorite parts over again, but that's it. I conquer a book, then move on to the next. I'm promiscuous that way. Always searching for a new literary lover."

Jasper chuckled, leaning back in his desk chair. Violet smiled. "You're not?"

"Well, I wouldn't put it that way, but... Maybe I'm more monogamous in my literary affairs? I stick with a book for a while if I enjoy it. I might read it two or three times within a month of finishing it. Sometimes it's difficult for me to move on if I'm captivated by something."

"I believe they call that a 'book hangover.' What's the last book that captivated you?"

"Hm... Probably *Secrets of the Gemini*."

Violet brightened. "I've heard of that. I keep meaning to pick it up—the one about the timeless stone in Egypt, right? I love that kind of stuff."

"Yes, it's phenomenal. It starts in 31 BCE with a jewel owned by Cleopatra. It's fictitious, of course, but it gives this lustrous account of an object's unique passage through history and time. You get to see how it's circulated from one person and situation to another, the object remaining the same but everything around it constantly changing. It was a poignant and beautifully written account of life and humanity."

"It sounds amazing. Is there any romance?"

"Um, no. Not really."

"That's too bad."

"There are plenty of romance books?"

She walked back to the couch and plopped down onto the cushions. "Romance books are nice. But I mean... I want a meaty, thoughtful plot and with good, romance elements. I don't want the woman to be objectified at all—and I want the guy to have *substance*. Lately the guys in romance books I read feel the same to me. Almost, formulaic?"

"That's because everyone wants the same thing, Vi." Jasper shrugged. "Someone tall with a square jaw and lots of testosterone. Maybe washboard abs, and a primitive mind and disposition... Someone like Freddie."

Violet narrowed her eyes at him in amusement. "That's *not* what 'everyone' wants."

"Or..." Jasper brightened, stroking his chin as if he were deeply contemplating. "A 'bad boy'? The one who treats everyone terribly and is justified because of his troubled past. Obviously, he is also tall, has a square jaw and is blessed with washboard abs. Those are standards—like flour, eggs and sugar in baking a cake."

"Jasper, not everyone wants a Fabio stereotype. *I* don't want that."

"I'm not sure if Fabio is relevant anymore? The new standard is probably Chris Hemsworth. Chris Evans or some other Chris."

"I do like Chris Pine..." Violet shook her head. "Anyway, that's why I don't read romances so much anymore, because a lot of the characters were starting to seem like cardboard cutouts of the same stereotype and always, always making poor choices. But in Ambrose Marcello's books, the characters feel more real. There's never a delicious romance, though—"

"Marcello is not a romance writer."

"Not strictly, I know. But there are always hints of romantic elements? I like his intricate plot lines, the descriptive locations, and that he always has ethnically diverse, thinking and feeling characters. His female leads are lively and smart, too."

In a rare occurrence, Jasper sat staring, simply blinking his dark lashes behind his reading glasses. "Well, maybe... romance isn't his strength."

"I suppose. I don't know. I just think if he ever put out a book like that, it'd be glorious. He takes such care with everything else—you know what it is about his characters?"

"Mm?"

"It's like he bases his characters off of real women that he knows, instead of wistfully creating a slew of svelte, big-breasted chicks from his man fantasies."

"Svelte?"

"Do you get what I mean?"

He grinned. "Yes—I just think 'svelte' is a very peculiar word choice. Archaic. I know I'm the one who doesn't leave my house, but your references feel outdated. Next you'll be telling me to come hither."

"Yes, that's right." Violet chuckled, lifting her arm in a dramatic fashion. "Come hither and rest yon weary bones on ye olde couch."

Jasper shook his head, smiling as he brought his mug to his mouth and faced forward once more. A small part of Violet had been serious. She'd been visiting him for a month, and it almost felt as if he was intentionally maintaining a healthy distance between them. They'd been so close when they were young—both emotionally and affectionately. It had been an easy, comfortable thing, like slipping your feet into a pair of warm, fuzzy house shoes.

"Someone broke into the greenhouse last week and stole all of Gram's marijuana."

Jasper flipped his head toward her so quickly, she thought his glasses might fly right off. "Are you being serious?"

"Yup. Broke through the glass, unlocked the door and took every last bit of that section. They also tried to take Gram's chest, but it's heavy and they couldn't get the padlock off. They took some basil, too—like they planned to make some spaghetti after smoking the weed."

"Why didn't you say something sooner? Did you call the police?"

"Um, *no*," Violet said. "Who calls the police about stolen, illegal marijuana? And it happened a week ago. What should I do?"

"Hm, I suppose... Well, it's gone now, so it's not like they would lock you up over something you don't technically possess? And that greenhouse has been there for decades. Why would someone do this now?"

"The town has expanded in recent years. We have new transplants..."

"Maybe," Jasper said, frowning. "How would they know about your weed?"

"Word gets out? There's also Freddie. He's come by the cottage twice now, banging on the door and saying he wants to talk with me."

"Why would Freddie steal your weed?"

"Why would Freddie want to talk to me? And stop saying '*your* weed.' It's not mine. I didn't grow it."

Jasper laughed openly, tilting his head back. "It was bequeathed to you."

"You tease me about 'svelte,' then turn around and use 'bequeath'?"

"Touché."

"Maybe because Gram, the official weed keeper, is gone? He felt bad stealing from an elderly woman, but doesn't mind stealing from me—whom he hates. Eternally."

"I don't know, Vi. Yes, you and Freddie have a checkered past, but it doesn't make sense for a person of enough moral standing to refrain from stealing from old ladies, to turn around and steal from a single woman living alone. It doesn't add up."

"Well, I'm not writing it off. I don't trust him. Never have and never will. He's a bully and a pig."

"I won't argue that," he said, his eyes softening. "Are you really okay?"

Standing again, Violet grabbed her cold, empty mug from the low table. "I'm alright. It was unsettling—a kind of violation, you know? Someone broke into my safe space. But the last two nights have been quiet, and I got the doors fixed pretty quickly. I don't think they'll come back since they cleaned the marijuana out. And some of the basil."

"If... if you need help with something, let me know," Jasper offered. "I can't leave the house for too long, but I want you to feel safe."

Violet smiled, something in her heart glowing dimly, like a

firefly. "Thanks, Jas. I'm okay, but I'll let you know." She tilted her head, watching him. As usual, he shifted his eyes away, resting his fingers against the laptop keys. She moved around the table and took a few steps toward him. He looked tired, actually. A little too pale and a tad gaunt.

"Hey, how about next week I make us some lunch? I made lasagna a few weeks ago and it turned out really well. I could change the recipe and make it vegan or veggie for you?"

He looked at her from the corner of his round eyes. "Why vegan or vegetarian?"

Violet smirked. "*Because* Jasper, I shop for you. You never put meat on the grocery lists, and when we were little, you were so into animals and bugs. Of course you don't eat meat. Or bugs?"

He chuckled. "No, no bugs. I'm not strictly opposed to meat but I do tend to avoid it. You don't need to do that, Violet, I'm fine—"

"I know, I know. You're perfectly fine and you don't need or want anything. But *I* want to eat with you, so…" Violet paused, watching him. "You don't have some sort of digestive ailment, do you? You're always just snacking."

"I don't."

Violet clapped, her previous vigor restored. "Alright, it's happening. Just leave it to me." She paused, waiting for him to object again, but he didn't. He only smiled his crooked grin and turned—tapping away on his keyboard in the comfortable silence.

12

NOW

"*V*alerian is used to help with sleeplessness and anxiety, Violet. Not to poison people." Simone's perfect brows drew together in concentration as she held a glass jar up to her nose. "I doubt Gloria has deadly nightshade just hanging out in her pantry. This isn't Macbeth."

By mid-November, Violet had decided it was time to take the bull by the horns and deal with the pantry. It was chock-full of herbs, roots and all manner of dried things in glass jars or porcelain pots, plastic bags and containers. She'd called up Simone and together, they pulled all of Gram's herbs out to take inventory. Some were labeled, some were not. A few things were obvious while some were a complete mystery.

Simone Bisset was the perfect person to help. Violet had gotten to know her well over the years, and Gram had even written that Violet should contact her (another bullet point on the handwritten list of final instructions). Simone had moved to the village after Violet left for college. She'd opened an adorable tea and cake shop in the town square, and Gram had provided Simone with fresh, locally sourced herbs, fruits and ingredients for her baked goods.

Violet often visited the shop when she came home during the holidays or on weekends, enjoying both the lemon meringues and conversation of the owner in equal measure.

"I don't know, I found a bunch of witchy things in Gram's chest. It's feeling more and more Shakespearean around here with each passing day." Violet opened a container, lifting it to her nose. She dry-heaved. "*Oh God,* wh-what is this—"

"Put the cap back on." Simone urged. "All caps stay on. All containers remain closed unless otherwise instructed."

Violet obeyed, swiftly closing the jar and pushing it across the kitchen table. Simone grabbed it, then brought the glass to her nose and sniffed. She held the jar up to the light. "This is Crown Imperial… Commonly used as a diuretic, or to help new moms produce breast milk."

"It smells like skunk."

"Yes, well, nobody told you to snort it, did they? Growing it in a garden helps keep rodents away. It's a pretty flower, though. A natural pest control."

"You being able to smell and identify these things so easily is incredible. Meanwhile… I think I singed my nasal passage." Violet stood, rubbing her fingertips against her nose. "Do you want coffee?"

"Sure," Simone said, twisting jars against the table and examining their contents. "You know, this spread is extraordinary. Anise hyssop, calendula and chaga… I didn't even know she had these. Gorgeous herbs. Are you sure Gloria wasn't secretly Wiccan?"

"No, she was an herbalist."

"Hm." Simone picked up a jar filled with pale green leaves and pressed the glass to her nose, inhaling. She broke her own rule and unscrewed the top. "Clary sage. It has antidepressant and estrogen-enhancing elements, so it can be used as a tea to help with menstrual cramps. It can also have a narcotic effect. Sometimes brewers use it in beer in lieu of hops."

"Ooh, leave that one on the counter," Violet said, busy pulling out all the necessary items for a strong pot of coffee.

"Plants are extraordinary. Some argue that they're the oldest tools of magic. They were established on Earth long before humans, and they continuously give and spread life—to us and the air we breathe, to each other, to animals. Completely self-sustaining. We think of them as these stationary, soundless objects, but truly, they're vital. Plants could go on forever without us, but we wouldn't last very long without them."

Violet turned, smirking. "Tell that to the peace lily in the front window that looks awfully sad if I don't water her every six days. Simone, are *you* Wiccan?"

She winked. "I just dabble. I'm fascinated with plants and their healing properties, and the idea that they draw on and embody the four elements of water, earth, air and fire. It's why Gloria and I got along so well. We'd lose track of time talking about the things in her garden and plotting new, seasonal recipes. I miss her so much."

"Me too..." Violet exhaled a sigh, the weight of sorrow settling on her shoulders. She'd been distracted lately: exploring the poppy chest and its mysterious contents, working through the pantry with Simone, meeting with Jasper and thinking of starting her art again. But now, grief pushed to the forefront, as it often did, unexpectedly. It was always there, though. Lingering. Waiting in the wings for the right moment to take center stage.

"You know, back in the day, the Ainsworth women were a force to be reckoned with."

Violet frowned as she pulled the cabinet door above her head open and removed two mugs. "What do you mean?"

"Are you serious? Your family practically ruled over this village as a safe haven during the Fifty-Year Witch Cleanse back in the 1800s—that is, until the Laurent family showed up with their caravan and decided to settle here."

Violet turned and faced Simone. Her friend was looking back at her as if she'd just declared bees like honey. "What?" Violet said. "What are you talking about? Are you kidding me?"

"Are you kidding *me*? How do you not know this? It's documented in the historic records of Libellule village. The Ainsworth witches were fierce—and they had *major* beef with the Laurent family… That Jasper is sweet, though. He always sponsors a booth whenever we have a festival in the town square. I'd love to meet him in person one day."

With the coffee brewing, Violet moved back toward the table, feeling a bit spellbound. When she plopped down, Simone laughed. "How do you not know any of this? It's your family's history."

"I don't know, I mean… I knew about Ginger Ainsworth, my great-grandmother. Gram rarely spoke of her, but I heard some things from kids and families around town when we first moved here. You know how people talk and tell silly stories. But I've never taken any of it seriously… And of course Dad never mentioned it because he's a man and men don't talk about *anything* unprompted. How am I supposed to know what happened in my family hundreds of years ago if no one tells me?"

It was like how people who lived in Paris never cared to go inside the Musée du Louvre or to the Eiffel Tower. You just existed in a space, more focused on the day-to-day tasks than the highlights or the historic landmarks. "Gram mentioned the Witch Cleanse once when I was little," Violet went on. "But as I got older, I figured it was something steeped in propaganda, you know? Like, *of course* they weren't trying to cleanse witches and 'magic' from the world. More likely it was rooted in some misogynistic, religious stuff."

Simone scoffed. "Well, it was definitely those things, too. You should read up on it—get a better sense of the blood that runs through your veins." She stood from the table and moved into the kitchen, likely to take over the task that Violet had abandoned.

"Maybe I should..." She absently watched Simone as she walked. She wore a pretty, mint-green sweater that complemented her rich brown skin and slim figure. Her hair was braided and piled atop her head like a crown. "There was one time—only once—when me and Rosie were little... Gram told us a funny story about Ginger. She said she used to take Gram into the woods to forage, teaching her about herbs and spices, the medicinal plants and flowers there.

"They came across a rabbit with his hind legs caught in one of those awful traps. It wasn't moving at all. They took it out from the teeth, then Ginger bent down, laid her hands on it and spoke some words Gram had never heard before—couldn't understand them at all. She said it was incredible but scary when the rabbit's red, marble eyes flickered open and its body twitched. It flipped itself upright and hopped away."

The kitchen fell silent. Rosie had repeated that same story to their father when he'd returned home from work, and he'd been so angry with his mother that Gram had never said another word about Ginger Ainsworth again. The story, though it seemed totally unbelievable to her adult mind, had always stuck with her. Always loomed somewhere within her psyche, making her question its relevance and validity.

Magic isn't real. Why would she tell us that story?

She looked up and Simone was staring back at Violet with wide, chocolate eyes. Simone shivered, her entire body shaking dramatically.

"Oooh, that's *creepy*. Don't tell me anything else like that! Why did you tell me that?"

"I don't have any other stories, so don't worry," Violet assured her. "But that's all I know about my family's history on my dad's side."

"I'm going to have nightmares about red-eyed zombie

bunnies now... living in this obscure country village where weird things happened."

Violet smiled, then considered something. "Simone, why did you move out here? What brought you?"

Simone lifted the coffee pot and poured the dark contents into her mug. "Well, living in the city was exhausting. But out here it's pretty and quiet, and I have learned that I simply prefer my own company."

Violet nodded, understanding completely. "The city is noisy and dirty. People are rude, and it feels like everyone around me is frantic—racing toward something, but I honestly can't figure out what. I don't want to be part of it anymore."

Simone returned to the table, two mugs in hand. "Then don't. Stay here in town. I love it here and people are pretty nice... Even that one guy—the town hunk who comes into my shop for his morning coffee and is always really sweet to me."

"The town hunk? Are you talking about Freddie?"

"Yeah, that's him."

"Blegh." Violet scowled. "He's always been a jerk toward me. He's like the town mascot."

"Right? He totally is." Simone laughed, clasping her mug within her palms. "That's why I'm surprised he's so chill with me."

"Why wouldn't he be?"

Simone's face fell flat. "Seriously, Vi? Gee, I don't know—maybe because I'm a trans-woman, and he looks like a model they'd hire for a hunting and fishing shop advertisement if they were trying to attract more business from straight, single women under thirty-five."

Violet laughed. "That is so weirdly specific and spot-on."

"Isn't it? He must not realize I'm trans."

"Aw, Simone, don't think like that—"

"Violet, please. I grew up in the city and witnessed very bad things happening to people just like me. Let's not pretend otherwise." Simone took a long pull from her mug. Violet folded her arms in a huff.

"People are stupid."

"People aren't stupid," Simone smiled, setting her mug down. "They're just terrified. They want everyone to live the same grayscale life, abiding by the same black-and-white rules because it makes them feel safe. Unchallenged to change or dig deeper inside themselves. Anytime someone who lives in vivid color comes along, it threatens their boring little life and they don't know how to deal with it."

Violet smiled. "That's very astute and all, but I think they're just stupid. You're too kind."

Simone shook her head, grinning. "Because they don't matter, do they? I'm busy digging deeper, knowing myself and living my colorful life, fulfilled. But they're busy being miserable, insecure and worrying about me. I feel bad for them."

Sighing, Violet rested her elbows on the table, chin cradled within her palms. "I want my life to be more colorful."

"Well, let's dig deeper. What's your dream? What are you passionate about?"

"Uh…"

"Let's back up—what do you like?"

"Hm." Violet folded her arms, but it only took a moment for something to pop into her head. "Lately, I've been thinking about painting. When I was little, gram got me started with watercolors because she said they were made with more natural ingredients. I didn't even understand what that meant back then. I just loved creating palettes and mixing colors, drawing everything and everyone around me in my sketchpad. I took a few classes in college for fun, and I would even volunteer at the local kindergarten once a month and do art masterpiece classes. That was a blast. But I could never pursue it seriously. Everyone knows artists don't make money."

"That's not necessarily true. I consider myself a type of artist and I do alright. Have you ever researched ways to make your art profitable? With social media, things aren't like they were before. There's so much opportunity for exposure."

Violet sighed, tracing her finger along the rim of her coffee cup. "I haven't. I've only ever looked at art as a silly hobby. I've been on autopilot, you know? Graduate high school, go to college, get a job, work the job… Work the job some more. But then what? What's next? Get married and have kids? I don't even know if I want that."

"I think you're definitely asking yourself the right questions. I've always loved baking—before I was old enough to properly use a stove, I was making snow cakes and mud pies in the backyard. Now, I *love* playing with fruit and fresh, local ingredients. Getting creative, like improvisation. It's my art. You just need to open your mind to the possibilities."

"I do… you're right." Violet turned it over in her mind. What could she produce, given the freedom and opportunity to do so? She liked the feel of it: returning home and exploring her true desires in this place that she loved. Opening herself to possibility.

13

NOW

1656—1820.

Ainsworth, DeRose and Zabelle. Three
native clans traditionally occupied the
Libellule province. Prior to 1789, the
province fell beyond the geographical
domain of Queen Francesca-Marie Au Clair
Dupont. As such, the three clans held
full authority over the land and were
said to have existed harmoniously within
their community, and with nature.

Libellule was diminished to a village
following the Queen's victory within the
Holy Damascus War of 1787—a civil
conflict which dramatically changed the
country's landscape and territories.

"*D*eRose and Zabelle," Violet considered. "I've never met anyone in this town with those surnames..." She adjusted against the stiff wooden back of the chair. In the silence of the library, the thing creaked loudly, as if its screws were protesting their very purpose—they hated this job and they wanted out.

It was Saturday morning, but the library wasn't busy at all. On the rare occasions Violet had dared to enter the local library when she lived in the city, the atmosphere was more akin to a zoo rather than a quiet place to read and study. Children ran around everywhere, mothers stood talking together with zero concern for said children running amok. The espresso machine within the café buzzed and whirred constantly. All manner of people came and went. It was a lavish and cutting-edge space, but for Violet, ineffective for accomplishing any actual reading.

Libellule Community Library was a different beast. If the library in the city was a giant dragon with bright, shiny iridescent scales and magnificent spikes, LCL was a soft furry thing. It was cute, and if you petted it (because it would definitely let you, on good days), it might roll over to reveal matted and dusty fur.

The librarian, Rochelle, just so happened to be the daughter of the former librarian, Mrs. Blanc. But that was the way of things in Libellule. Violet noticed that most families just stayed here, as if they were holding down some invisible fort. Generation after generation.

Stretching her arms up, Violet glanced around at the filmy windows, the squat rows of dark bookshelves and the old furniture that hadn't been replaced since she was a child. The walls of the library were cornflower blue, which, to Violet, gave the space an oddly cheerful disposition. Crown molding lined the upper walls, creating an elegant transition to the stark white ceiling.

She looked back down at the history book, intrigued when a surname she recognized besides her own jumped out at her.

...1819 led by Xavier Charles Laurent. The terms of the Queen's post-war treaty allowed for affluent Northern families to claim what was regarded as unoccupied land within certain boundaries. According to the royal records of 1788, Libellule was deemed as an area with "rich, undiscovered resources" and "prime for the establishment of modern civilization and cultivation."

Xavier Charles Laurent and his caravan were immediately met with opposition upon arriving at the village. His key rival, Victoria Ainsworth, led the fight against the caravan and their ideals of purity in moral living. The contest waged on with fierce hostility until the spring of 1820. The native clans had held strong until then, and although the surrounding circumstances are undocumented, it has been said that a betrayal within the clan's ranks led to the eventual capture and burning of Victoria Ainsworth.

The remaining natives conceded to Xavier Charles and his ideas for the commune's prosperity and development. However, by 1821, very few of the original clans' people (Ainsworth, DeRose and Zabelle)

were documented within the town's census
record. The youngest son of Victoria,
Noel Ainsworth, was

"They were witches."

Violet gasped and jumped in her seat, making the chair's screws truly hate their task of keeping her off the floor. She scowled. "Rochelle, don't sneak up on people!"

"I didn't sneak. I walked." The waify woman pressed her glasses further up the bridge of her nose, making the top of the rims hit the dark, heavy bangs stretched across her forehead. "Anyway, Ainsworth, DeRose and Zabelle? They were witches. It was a coven. One of the most powerful in Europe at that time."

Violet adjusted in her seat. "Well, that's certainly fascinating."

"But the writer doesn't *say* that. It irritates me. Even the half-baked academic accounts that glorify that snake Xavier Laurent acknowledge the natives as witches. I like this book because it's one of the very few that even lists the indigenous people by name. The author went through all the trouble of digging up information, objectively trying to show their side, but then he ignores the elephant in the room. The witch in the room."

"Maybe he didn't want to vilify the natives like those other books do? He was trying to be politically correct."

"They weren't villains, but a spade is a spade."

"Some people don't believe in magic and that kind of stuff. Especially academics."

Rochelle turned her nose up. "And that's their deficiency. How can you really know anything about anything when your mind is so small? They claim to be these 'knowledge seekers,' but no *true* knowledge can get into the tiny, narrow space of their own entitled, biased existence."

Violet sighed. Rochelle grew up two years below her in grade school, so she never spent much time with her when they were kids. But when Violet came home from college for long weekends and studied in the library, Rochelle was always here. Just like this. Mrs. Blanc was the exact same way.

Wanting to lighten the topic, Violet smiled. "Are you going to the Welcome Winter Festival in the town square tomorrow?"

"No."

"Aw, why not? It sounds fun."

"Because people will be there. And I hate people. You know what else I don't like about that book?"

Violet raised an eyebrow, her effort to lift the conversation thwarted. "I thought you kind of liked the book?"

"Forty percent in favor, which is a lot coming from me."

"I gather."

Rochelle pointed at the book on the table, her nose upturned once more. "This writer doesn't even know what really happened. The Ainsworths, DeRoses and Zabelles were holding their ground against the Laurents, right? But he doesn't say what went wrong. Nothing about the breaking point. It's just empty conjecture. Annoying. That book creates more questions than it provides answers. It fails."

Flipping to the front cover, Violet read the author's name. "Alain Foxfort—wait, is this the same Mr. Foxfort that taught tenth-grade English at Libellule High?"

"Yes."

"Oh wow, why don't you just ask him about it?"

"He's dead."

"Oh…"

"Look, follow me." Rochelle stepped back, gesturing for Violet to stand. "There's another book that tries to cover our village history without blatant racial bias. Fifty-percent approval rating from me."

Violet pushed herself up from the creaky chair. "That's still pretty low, but a marked improvement."

"Nothing gets over a fifty-percent approval rating from

me. Well, with the exception of Simone's cranberry macadamia scones. But she only makes those between October and December, which is annoying. I have to eat so many because she only makes them for a limited time and then I feel sick."

Violet shook her head as she followed Rochelle around the corner of a bookshelf. "You don't *have* to eat so many."

"Of course I do. They're one of the few joys I have in this life. By the way, I heard your greenhouse got broken into."

"How do you know about that?" Violet hadn't called the police, and she'd only told Jasper and her sister.

Rochelle shrugged, then pulled a faded red hardcover book from the shelf in front of her. "People talk. Which is yet another reason why I hate them."

LATER THAT AFTERNOON, Violet stood on the front porch of Laurent House, grocery bag in hand. When Jasper opened the door, she couldn't contain her fervor.

"Did you know our families were basically sworn enemies?"

Jasper blinked. "Well, good afternoon to you, too."

He opened the door wider and Violet stepped inside. "Hi— I'm serious. Apparently, way back when, my great, great, great... great?... grandmother was an amazing witch and herbalist in this village, and as such, was a huge target for the northern settlers when they arrived here. Your family is written in the history books as her primary accusers. Jas, we are *literally* like the platonic version of Romeo and Juliet."

"Oh me! What fray was here? Yet tell me not, for I have heard it all." Jasper plucked the grocery bag handle from her grasp and turned, walking toward the kitchen.

Violet stared after him. "We-We're quoting Shakespeare now? I'm sensing a weird theme in my life lately." She shuffled forward to catch up to his long stride. "You don't own any deadly nightshade, do you?"

"What? Of course not."

"Did you already know about all this stuff with our families?"

In the kitchen, he set the bag on the countertop and started rummaging through. "Yes. You didn't?"

"Not at all," she said, falling into their established routine and moving toward the stove, turning the fire up high. "I had no idea. I mean, no one ever said anything. Your parents were always pretty nice to me—"

"Because that was four hundred years ago, Vi. You and me, we don't have anything to do with it."

Violet grabbed the cups from the cabinet and the tea bags from the white canister. "But still. My great, great-great—her name was Victoria. She ended up being burned at the stake in the center of town. It was a gruesome thing, in the midst of a famine and typhus epidemic. There was a lot of bad blood between my family and yours. Very old grudges like that... Do they just die out?"

The kettle on, Violet turned to watch Jasper. He was busy digging in the bag and removing his groceries. He almost seemed too focused on the task, with his dark brows drawn tightly together. She sighed. "It's just been eye-opening, but I'm—"

"Did you get more pumpkin seeds?"

"Did you eat the entire bag I bought last week?"

"Yes... So, no?"

"No, Jas, that was a giant bag. I got you a bigger bag than usual, so I didn't think you'd need more that fast. You're going to turn into a pumpkin if you don't slow down."

"The list is the same every week. Everything, every time, please?"

Violet rested her hands on her hips. "Jasper Oliver Laurent, are you scolding me?"

"N-No... When you say my full name like that, though, it feels like you're scolding *me*."

"I might be." She winked, smiling. "I'll make an extra trip and bring some tomorrow—"

"You don't need to do that, I'll just wait. Or I can go myself."

"I'll take care of it," she assured him, turning back to the stove. "But as I was *saying*, reading about the town's history has been interesting. And even though our families didn't get along, I'm glad we're friends, and that we can do mundane things together... like me screwing up your grocery list without anyone being burned at the stake." She peeked over her shoulder to catch him watching her. He rubbed his fingers against his scalp and through his thick hair, glancing away.

"I'm glad, too. Thank you for helping me."

The teakettle whistling, Violet turned and shut off the heat. When everything was arranged on a tray, they went to the study. Violet had brought her laptop and charger this week, wanting to do research and get Jasper's opinion, because friends sometimes saw things clearly that you yourself couldn't discern. She settled onto the leather couch, sinking down in the smooth softness of it and leaning back with her computer on her thighs. As usual, Jasper sat at his desk just a short distance away and near the curtained window. The weather was even colder now, so he'd lit the fireplace, casting the room in warmth, orange light and shadows.

"Do you think," Jasper began, "that if cockroaches were furry, people would like them?

Violet's stomach lurched. "I think I would like to burn *you* at the stake for putting that image in my mind."

Jasper laughed. "I'm serious. Furry things get such positive PR. Caterpillars, bees, all manner of woodland creatures. Squirrels are rodents, but they have fluffy tails so people like them.

They don't call squirrels, hamsters, guinea pigs or gerbils 'pests' like they do rats and mice. It's because of the hairless tail and lack of fluff. So maybe the fur factor would help roaches?"

"I don't know where this is coming from—usually I encourage random introspection like this and am admittedly guilty of it myself—but this is making me nauseous."

"Okay, okay," Jasper conceded, but then folded his arms. "So that's a 'no' on my theory?"

"A resounding no. And I don't think mice and rats are bad. They're just associated with diseases, sewers and would potentially eat people or other rats if it came down to it. You don't hear that about squirrels?"

Jasper frowned. Violet wasn't sure, but it almost looked as if he was pouting? "*Any* mammal can get rabies," he said. "Or eat something they normally wouldn't if food is scarce."

Violet shook her head. She rested her fingers against the keys of her laptop, then looked down at the glowing screen. An Internet search engine poised and ready for every possibility.

"If I quit my job," she began, "what would I do with my life? How would I create enough income to address my basic needs?"

"Do you have savings?"

"I do. A decent little nest egg."

"Gloria has presented you with a lot of options," Jasper acknowledged. "A greenhouse, dried flowers and herbs of every kind and clients who want to buy them. Land, a house. Would you want to pick up anything she left behind?"

"I don't know. I do like learning about the herb stuff—for instance, I made dried valerian root into tea the other night. I had to soak three grams of it in a cup of hot water for fifteen minutes."

Jasper grinned. "How did that go?"

"It tasted like feet."

He laughed. "That's because you need to blend it. Gloria

used to make some for me, but she'd blend it with orange blossoms and lemongrass. Did you sleep, at least?"

"I did. My breath was like dirty socks the next morning but I slept well."

"I'm not sure the end justifies the means."

"What about teaching art at the local kindergarten? I used to do that in college once a month and I loved it. It wouldn't pay the bills, if anything at all. How could I make that sustainable?"

Jasper leaned back, his arms still folded across his black sweater. Something about him looked a bit neater lately. He appeared slightly less like an active member of the dust bunny community. "Hm, I remember you were really good at sketching and painting... but anything in the arts is difficult to break into and make a sustainable living—unless you're very high-level. It could take a while to make headway."

"I know. I'd still like to do that in some capacity, though. Okay, let's table that. What else? Knowing what you know about me, what can you see me doing?" She met his eyes, and for once, he didn't glance away.

"I think... you can do anything you want, Vi."

She pursed her lips. "That's nice and very 'after school special' feeling, but I need something more tangible. More specific?"

"But it's the truth. I think whatever you try, you can do it well. When you make up your mind about something, you do it. It's an amazing quality about you. If you want to do the art masterpiece classes and paint, I think you'll do it and make it work. If you decide to take over Gloria's business dealings and learn more about plants and herbs, you'll accomplish that, too. It's just who you are."

Violet sat, processing. "Huh. In the end, I liked that speech very much. Honestly, that's the way I've always seen Gram—ambitious and free-spirited. Taking control of her own life and doing what *she* loved. If I embody even a small bit of that, I'm glad."

Jasper shrugged. "You embody all of it. You're a lot like her in the way you think and live, but you're young and Gloria was much older. Give yourself some time and try not to stress. You'll get to where you want to be."

He turned away, focusing on his laptop. But the warmth of his words quietly swelled in Violet's chest. Jasper was always like this: saying what she needed to hear. Giving her broader perspective when her own vision had narrowed and tunneled. She placed her laptop on the coffee table in front of her, then stood and stretched. "If my sister could hear you, she would not be pleased."

His eyes flicked over to her. "Why? I would *not* want to upset Rosie."

"Because she already thinks I have you placed on a pedestal. And then you say encouraging and sweet things to me, and it just raises the bar higher and higher."

"Why would someone like me be on anyone's pedestal? That makes no sense."

She walked over to the desk, standing at his side while he typed on his computer. As usual, there were emptied shells of various seeds on a napkin, as well as raisins and a dried-out apple core. Sometimes there were shriveled-up orange peels, blackened banana peels or cherry pits and stems. Always snacking...

"Why wouldn't you be?" Violet looked down at him, examining his features up close: the dark, curly mess of hair, matching eyebrows and very straight nose. Jasper wasn't glamorous. Not at all model-like or chiseled in the sense of society's conventional beauty standards (no Chris by any means).

But something... something about him whispered soft. Safe. Steady and reliable in the way of a thing you loved. A favorite cozy hoodie or blanket. The one with that rare element of subtle perfection that you adored, and every time you touched or held it, a spark glimmered in your heart.

And something unknowable quietly buzzed around him with warm energy—like electricity. He naturally radiated an imperceptible air, even though physically, he always seemed to be shrinking away. Trying to, at least. Constantly hiding and isolating himself on his own dreary island.

Without thinking, she reached down, gently fluttering her fingers within the wild, floppy curls at the back of his head. In truth, she'd always wanted to do this. Jasper's hair was its own entity, like the waves of a dark-chocolate ocean swirling and crashing into each other. Beautiful and chaotic.

She softly threaded her fingers within the silky strands just along his hairline at the back of his neck. "Should I make lunch for us again today? You didn't eat much, but you enjoyed it the last time, right?"

He stopped typing and glanced up at her with his gray eyes widened. His demeanor stiffened, completely frozen for only a moment as they watched each other in the dim light. Jasper always kept the house shadowy with curtains drawn, as if direct light and sunshine would cause him bodily harm. Slowly, he stood, shifting himself away to create space between them. Violet blinked, surprised by his movement. "You okay?"

"Don't—please don't do that."

"Do what? What did I do?"

"I think you should go for today."

Violet drew back, blinking. "But I just got here. What—"

"I apologize. I'm not feeling well, suddenly." He lowered his head, taking a breath. "I would appreciate it if you left for today. Thank you for the groceries."

Violet stared blankly, feeling like her throat was clogged. Her chest was tight. *What just happened?*

"Jasper, I'm sorry if I offended you—"

"You didn't, I... I just need to rest. Thanks for understanding."

Jasper turned and walked through the room and toward the hallway. In the doorframe he paused, waiting for her there to escort her out of his home. Stunned, Violet quickly moved to the coffee table, closed her laptop, picked it up and stuffed it into her bag. She followed behind Jasper without a word, the two of them walking in mutual silence.

At the front of the house, Jasper pulled the door open for her. He smiled. The gesture was genuine, without any discernible malice. "Thank you for today—and for the groceries. I appreciate it."

"Sure, of course..." She crossed the threshold and walked into the wintery afternoon. She half expected him to immediately slam the door behind her, but he didn't.

"Goodbye, Violet."

She turned, glancing over her shoulder, her mind a mess of confusion and embarrassment. "Bye. See you next week?"

He simply smiled. A sad gesture without warmth. When she was at her car and about to sit down in the driver seat, he closed the front door.

Inside the quiet vacuum of the cold vehicle, Violet swallowed hard. She watched as very fine snowflakes drifted down in the sunlight like glitter all around her.

What's wrong with you? Why won't you just tell me...

14

THEN

"Jasper... have you ever kissed anybody?"

Violet stared at her friend as she sat on the floor of Gram's front room, the fireplace crackling loudly as she waited, a large box of Christmas tree baubles just beside her. The glass orbs shone in every color, like a fancy arrangement of oversized hard candies.

Jasper was standing in front of the tall fir tree, frozen with a single iridescent-pink bauble in his hand. He was staring at her like she had snot on her face. "I'm *eight*." He frowned.

"So?"

"Eight-year-olds don't kiss—we're too young!"

"I don't know..."

"Well *I* know," he assured her. "We're too young." He turned, skillfully placing the looped ribbon on a branch as he cupped the glass sphere with his other hand. Violet decided a gold one should be next, so she lifted it out of the box, placed it in the concave of her folded legs and started tying the ribbon.

"Well, Rosie kisses all the time," Violet said, making a small bow at the top as a finishing touch. "Boys *and* girls."

"She's eighteen. She's way older than us so she can kiss whoever she wants."

"Hm. I guess."

Jasper stepped toward her. Violet raised her arm and transferred the gold ornament over to him. When he turned and walked away, she lifted from the ground slightly in the opposite direction, stretching her arm over to the coffee table beside her and grabbing another gingersnap. Gram's gingersnaps were the best because she always frosted them with a lemony drizzle.

"Why are you thinking about kissing?" Jasper stood on tiptoe, placing the bauble on a high branch. Dad and Rosie had already strung the tree with white lights, so they twinkled like starlight all throughout the thick brush.

Violet took a big bite of her cookie and spoke around it. "I don't know. I was just... Rosie left earlier with Art to go to the movies. When she came downstairs, she kissed him, like it was no big deal."

"She's eighteen. What color is next?"

"Mm... how about blue?" Violet quickly shoved the last bite of the cookie in her mouth, picked up a dark blue bauble and tied the ribbon. As she secured the bow for good measure, Jasper's voice was low.

"Do you *want* to kiss someone?"

"Yeah, maybe?" Violet lifted her arm again, handing him the orb. He took it, then turned toward the tree.

"Who do you want to kiss?" he asked.

Violet reached for her mug of warm milk with cinnamon, careful to lift it from the table. "*You*, silly."

"Me?" Jasper started. He turned, his big eyes even larger than usual.

"Yeah. You'll be my first kiss ever. Do you want to kiss me?"

He flipped back around, facing the tree and turning the blue ornament in his fingers. The movement reminded Violet of spider legs crawling around a ball. "Well, yes... but not now. We're too young."

Violet held the warm mug with both hands, smiling. "So when we're older? When we're eighteen?"

"Maybe... maybe a little sooner than that."

"Sixteen?" Violet brightened.

"I don't know—"

"Thirteen?"

"Violet, I don't know! We can decide *later*."

"I'm excited." Violet grinned, bringing her milk up to take a long sip.

"I—I'm... excited, too."

"Will I be your first?"

He nodded. "Yes... Yeah."

When he turned and was standing over her again, she beamed up at him. "Jasper Oliver Laurent wants to *kiss* me."

He frowned, his eyes shifting away and his face pink in the firelight. "You have milk under your nose. Would you just give me the next ornament, please?"

"Which color? How about purple? You like purple things." She lifted her chin, flashing a toothy grin. "Like my name—"

"The purple one is fine."

15

NOW

*A*t first, Violet felt confused. Then, embarrassed. This was quickly followed by frustration and indignation, which, soon, were wholly replaced with panic.

In her hasty exit from Laurent House, she'd forgotten her laptop charger. It was still plugged into the wall beside the brick fireplace. The cord hadn't been long enough to reach her position on the couch, so she'd abandoned the effort and told herself she'd plug it in later if needed.

"Ugh, I don't want to go back there right now..." She slouched on the sofa, an empty wine glass on the low table in front of her—her second glass of the evening. It was dusk and still snowing, sizable flakes now. Wet and heavy. The sky was overcast, but there were soft breaks in the clouds to show the pink-orange watercolor hues of sunset. She paused, squinting and blinking at her watch through her inebriated haze: 6:04 p.m. It was already well outside of Jasper's two to five o'clock visiting hours, and he'd booted her out. Violet groaned.

"What am I going to do? I need that stupid thing."

Why had he kicked her out so abruptly? Because she'd offered to cook for him again? Because she'd touched his hair?

Was he averse to touching? If that was the case, fine. But he should have communicated as much instead of throwing her out. What kind of sickness did he have where touching him was a heinous crime?

In truth, the more time she spent with him, the less sickly he seemed. Aside from being underfed (likely due to his steady diet of leaves, nuts and berries), he presented as energetic and strong. Astute and witty. If you took away the dusty old house and his lack of concern over his wardrobe and general appearance, a seemingly healthy young man remained. The house and his unkempt appearance were starting to feel like theatrics—props to aid him in his self-appointed role as a sick person.

It was all so confusing and Violet wanted to understand. Weren't they getting along well? The initial start had been a bit bumpy, but the more they met, talking to him felt easier—just as it had been when they were little. No subject had been off limits back then, the conversations and questions always flowing freely between them. Without judgement or rebuke. Without shame or tension.

In the past month of being reunited, Violet had felt as if things were still the same, even as adults. But this sickness of his was untouchable: an impenetrable wall between them.

She sighed. "I need my charger." Violet abruptly pushed herself up from the sofa, but paused when the floor seemed to tilt underneath her. "*Whoa...* Move slowly, Violet."

After a moment to get her bearings, she walked to the front door, slid her emerald peacoat onto her body and fluffed out the curly mass of her hair from underneath the collar. Given her wine-induced state, she decided to walk and take the path through the woods to Laurent House.

A quick check in the hallway mirror before she grabbed her house keys and headed out the door and into the snowy evening.

~

"HELLO?" Violet called out into the frosty air. It was darker now, the only real light source was a dim yellow lantern glowing like a soft halo at the front door of Jasper's home. The scene felt too quiet. Secluded, with no easily accessible neighbors in this more rural area of town. The vast apple orchard beside the estate, with its naked, crooked tree limbs motionless and stretching out into the night, did little to settle her nerves.

She'd knocked loudly three times with no response. It was cold and she was getting wet from the snow. She could feel the weight of it penetrating her curls.

"I'm sorry—I just need my charger."

No response. No obvious movement in the house.

"What a pain…" Maybe Jasper left in the evenings? Maybe he had treatments at the local hospital? Or overnight visits where he needed special assistance.

Violet pulled her coat a little tighter. She had a late start for work tomorrow and needed to go into the city around noon, but with Jasper's visiting hours being so strict, she'd miss his window, and she definitely wanted her charger now.

She exhaled and rolled her shoulders. She'd be in and out, quickly. *No harm in that, right?* With half a bottle of wine fueling her, it all made perfect sense.

Violet knew that the French doors off the kitchen were typically unlocked since they led into the back garden. There was the problem of the wooden door leading into the backyard, which might be bolted shut, but she figured she'd take a chance.

Following the perimeter of the house, the grass was wet and slippery underneath her feet as she turned a corner. She looked over her shoulder and at the silent rows of still apple trees. Unexpectedly, she sighed. Memories of spending long afternoons in the orchard with Jasper, his mother and father, sprung to the forefront of her mind.

The warm autumn sunlight, the distinct *snap* of an apple being yanked from its stem as the branch and leaves rustle and recoil. Taking that first sweet and tangy bite. Running the narrow lanes and laughing until she was out of breath. Carrying heavy baskets and being rewarded the next day with a hot, buttery, freshly baked pie.

Some memories, when they were strong enough, were like an enchantment. She didn't see the decrepit, ghostly orchard stretched out beside her. She saw beyond it, remembering what it was—what it could be if given some love.

The wooden door into the back garden stood taller than her five-foot-five frame. She wrapped her fingers around the icy iron handle and gave it a tug. There was a loud *clink* in the silence, and the door instantly opened wider—its broken chain dangling and hitting against the weather-worn wood.

"Huh." Violet blinked, surprised. She wondered if this was officially considered breaking and entering, but then decided she would tell Jasper about the broken lock the next time she visited (if she were allowed, anyway).

The garden path was laid with small square stones, one placed after another. It'd been perfect when they were little and pretending to be frogs jumping onto lily pads. It hadn't been perfect when Violet had mis-stepped one summer and came down hard on her knees. But that was almost always the way in her adolescence—falling, breaking, bumping and scratching. It seemed unfair to blame the stones when she herself was the common denominator in a long series of unfortunate incidents.

Just like the front of the house, practically everything in the back garden was dried up and skeletal. In the past, the space had been filled with beautiful rose bushes, lavender and red poppies. A lively bird bath wrapped with ivy had sat in the center, welcoming all manner of feathery friends. As with the orchard, Violet could see past its current state and remember its former glory. However, that didn't ease the low hum of melancholy in her heart—the loss of joy in a place where there had once been an abundance.

She stepped up to the French doors and tried pulling one open. It gave, creaking loudly in the silent, snowy night. She stuck her head through the crack. "Jasper? It's Violet."

Nothing. The wind whipped from behind, pushing frantic snowflakes into the kitchen as she stepped inside and pulled the door shut. "I just need my charger," she called. It felt ridiculous to speak out loud like this, but just in case...

The house was dark and even colder than usual. She shivered, patting her coat and hair to rid herself of snow before walking toward the study. It was quiet as she moved. So much so that one would think the house was abandoned—that there hadn't been any inhabitants for decades.

I guess he leaves at night... She turned the corner into the hallway and was surprised to see a soft orange glow radiating through the open doors of the study up ahead. She knew this was Jasper's favorite room, or at least where he seemed to spend the most time. But it felt odd that he would leave the house with the fireplace burning.

"Jasper?"

She slowed her pace. No response. Anxiety stifled her chest and her throat was like cotton. Afraid of what she might find in the study, her imagination suddenly ran wild. But she shook her head and trudged forward. When she reached the door, she took a breath before peeking around the corner. No one. Jasper's desk was empty save for the usual hoard of trail mix and abandoned strawberry tops on a napkin.

Stepping inside, the low-burning fire popped and cracked as she looked around. "Maybe he only ran out for a minute?" Shrugging, Violet walked over and swiftly pulled her charger out of the wall, then looped the cord around her palm in her usual way.

Just as she placed it within her large coat pocket, she heard a sound. Something faint within the room that made her freeze. If the house hadn't been so quiet, so still, she probably wouldn't have heard it. But she had, and now her heart was racing as she scanned the floor. The source had registered low, so she stepped forward and past the coffee table, cautious, as if moving in slow motion. When she reached the opposite side of the couch, she heard it again and stopped.

Violet took a few careful, silent steps back and swallowed. She crouched down, gradually lowering to her knees far enough away from the couch so that whatever lay in wait wouldn't be able to assault her head-on. She bent, both palms on the floor, then lower, shifting to her elbows. A little lower and she saw it. And it saw her—staring back at her and frozen in place. Violet gasped in shock and the slight action made the little mouse spring into motion. Like a gunshot it darted from underneath the couch, the surprise making Violet pop upright with a yelp.

"Oh no oh no!" She took two long strides forward and quickly shut the double doors to trap it inside the study. Thwarted, the mouse raced toward Jasper's desk for cover. Violet's pulse pounded in her ears, but she needed to think fast. There was nowhere for it to run or hide now, so the task of capturing it should be easy enough.

Taking a breath, she scanned the room. "What can I use to—" She moved to the messy desk, but in doing so, the mouse retreated again, this time squeaking and running toward the open area behind the leather couch. She grabbed the wastepaper bin from beside the desk and chucked its contents onto the floor. Properly equipped, she turned and listened.

At first, stillness. But she waited, her eyes and ears alert until she received a clue. Soft squeaking sounds on the opposite side of the room near the bookshelves prompted Violet to walk forward. It was there, running along the bottom of the book-cases, frantically seeking an escape. But when it saw Violet, it backed itself into the corner of the shelves, almost cowering, as if understanding its inevitable defeat.

"I'm not going to hurt you, buddy, alright? Just don't make any sudden movements..." She crept forward and it actually seemed to obey. When she was close enough, she flipped the garbage bin upside down and gently placed it onto the floor for a successful capture. With this much done, she stood straight and breathed. *Of course this house has mice. Why wouldn't it? Good grief...*

Contemplating what to do next, Violet took a breath and glanced around. A book would be too thick. Paper, too thin. She walked over to Jasper's desk, looking over the surface. He had a couple thick folders in an upright organizer. Perfect. She removed the contents for good measure, laying them on the desk so that she could return them later, then walked back over to the mouse trapped underneath the trash bin.

Once there, she rested on her knees, only lifting the makeshift cage enough to slide the folder underneath. "Step onto the folder, little guy. Or girl?" When she felt the weight of the mouse on top, she slowly tipped the bin so that the mouse needed to crawl to the bottom. With the bin upright, she removed the folder, peering inside to get a closer look.

It was so small—smoky gray in color and with a starburst of white whiskers coming from its little snout. Dark marble eyes, roundish ears standing alert... and it was shivering in the corner of the wastebasket. Curled into itself like a furry little ball as it peeked up at her. Violet wasn't into rodents, but something about this little creature's visible terror made her heart ache.

"I'm not going to hurt you, but you shouldn't be in here." Violet stood, stepping toward the coffee table. "Little field mice belong outside in the orchard. I know it's cold, but you need to burrow into a tree trunk or something."

She set the basket on the table, then made quick work of

LOVE, MAGIC & MISFORTUNE

replacing Jasper's folder. Grabbing the bin, she walked back out into the hall and toward the kitchen. She stepped through the door to the dark garden, knelt down and gently tipped the bin so that the mouse could escape. Violet expected it to scurry off, happy and grateful to have been spared from any harm (or at least running away in terror). But in an odd turn, it just sat there, upright and on its back legs. Its tiny front paws curled as it looked up at her, lifting its snout and still shivering. She tilted her head.

"Hey... this is the part where you scurry off." The mouse settled down on all fours, then tried to move past her and back into the house. Violet turned and quickly pulled the cracked door all the way closed to block it.

"Seriously? I'm being kind to you. *Go.*"

The mouse paused again before turning. It looked back at her once, then hopped off the small step and scurried out into the dead brush of the garden. When she lost track of it, she stood and shook her head.

How strange. Could it have been someone's pet? She didn't think Jasper had a pet mouse. If he did, surely he would have mentioned it by now. Had she just released Jasper's secret pet mouse?

"It's just a field mouse..."

Within ten minutes, she'd cleaned up the trash, stopped in the kitchen on her way out to grab a handful of Jasper's blueberries and deposited them in a small pile on the back step before leaving Laurent House.

She'd done a nice thing in humanely removing the mouse. That was a *good* deed and she'd tell her friend that he needed to set some kind of friendly traps later on to help with the problem. Because, obviously, mice running around a person's house was a problem...

But as she drove home, she felt weird about it. Sad, somehow. She couldn't pinpoint why.

16

THEN

"Where's Jasper?"

Violet looked up. She'd been staring down at her arm in its sling as she sat motionless on the playground swing. "What?"

"I said, *where is Jasper?*" Freddie stared at her with searing blue eyes. They were only nine, but he was already so much taller than her—taller than everyone in their class. He towered over her like a mean giant, as if it was her fault that Jasper hadn't been coming to school lately. Actually, Freddie probably did blame her. He hated her.

Violet rocked her heels against the grass, making the swing move in a gentle motion. Having just one functioning arm made it difficult to enjoy such an activity. "I don't know... He's sick."

"Sick how?" Freddie demanded. "Why isn't he coming to school?"

"I don't know—"

"You're his *best friend,* aren't you? Shouldn't you know? What good are you if you just sit here with your stupid curly hair and your stupid broken arm not knowing anything—"

"Just leave me alone." Violet jumped to her feet, turned and marched away from Freddie.

"Wait—come back!"

She shook her head and kept walking. Violet didn't know what was going on, and when she'd tried to take matters into her own hands to find out the truth, she'd stupidly fallen from a tree. She'd broken her arm, gotten yelled at by her Gram (who forbade her from ever climbing another tree again) and she hadn't really discovered anything at all in the process.

It was a big mess. Her arm hurt and her heart hurt, and she was the loneliest she'd ever been.

When Violet reached her usual spot behind the school house, she plopped down onto the cold grass, resting her back against the brick wall. She was thinking that this was the part when Jasper usually came around the corner to sit with her. He'd talk to her and say something interesting to distract her and make her genuinely curious. Then they'd laugh, because they were always laughing.

But he wasn't coming. Violet knew that. The emptiness of it made her stomach hurt. She drew her knees up and rested her good arm on top so that she could put her head down. She took a deep breath, and then she cried. Even after the school bell rang to mark the end of recess, she didn't move. She just stayed there, all alone.

17

NOW

Bang-bang-bang.

Violet sat upright in bed with a jolt. She blinked, her eyes and mind both foggy from sleep and a little too much wine. She rubbed her palms against her face, groaning. After a moment, she dropped her hands in her lap and sat still, stuck in that strange space where she wasn't sure if she had actually heard a sound, or if she'd only imagined it. *Can you dream sounds?*

Bang-bang-bang. Violet started. "Okay, not a dream..." Lazy, she swung her feet over the side, then donned a robe and slippers. She moved into the hall and toward the front room, yawning. If this was another Freddie intrusion... Violet really should answer and make it plain that she had no interest in talking to him about *anything*. This was getting ridiculous.

Or maybe it was perfect? She could ask him about the greenhouse. Nothing had happened since, but if her number one suspect was standing on her doorstep, she should probably take advantage.

When she got to the front door and looked through the peephole, her jaw dropped in complete shock. It was Jasper.

Without a second thought, she unlocked the door and swung it open. He was wearing a navy-colored duffel coat with a large hood, the latter pulled up over his dark head.

His face. In all the time she'd known him (notwithstanding the fifteen-year gap in their relationship), she'd never seen this expression settled on his usually gentle demeanor. In his typically bright but serene eyes.

He was fuming. Startled, Violet swallowed. "H-Hi... What are—"

"Why were you in my house last night?"

Violet took a breath, the tone of his voice unfamiliar to her as well. "How—how did you know I was there?"

"Because I know. *Why?*"

"I forgot my laptop charger and I needed to get it. I'm really sorry, but I tried knocking, and—"

"Do not *ever* come into my house without me letting you in."

"I understand, but Jasper—"

"No," he said, his frown intensifying. "You don't understand, Violet. You just—" He took a breath, shaking his head as he lifted his hands, raking them through his hair and knocking his heavy hood back in the process. He looked truly exhausted. Without the shadow of his hood as a cover, the dark, heavy circles underneath his eyes and paleness of his skin made him appear ghostly.

He turned and took a step away, dropping his shoulders with his back to her. Violet seized his pause as an opportunity.

"I'm sorry I broke into your house, okay? I—It seemed like a good idea at the time, but that was definitely *not* socially acceptable behavior. I was wrong, but I needed my laptop charger for work later today and I'd forgotten it in your study. Jasper, honestly... It would be better if you just talked to me instead of being so mysterious and anxious—"

"Anxious?" He whipped his head to the side. "I'm *not*... Fine, I am anxious. Very. But I have *reasons.*"

"Okay, yes, and this is the mysterious part. How am I supposed to navigate your quirks if I don't even have a roadmap? I don't know how to avoid the landmines."

"Not breaking into my house is one surefire way."

"That's fair, I agree," Violet said. "But what did I do yesterday that made you kick me out? I have no idea."

"It's complicated. You *can't* know—that's why you... you shouldn't even be coming to my house. This is all because of Gloria's meddling and I shouldn't be doing this. I'm being a complete idiot and..." Jasper shook his head, but then his tired, steel-gray irises were serious when he looked at her. "Don't come to my house anymore, Violet. I can't do this with you."

They watched each other in the stillness, and something inside of Violet—something small and fragile that maybe never quite had a chance to properly heal—came rushing up to the surface.

As she took a breath to ease the tightness in her chest, Jasper turned and rushed down the path and away from the front door. Violet lifted her chin, shouting, "Jasper Oliver Laurent, come back here! We're not finished."

"I'm scolding *you* this time," he yelled over his shoulder. "Don't try to flip the script."

"Oh no, no, just wait—darn it." He was moving too fast and Violet was standing there in her robe, house slippers and not unlikely, with crust in the corner of her eyes. She slammed the door and went back inside to dress... And probably wash her face as well.

IF YOU WENT on foot and walked the path through the woods, Laurent House was less than ten minutes away. It was very cold out, and Violet considered driving, but the road wound along the perimeter of the forest, then through the town circle (where there were pedestrians, stop signs and other things that would inevitably prove a great inconvenience in Violet's present circumstance).

She brushed her teeth, threw on jeans, a sweater and her coat before trekking through the woods and over to Jasper's house. They weren't finished with this conversation. Not like this.

He'd disappeared from her life fifteen years ago. But not really. She always knew where he was. But he was so complicit in not seeing her. Not even trying to rebel against the adults' wishes (Violet would have fully supported him in staging a prepubescent coup).

They'd gone from four years of practically spending every single day together—afternoon picnics in the meadow with homemade croissant sandwiches and fresh fruit teas; sunsets in the forest, running and climbing when everything around them was drenched in firelight; holidays, birthdays and even mundane school days only made special by their being *together*. So much joy and camaraderie, and then absolutely nothing. Cold turkey.

It had taken so long to see him again—to achieve some semblance of healing in that vacant, painful space within her heart. This, in addition to the new hole in her chest from Gram's passing, was tipping the grief scale. It was too much.

If he didn't want to see her anymore, fine. She would accept that. But she wasn't going to let him walk away without some explanation. Some kind of closure so that she could move on and finally let him go.

When she reached the front door to his house, she knocked hard. "Jasper, I know you're inside. Please open the door."

She waited. Nothing. Violet growled. "*Jasper.* You cannot just —just brush me aside like I don't mean anything. Open this door—"

"Well, hello there."

Violet swung around with a gasp, nearly jumping out of her shoes. She pressed her back into the door and stared up at the tall, ridiculously handsome man before her. He was...

"Holy—you're Ambrose Marcello? Oh my God—"

"You know me? My, what a pleasant surprise."

He was impeccably dressed: a long tan trench coat over pleated slacks, a beautiful creamy knit sweater and the most elegant pair of brown leather wing tips she'd ever seen. His hair was dark, neatly trimmed and his eyes were like rich cocoa but... Violet tilted her head, examining. There was something captivating but strange about his deep gaze staring back at her. Almost infinite. She'd seen Ambrose Marcello in many pictures (not that she was regularly searching for images of him or anything), and had even seen him from a distance when she'd attended one of his writer's forums. But up close and in person...

"Wow," she breathed, beside herself. His nutty brown skin was so rich, it practically glowed.

He smirked, his thick lips teasing. "I could say the same thing about you," he said, his voice deep and smooth like a midnight river.

The door behind Violet swung open, knocking her out of her stupor and making her clumsily tilt backward. Immediately, she felt firm hands gripping her shoulders to catch her. She jumped, adjusted her footing and turned, feeling inept as she saw Jasper in the doorway behind her, his face still brimming with displeasure as he looked them both over. When his eyes settled on the tall, eloquent man beside her, Jasper lifted his chin.

"Why are you here so early?"

"Well, firstly, hello Jasper."

"Hey."

"Second, my meeting in the city was cancelled," Ambrose

cooed. "So I thought I'd stop by a little early. I had no idea you were expecting company?"

Jasper's stormy eyes narrowed on Violet. "I'm not," he spat.

"It doesn't appear that way to me." Ambrose tilted his head. "You know, most men only dream of having a beautiful, voluptuous woman beating down their door. And yet, here you are, seemingly displeased with such a rare blessing."

Violet stared at Ambrose, awestruck. *Whose child is this? What woman gave birth to this creature?* She stifled the urge to poke him, just to see if he was real.

Jasper's grunting made Violet turn her head back toward him. He was still frowning as he opened the door wider. "Just come in and spare me the guru drivel."

Ambrose smiled, then dipped in a little bow at his waist with his hand out. His coat sleeve moved up with his motion, revealing a shiny, expensive-looking watch on his thick wrist. "After you? Ladies first."

Hesitating, Violet looked at Jasper and waited. He rolled his eyes. "Come inside please, it's cold."

She stepped over the threshold, but she let her displeasure be known as she passed him, turning her nose up before cutting her eyes away from him. Ambrose's voice resonated behind her.

"I'm not sure why we're behaving like children, but I am *greatly* intrigued by this new development."

"There's no development," Jasper said, closing the front door. "Go sit in the study and I'll bring tea." Their gruff host turned, walking down the hallway and disappearing into the kitchen.

18

NOW

*V*iolet and Ambrose stared down the empty hallway. Soon, the sounds of cupboards being aggressively opened and closed echoed through the dim, dusty space.

"Interesting…" Ambrose said, blinking. "I don't think I've ever seen him like this."

"Like what? Being stubborn as a mule?" Violet huffed. "Me neither."

"Not just that. Perhaps I've never seen him express *any* raw emotion with such conviction… Well, there was one time. Anyway, you've certainly stirred him." He gestured, urging her to move toward the open doors of the study. "May I have the pleasure of knowing your name?"

She smiled, her previous excitement restored as she walked past the doorframe. "It's Violet. Violet Ainsworth. I'm actually a huge fan of your writing."

"Ainsworth, you say? You have deep roots here in this village."

"I've just started reading up on that, actually."

"Remarkable. So, you mentioned that you enjoy my books?"

"Oh, absolutely," she said, sliding her coat off her shoulders.

She went to lay it aside, but Ambrose approached, offering to take it along with his. He went back out and into the hallway, likely hanging them on the rack before reappearing. "I've read all of your books," Violet went on. "Your writing is so vivid and expressive. It makes me feel like I'm seeing the world through your words—like a movie in my mind. And your characters are always rich and layered, too. The women are so fun to read."

Ambrose sat in the armchair near the sofa, folding one long leg and resting his ankle on his knee as he settled. "Well, Violet, it is an absolute pleasure to meet you. You must forgive me though, as I am quite caught off-guard by this present circumstance. I'm not exactly sure how to proceed. May I ask how you know our dear Jasper?"

That was a weird thing to say... "We grew up together. Well, partially. We were very close when we were young. I recently moved back home, so I'm trying to help him out since he can't leave the house," she explained. Although, he could leave sometimes, apparently. To scold her.

Ambrose folded his large hands in the gap of his legs, threading his fingers as he examined her with dark eyes and a beautiful smile. If he ever grew tired of writing, he could easily be an actor or some type of model. "Hm, 'very close,'" he repeated. "Would you say you were his best friend as a child?"

"Ah, yes? I would say that—at least, that's my perspective. If you asked *him* right now though, he might disagree, and then throw me out."

At this, Ambrose laughed, a little huff that made his shoulders jump. "Incredible... Well, it seems that I am sitting in the presence of an integral wellspring of my own achievement. I thank you, Violet Ainsworth. I am truly honored to meet you."

"Um, sure. You too?" Violet frowned. She liked Ambrose Marcello, a lot. But she was starting to get an odd feeling about him. *Maybe he really is a weirdo like Rosie says...*

She realized her eyebrow was cocked in suspicion when

Jasper came into the room with a tray. She fixed her face, but it was too late. Ambrose laughed again. "Jasper, your lovely friend thinks I'm strange."

"Aren't we all a little strange?" he asked, setting the tray on the coffee table and distinctly avoiding looking up and into Violet's face. "I only have Earl Grey, but there's cream and sugar."

"If you need chamomile, I'll bring it next time," Violet offered without thinking. She'd been responsible for his food supply for a month now, and it was becoming second nature. But he stood straight and turned, walking toward his desk.

"You don't need to do that."

Violet rolled her eyes.

Ambrose unfolded his leg and bent toward the table to pour his tea. "Violet tells me you've known each other since you were children?"

"Yes," Jasper said, his arms folded as he leaned back in his desk chair.

"Hm. You once told me a beautiful story about a very precious childhood friend, and that she is the—"

"René, *stop*." Jasper abruptly sat upright, his gray eyes wide as he looked at Ambrose, then over at Violet. Slowly, he relaxed his shoulders. "Please... *please* don't do that."

"René?" Violet blinked, looking between the two men with her teacup paused at chin-level. "Who is René? Aren't you Ambrose Marcello?"

Quiet. Now they were all awkwardly flickering their eyes back and forth: Jasper at Ambrose-René and Violet, then Ambrose-René between Jasper and Violet. She felt as if she were in an intense mystery movie scene where one of them was definitely the murderer.

"My dear Jasper, I think it may be best to reveal the truth to your beautiful friend? She is obviously sharp. Attempting to deceive her will only elongate the present awkwardness of this impromptu meeting?"

Jasper fell back into his chair, groaning as he slid his palms over his face, then up into the floppy mess of his dark hair. Ambrose watched him with hawk eyes, bringing his teacup to his mouth. "I haven't known her for very long, but I am almost certain that we can trust her?"

"It's not about trust—"

"Isn't it?" Ambrose raised his eyebrow. "I believe all complex human relationships are driven by trust. It is the foundation of our every interaction."

"Would you please stop that." Jasper moaned, laying his head back.

Violet considered, suddenly seeing the situation from a new perspective. "Wait. Are... are you two involved?"

There was a slight pause. Jasper lifted his head and looked at her contemptuously, but Ambrose smiled. "Aren't we?" he said, then turned toward Jasper with a smirk. "*Involved.*"

Jasper frowned at him. "Not like that."

"And not from a lack of effort on *my* part, mind you, dear Violet." He shifted his evocative eyes to her, still grinning as he took a sip of his tea.

"Oh..." Violet blinked. Well, Ambrose was a beautiful, outwardly elegant and luxurious man—currently existing in direct conflict with his surroundings. A cluttered and dusty library within an old, run-down country chateau. He belonged in an expensive high-rise condo in the city. The ones with all the glass windows and no discernible privacy. She doubted many people ever refused his advances.

Jasper sighed and met Violet's eyes. "Ambrose and I work together. Ambrose isn't his real name. His real name is René. You know authors typically have a pseudonym?"

Violet nodded. "Yes, of course."

"So, there you go." Jasper sat back again, folding his arms and turning his body slightly away from them. End of conversation. Ambrose laughed, but the sound registered as disbelief rather than genuine amusement.

"That's... pretty bare bones, my friend."

"It adequately explains the situation while clarifying any misconceptions," Jasper stated.

Violet looked at Ambrose. "What is he not telling me that lies beyond the bones?"

Now it was Ambrose's turn to avoid Violet's gaze. He brought his teacup to his mouth once more, tilted his head back and finished the contents before making a satisfied sound. He placed the cup back on the tray and stood. "Well, Violet, that puts me in a predicament. I think in this situation, any revealed truths should come from our forlorn prince here."

Ambrose walked over to Jasper, reaching in his back pocket and pulling out his wallet. When he was standing over Jasper, he handed him something that looked like a check. "Your cut of the spoils from last month, kind sir."

Jasper rolled his eyes, but took the check, then placed it in a desk drawer. "Thank you."

Ambrose looked between them. "Well, Monsieur Laurent and Mademoiselle Ainsworth, I'm leaving. The tension in here is so thick that even saying it is redundant. Clearly, we need to do some talking?"

"I would love that," Violet agreed. "But it seems I've made one too many mistakes, so I doubt that will happen."

Jasper sighed, closing his eyes and massaging the center of his forehead with his long fingers. Not a word.

"We've had the pleasure of knowing each other for some time now, Jasper," Ambrose said, his deep voice warm and unruffled. "I don't know exactly what's happening here, but... I do hope that you'll try being open to it. This seems *very* good, for you—"

"I'll walk you to the door." Jasper flashed a tight grin as he stood and moved past Ambrose. When he was gone and out in the hallway, Ambrose breathed in a quiet laugh.

"I've upset the boss. Violet, it was wonderful meeting you. I hope we cross paths again, soon? Under less strained circumstances, of course."

"Well, we'll see. This may be my last time here, but it was very nice meeting you, too."

"Pity. I certainly hope that isn't the case. Shall we take control of our destinies instead of relying on chance? Here." Ambrose reached for his wallet again as he went to her. This time, he pulled out a business card. "I'll be in the city again next week for a book signing. Let's have coffee? Here, in your charming village. I always come straight to Jasper's home when handling our business, but I'd like to see how the town has changed. It has been a long while since I've looked around."

Violet nodded, turning the card over in her hands. "Sure. I'd like that."

Graceful, he took her hand, then kissed her knuckles before departing.

As Violet waited in the silence, she checked her watch: 9:25 a.m. She had plenty of time before she needed to start the drive into the city, but she didn't want to stay where she wasn't welcome.

When Jasper came back into the room, Violet stood and took a deep breath. "Listen, I get it. I've intruded on your space, I broke into your house, crashed your meeting with your colleague... I'm like the character I told you about that's always in romance novels and making poor choices. You don't want me here, so I'll go."

She paused, bringing her palm to her forehead and swallowing hard. "Maybe... maybe I was hoping to rekindle something that I thought was important between us—something that honestly meant a lot to me. But it's not there anymore, right? I'm chasing a ghost. So I'll stop. I won't come here anymore."

Jasper listened, watching her with his round eyes. Violet took a step forward to go and he finally spoke.

"You *don't* get it. At all. Would you sit down, please?"

Surprised by the sudden shift in his attitude, Violet nodded once, then sat back down on the couch. Jasper went to the armchair that Ambrose had previously occupied. When he sat, she noticed again how utterly exhausted he looked—the dark heavy bags, the pale discoloration of his skin.

"Jasper, if you feel bad, can I drive you to the hospital? Or I can leave, and we can just try talking another time?"

He ran his palm down his face. "I'm fine. I just... this is normally my sleeping time, so I've been up for almost twenty-four hours. Will you listen to me?"

"Yes."

"You haven't intruded or crashed anything. I let you in here, remember? You shouldn't have broken into the house last night, and I sincerely ask that you never do that again—"

"I won't. That was wrong of me and I'm sorry."

"I understand why you did it, but... Violet, I'm not supposed to be around anyone. The way things are for me, I have a responsibility, and part of that charge is to remain isolated. It has nothing to do with you. You are... radiant. You've always been like bright sunshine to me and I really, really enjoy being in your presence. Feeling your glow and energy is life-giving. But I *shouldn't*. I really..."

He looked down at his hands resting on his thighs, then took a breath. "And please don't say—or even think that I'd brush you aside. You're not nothing. You're *everything*, Violet. To me. Everything I could ever hope for in a friend. You can't imagine how much I care about you and think about you. But I shouldn't be. So..." He shook his head and ran his fingers through his hair.

Violet's heart was so warm and her throat so tight, it was hard to speak. When she did, her voice came out quiet, cautious. "Jas, why shouldn't you? What's the reason?"

He finally looked up, his watery eyes meeting hers in the dim light. "I can't tell you."

"Why?"

"I just—I can't. I'm sorry."

The silence settled over them and it felt cold. Lonely. It was the same sensation she felt when she looked at the run-down state of Laurent House. When she took in the barren apple orchard and the withered rose garden. The loneliness was like a black, inky bubble around this house, radiating outward in a giant malevolent sphere. In the center of the misfortune and despair was Jasper. Her lovely, smart and sweet friend with his bundled-up secrets. Crouched there, all by himself.

"You don't need to be sorry." Violet broke the silence. "But, what now? What... are you comfortable with?"

He lifted his head, meeting her eyes again. "I enjoy having you here and our visits. I think it's much more than I deserve. But I just need some boundaries if I allow myself to do this. Can you understand? I don't mean to insult you. That's not it, so please don't take it that way."

"Okay, but if I do something that upsets a boundary, can you tell me? It's hard to not take things personally when I'm immediately escorted off the premises without explanation."

He scrunched his nose, playful. "I may have overreacted a bit."

Violet mocked his expression. "Mm. Just a little."

He smiled, leaning his head back and closing his eyes. He was obviously tired, so Violet stood, grabbing her purse as she did so. At the sound of Violet's rustling, Jasper lifted his head again, his heavy lids opening.

"I'll go," she assured him, smiling. "You need some sleep. And for the record, you're everything to me, too, Jas. You're someone that I always want in my life—no matter how old we get. I care about you, too, and I love you. If you ever decide you want to tell me what's going on, I'm here."

Jasper's eyes went ridiculously wide before he closed them tight and held up his hand in a stop motion. His face flushed in deep rosy red. "Boundary. Don't do that."

"Do what?" Violet frowned.

"What you *said*. Don't—"

"I said a bunch of stuff. You don't have to tell me what's really wrong with you—"

"Not that part."

"Then what? That I love you?"

"*That.*"

Violet blinked, confused. "But I do—why? I can't say that I love you, now? You're my best friend. You don't love me?"

The rosy flush of his skin deepened as he shook his head. "I'm—I... Violet, *please*. I'm exhausted and—"

"Alright, Jasper, *alright*. Ugh. Men." She shook her head and moved toward the hallway. "I'll see myself out. Should I visit with food next week?" Pausing, she turned to look at him. He was slouched down in the chair, his hair even messier than usual as he stared at her with his flushed face. He looked hopeless. And adorable.

"Yes, please," he said, a little smile on his lips. "You don't have to wait until next week. If you have time..."

Violet lifted her chin, her nose upturned in a teasing gesture. "I *might* have time. If you're lucky."

"I'm not lucky." He grinned. "But I *would* be if you did."

"I'll let you know. Oh, you don't have a pet mouse, do you? Cute little gray guy—or girl?"

Jasper went still, his face flat as he watched her. "No."

"Hm. Well you might have some tiny roommates living here rent-free and scurrying around at night. You should probably investigate that—or at least charge them? You'll also want to get a better lock on the back-garden gate. I'll reimburse you if you give me the receipt."

19

THEN

"Hey Gram!" Violet called, bouncing up from the blanket and onto her knees. Her sundress fluttered out with her sudden movement, drifting into the plate of sandwiches and strawberries in front of her. Jasper leaned forward, pushing the material back and tucking it into the crevice between her knees and the blanket.

"Yes, sweet pea?"

"Is magic real?"

Gram paused and sat up straight from her crouched position. She removed a thick gardening glove from her hand to wipe the sweat accumulating on her forehead underneath her wide-brimmed hat. "Why do you ask?"

"Because I'm telling Jasper the story you told me and Rosie, and *he* says it's not real."

Violet looked down her nose at the skeptical boy sitting across from her. He was holding a big strawberry by its green top and taking a bite. When his eyes met hers, he shrugged and kept eating.

Gram stood, groaning as she did so. Carefully, she stepped through the spread of wild flowers and herbs in her garden. It was early summer, the sky bright and cloudless but the temperature still cool. Gram had made Violet wear a light sweater with her sundress when she'd first come out for lunch with Jasper. Eventually, she'd shed the garment and tossed it aside, letting the gentle heat of the sun warm her skin. The cool breeze caressed her shoulders.

When Gram was standing over them, she put her fists on her hips, one hand clenching her gardening gloves. "I thought I told you not to repeat that story, missy. Your father doesn't like it."

"I know... but he's not here right now, so how's he gonna know?" Violet bounced against her knees, grinning.

"Hm. True." Gloria bent slightly at her waist, whispering. "Alright, but it has to be our secret."

Violet clapped as Gram sat down on the edge of the blanket. Jasper picked up another strawberry.

"Magic *is* real," Gloria said, gripping the brim of her large hat with her fingers and slowly pulling it from her head. She bent forward, keeping her voice low. "There's just much less of it in the world now, so it's hard to find."

"I *knew* it," Violet whispered against the breeze.

"So what happened to it?" Jasper asked. "Why is there less? Where did it go?"

"The people who knew how to use it were treated very badly—"

"Persecuted?" Jasper blinked.

Gram sat back. "Well, that's a big word for such a little boy."

"Jasper knows lots of adult things—keep going!"

Gloria hunched down again, shifting her eyes back and forth between them. "Yes, persecuted. Long, long ago, magic flowed abundantly and freely throughout the world—streaming and moving through the air like a rushing river, free for anyone to reach out and harness some of its power." Gram moved her arms gracefully to mimic the flow of a stream, then reached her arm out and clenched her fist, quickly snapping it shut. Violet's eyes were wide, and when she looked to Jasper, his mouth hung open.

Gram straightened her posture. "But then, there were wars and disease. People were angry with those who had magic—with those who lived differently and in ways that were difficult to understand. The magic wielders became angry, too, and started using their powers for evil. This upset the Earth, and slowly, the magic stopped flowing. The river was cut off and the stream of energy dried up."

"So…" Jasper began, his face filled with melancholy, "it's all gone now? There's nothing?"

"Oh, there's still magic." Gloria reached over and gripped his small chin with her fingers, lifting his head. "It just exists in more subtle forms now—inside of us… There's a lot inside of you, my child. You're practically brimming with it." Gram tilted her head, her brow creased as she exhaled a sigh.

Violet brightened at this development. "Do I have magic inside me, too?"

"Of course you do, sweet pea. We all do."

Jasper folded his arms. "But not *real* magic."

Gram frowned. "Yes, real magic."

"Okay, so that means the next time Freddie tries to say something nasty to Violet, I can zip his mouth shut with my mind? Or maybe make him trip and fall…"

"Not necessarily." Gram smirked, standing up.

"Jas, that's evil magic. The Earth doesn't like stuff like that."

Jasper pouted. "How is it evil if I'm using my magic to help *you*?"

"Violet doesn't need you to fix her problems, dear." Gram dusted off her pants. "She just needs you to be a good friend and listener when problems come up, so she doesn't have to hurt on her own."

Looking to the side, Jasper considered that for a moment. He nodded. "Okay, I can do that."

"No violence against Freddie Martin, please," Gram said, stern. "Promise me?"

"I won't," Jasper agreed.

"Good. Finish your sandwiches and then we'll take a walk out to Pont du Coquelicot."

At this, both Jasper and Violet turned to each other, grinning. Poppy Bridge was their absolute favorite place in the entire village—a small arched structure made of gray stone, idyllic and serene in a clearing surrounded by a sea of red poppies and wildflowers. It was very deep into the woods, and they were not allowed to walk such a great distance alone. Not at their age.

They both turned their attention to the sandwiches, fruit and tea, bubbling with excitement as they finished their lunch in the golden sunlight.

20

NOW

[Janet: I have a fun idea for this year's holiday party and I couldn't wait to tell you.]
[Janet: Are you ready? A pool party! A holiday splash!]

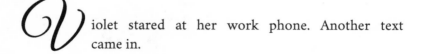iolet stared at her work phone. Another text came in.

[Janet: Reach out to that adorable new boutique hotel downtown on Monday. See what the cost is to privately reserve the indoor pool and some rooms.]

Slowly, Violet placed the phone facedown on the small table beside her. It was best to deal with that later. Or never.

"You've been painting? I approve." Rose examined the colorful canvas on its easel. "Just this one?"

"No, I'm working on a couple others." Violet turned another page in Ginger's journal, skimming.

"Like what?"

"Well, I'm starting with acrylic since it's so versatile, and it's been years since I painted anything at all. I'm painting Poppy Bridge from memory. Since winter is settling in, I'm positive that it's all cold and ugly out there now, and I haven't been since I was a kid. I sketched a portrait of Gram, too, but I haven't started painting yet. I want to do that one in gouache, but I need to play around with paper types to see which one holds the paint the way that I want." Violet had another project in mind, but she decided to keep that one to herself.

Rose ran her fingers across the surface of the dry canvas. It was another cloudy, late November day on the back porch and Rose had driven up Friday night to visit for the weekend. Violet sat in one of the large wicker chairs at the end of the enclosed patio space, two cups of hot chocolate set on the small table beside her. The heat of the liquid swirled and danced in the gray light.

"Paper matters?" Rose asked.

"Oh, absolutely. The dispersion of the pigment—even the color of the paint can present differently depending on the content of the paper. I tested out one pad, and it made the black present as blue. Of course it was a cheaper block of paper. So I'm going to need some higher-quality canvases."

"It sounds tricky," Rose said. "I was always so impressed with your talent growing up. I remember you saying you wanted to paint a particular person's portrait, but you were sad that you never had the chance."

"Huh." Violet shifted her gaze, intentionally obtuse.

"So you're not doing a portrait of your shut-in friend? Now that you're reunited?"

Violet didn't answer, only picked up her hot cocoa and took a long sip.

Rose turned, smirking. "Well?"

"You looking to start a fight?"

"No." Rose laughed. "I don't know why you think you can

hide anything from me. You never could. You should have him sit for you—"

"Jasper would *never* sit for me and let me paint him. Bah."

Rose raised her eyebrow. "If he's anything like he was when you were both little, I think Jasper would do just about anything for you. The two of you were inseparable."

"No." Violet shook her head, resolute. "We're rekindling our friendship, but he keeps me at arm's length. There are some hard boundaries established and if I broach them, he gets prickly with me, fast. It's not what you're thinking."

"Hm. I'm not convinced."

Violet's work phone buzzed on the table. Against her better judgement, she flipped it over and casually leaned to look at the screen, watching the messages pop up in succession.

[Karen: What are we doing for the holiday party?]
[Karen: It's already November 23rd!]
[Karen: Should we just book a restaurant?]
[Karen: That sounds expensive...]
[Karen: What if we got a food truck?]
[Karen: We could do a thing in my backyard.]
[Karen: I know a guy and we can rent heaters?]

Rose lifted her chin, gesturing toward the journal in Violet's hands. "Why are you looking at that?"

"Because it's interesting. I think it's a grimoire. There are lots of lists of ingredients and their magical intent, sketches of what look like amulets and talismans... There are even some Latin phrases in here and other symbols I don't recognize. Maybe spells?"

"I can't." Rose waved her hand, dismissive. "I wouldn't even *touch* that. Everything about it makes me uncomfortable—we should throw it away."

Violet laughed, turning a page and finding another complex-looking formula in an unknown script. "This feels like the kind of thing you'd throw away one night, but the next morning—"

"Don't even *say* it—"

"You'd wake up and it'd be sitting on your nightstand."

Rose groaned loudly, pressing her palms flat over her ears. Violet chuckled once more. "I think you'd be cursed if you tried to get rid of this. It's a relic from the past. Plus there are actual curses in here, I bet."

"I'm not touching it," Rose said, walking toward the wicker chair on the opposite side of the small table. She sat and grabbed her cocoa, but then dramatically leaned away from Violet and the book.

Violet shook her head. "You goofball. Anyway, I'm thinking of taking it to Simone so she can go through it. She might be intrigued since she's kind of into this stuff."

"Simone… Oh, the pretty baker lady?"

"That's her. Aw, I hope people say cute things like that about me and not like, 'Oh, that freckly mixed girl with the frizzy hair?'"

"Your hair isn't frizzy. Today."

A loud knock at the front door made them both jump. When it was silent again, they stared at each other.

"You gonna go get that?" Rose asked.

"*You* go get it. You're older."

"This isn't my 'cozy cottage' so it couldn't possibly be for me." Rose sat back, bringing her mug to her mouth in stern protest. Violet sighed, stood and headed toward the door. She hated answering doors. It always felt like the epitome of "stranger danger."

When she got to the front and looked out the peephole, of course it was Freddie Martin. Violet looked at her watch: 5:32 p.m. *Why isn't he at the grocery store?* She rolled her shoulders, unlocked the door and whipped it open.

Freddie stood there, tall, blonde-haired and blue-eyed, in his

Chris-like glory. He wore a check shirt that fit his square shoulders perfectly. Jeans that neatly hugged his narrow waist and muscled legs. He looked like a real-life Ken doll and Violet despised him.

"What *is* it?" she spat. "Why do you keep coming by here? Did you steal Gram's weed?"

"What?" Freddie drew back, his chiseled features contorted but still vulgarly handsome. "Who answers a dang door like that? I didn't steal any weed—what are you *talkin'* about?"

"Gram's greenhouse was hit and someone broke in here. Who else would it be besides you? You putz."

"I wouldn't ever take anything of Gloria's. She was a real good customer to me and my dad for years. Why would I steal from her? I don't steal."

"Right..." Violet eyed him viciously, unconvinced. He may not have stolen the weed, but he was definitely guilty of something. Being a jerk, for starters. "What the heck do you want?"

He took a deep breath and dropped his shoulders. "Can you stop being so hostile toward me?"

"Are you kidding? You teased me for the duration of my *entire* adolescence and made my school life miserable. The minute I move back home, you tell me my hips match my hair. No, I don't think I'll stop being hostile toward you. I have *years* of hostility to inflict—"

"Look, I'm *sorry*—and your hips do match your hair. But it's nice, alright? You have a good full body, like a little hourglass."

"Are you done?"

"No." Freddie groaned, running his hands up through his hair. "That's not why—just *listen* for a second. I wanna talk to you about something. My therapist says it's important that I have a talk with you but... but right now I'm worried and I want you to go see about Jasper."

Therapist? Violet frowned. "Excuse me? What did you do to Jasper?"

"I didn't do anything to him! It's just—on the second Friday of every month, we get a shipment at the grocery store. I usually take the heavier things that Gloria didn't wanna wrestle with over to Jasper's. He always buys household stuff in bulk from us to help support the business—"

"Why didn't you tell me? I could have taken it over."

"I don't mind doing it, woman. Do you need to take *everything?*"

Violet paused at that, taking in his frown and the poignant tone of his voice. "I guess I don't. Go on."

"Like I was saying, I go over there every second Friday in the afternoon—in his scheduled free time, I guess. Usually I knock, he doesn't answer, so I walk away and go hide behind that big ole tree off to the side and near the orchard. He always opens the door about five minutes after he thinks I'm gone and brings the stuff in the house."

Violet shook her head. "You're a real creep, you know that?"

"I'm *not,*" he spat, rubbing his palm against the back of his neck. "I just like to know he's doing okay. But yesterday I waited for fifteen minutes and he never came out. I went over there just now and the stuff I delivered is still on his porch."

Freddie exhaled a deep breath. Now that she wasn't wholly occupied with detesting him, she could see that he was genuinely distressed.

"I've been helping him and Gloria for years and he only did this one other time," he went on. "I told Gloria and it turned out he did need some kinda help. She wouldn't say what happened when I asked but... Could you check on him? He might be in some sort of trouble."

He stared at her, blue eyes focused. Waiting. Violet shook her head, snuffing out a sudden thought that glowed to life within her mind like a tea candle.

"Okay, Freddie, I'll go right now."

"I need to get back to the store. Just let me know later if he's alright, please?"

Violet nodded. "I will."

"Thanks." Freddie turned and strode down the path toward his car. Violet looked after him with her hands on her hips, the cogs in her mind spinning when her sister's voice registered behind her.

"Did he just confess to you or something? I swear he likes you..."

Violet sighed. "Not quite. I need to go and check on Jasper. I'll be right back."

∾

WHEN JASPER HADN'T ANSWERED the door after three loud knocks within a ten-minute span, Violet was faced with a conundrum.

She hated to admit it, but she now shared Freddie's concern. However, she absolutely, positively *would not* go into his house uninvited again.

"So what now?" she said, then huffed out a breath in frustration. A rattling sound in the bushes made Violet jump. She watched, and just like before, out came the black cat with white paws. It strutted confidently now, the bandage on its front paw gone. But it had something firmly lodged in its mouth. Violet drew back, recoiling when she saw the long rodent tail and the small limp, unmoving body it was carrying.

"Ick." The cat ignored her and moved toward the back of the house. Violet followed.

The wind was bitter and blustery, making her nose burn as she walked against it. When she reached the back of the house, the cat scurried off in between the orchard trees with its prize. Violet turned her attention to the garden door, which gaped open, quietly banging against the frame in the winter breeze.

Looks like we didn't get this fixed yet. Technically, going into the backyard wasn't the same as breaking into the house. She'd just have a peek into the kitchen and go from there—maybe call the local police.

The garden was exactly the same as before, but a little less sinister in the overcast daylight. As she focused on the double French doors, she tripped, forgetting about the small step there. But she caught herself, took a breath and moved closer to the house.

At first, she didn't see anything. Just an empty, shadowy kitchen like always. But something on the floor caught her eye. She sucked in a breath, her mind bending and frantically trying to make sense of what she was looking at... What on Earth *was* she looking at? Was it even from Earth, or from some other planet or universe entirely? She was perplexed and shaken by it. As if in a trance, she reached up slowly and knocked against the glass, willing the form to move. When the thing twitched, Violet started. Her entire body shuddered with fear and unknowing.

Without thinking, she stepped back. Of course, she hadn't remembered the small step there, so when she missed it completely, there was no opportunity to catch herself in the fall.

She tumbled backward, barely seeing the world sweep and turn from underneath her as she fell. She hit the ground cold and hard.

21

THEN

The surrounding woods were silent aside from Jasper and Violet's feet crunching twigs, gravel and underbrush as they walked along. The occasional call of a raven echoed across the sky. Violet looked up. The trees were tall and imposing in the late afternoon light, standing strong like nature's guardians.

Jasper held her hand firmly, pulling her along. Determined.

"Jas, what are we doing? You know we're not supposed to go to Poppy Bridge by ourselves."

"Gloria made that rule when we were six. That was three years ago—"

"But still. And it's getting late. Why right now?" The sun was already setting, pinkish and yellow with light streaming in between the thick tree trunks. The sky reminded her of cotton candy.

"I don't know," Jasper said, soldiering forward and gripping her hand tightly. "I just... I want us to go there again. It's our favorite place, right?"

Violet nodded, keeping pace behind him with her eyes focused on the back of his head.

Jasper sighed. "Things are getting weird at home."

"Is this because of the itching?" Violet asked. "You said your mom took you to the doctor, and they said that everything was fine. You even had tests done."

"Yeah but it still hasn't gone away. It's getting worse and it feels like spiders are crawling all over the inside of my body. Dad is really quiet about it. He doesn't say *anything* and just keeps looking at me like he's about to cry. And Mom is freaking out. I—I don't know what's going on, but it doesn't feel right."

When the path opened up, Jasper stopped. Violet stood beside him, her eyes sweeping over the tall, yellowed, flowerless grass of the clearing. The trees seemed even darker here, lining the perimeter of the glade like an army closing in on its enemy. Now, it was totally silent. Violet's heartbeat drummed in her ears, her breath shallow as it passed in and out through her mouth.

Jasper let go of her hand and walked to the arched stone bridge. It stood like a beacon, with a tiny stream of fresh water trickling underneath, winding its way through the clearing and then deep into the forest. Sometimes, the water didn't even flow and the brook was dry. But with all the rain they'd had over the summer, it flowed smooth and steady.

At the top of the bridge, Jasper leaned with his palms against the side, looking over and into the narrow stream. Violet followed and stood with him.

"Where does it itch the most?" Violet asked.

"It's just all over. It feels warm, too, but I can't scratch it."

Violet moved behind him, scratching her fingers against his shoulder blades. Then up to the tops of his shoulders before trailing down his spine. "Maybe *I* can?"

Jasper laughed, squirming. "No, when you do it, it just tickles." When she moved to his lower back, he wriggled a little more, hunching his shoulders. Violet smiled and looked up at the very dark swirls of his hair. She really wanted to put her fingers in it. Jasper's hair was always so shiny and clean-look-ing, and his mother kept it very neat—but Violet dropped her hands. She shouldn't mess that up, probably.

"Violet?"

She blinked, realizing she'd been staring. "Yeah?"

Jasper turned and Violet's breath caught because he was a little too close. They were always close, but... her heart was beating in her throat for some reason—heat glowing to life in her cheeks.

He smiled, his gray eyes glassy in the setting sunlight. "Thank you for coming here with me, and if anything happens... I mean, something where we can't be friends anymore—"

"Jasper, nothing is happening. You just feel itchy, and the doctors say you're fine—"

"I know, but, you... you let me talk about anything. Every-thing! And you don't think I'm boring or weird or stuck-up, and you never say that I'm 'rich and spoiled' like the other kids at school do. You're my best friend and you'll always, *always* be. No matter what. Okay?"

Violet stepped forward, wrapping her arms around his shoulders and pulling him into a tight hug. "I know, Jas. You're my best friend, too. And the kids at school are stupid. They laugh when Freddie makes fart noises with his armpits."

Jasper mumbled within her embrace. "That's *not* funny."

"It's gross," Violet confirmed, hugging him a little tighter. "You're okay, Jasper. Don't worry."

The wind swept through overhead, rustling the leaves as if the trees were whispering and sharing secrets in their own ancient and unknowable language. Jasper lifted his head from the embrace and took a deep breath, his smile bright. "I want to show you something on the way back. I think you'll like it."

As they walked down the long wooded path and toward

LOVE, MAGIC & MISFORTUNE

Gram's house once more, Violet grabbed his hand and clasped it tight.

Quietly, she kept sneaking glances at her friend, noting the straightness of his nose and the glimmer of his pale eyes. She didn't know why, but she was wondering if, just maybe, she could convince him that they should try kissing sooner. Perhaps, even before they were thirteen?

22

NOW

*W*hen Violet opened her eyes, the light of the room practically blinded her. Everything was white and fuzzy, like someone was holding a piece of printer paper too close to her nose. Her head throbbed and she groaned.

"You're awake?" Rose's voice rang out from her side. Literally rang, making Violet clench her eyes shut. She moved her head, instantly regretting it as the wave of nausea washed over her.

"The doctor says it's just a good bump on the head," Rose stated. "Maybe a very mild concussion. At least you didn't break anything this time?"

"Ugh... too bright."

She heard Rose stand, shuffle away, and soon the room was much darker. Violet opened her eyes, feeling a little relieved. "Thanks."

"You're welcome. What the heck happened? I got a frantic call to the house from Jasper, telling me you fell and he'd called an ambulance. Speaking of, I should call and tell him you're awake. Poor guy sounded beyond distraught."

Violet stared at the ceiling, her head still throbbing with its own pulse and intention. It was as if her skull had transformed into a subwoofer while she'd been sleeping.

Gradually, the image of what she'd seen before she fell came back to her. She sucked in a breath and closed her eyes. Her entire body trembled.

"Vi, what happened? Do you remember?"

For a long moment, Violet didn't say a word. She didn't know how to process what she'd seen. What it meant, or who or *what* it had been. She took a breath, pushing down the intense swirl of confusion. "I just tripped and fell backward. You know how I am, Rosie."

"I do, but I thought you'd gotten better about that. Sheesh, Violet, you have to be more careful."

"I know."

"How do you feel?"

Violet considered. "Like I have the worst hangover in the history of hangovers—but without the wild partying to validate it. Feels like my elbow is burning, too?"

"Yes, you caught yourself on your elbow and saved your skull, thankfully."

Violet tried moving, just a little, stretching her spine against the hospital bed. She took inventory. Aside from the massive headache and tingly elbow, everything else seemed to be in working order. "So, Jasper called you? He—he's alright?"

"Yeah, after he called the ambulance," Rose confirmed. "He was panicked. Why wouldn't he be alright? Was something wrong when you got there?"

Violet shook her head, which was a terrible, terrible idea. "*Ah*—no. Ouch. Everything was fine, I just feel a little woozy. Confused."

"The doctor said that's to be expected. You've been out for about thirty minutes. Let me call your friend and let him know you're awake so he's not freaking out anymore." Rose stood, pulling her smartphone from the pocket of her blazer, then walked into the hallway just outside the room.

Violet sucked in a deep breath and blew it out. She stared up at the ceiling, her mind thick and heavy like a dense fog.

"What in God's name is going on?"

VIOLET WAS RELEASED and sent home the following morning with firm instructions to take it easy over the next week. Rose helped her into bed, then drew the curtains and provided her with a cold, damp compress and a big glass of water. When Violet was settled and warm underneath the quilt, she smiled.

"Do you think a mild concussion is a good enough excuse to get me out of planning a 'Holiday Splash' pool party?"

Rose giggled, but frowned as she finished folding the basket of clean, cold laundry that Violet had abandoned the day before. "When we're excited about a mild concussion because it can get us out of work, maybe it's officially time to look for a new job."

"Oh? You told me to stay the course before."

"Well, stay the course but in a different car? You can change jobs. Why are we having a pool party in December? Is this for a bunch of teenagers?"

"No. Professional adults."

"There's no way I'd let anyone in my law firm see me in a situation requiring anything less than business casual," Rose snarked. "What a nightmare."

"Thank you for validating my concerns."

"Are your crazy bosses wanting to do this?"

"It sure as heck isn't me."

"Gosh," Rose said, shaking her head. "Why can't they just do things normally? They have seventy-five employees, but they're always trying to do these weird events like they used to do when your company was smaller. What did they try to have you do over the summer? Something about a sidewalk barbecue?"

Violet grinned. "Oh right. They wanted me to rent plastic tables and chairs for a 'parking lot picnic' in the middle of a heat wave. That really stressed me out, talking them out of that."

"Legally, they don't even own the building where your office space is. It's a commercial property with a restaurant next door. What were they thinking?"

"I've been working for them for three years and I still have no clue. It's a mystery."

"They set you up for failure with half-baked, outlandish ideas and then get mad at you when things don't work out. You need a new job. Or... what if you took this painting thing more seriously on the side? See if you can make it profitable so you can get the heck out of there."

"Wow, you've changed your tune," Violet said.

"Well, that's because before, there was no other option. You were talking about quitting your good-paying job to 'find your-self,' like some college drop-out backpacking through Europe and living off Daddy's trust fund. But painting is tangible. And you're amazing at it, Vi. You have a unique point of view and solid taste."

Violet pursed her lips, doubting. "I'm rusty. And nobody wants to buy my sketches—"

"Be positive. You have an eye for subtle details, and it makes your drawings feel alive. If you did it more intentionally, with serious practice, I bet you could sell some pieces."

"I don't know. I was going to focus on creating an art masterpiece course for the local elementary school. Maybe pitch it to them?"

"Well, do that too. Yuck. Small children."

They both fell silent, looking at each other in a pause.

"Did you hear that?" Rose asked.

"Maybe someone knocked? Go see..."

Rose finished folding the last towel, then turned and left the room. Violet relaxed into the pillows propping her upright, letting her mind revel in the cool quiet around her, listening for the faintest of sounds. Soon, she heard Rosie and a second, much quieter voice. A voice she knew well.

Rosie reentered the room, her eyes wide in a surprised expression only Violet could see. A moment later, Jasper appeared, cautiously, as if some alarm might go off because of his presence. Violet sat a little straighter, amazed. He looked exhausted again—pale and with dark circles. Except this time, there were raw but faint scratches on his face. He stayed inside the doorframe.

"Hi... are you alright?" His tired face was riddled with concern and other things, too. Stress? Fear? Several emotions not clearly discernible.

"I'm alright," Violet answered, unable to pull her gaze from him. "Rosie, can we have a little privacy, please?"

Rose lifted her eyebrows and turned slowly. "*Suuure*... I'll make some tea." Jasper stepped aside to let her leave the room, but remained in the doorframe once Rose was gone. He stuck his hands in his coat pockets as he looked at the floor.

"You can come in," Violet said, her voice soft in the stillness. Jasper shook his head.

"I shouldn't. I'm not staying. I just wanted to make sure you were okay—"

"Jasper, what did I see?"

He looked up at her now, tired gray eyes full of apprehension and sorrow. "I don't know what you saw."

"Why is your face scratched up? And why do you look so tired like this sometimes? As if you haven't slept in days. Jasper, what the heck—"

"Did you tell anybody?" He took a hesitant step forward, his voice quiet but urgent. "Rose or anyone at the hospital, about what—what you saw?"

Everything about his demeanor read frightened and anxious. It made Violet's heart ache in the midst of her wild confusion. "No," she said. "Of course I didn't. I don't even understand what I saw to repeat it."

He relaxed, visibly. His shoulders dropped as he retreated a single step back into the doorframe. "*Please* don't say anything to anyone. I'm sorry that I... I shouldn't have let things get this far. I'm so sorry you had to see that."

Violet was about to tell him to come closer and sit, but Rose popped up behind him, making Jasper jump at the sound of her voice.

"Do you prefer honey in your tea, Mr. Laurent?" she asked.

"Thank you, but I'm not staying. I just wanted to make sure Violet was alright." He took a deep breath. "I'll have my groceries delivered going forward—you don't need to do that for me anymore. Let's just end things here. Thank you for helping me, Violet. It was really nice to see you and talk to you again."

Without another word, he turned and disappeared down the hallway. Rose scoffed. "Did he just fire you from your volunteer work?"

Violet gripped the plush comforter in her fists and took a breath. "Yeah, I think this is the third time he's fired me? It's our comedic routine, don't worry."

"It didn't look very funny. Why does he call me, hysterical and worried about you, come over here to check on you, but then tell you he doesn't want to see you anymore?"

Sinking down further into the bed, Violet closed her eyes. "That's the question, isn't it? I don't know, Rosie. I think I'm done. I'm not going to fight him on this anymore. If he wants to be guarded and isolated, who am I to stop him?"

"Well, you said this is the third time he's fired you. Maybe third time's the charm? But Gram did tell you to be patient with him."

Violet's eyes flickered open, and she frowned at her sister sitting on the edge of the bed. "I'm confused. *You* are the one who has been nagging me to let go of Jasper for the past fifteen years. I'm finally in agreement with you and now you flip sides? What is this treachery? What's with you today?"

Rose drew back slightly, her perfectly arched eyebrow raised. "Well, I—you *could* walk away. That would be fine, too. Maybe for the best. But I don't know... He was so distraught when he called. It was sweet. And then he shows up here looking pitiful with a face full of scratches and that messy bedhead. I feel a little sorry for him."

"When did you grow a heart?"

Rose chuckled. "I know, right? I blame Jillian. Even though she's working way too much lately."

"She's back from Paris, right?"

"Yeah." Rose sighed. "But now she's talking about some huge meeting in Berlin. I don't know. Everything feels so vague and secretive with her lately. I'm trying to trust it, but I have this nagging feeling."

"What if she's been lying all this time and is doing something completely off the rails? Like a high-end male brothel."

"Random. Can we have a variety of genders in this hypothetical brothel?"

Violet shrugged against the bed frame. "Sure. And everything is consensual. Everyone wants to be there."

"In theory this sounds exciting, but in practice maybe this would not be sexy... and also a legal and logistical nightmare."

"Oh, it's definitely illegal. Nobody said it was legal—hence the secrecy."

Rose sat straight and folded her arms, pouting. "I think I would be mad if she kept that from me. Why leave *me* out of the illegal fun?"

"You're a lawyer."

"I'm not a cop though, and I'm a family lawyer. Why are you

making me feel upset over my girlfriend's non-existent prostitution ring?"

Violet giggled. "Sorry. Maybe in the end, she'd be getting lots of new clients for *you*."

"Dislike," Rose declared, her face softening as she looked at her sister. "Try one more time. With Jasper, I mean."

"We're back to this again?"

"Would you rather go deeper into this imaginary gender-nonconforming-brothel rabbit hole?"

"Yes, actually."

Rose shook her head. "He just seems so gloomy and lonely. His dad died and nobody has seen his mom around town in years. I don't know... I realize that I've pushed you to get over him, but you're living here now. Maybe he needs a friend?"

Exhaling and nestling deeper into the warm bedsheets, Violet pulled the comforter up, physically shielding herself from Rosie's unexpected encouragement. Violet closed her eyes and turned onto her side. "I don't think he wants one."

23

NOW

When Violet walked into Le Petit Sweet Bakery and Café a week later, she waved to Simone. She was radiant as usual and standing behind the curved glass case full of colorful, elegant pastries and freshly baked breads. Violet took a seat near the window, basking in the gentle sunlight of the wintery day—the first of December. It warmed her face, and after days of lying in bed, she was glad to be feeling more like herself again.

"Hello, dear. Are we treating ourselves today? You feeling better?"

Violet opened her eyes at Simone's question. Her braids were down, falling all around her shoulders like twisty little ropes. "Mm, yes and yes. But I'm meeting someone."

Simone smiled. "Oh? Is Jasper coming out today?"

"No."

Silence. Simone shifted her weight. "Ooookay... Anyone I know?"

"Have you ever heard of the writer Ambrose Marcello?"

"The author, right? I've never read anything by him, though. Isn't he a self-help guru type?"

"Yes, privately. But he writes fiction. He knows Jasper for some reason and we ran into each other at his house. He wanted to have coffee together—ah. I brought this for you." Violet turned and reached into her tawny brown bag. She pulled out Ginger's journal and handed it to Simone. "I thought you might find this interesting. It's full of witchy notes and things."

Simone's eyes grew wide. "A little Saturday night intrigue. Excellent. Can I get you anything?"

"How about a generous slice of lemon meringue?"

"Smart girl."

Once Simone was gone, Violet glanced around the café. There was a healthy crowd—not so many people that the small space felt congested, but just enough to help emphasize its coziness. Rays of sunlight, a low humdrum of lively chatter and the smell of powdered sugar and fresh coffee wafted through the air.

Glancing out the window, Violet's mind wandered. First, to the failed pool party attempt at work. She'd been grateful to learn that the hotel was booked full through the end of the year with no option to rent out their pool. She'd had to try three more hotels before her boss gave up on the ridiculous idea. In its place, they were treating everyone to dinner and drinks at a locally owned restaurant. An event appropriate for professional adults.

Then, despite herself, Violet's mind wandered to Jasper. *Again.* She wanted to stop thinking about him—to stop trying to figure him out. There were moments of success. Temporary distractions. But Simone's mentioning him had yet again unleashed the flood of confused thoughts in her brain. The anguish of frustrated emotions in her heart.

What would it be like? To sit in this café drenched in winter sunlight and talk with him. To laugh and smile, carefree and with no secrets between them. Like normal friends—normal people who genuinely cared for each other. Why couldn't they get there? They'd had it once. Even now, it didn't seem *so* far off. Not impossible, anyway.

"Let it go, Violet," she mumbled. It was over. Yes, Gram had told her to be patient, but for how long? Rose had unexpectedly switched sides after years of telling Violet to move on, but so what? She wasn't the one being rejected and pushed away at the drop of a hat. Rose had become more adamant when a large bouquet of lavish flowers had shown up on the cottage's front doorstep. Violets, richly colored in gorgeous dark and light purple hues. They'd included a message: "Thank you for every-thing." From Jasper.

Rose always got roses from everyone she'd dated. Perpetu-ally, like a rite of passage and in any and every color—to the point where it had become inane. "A rose for a Rose." Her sister gagged at the unimaginative irony.

But Violet had never once received violets. No one had ever put two and two together for her. She'd gotten roses once or twice, and daisies. Even eucalyptus (that had been an odd and short relationship). But never violets. It wasn't something she was waiting for, or some monumental act. It was simply nice. Thoughtful.

Violet sighed, shaking her head.

"You could sail ships with that sigh."

She looked up and Ambrose was standing over her: poignantly tall, dark, handsome and fashionable, like a cliché or a model from an expensive men's clothing catalog. Today's trench coat was pewter gray, layered over a buttermilk-colored cashmere sweater and dark slacks. "Are we having a bad day?"

"Oh no, I'm fine. Hi, again." Violet smiled, shaking off her self-imposed melancholy. Ambrose moved to the chair opposite her, pulling it out and sitting with the grace of a swan.

"Are you sure?" he asked. "We can't allow our muse to exist in a state of discontent."

"Our muse?" Violet frowned. But Simone walked up, setting

down a plate decked with a large slice of fluffy lemon meringue, and topped with her signature torched whipped cream.

"My angel."

Both Simone and Violet stared at Ambrose as he stared up at Simone, his face that of a man who'd just seen heaven's gates.

Simone frowned. "Um, can I get you something?"

"Your name?"

"Seriously?"

"Hello, Seriously."

Violet laughed. Ambrose winked at her before focusing back on Simone. "What is someone like you doing in a small country-side town like this?"

Simone drew back, guarded. "Someone *like me?*"

"Yes. Royalty."

"I actually agree with him on that," Violet chimed in, picking up her dessert fork. "You're always so perfectly put together. And you have such long legs—"

"Eat your pie," Simone spat. She looked at Ambrose again, distrust coloring her expression. "I'll let you look at the menu a little, first."

"I look forward to seeing you again." Ambrose grinned. Simone shook her head and walked away.

"Didn't you try it with Jasper, too?" Violet asked.

He smirked. "There was a specific purpose in my actions toward Jasper—a paltry attempt to pull him from the depths of despair. And anyway, I appreciate beauty in its infinite and unique forms."

"Sounds like something a player would say."

"Or perhaps someone with a broader view of the universe and how it works? But this one... Does she own this shop?"

"She does."

"Amazing. This village. This is fate. I'll have to stop here in the future after my business dealings with Monsieur Laurent."

While he contemplated, Violet shook her head, staring. Something about him...

"What kind of business do you conduct with Monsieur Laurent?" she nudged. Ambrose had shot her down before when she'd tried probing him for answers, telling her that any truths expressed should come from Jasper. Even still.

"Yes, well, to be honest with you, I have ulterior motives in requesting this meeting with you. I do wish to instigate, just a bit."

"Instigate what?" Violet asked. "There's nothing going on between Jasper and me. So if you—"

"*Of course* there's nothing going on." Ambrose chuckled. "I have gotten to know Jasper fairly well in the past five years of our business dealings, which is exactly why I wish to instigate."

Violet rested her hands on the table, dessert fork frozen between her fingers. She blinked. "Okay, so?"

"I imagine that you are losing steam. When I met you and sensed the tense atmosphere between you and Mr. Laurent, many things became evident to me all at once and I thought, 'This is *her*.' Our muse in the flesh and before my eyes."

"You know... No offense, but, you're saying a lot of things without really saying anything."

Ambrose laughed, flashing his brilliant white teeth. "You are refreshingly astute. Apologies. I do have a flair for the dramatic."

"It shows."

He leaned with his elbows on the table, keeping his deep voice low. "May I divulge something of the utmost confidentiality? I feel that I can trust you..."

"Of course."

"First, my name is René Janvier and I am an actor—hence my love of drama. Second, I work for Jasper because he hired me to represent him."

"To represent him how?"

"In public. In interviews, panels and discussions, book signings, television appearances, and so on and so forth. I am Ambrose Marcello by face, but Jasper is Ambrose Marcello by pen. *He* is the true writer of the books you so adore."

Dropping her fork, Violet sat back, feeling like the wind had been knocked out of her. She repeated Ambrose's... René's words in her mind, turning them over, twisting them and examining them from multiple angles.

"You had no idea?" he asked.

"*No*. How—oh my gosh. I've literally been criticizing his work and fawning over you and his characters for almost two months."

He waved his hand, dismissive. "Jasper is not motivated by ego. I'm sure he doesn't mind. But I must tell you that I find there to be a beautiful irony in this. An author's work unknowingly touches the very person he is inspired by."

Massaging her forehead with her fingertips, Violet paused. "What?"

"Ah, now we have arrived at my true intention. My *instigating*. Jasper has won literary awards for his books—particularly with regard to the handling of his female characters."

"He won the Lighthouse Award for *A Tanzanite Sky*... that was the first time they ever gave that award to a work of fiction. Olivia was such an amazingly complex character—I heard they're in talks for a movie."

"Yes." René grinned. "And he won the Baudelaire Prize for *The Dagger of Leti de la Croix*. He received both of those prestigious awards with critical acclaim for his female leads. I once asked Jasper what inspired him to create such dynamic characters—these larger-than-life women. He proceeded to tell me the most endearing story of his childhood friend. His *best* friend.

"He told me about her vibrant energy, and that she was like the sun, and that she was funny and brave. She climbed big trees he would never climb, and she listened and showed him infinite kindness. He told me that essentially, all of his characters are a reflection of her. Of *you*, Violet. And although I've been in your presence a very short time, I can easily see it."

The light of the café shifted, a passing cloud briefly blocking out the bright sunrays. Violet sat in a daze as Simone came back to the table, the banter between her and René muffled and far from her awareness.

Why? The question floated in her mind like a small bubble in a vast black lake. A simple question surrounded by mystery. Hints and clues but no direct answers. She'd grown tired of feeling confused—of pushing up against a wall that wasn't giving way.

But here she was, being pulled back in. Rose. The bouquet of violets. Now Ambrose. The signs were getting stronger and harder to ignore. But at the same time...

"The phone number to the shop is in the directory," Simone said, "and business hours are between six and—"

"But what about *after* business hours?" René pleaded, blinking up at Simone with very dark lashes. "Dinner hours? You are obviously talented in the dessert arena, and I am very skilled in buying dinner. It could be a wonderful pairing?"

"I'll have your cappuccino right out." Simone shot Violet a look that said "Who is this and why did you bring him here?" before stalking off.

René moped, grumbling to himself. "I don't think she likes me. Perhaps I'm misreading something? It is unfathomable that I have been led back to this village—"

"René, what am I supposed to do?"

"What do you mean?"

Violet took a moment to clear her thoughts. To ease the tension in her heart. "You've told me all these things... things Jasper would *never* tell me himself. But... I don't know what you expect me to do now? I'm not going to save Jasper from anything. That's not... This isn't some fairy tale. I'm not his knight in shining armor."

René sat forward once more, his face serious. "No, Violet. I'm not suggesting that you can or should solve his problems. My message to you is simply this—don't let him push you away because *he* thinks that's best. Because he's wrong. Pushing someone he loves away is not the right answer. Whether he's trying to protect himself, or even you. He's wrong. I've seen the way he lives. I've borne witness to it for the past five years, and it's no way for a person to exist. This thing that he's doing... It is *not* the correct answer."

"I can't keep forcing myself on him—"

"That's not it, my dear. Even though you two were in the middle of some kind of tiff when we first met, the feelings Jasper expressed were amazing. I'd never seen him so alive. *Angry.* A nice, healthy emotion. Glorious. My typical visits with him are nothing like how that day was. Usually he's skulking about, quiet, too thin and dusty like the ghost of a young man rather than a living one. The only other time I've ever seen him exuding such raw emotion was when he told me the story about you, which was how I could easily put two and two together."

"Do you know what's wrong with him?" Violet asked, desperate for an answer.

René paused, the stillness of the moment emphasized by the intensity of his deep, deep eyes. It was as if everything around them fell into shadows and silence, and Violet couldn't see or hear anything else.

"I do," he said. "But he does not know that I know. And he should not."

Violet sucked in a breath, her heart pounding. "Can... Can you tell *me?*"

He shook his head, his lips turning up in a soft smile. "It is not my place."

"But you just told me everything about your arrangement. Why not this, too?"

"Because these trivial worldly matters are of no consequence, and I would not have them stand in the way of a greater reckoning—particularly one that is long overdue. And the signs are unmistakable."

Slumping back in her chair, Violet let the weight of his enigmatic declaration sink in. Reckonings and signs. It all sounded like things a fortune teller might say while trying to assure a person that they haven't just wasted their money. She looked up to find René staring back at her, his rich irises drawing her in. *They're like... an infinity mirror.* Innocently looking at her on the surface, but watching her from the depths of an unknowable scrutiny.

She straightened, knowing he wouldn't speak more about Jasper's condition. She felt it instinctively, somehow. That path of conversation was closed off. This sickness was the root of everything: an impenetrable force field she couldn't vanquish. And what Violet saw on the kitchen floor that day... That unexplainable thing.

"How did you and Jasper meet?" Violet asked. "How did this arrangement come about?"

"He put an advertisement for an acting job in the city paper. Apparently, I am the third person he interviewed. Third time's the charm?"

"So they say..."

"After we got to know each other a bit, he told me he needed someone very good-looking, mannish and tall, because, quote, 'that's what everyone likes.' I always found that statement amusing. As if Jasper himself in all his endearing, innocent and gangly glory wouldn't be enough. But... I suppose this is partly attributable to his condition."

"Listen," Violet said, folding her arms, "you're not allowed to casually refer to his 'condition' if you're not willing to tell me what it is."

René lifted one brow, scrutinizing her again with his inexplicable stare. He grinned. "Understood. Violet Ainsworth, I do love your tenacity. You remind me of someone I knew a very long time ago. He possessed the same fiery temperament. And freckles."

24

NOW

"Oh no..."

As Violet approached Gram's cottage, she recognized the vehicle parked out front and sighed—all hopes of a relaxing bath and glass of wine upon entering the house, dashed.

She'd gone around town after her strange but mildly insightful coffee date with René, making stops at the artisan market for her favorite wine and cheese, and The Clean Chemist for some new candle scents, herby soaps and bath salts. The owner of the small, eclectic shop had regularly consulted with Gloria for inspiration on mixing new fragrances. Violet left the shop as the proud owner of a gorgeous hand-poured candle set in a powdery pinkish glass jar.

The scent was peony and eucalyptus—the last combination Gloria had suggested before falling ill. The shop owner gave it to Violet as a gift.

She pulled up behind the little red pick-up truck, parked, then made her way to the cottage. Once she was staring her uninvited guest in his blue eyes, she tried hard not to frown. "Can I help you with something?"

"Can we talk?" Freddie asked. "Just for a darn minute."

"Why aren't you running the grocery store? It's Saturday—"

"I have employees, Violet. I don't need to be there every second. Can I have a little of your precious fancy-pants time?"

"Not if you ask like that." Violet huffed, moving past him and toward the front door.

He'd been sitting on the small steps, but abruptly stood. "Sheesh, I'm sorry—*please?*"

Unlocking the door, Violet paused as she pushed it open. She didn't look back at him, but said, "Ten minutes." She went inside. Freddie followed.

Violet dropped her bags on the hallway table and went straight to the sitting room. Once there, she plopped down into the soft armchair perpendicular to the couch, not bothering to remove her coat. She slouched as Freddie turned the corner. He looked all around, his head turning from side to side in wonder like a child at a dinosaur museum.

"It's real cozy in here. Nice place. So, are you going to stay in town for good? It's been two months now." He paused and looked at Violet for a response.

"Nine minutes and twenty seconds."

"Geez, woman. *Alright.*" He sat down hard on the couch and raked one hand through his blonde hair. "I—I started seeing a therapist a little over a month ago, right after you moved back here."

"Are you blaming *me* for some type of psychological distress in your life?"

"Well, yes... and no. Not blaming you, alright? You're just like, a trigger? But it's not your fault. That's not what I'm trying to say."

"Then what are you trying to say?"

He took a deep breath, his square chest rising and falling underneath his red plaid shirt and brown leather jacket. "I was jealous of you. I *am* jealous of you. Growing up. And now. So I treated you badly because I couldn't deal with that."

"Jealous of *me?*" Violet frowned. "Mr. Popularity? Mr. Class Clown with everyone in school fawning over his every action and word? Jealous of me, the misfit transplant with my one friend—"

"Yeah, *exactly*. The one friend that I really wanted. The one person who ignored me like I didn't even exist—ignored everyone until the day *you* showed up."

"Oh my God." Violet slouched even deeper into the armchair. For someone who tried so hard to hide himself, Jasper seemed to attract an unreasonable amount of attention.

Freddie grinned, rubbing his palms against his jeans. "I don't know what it is about him. The Laurent family is famous in this town, historically... His great-great-great-grandfather was one of the original founders."

"Um, *no*. The Ainsworth family was here first, foraging the land and—"

"Nah. That's just a spooky old folktale about witches. I'm talking *real* town history, like in our school textbooks."

When Violet stared at him, unblinking, Freddie frowned. "Why are you looking at me like that?"

"Because I was trying to say something, but you cut me off and just bulldozed—"

"No, I didn't. I—" Pausing, Freddie set his shoulders back as he nodded in Violet's direction. "Sorry. Mama gets really mad when I do that to her."

"Mmhm."

"I... I was just trying to say that the Laurents were a huge success in this town—especially with running the orchard when we were kids. They seemed untouchable, and Jasper..." Freddie blinked, mesmerized as he spoke. "His clothes were always a little bit nicer than everyone else's. He was so freaking smart in all our classes, and he used big words I had never heard before. Sitting alone by himself and content in his own world all the time. He seemed magical to me. Special. With that dark, curly hair and those eyes. Like... prince of the faeries."

"Oh wow. Okay..."

"So I *hated* you." Freddie turned, his eyes fiercely meeting her surprised gaze. "I couldn't figure out what made you so special. Why did the most remarkable kid in our class suddenly open up to you?"

"Freddie, everyone teased Jasper. Kids would say he was weird, too quiet and stuck up because of his family."

"*I* never said those things. I never once teased Jasper."

"You dummy, you teased *me*. I was his only friend and you constantly attacked me. Of course that wouldn't help your case."

"I know, I *know*." He leaned forward, elbows against his knees as he ran his fingers deeper into his hair. "It was stupid—I know that now. I knew it then, too, but I couldn't stop myself."

A tense lull washed over them. Freddie massaged his head, tormented. Violet sat a little straighter in her chair, watching him carefully. "Maybe I'm overstepping here, but are these feelings toward Jasper coming from a romantic place?"

"I don't know," he said, head still lowered. "Hence the therapist."

"A therapist will not 'fix' your potentially being queer, Freddie."

He snapped his head up, his face pained. "*No*. It's not like that. I just need to talk to someone so I can sort out my feelings. I've been even more peeved since you came back, and I keep going over to Jasper's to try and talk to him, but he never answers the freaking door. And then I'm jealous *and* worried." Freddie flopped back against the couch and blew out a deep breath. He turned his head to meet Violet's eyes. "I just want to talk to him. I've never even had a conversation with him before.

Can... Can you please help? He's always been so open with you. If you ask, he'll do it."

Freddie watched her with a look she'd never seen on his face before. This face that she'd loathed all her life was pleading with her now. Sincerely. Violet decided to be honest with him.

"Listen, Jasper and I were close a long time ago, but things are very different now. If I go over there, there's a big chance he won't open the door for me, either."

Freddie shook his head, his blue eyes steady. "No way. If you go, he'll let you in. He's in love with you. Like, *crazy* in love."

Violet's breath caught, her body tensing. "Wh—you don't know that. You don't know *anything*—"

"Of course I do. I spent all of primary school watching him watch you. I know I'm not the smartest in the bunch, but it would take a real potato to miss something so obvious."

"A potato, huh?" *Gram, Rosie, Ambrose and now Freddie of all people? Give me a break.*

"Will you help?" he asked. "My therapist said I should talk to both of you. But I don't think I can talk to him without you puttin' in a good word, first."

The universe was officially beating her over the head with a mallet, but Violet was her own woman. Wine and a hot bath were calling and she was not leaving this cottage until she was sufficiently soaked and boozed. "I'll help, but not today. I'll let you know. Your ten minutes are up."

He flashed his Mr. Popular smile, his eyes soft. "Alright, I appreciate it. Thanks for listening... and I'm sorry I made your life hard growing up."

"Whatever," Violet said, standing. "Get out of my house."

TWO DAYS PASSED before Violet built up the nerve to go back to Laurent House.

Saturday night's hot bath and wine had been followed up with homemade baked veggie lasagna and the reading of a new book by the fire. All the while, a brilliant bouquet of rich violets kept her company—gracing the atmosphere with a quiet splendor and softness. A gentle reminder of a situation yet to be addressed.

Sunday, she spent the larger portion of the day re-sketching Poppy Bridge. At first, her intent had been to paint it the way she remembered it fondly in her mind: surrounded by a field of wild poppies in summer, perfectly enclosed by tall green trees humming with wildlife. Beautiful and unflawed.

But something in her wondered about its current state: Poppy Bridge in winter. Poppy Bridge as it was now. Maybe it wasn't as picturesque as the rosy memory encapsulated in her thoughts, but perhaps it held a new beauty? Aged and withered, having faced the inevitable hardships of time. Maybe there was something to be appreciated in that. Something worth capturing.

Violet decided she'd go out there the following weekend. Braving the cold, she'd start out early and follow the overgrown path, sketchpad and blanket in hand. It would be an adventure, and she hadn't had one of those in a while.

That is, if you didn't count the journey up the walkway to Laurent House. Somehow, it felt plenty challenging as Violet stepped out of the car. The wind whipped at her wool coat and loose hair, pushing the thick of it around like a playground bully. She took a deep breath.

Alright, this is it. One last try.

Even after all the ridiculous encouragement over the weekend, the truth was that Jasper still might not even open the door. Violet could be met with harsh silence. Another rejection. It would be the end for her this time, no matter what anyone said.

She made her way up the path, pulling her coat tighter

against her body. When she reached the porch, she took a breath and lifted her fist. The door automatically creaked open, leaving Violet standing there with her fist midair and her eyes wide. Jasper peeked through the crack in the door, a polite smile on his face.

"Hello..."

"Hi..." Violet dropped her hand and swallowed. "Freddie wants to talk to you. He's getting upset because he comes over here, but you don't open the door."

"I never open the door when Freddie comes here. It's what we do. He brings me bulk items and sets them on the porch, I open the door after he leaves. Why is he showing up more often? Why should things change?"

Violet held back a laugh. "I don't know—because sometimes change is good, Jasper."

"Even if Freddie is involved?"

Violet shrugged. "I'm just the messenger."

"Since when are you a messenger for Freddie Martin?"

"Since he apologized and told me he's seeing a therapist."

"What?"

"Don't ask."

"Alright..." Jasper smiled timidly. "How is the messenger? Are you feeling better now? You look much better."

"I am. Thank you for the flowers. They were really pretty."

"I thought they suited you. Perfectly." For just a moment, he looked at her from underneath his dark lashes, those slate (faerie prince) eyes, but then looked away and breathed a heavy sigh, shaking his head. His face was suddenly heavy with anxiety and sadness.

Violet folded her arms. Enough was enough. "Jasper, are you intentionally playing games with me?"

"Of course not."

"So, what are you doing, exactly?"

His gaze flickered to hers before shifting away again. "Honestly, Violet... I have no idea what I'm doing."

"In that case, I propose you let me in. Then maybe we can figure this out, together?"

He paused, only for a moment, before standing straight. He slowly pulled the door open and stood to the side to let her in.

25

NOW

*V*iolet sat still on the sofa, listening to the crackling fire to her immediate right and Jasper clanging dishes far off in the kitchen. She was inside again. Somehow.

When Jasper rounded the corner with the small tray of tea things, Violet watched him. He stopped in front of her on the opposite side of the coffee table. As he set the tray down, she said, "The scratches are almost gone."

He blinked up at her, briefly, in a passing moment. "Yeah..." He poured her tea, then set the cup just before her on the table and smiled coyly. "I need to hear the story of how Freddie apologized and told you he's in therapy. Good for him."

"It is an interesting story, but... I think it would be best if you were honest with me about yourself, first."

His smile dropped as he stood straight. "Is there any way we could just carry on like before? Without me talking about this?"

"I don't think so," Violet said. "If you want me here, it would be nice if I knew the truth."

"What if I want you here, but the truth might drive you away and that possibility scares me? Or what if deep down, I know you *shouldn't* be here, but I'm too selfish and stupid to hold myself to it."

Violet tilted her head, staring up at him. "You're not selfish or stupid, so don't say those things about yourself. And is that what you're doing, Jas? Pushing me away any time I get a little closer to the truth?"

He rubbed his palms against his face, his voice muffled. "I *don't know* what I'm doing."

"Okay, so let's figure it out."

Jasper walked toward the draped window by his desk, pulling the thick, dusty curtain aside. Silver light peeked in through the slit, revealing a frenzy of fine snowflakes dancing on the other side of the glass.

Violet waited. Watching his slender back as he stared out the window until his mellow voice broke the silence.

"I'm not sick. I'm cursed."

He turned slightly, glancing at Violet from over his shoulder, the cool light making his profile glow. "Did you hear me?"

"Yes," Violet said. "Do you mean... in a metaphorical or poetic sense?"

"No. In a very real sense. In a physical, 'every day my life is a living hell,' sense."

"I don't understand."

"Exactly. How could you? How could anyone?" Jasper took a deep breath and raked his fingers through his messy curls. "It's illogical and preposterous—but real. *Painfully* real."

"In what way are you cursed? What is—"

"It's magic, Violet. Very old, powerful and vengeful magic that has lasted for centuries. Everyone thought it was over—nobody had carried the curse across two generations. But surprise! Here I am."

Holding her palms up, Violet shook her head. "Jasper, stop. Just... Let's back up. *Magic?* Like hocus-pocus, pulling a rabbit out of a hat? There's just no way. I can't—"

"Again, no. That's illusions and mind tricks. This is *witch's* magic. Stuff harnessed from the earth and spirits and formidable intent. This curse is real, Violet. Magic is real. It exists."

Violet stared at Jasper's frame silhouetted against the window, unaware that her mouth was gaping open. She hadn't known what was wrong with Jasper, but she wouldn't have guessed it was this. What rationally-minded person could have guessed this? She'd genuinely thought that maybe he had lupus or some rare genetic ailment that he was ashamed of. But *magic?*

"You're looking at me like I'm insane," Jasper said, his eyebrow raised above a cynical smirk. "Of course, you should. This is why I don't tell anyone. Why I shouldn't ever—"

"Jasper, what is the curse exactly? How... How does it impact you?"

Jasper sat down against the window's narrow ledge and gripped the edge with his palms. "It makes me change. Every day."

"Change how?"

"Grotesquely. Agonizingly. It started when I was almost ten. Back then I would only change for three hours in a day. But the older I get, the longer it lasts. By the time I'm in my forties, I won't be anything like myself anymore. I'll be gone."

Violet lifted both hands and rubbed her temples with her fingers. "I'm so confused and I have so many questions."

"You asked for this."

"You keep saying that you 'change,'" Violet said, dropping her hands. "*How* do you change?"

He looked away again, shaking his head. "That doesn't matter."

"It does. Jasper, if you're going to tell me the truth, tell me the whole truth. Stop keeping secrets—"

"A *rat*, Violet. I change into a rat. Every day since I was ten."

Violet blinked, turning the information over in her mind. "A rat? Aw..."

"*Aw?*" Jasper drew back, incensed. "*Not* 'aw.' That's your first reaction? This isn't some Disney movie."

"I mean, just generally speaking, rats aren't so—wait a minute..." Violet sat up straight with a jolt. "Did... Did I put you outside a few weeks ago? Oh dear God, was that you? That little gray mouse?"

Jasper narrowed his eyes in unquestionable scorn. "*Yes.*"

"Oh, oh my gosh, I am so sorry, Jasper. I had no idea—how could I know? I thought I was helping."

"You shouldn't have been in here."

"I know, please don't get mad at me about that all over again. God, I'm sorry... You were so cute though. You're not a rat—"

"Stop it. I'm not cute. I'm *disgusting*. The first time I changed, my father was on a business trip and it was just me and Mom here. The whole thing was horrific. I didn't know what was happening to me and it hurt like hell—my whole body contorted down, cracking and shifting in ways that aren't humanly possible. Mom screamed bloody murder the *entire* time, and when I had finished changing, she scooped me into a bucket and dumped me outside. I was terrified and alone in the dark in that stupid garden, half confused and half worried I'd get eaten by an owl or a snake. Nothing about this is *cute*."

He rubbed his palms against his face again, his shoulders rising and falling in a deep breath. Violet lowered her head. She couldn't imagine what he'd been through—what he was still going through, being saddled with this bizarre, unbelievable thing. She couldn't fathom the depth of his trauma.

"I apologize, Jasper," Violet said. "I don't mean to make light of something serious... it's just all very surprising. Magic and curses and a little gray mouse."

Jasper lifted his chin, nose upturned. "Your tone reads 'this is very cute.'"

"How? You can't be mad at me about my tone. That's not fair."

"You're supposed to be horrified by this! It's crazy and disgusting—"

"Well, what if I'm not horrified? It's... definitely unexpected, but not disgusting."

"Unexpected?" Jasper mocked. "Unexpected is when you get a package delivered a day early. Unexpected is when you buy something and it rings up for less than the price tag. Not a dark, malevolent curse on a family's entire male lineage."

"I mean no disrespect to the seriousness of your curse, Jas, but 'dark' and 'malevolent' don't equate to 'little gray mouse' in my vernacular."

"I'm a *rat*."

"I disagree. Have you seen yourself? Seriously, have you ever looked?"

He stared at Violet, shaking his head. "You're unbelievable."

"I'll take that as a compliment," she said, folding her arms and sitting back against the couch. "To summarize, magic is real, you're cursed—not sick, technically—and you don't leave the house because you turn into a mouse?"

"Rat. And you're trivializing."

"I'm not. I'm trying to understand."

There was a long pause where neither moved or said a word. Eventually, Jasper spoke, his voice serious. "Can you imagine what would happen if people found out about this?"

If people found out...

Chaos. Unquestionably, Jasper would be dragged away, put under a microscope and studied in a lab somewhere. Examined and prodded with no concern for his actual, meaningful humanity. Maybe he'd be feared and loathed by everyone around him, or a relentless target for crude tabloid fodder.

She looked up at him, her eyes sincere. "I can't imagine. Nothing good would come from it."

"Right. Keeping my mother quiet was hard enough. Growing up, every day I waited for men in white coats to show up at the door and drag me out of the attic, kicking and screaming. I think the only reason they didn't was because of Dad. He kept her calm enough until he gave in and they moved away when I turned eighteen."

"Your mother, she wasn't supportive about this?"

Jasper scoffed in a bitter sound. "'Wasn't supportive,' is putting it nicely. She rejected me after I changed that first time —refused to be in the same room as me and made me go in the backyard whenever the change started to happen. Actually, the day you climbed that tree and fell? The last time we saw each other as kids? That was my third time changing. If you'd arrived about twenty minutes earlier, you would have gotten a real horror show."

"Sh-She made you go outside in the yard? It was so cold that day."

"Yes. Eventually Dad talked her into letting me change in the house. But I had to stay in the attic where she couldn't hear my bones cracking and shifting, or me crying because it hurt so badly. She didn't want anything to do with it and I don't blame her. It's horrifying." Jasper shrugged, his arms folded as he watched her.

With that story, Violet's perception of the entire situation shifted. Any "cuteness" was gone, replaced by something darker and weighted. Traumatic. She swallowed hard. "So, changing… it hurts that badly?"

"I'm used to it now," Jasper said, matter-of-fact. "But back then, in the early days, yes. It was very bad."

"And your mom *never* helped you? She never came around?"

"No. She wouldn't even look at me. Barely spoke to me. Dad sat with me as much as he could. But that created problems for the orchard and his business. He started spending all his time looking after me—making sure I was fed and clean, which of course drove a wedge between him and Mom. Eventually he let the business die off. He settled his debts, paid his employees what they were owed and sold some of the used machinery, but that left us in a kind of poverty. Mom wasn't thrilled about that, either. She went from being at the top of the socioeconomic ladder to being near the bottom, and with a cursed son that she despised."

Violet hadn't realized. She'd known that things had changed and that the orchard had closed down by the time she was in high school, but she hadn't known why. Of course, everything about the Laurents became shrouded in mystery after Jasper's "sickness." The orchard shut down, they stopped attending village events and Jasper was nowhere to be seen—never attending school or even having the occasional doctor's appointment.

This thing... This curse had ravaged their family. It made a brilliant, curious boy who'd been full of life into an insecure shut-in. It led to his mother rejecting him, and pitted his parents against each other before driving them all into financial ruin.

"It's not cute. None of it," Violet said, speaking over the lump in her throat. "I'm so sorry I made light of the situation. I'm sorry for everything you've been through."

Jasper shrugged again. "It's a curse, Violet. It's meant to do harm. That's the nature of the beast."

"But why? This all seems so... How did this happen? And why *you?*"

"I have ancestors who did some very bad things to the people who were indigenous to this village. They were greedy, condemnatory and selfish, so they paid for their sins. I'm still paying for them. It's just the way it is."

"Can't—isn't there anything that can be done?" Violet asked, her heart aching. "You didn't do those bad things. Why do you have to pay generations later? Can't this be broken?"

Jasper sighed. "Gloria tried—a bunch of things, actually. Weird things I questioned, but she felt so passionate about it—"

"Stop. Gram *knew* about this? She knew you were cursed?"

"Yes."

Violet scoffed, undone. Her world kept being flipped upside down and all around and it was getting harder to keep up. "How... How did she know? Did you tell her?"

"My father did, right before they moved away to the city. He asked her to look after me."

"Oh my God. Gram wasn't a witch."

"She was not."

"So why on earth was she trying to break your curse? What made her think she could do something crazy like that?"

Jasper huffed a laugh through his nose. As far as Violet could tell though, nothing was funny.

"Well," he said, "she thought that since her ancestors were the ones who cursed me, that maybe she could do something? She was wrong though. Nothing worked."

"Her ancestors? Do you mean *my* family? The Ainsworths?"

Jasper turned his head, gazing out the window and at the blustery snowfall. "Yes. That's exactly what I mean."

26

NOW

*M*y ancestors did this...

Simone had told Violet that the Ainsworth women had been a force to be reckoned with. The statement was so assured, so captivating that it had pushed Violet to research the town's past. A past that varied depending upon which book or memoir she was reading.

Some versions claimed that the Laurent family had founded the village of Libellule. They'd bravely traveled in a caravan with four other families from the north and settled here—building modern structures and establishing trade and commerce with nearby towns. In these versions, there was only small mention of the indigenous people: that they were made civilized and their lives bettered. The settlers had brought new, useful materials to the locals and "clean" morals, and everyone had lived happily ever after.

Of course, the town's history was much different when told from the perspectives of those indigenous to this land. Those accounts weren't represented in the glossy hardcover books that local students received in school. Those stories were harder to find: tucked away in private memoirs or independently published projects. Indeed, the Laurent family and their caravan had come to the village, but they'd taken over—disrespectful and trotting over sacred ground, digging and building indiscriminately. Any native that had objected or refused to conform to the modernization of the village had been brutally terminated and made to be an example.

In both stories, the Laurents reigned victorious, leading a life of prosperity, wealth and happiness in the thriving little town they'd helped to establish...

Or so the books had led Violet and everyone else to believe.

"I... I can't believe Gram knew about all of this and she never told me."

"You weren't supposed to know. Gloria shouldn't even have known, but Dad—" Jasper took a deep breath, bringing his palm to his forehead. To Violet, he looked as if he were physically trying to hold his mind in place. To keep it from falling apart. He closed his eyes. "Dad was always worried about me. Obsessively so. It's like he worried twice as hard to make up for Mom hating me. Things had gotten so toxic here before they left, but he refused to leave me alone. He told Gloria because he thought it would be better for me if I had someone to talk to, at least sometimes."

Jasper ran his hand up into his hair, his eyes downcast. "After they left, Dad would still visit me once a month, for a while. But then his health kept deteriorating—probably from all the stress and worry. He worked a few jobs, too, to help support me and Mom. The first year, he'd come see me every month, the next year, every other, then every three. The last two years he was alive, he only came and spent Christmas Eve with me. He was too weak and Mom didn't want him here, anyway."

Jasper rubbed his fingers against his scalp again, mussing his hair. He clenched his eyes shut, and Violet could see the tears streaming down his pale face. "Mom... wouldn't let me come see him when he was in the hospital. She—she wouldn't even let me come to the funeral. He gave up *everything* for me my whole life and I couldn't even say goodbye—" Jasper gasped, the tears rolling heavy from his eyes as he shook his head. His face contorted in sorrow.

Violet stood and walked over to him at the window. She reached for his hand and held it gently. He jolted, but as Violet shifted down to sit against the floor, Jasper allowed her to pull him down as well. Soon, they were sitting side-by-side underneath the window, their backs pressed against the wall. Violet held his hand a little tighter, and after a moment, he reciprocated, accepting the gesture.

The house around them felt still, like a hollow shelter. He rubbed his face with his free hand and cried quietly, and Violet let him. When she blinked, her eyes had welled up, too, so she wiped them with the tips of her fingers and sniffed. They sat together this way for an unknowable time, listening to the blizzard wind whistle through the gaps in the window overhead.

"I was also really sorry that I couldn't come to Gloria's funeral," Jasper said, his voice low and dry. "I wanted to be there, but I—I shouldn't be around other people, and you were there and I—"

"But *why*, Jasper? It's not like the curse is contagious, is it?"

"Not physically, but it's a *curse*. It's dark and rooted in hatred like an evil spirit. Even if you can't 'catch' it, it still impacts the people around me. Look at my mother and father. Gloria had to keep secrets from you, and now you're here when you definitely should *not* be."

Violet turned to look at him, frowning. "Why shouldn't I be?"

Jasper scoffed as if she'd asked something ridiculous. "Violet, this isn't what you should be doing—sitting in this dingy old house with some pathetic and gross monster. You deserve a life that's full of everything you yourself embody. Radiant energy and love, kindness and real beauty. You should be in the city and *happy*. Gloria shouldn't have asked you to come here. I don't want any of this for you."

"Is that why you always write me as an international adventure woman in all your books? Because in your head, that's what I should be doing?"

At this, Jasper slowly turned his head, the look on his tearstained face something like dread. "What?"

"René told me everything—about how you're actually Ambrose Marcello and write all the books but pay him to represent you in public, and that you told him all your female characters are based off of me."

Jasper jerked, his eyes wide with disbelief. He shifted to stand, but Violet gripped his hand and tugged him so that he tumbled back down into his seated position beside her. She smiled. "Stay calm."

"*No*," Jasper exclaimed. "This—this is a severe breach of confidentiality. He isn't supposed to tell anyone these things. What purpose does he serve if he tells people?"

"Not 'people.' Only me," Violet argued, their hands still clasped as she watched him.

"God…" He covered his face with his free hand. "Humiliating."

"I think you're very sweet and incredibly talented. Good grief. How can you write such descriptive books about places and smells and scenes when you never leave your house? You haven't been to any of these places, have you?"

He dropped his hand, staring straight forward. "Research. I have a lot of free time."

"You do wonders with that time."

"Mm," he groaned, then laid his head back against the wall with his eyes closed.

"I won't tell anyone that we have an internationally recognized and critically acclaimed author living in our small town." Violet smiled. "Or that you're a mouse."

"Rat."

"You're wrong. Should I kiss you? Will that break the curse?"

"I already told you this is not a fairytale."

"Could be worth a try though?"

"No."

Violet snorted in a laugh. "Are you officially saying 'no' to me kissing you?"

"Yes. You shouldn't even be here. I have nothing good to offer you—nothing even close to what you deserve."

Sneering, Violet reached over and poked him in the waist, making him flinch away, but she kept a firm hold of his hand in hers. "*I'm* the one who decides what I want and deserve. Got it?"

"Hm," he grunted, still leaning away.

"Jasper Oliver Laurent—"

"*Alright.* I hear you."

"Can we go sit on the couch together near the fireplace? It's cold under this window."

Jasper nodded, shifting to stand. He helped pull Violet upright as well. "I... I'll make a new pot of tea. This one is probably cold now."

IN THE END, they decided to have coffee instead, and Jasper sat in the armchair, markedly isolated from Violet's position on the couch. But she didn't say anything. The fact that he was opening up to her at all was a true miracle. A small kind of magic in and of itself.

She held the warm coffee cup between her palms and against her thigh, mulling everything over. Jasper sipped from his cup. Despite the silence, the atmosphere was peaceful. Comfortable.

"Why was your mother so..."

"Disgusted?" Jasper offered. "Repulsed?"

"Yes."

"Well, I'm a rat, for one. And two, the change itself is gruesome to watch. She only half-watched the transition once and it traumatized her. It's not bibbity-bobbity and *poof*, a puff of smoke later I turn into a rat."

"What actually happens?"

"The magic..." Jasper paused, sliding his fingers across his scalp and mussing his hair. "The curse is such that my body shrinks down and contorts at the same time. The entire process lasts about an hour. The first thirty minutes are slow and innocuous—I get that spidery feeling in my veins and little things happen. Some fuzzy hairs over my skin and my eyes change. The last thirty minutes are the worst and most painful. That's when my body fully shifts. When I was little, Dad always sat with me through the transition. He... He'd hold me and rock with me through the pain. Sometimes he cried, too. But he never screamed. He wasn't afraid."

"Your dad was so supportive. It's wonderful."

Jasper nodded. "He was. I wish he could have had a better life, you know? I think Mom was right. They should have left me sooner and lived their own lives. Enjoyed themselves."

"No." Violet shook her head. "Knowing the kind of person your father was, he wouldn't have been able to do that. You're his only son and he wanted to make sure you were okay. He probably blamed himself—maybe even wished it was him and not you. But it's not his fault or yours, Jasper. It's just the curse."

"I don't know. Maybe if I had been less selfish and pushed him away, he'd still be alive now? Maybe he wouldn't have spent so much time worrying and stressed. Even if I couldn't see him, knowing he was still here, *somewhere*—"

"If you pushed him away, you would have made it worse, because then he would have been worried about you *and* heartbroken. Again, it's not your fault. The time you spent with your dad... it's priceless, Jas. All my memories with Gram are what help me through the pain of losing her—knowing we at least had that time together. Of all the people she could have loved and spent time with, she chose me. In the same way, your dad chose you. Over and over."

Jasper stared down into his coffee. Violet wasn't sure if her words were getting through to him—through the thick wall of guilt and insecurity set firm within his mind.

"And..." Violet began, cautious as she watched him. "Maybe you don't need to hide yourself so strictly? Being around other people won't automatically bring them misfortune. Do you know for certain if that's part of the curse?"

"Well, eventually, I'll lose all of my humanity and be a rat permanently, so I figure the fewer people I interact with, the better."

"Wait—how?"

"I already told you. The older I get, the longer I stay in rat form. When I was ten, it lasted for three hours a day. Now, I'm at twelve hours—literally half the day I'm a rat. Well, technically all night, since the change starts around five in the evening. By the time I'm in my mid-forties, I'll be a rat full-time. Until something catches and kills me."

Sitting back against the couch, Violet's heart sank. *No...* The lump reformed in her throat, her chest heavy and her face flushed with stress. She shook her head in refusal.

Jasper pointed at her, his eyebrow raised. "See? That's why you shouldn't be here wasting your time. Look at your face."

"Jasper, this isn't funny," Violet spat, swiping away the renegade teardrops forming at the corners of her eyes.

"I'm not suggesting that it is," he said, his words contradicted by a weak grin. "But I'm the very last male Laurent in existence. So at least this curse ends with me. Nobody else needs to suffer."

Taking a breath to calm her emotions, Violet steeled herself to ask the obvious question. "There's nothing that can break this? *Nothing* can help?"

"Nope—" He tilted his head, considering. "Well..."

"Well what?"

"It's not a matter of breaking it but... Whenever Dad was home with me, my mind was always sharper when I turned. When I'm a rat, I experience something like... rat-brain? Where I lose consciousness of my humanity. After Dad left with Mom, rat-brain became harder to fight off. I still did it though, a little. Gloria's visiting once a week helped some, too."

"So, when you're a mouse—"

"Violet."

"Nope. We're just going to have to agree to disagree on this point. Anyway, when you change, you still think like a person?"

"Sometimes."

"That night I came into the house, you recognized me, right? Even though you were a mouse."

"Yes. But my view of you wasn't sharp. Think of it like looking through a foggy car window. I know your smell, too, so those things helped me to discern you through the haze of rat-brain."

Distracted, Violet smirked. "What is my smell, exactly? Is it good?"

"That's... Can we not focus on that right now, please?"

Violet huffed, folding her arms and sitting back. "Fine." *When his dad was around, Jasper's mind was sharper. When he was left alone, he was more mousey...* As she considered, the answer became crystal clear. "Jasper, you *need* to be around more people."

He stared blankly. "Have you not been listening to me at all?"

"I don't think you're listening to yourself. You basically just told me that when you're interacting with people, you're less mouselike when you change. Don't you think that's significant?"

He paused, shifting his oversized gray eyes away in contemplation. "I don't think that matters. Even if my mind is sharper as a rat, I'm still a rat, Violet. Nothing will change that."

"Alright, okay. But what if... I don't know, you tried to enjoy your life, while you have it? Indulge in your humanity while it exists."

"What does that mean? What would I do?"

Violet inhaled and exhaled a deep breath, thinking. "Well, that's for you to decide. But you've been hiding yourself away for the past fifteen years. You don't have to do that, Jas. Nobody is imprisoning you here. And you already know your time as a human is limited, so why not try something different for the next fifteen years or so?"

Jasper put his coffee cup down and stood, stretching his arms as he walked toward the fireplace. He stared into the low-burning flame, not saying a word.

"Is this a terrible idea?" Violet prompted.

"No, it isn't. But I can't go on a world tour because the transition itself is hard on me. I've only changed in my own house, so I don't feel comfortable doing it anywhere else—like in a hotel or on an airplane. That would be an absolute nightmare. I also don't sleep when I'm a rat, so I need to sleep during the day. My window of alertness and good health as a human is honestly very short—and getting shorter."

"Why don't you sleep at night?"

He turned, facing her. "Rats are nocturnal. Of course, I'm capable of sleeping at night. I did when Dad was home with me. Everything was better then. But I like to be alert and aware when I'm vulnerable. Perfect example—the other night, a giant outside rat somehow got into the house. I spent the entire night running and fighting with that evil thing. When I changed back, it took me the entire next day to find him and put him outside. So again, no sleep. I ended up passing out on the kitchen floor. I couldn't even go upstairs to transition like I usually do. I was too exhausted."

"The scratches on your face..."

"From fighting with a stupid rat that was much bigger than me."

"Yes, bigger because you're a *mouse*, and I'm pretty sure a cat got to it. Jasper... is—is that what I saw that day in the kitchen? The day I fell and hit my head?"

It was a tiny, almost imperceptible shift, but his entire body went rigid. He took a small step back and closer to the fireplace. He didn't say anything.

"Jasper?"

"I don't know what you saw."

"Don't do that." Violet shook her head. "It's just a yes-no question."

"Can we forget about that? You shouldn't... I don't want you to think about that anymore. Let's not talk about it."

"Alright, but it's a major part of you and everything else we're talking—"

"*Please.*"

Violet nodded. "Okay." Hard boundary. But she understood. Lots of trauma there. "What are you doing this coming Sunday?" she asked, trying to shake off the sudden tension between them.

"What am I doing?" he said, his eyebrow raised.

"Do you plan on having epic rat battles in here, or would you maybe like to accompany me out to Poppy Bridge?"

"It's too soon to joke about. Why are you going out there?"

"I'm thinking of a new project to paint. I want to see it in winter so I can sketch it. I don't think I ever have."

"You're painting again? That's lovely."

"Yeah, thanks."

"I think a walk would be nice."

"Great." Violet smiled. "You can meet me at Gram's house Saturday morning? It's not travelling the world, but it's a start."

27

NOW

"$\mathcal{H}$ere you are." Simone held out Ginger's journal as she stood on the porch wrapped in a deep red shawl. "I thoroughly enjoyed that. Happy Friday."

Violet smiled. "Happy Friday, and I figured you would." She stepped aside to let her friend pass. As Simone strolled through the door, Violet asked, "You didn't happen to come across any entries about breaking curses in there, did you?"

Simone paused, her brows drawn together as she looked over her shoulder. "Um, *that's* a weird question. Does someone have a curse that needs breaking?"

Violet tensed. "No. I don't know, I... I'm just reading too many books lately."

"I want these books if they talk about curses. Sounds fun." Simone winked. "I did find some valuable herbal remedies for simple ailments—stomachaches, sleeplessness, headaches and cuts and bruises. Ingredients I can find in the local forest, apparently. Come spring, I want to try a little foraging. Come with?"

"I would love that. I'm in."

"Gloria would be proud of us, I think." When Simone turned

the corner into the sitting room, she gasped. "Look at you. You've been busy." She walked over to the row of canvases that Violet had on display. They were placed on the floor along the wall: an impressionist-style portrait of Gloria in gouache earth tones, then three others in the same medium, but brighter depictions of detailed landscapes—a field of wild red poppies against a stormy sky, a magnolia tree in full bloom and the third, a charming chateau juxtaposed against a flourishing apple orchard.

"I'm just trying to get back into it," Violet said. "It's been years so I feel rusty. Wine?"

"Rusty? Are you kidding? These don't look rusty at all. This looks *just* like Gloria. And I love this one in the center—is it a magnolia tree?"

"Yes. There was one in the park near my place in the city. It was stunning and I loved taking walks there in the spring. Just looking at it and smelling the flowers in the air gave me a sense of peace."

"You did this from memory? The colors are so rich and vibrant, and the way you've done the shadows and sunlight through the branches... Wow, Vi. You're seriously talented."

"Aw, thanks," Violet said. "Do you want wine? Red or white?"

"Red, always. Are you selling these?"

Violet moved toward the kitchen, grabbing a bottle of cabernet sauvignon from the wine rack just outside the wide, open doorway. "Not at all. Who would buy them?" She swiftly uncorked the bottle and poured two glasses.

"Lots of people," Simone shouted from the sitting room. "Me, for starters. How much for the magnolia tree? It'll look so beautiful on the wall of my shop—and it's by a local artist."

When Violet made her way back into the sitting room, Simone was already relaxing on the couch. Violet handed her a glass. "Oh please. You can just have it. It's not a big deal."

"Yeah, *no,*" Simone said, accepting the offering. "Vi, you are gifted and I firmly believe in paying artists for their hard work and talent. The painting has so much vibrancy and character—the colors of the petals have a subtle gradient, even though each one is so small..." Simone stood with her glass and walked over to the paintings again. She crouched, examining the magnolia tree. "Can I have another one that matches this? Like a sister painting? It can be whatever you want. I'll give you a thousand for the pair."

"*What?*" Violet jerked, almost spilling her wine. "There's *no way* I could—I'm just dabbling. Playing around."

"Well, I'm excited to see what you create when you get serious." Simone looked over her shoulder. "This could be a thing, Vi. The beginning of your colorful life. How long have you been painting?"

"I... Well, as far back as I can remember. I've been drawing and painting as a hobby since Mom died. I've taken some formal classes for fun, here and there. But I've never thought to focus on it as a profession. It just gives me joy, you know? Creating and mixing colors. Especially if I'm down or having a hard time. It's my happy place."

Moving back toward the couch, Simone smiled. "I can feel the joy in these paintings just by looking at them. Listen, let me set up a social media account for you. Paint a few more—whatever interests you. No pressure. And just... let's see what happens. I've done this for the bakery, so I have a pretty good handle on what I need to do. I'll just alter everything slightly for *your* specific art form. Will you let me?"

Violet considered for a moment. Simone was her friend, so of course she'd say kind things about her art. That's what good friends were—supportive. She supposed there couldn't be any harm in letting Simone set up an account.

"Yes, you can." Violet nodded. "But don't be disappointed if nothing happens."

"Don't be too shocked when something does." Simone

winked, raising her glass. "Cheers to your new business, Violet. And to having your first customer—me!"

Violet couldn't help but smile as she raised her glass. "Alright, cheers. And thank you."

They clinked their glasses, and as Violet drank the bold, smooth liquid brimming with notes of fig, dark cherries and espresso, she couldn't deny the flush of warmth in her cheeks. The rush of excitement and sincere gratitude. She thought of Gloria—always dabbling in what she loved, experimenting and trying new things. Gloria had cultivated a rich life for herself, like a vibrant quilt made up of unique, interesting patchwork. Could this be the first patch on Violet's own unique quilt? A bright splash of color in an otherwise gray existence?

"You really think people will want my paintings?" she asked.

"Oh, I *know* they will. What style is this? What kind of paint?"

Violet sat straighter, excited about the nerdy details she almost never had the opportunity to divulge. "Well, the paint is gouache and the style is impressionism—like Degas, Renoir and Monet. You've heard of them?"

"Degas did the ballerina ones, right? I always liked those."

"Yes." Violet beamed. "Degas is famous for ballerinas and Monet for lilies. This is my favorite style because it just feels airy and light. Whimsical? But I like to experiment—so I've also done realism in acrylic, oils and watercolors. I tried abstract but I struggled. It's like my brain doesn't really work that way. I'm too literal and straightforward. I actually want to start doing more charcoal. Maybe a portrait? I've seen some that are really haunting and beautiful, and it feels so different from what I'm used to. I want to get my hands messy and give it a try."

Simone took a long sip of her wine. "And you should. You're already so alive just talking about this. Don't brush that feeling aside, Vi. It's important."

"You're right. I shouldn't."

"You seemed a little off when you came to the bakery last weekend with that ridiculous author man. Is everything alright?"

Violet snickered. "Why is René ridiculous? He has a flair for theatrics, but he's nice. And I'm fine. Thank you for asking."

"'Flair for theatrics...'" Simone sneered. "All that flirting and carrying-on. He's way too good-looking to be trusted. And I thought you told me his name was Ambrose?"

"That—that's just his author name. His real name is René. Why do you think good-looking men can't be trusted?"

"Because society has taught them that they can pretty much have anything they want and get away with everything. So they do."

Violet laughed. "Nah, not all—plus, there are different kinds of handsome."

"Well, I'm talking model-esque, 'likely to be cast as a heart-throb in a steamy romance' handsome, like your friend Ambrose or René or whatever."

"You should give him a chance. Maybe he's being sincere toward you?"

"Please. He doesn't have a sincere bone in his body. And anyway, I moved out here to run my little bakery in peace and solitude. I don't want to deal with all that anymore—feeling anxious about disclosure and worrying about what someone thinks of me. I'm over it. I just want to be *me* and be happy."

"Your colorful life."

"That's right."

"I hear you... René seems pretty open though—"

"Enough, woman," Simone scolded, playful. "What's happening with Mr. Laurent? Are you still seeing him?"

"Not seeing, exactly. But yes, I visit with him. We're friends."

"So what's his deal, exactly? I hear he's sick, but nobody seems to know what he has. In the seven years I've lived here, I've never once *seen* him. I don't even know what he looks like." Simone watched Violet now, pointedly. Requiring answers.

"Um… well, Jasper is average height, but taller than me. Oh, so Freddie, the town mascot who runs the grocery store?"

"Yes, Ken Doll. Another one too handsome to be trusted."

Violet rolled her eyes, smiling. "Jasper is just a smidge shorter than Freddie, maybe? But Jasper's features are dark. His mom is from Portugal and he has her same coffee-colored, kind of loosely curled hair—which is almost always a mess. His eyes are really pretty. Like giant gray marbles."

"Aw, he sounds like a cutie."

Violet snuggled a little deeper into the couch with her wine, her heart warm. "*I* think he is."

"I guess he's sick, but… Why does he stay locked up in the house all the time? Does he work?"

"Yes, he works. He has his own business."

"Does he date or have a partner?" Simone asked.

"No. Not that I know of."

"Vi, you're straight, right?"

"Hmm, straight sounds so boring. Can I be curvy?"

Simone laughed. "Yes, you can be curvy. You *are* curvy."

Violet wiggled her hips, grinning. "I am."

"Jasper sounds interesting, I wish I could meet him. He always gives very generous donations to the winter and summer festivals every year." Simone took another quick pull from her glass before eyeing Violet once more. "So, make things plain for me…"

"Okay?"

"You always say he's your friend, but do you *like* him? If he were open to it, would you be seeing him romantically?"

"I… Hmm. It isn't that I *like* Jasper. I love him. Fundamentally and as a person. Who he is and what he means to me are so deeply rooted in my heart that I will always feel for him, no matter what. Does that make sense?"

Simone blinked, staring. "Wow, that's beautiful, Violet."

"That's just how it is." Violet shrugged. "He was a sincere and kind friend to me at a time in my life when I needed that more than anything. Even if I met someone and started a relationship, married them or whatever, Jasper would still hold that unique place in my heart. It can't be undone. I've tried to unravel it—to let him go. Multiple times. But it doesn't budge, so he's just part of me."

"So the answer to the romance question is a resounding 'yes,' then?"

Violet laughed. "Not *resounding*, but... If I thought Jasper was open to me romantically, yes, I would walk that path with him and see where it takes us. I would be open to doing just about anything with him. He's very different from most people. I just trust him."

"Well, now I *really* want to meet him. Can we set this up somehow?"

"I don't know, he's pretty introverted." When Violet had suggested that Jasper start living his life with a little more enthusiasm, he hadn't rejected the idea. They were planning to walk together tomorrow morning, which was promising. But adding someone new to the mix and so soon...

"His birthday is coming up on Christmas Eve." Violet considered. "I was thinking about asking him over for dinner. Maybe you can join?"

"Ah!" Simone clapped. "I think that's fantastic. Why not make it a little holiday party? Maybe the week before, since Christmas might be busy for others?"

"Um, Jasper gets worn out pretty easily—"

"How about a pre-birthday holiday brunch? I can bring sweets, of course, and if we invite a couple others, they can bring dishes? We'll keep it short. An intimate little gathering."

Violet bit her lip, absently twisting the stem of her wine glass between her fingers. "I'll—Let me think about it."

"We could decorate, too," Simone went on, her brown eyes sparkling with excitement, "and make the cottage all bright and cozy. Gloria used to have this place decked out around the holidays... Speaking of, why haven't you decorated in here yet? Where's the Christmas tree? Some lights? I got the shop all lit up and the halls decked Saturday night last week, so I'm ready. You have to come back and see."

Sighing, Violet nodded. "I will, and I—this is the first Christmas without Gram here. I haven't been in the mood to decorate and do all that stuff alone." Spending the holidays with Gram was always the best time, rivaled only by summers together in the greenhouse, or sitting on the porch drinking blueberry lemonade and listening to the echoes of cicadas buzzing through the forest canopy as the sun was setting. When the sky was ablaze with orange hues and the air was warm and sticky against Violet's skin.

But now, without Gram... Without her strutting around and singing too loudly to lively holiday music, or the smell of lemon-glazed gingersnaps baking while they laughed in front of the fireplace, or the tree full of twinkling lights in the corner... What was the point? Why even bother with any of it?

Violet sat still, breathing slowly and feeling like she was a blank slate—an empty canvas drained of all color. She stared, not knowing how much time had passed when Simone's voice registered softly in the silence.

"I have an idea," Simone said, gently wrapping her fingers around Violet's wrist. "I'll have a tree delivered for you, and I'll help you decorate before the birthday brunch party. What do you think? Lots of people, and you won't be alone. You're not alone, Vi."

Pulling herself back to the present and away from the empty void that had taken hold of her (as it often did, unexpectedly), Violet considered Simone's suggestion. A birthday brunch with spiced comfort foods and a house humming with people. The thought made her smile, just a little.

"Well?" Simone prompted, affectionately squeezing her wrist.

"I like the idea. Let me ask Jasper about it. He's not used to parties so I don't want to overwhelm him. Even if he doesn't want to come, though... I want to do it. It would be nice to have something to look forward to."

"Perfect. We're definitely doing this. And if his feelings toward you are anything like yours are toward him, I think he'll want to be there. Who would want to miss an opportunity to be in your lovely presence?"

"I could say the same about you." Violet smiled wickedly. "I think I'll invite René."

"Oh shoot. Something's suddenly come up. I don't think I can make it."

Violet smacked Simone's shoulder as they broke into a satisfying fit of laughter.

Simone grinned. "Invite Ken Doll, too. He's nice to look at."

"Meh..."

"You told me he apologized to you?"

"That doesn't mean I want him in my house."

"It's time to forgive, my dear. Let's make this gathering the beginning of your prosperous and good life here—a new creative business, a friendly community and maybe a little romance with a very special friend that we love?"

"Ah, only two out of three are within my control."

Simone's smile fell flat. "I need you to be more self-assured about this. Positive energy, Violet. Positive energy."

"Only if you're positive about René?" Violet clenched her teeth in an awkward, knowing smile. Simone glared with one eyebrow raised as if she wanted to call Violet by some name that started with "you little..."

28

NOW

allen leaves crunched loudly underneath their feet as they walked—to the point where they had to shout a little to be heard over the noise of it.

"It was awkward," Jasper said. Violet couldn't see his face since she was walking ahead of him on the path, but she could hear the displeasure in his voice. She could imagine his little mouth downturned and frowning.

"Well, that was to be expected, wasn't it?" she answered. "Had you ever sat down and tried to have a conversation with Freddie before yesterday?"

"No," Jasper confirmed. "And it served as a profound illustration as to why that's the case."

Violet snorted in a laugh. "He told me he wanted to talk to you. I thought he would have some important things to say?"

The air around them was crisp as they walked through the woods, the sun high and filtering brightly through the naked canopy of bare branches overhead. Violet could already see the opening into the clearing. Just a little further.

"He left within ten minutes," Jasper said. "Which I am pretty pleased about. He just asked me how I was feeling, and if there was anything he could do to help or bring up from the store. It was weird. And his eyes kept darting all around like he didn't want to look at me."

Violet never would have thought that she'd have *any* kind of sympathy for Freddie Martin—her childhood bully and therefore lifelong antagonist. But she'd also never imagined her best friend being cursed to turn into a mouse, so... Silly her for thinking she had a firm grip on reality and the way the world worked.

"I don't have to do that again, do I?" Jasper asked as they stepped into the clearing. "Can I go back to *not* opening the door when he comes over?"

"That's entirely up to you." Violet took in the scene before them. The clearing, which had seemed so large when she was a child, felt small now—intimate, like a woodsy hideaway. Violet imagined that it'd be the perfect place for a secluded little cottage. There were no flowers, and the grass was long: brittle and wispy in some places, but shorter and patchwork in others. Poppy Bridge itself remained the same. The arched drystone structure was still full of character with its intricate hand-layered rocks and speckled form. A bubbling stream flowed underneath, winding through the clearing and disappearing into the thick woods surrounding them.

"How about we set up over there?" Violet pointed. "Just beside the stream?"

"Sure." Jasper strode forward with the quilt tucked underneath his right arm, a thick book in his left hand.

After finding a patch of shorter grass, they spread the blanket out and made themselves comfortable. Violet sat upright, sketchpad in hand as she focused on the bridge and its surroundings. She examined her subject in silence, mentally deciphering the unique details of each stone, the overall shape of the arch and the flowing water underneath. Meanwhile, Jasper settled on his back beside her, eventually holding his novel above his face to read while simultaneously shielding his eyes from the sun overhead.

"Is my favorite author writing anything, currently?" Violet asked quietly.

Jasper breathed an amused laugh. "No. I don't write in December. Generally speaking, it's my month off."

"What are you reading?"

"*Secrets of the Gemini*."

"Second time?"

"Third."

They both chuckled as a cool breeze swept through the clearing, causing the yellowed clusters of grass to bend and sway, the tree branches bouncing and creaking. Remarkably, the weather was clear, with the sunlight creating just enough warmth to abate the brisk winter wind.

Violet almost always wore her wristwatch, but not today. It was nice, being unaware of time passing. But it did, slinking by peacefully with Violet in a kind of trance as she scraped her pencil across the page, both in long, sweeping movements and short, clipped strokes—creating shadows and hard outlines. Capturing the details of the scene before her. Sometimes, she'd notice the boisterous caw of a crow overhead, or the soft, melodic whistling of a bird she couldn't identify in a nearby tree.

When the sun was positioned more in the west than east, Violet finally roused from her engrossed state. Jasper had been so quiet, the atmosphere so comfortable, that she'd allowed herself to become completely absorbed. She looked down at him and he'd turned over on his side, facing her hip with his eyes closed.

Her gram had left her. But then, another person had immediately returned by way of some strange, cosmic exchange. Why was life like this? This constant push and pull of death and life: doors closing and then opening, chapters ending and then beginning anew. It always seemed to happen this way, as if the world needed to maintain some divine balance.

She'd spent more than a decade worried about this person, wondering whether or not he was thriving, while simultaneously dreading the inevitable call from Gram someday to tell her that he was no more: the hope of reuniting with him replaced by the pain and promise that she would never see him again.

But he was here. Right now. Sleeping peacefully beside her.

Violet had the urge to lift her hand from the blanket and trace his hairline—just a delicate sweep of her fingertips against his skin and the heavy curl of his wonderfully dark hair. However, knowing better and recalling his established boundary to the forefront of her mind, she didn't.

When Jasper's eyes lazily opened, Violet froze, her body tensing as if he'd somehow sensed her incriminating thoughts. His gaze met hers before he reached between them, timidly sliding his hand over hers against the blanket. Understanding, she turned her palm up. He laced his fingers within hers, then pulled her hand closer so that Violet's knuckles brushed and rested against his nose and mouth. He breathed in deeply, then out in a sleepy sigh. He closed his eyes, but kept her hand pressed against his skin.

Violet's pulse thumped throughout her body, the cool breeze whisking past her no match for the heat rushing up her neck and to her cheeks. When she gripped Jasper's hand a little tighter, he gently squeezed her hand in response.

"Isn't this normally your sleeping and recovery time?" she asked.

"Mm," he breathed, his eyes closed. "But it's okay."

Violet nodded. "I was thinking, this is... Well. It's my first Christmas without Gram."

Jasper opened his eyes, but he didn't speak so Violet went on. "Simone wants to have a little gathering of people. A holiday brunch, early in the day. Maybe I'll ask René to come—I think he likes Simone, although Simone is convinced he's some kind of narcissist because he's 'too good looking.' She also wants to invite Freddie, even though I'm not sure I'm finished despising him. But anyway, she wants to meet you, too. Plus, your birthday is coming soon..."

Jasper remained still beside her, staring at her hip. Violet took a nervous breath.

"Everyone knows you're sick, so you don't have to do this. I just thought... well, you know me and René, and Freddie... that doesn't help—but Simone is lovely."

"René isn't a narcissist," he said, his lips and breath tickling the back of Violet's hand. He lifted his face slightly to watch her. "Actually, he's really sensitive to other people. Did he tell you he was homeless when I hired him?"

Violet drew back. "No. Not at all."

Jasper closed his eyes again. "He grew up in a single-family household with his mother, little brother and two little sisters. His dad died when he was a kid. I guess the apartment was small, so he moved out with the intention to work and send money back to them, but things didn't go so well and he ended up on the streets. If he wasn't so busy representing me, he'd do well to write and sell his own memoir. I think he's ashamed of it, though, so he probably won't."

"Oh wow. I had no clue."

"I think that's why he does all that stuff—wears high-end clothes and speaks in that flowery, uppity manner. I think he's trying to compensate for his past. Distance himself from it as much as possible. He said he did things he's not proud of to get by."

Violet blinked, processing. "He didn't mention anything—I mean, I guess he wouldn't since we don't know each other very well."

"Well, he was too busy telling you *my* secrets. And he can't talk about it, anyway. Not really. It's messy now since his success is tied up in my books. But I don't script him when he does speaking engagements and appearances.

"He just reads the books, talks to me about them and does his own thing. I don't police him because I don't necessarily care about the attention and awards. I just like writing and researching. But René is naturally good at public speaking, and people like him. I let him have all the profits for speaking engagements, while I keep the money for the books—well, that's how it *should* be. He insists on giving me thirty percent for appearances. He says he doesn't feel right taking it all since he wouldn't be making the money if it weren't for me. I just put that money back into the town or some charity somewhere."

Her heart warm, Violet leaned toward him, just a little. She let go of his hand, then softly slid her index finger between his eyebrows and down the straight path of his nose. "For someone who's stayed inside a house for the past fifteen years, you do quite a bit of good in this world."

He shifted away and looked up at her with suspicion. "Are you petting me because you're thinking about how I'm a rat?"

"Uh, no, I was not. And you are not a rat—"

"Not at this moment, but I will be. Later."

Violet paused, then flicked his forehead with her finger.

"Ow—"

"Nobody was thinking about that, you silly man."

Jasper pouted, his palm pressed to his forehead as he lay on his back. "You *should* be thinking about it. I'm cursed, Violet. Don't ever forget that."

"I know you're cursed. It's not something I would forget. What are you really trying to say to me?"

"That… That you shouldn't get too complacent."

Smirking, she leaned over him, resting her palms on either side of his shoulders so that he was trapped underneath her, unable to avoid her gaze. She lifted her chin. "And what happens if I get complacent? Tell me."

In a surprise move, Jasper rolled, catching Violet's arm so that he broke through her barrier, nearly making her fall face-first into the blanket. But she caught herself. When she looked over, Jasper was sitting straight, looking down at her. "Nothing happens. Ever."

Violet sat upright, brushing her palms against her thighs. "Why?"

"Because it can't."

"Because it can't or because you don't want it to?"

He turned his head toward the distant trees, his expression unreadable. "Both."

Something about that felt like a door being slammed. Another hard boundary. Violet nodded, picking up her sketch pad and standing. "Understood. Should we head back to the cottage? It's getting cloudy and colder." Violet stretched her arms, but Jasper only stared up at her with his marble eyes. He didn't budge.

"What is it?" Violet asked.

As he stared, his cheeks warmed to a rosy red. "Because you *don't* understand. Violet, you—"

"Listen, you don't need to give me a big speech right now," Violet said, holding her hand out flat to stop him. "I respect your boundaries, Jas. You're worrying about something I didn't even technically offer, so get your narrow behind up and let's go. I'm cold."

The rosiness shifted into bright crimson as he stood straight, his forehead furrowed. He bent to grab the blanket. "I wasn't suggesting that you were offering me something." He shook the blanket out a little too hard, sending dead grass and debris flying such that Violet had to take a step back.

"I would never be so presumptuous," he fussed.

"Mmhm. Right."

He stopped dead, blanket ruffled in his arms and face disgruntled and flushed. Despite herself, Violet smiled. She moved closer, then bent to grab the bottom edge of the quilt to help fold it. "You're really cute, all flustered and indignant like this."

He snatched the blanket from Violet's grasp, but his mouth broke into a crooked smile. "The answer is *yes*," he said.

"Yes what?" Violet turned her nose up, but then smiled. "What was the question?"

"To the party thing... Yes. I'll come."

29

NOW

hen Jasper and Violet rounded the corner at the front of Gram's cottage, she stopped in surprise. "My God, she works fast."

"There's a tree on your porch," Jasper said.

"It's my Christmas tree, apparently. Courtesy of Simone. Sheesh, she just mentioned ordering it last night." Violet walked up the stone steps and onto the small porch space. She reached out, stroking the needles encased in thick twine. "Soft pine." She leaned in and sniffed. It smelled wonderful.

"It came with a stand."

Violet looked over to see Jasper staring down at a large box and reading the label. "That's handy," he went on. "Can I help bring it inside?"

"Sure, thanks. Let me grab us some gardening gloves from the pantry."

About fifteen minutes and a bruised elbow later, they'd wrestled the tree inside. Presently, it was still wrapped tightly in twine. They'd leaned it against the brick fireplace near the front picture window.

Jasper sat on the floor with the box open and various tree-

KARLA NIKOLE

stand materials scattered about, reading instructions and looking as if he were in his element—a new puzzle to be solved. Violet plopped down onto the couch with an ice pack pressed to her elbow, trying very hard not to cry.

"Do you need help?" Violet asked.

"No, you take care of your elbow. You should have let me walk in backward like I said."

"Well, hindsight is twenty-twenty, isn't it?"

"You're stubborn."

"Am not."

Jasper looked up at her, grinning openly. So much so that it reached his eyes, which was rare. "Are you intentionally proving my point?"

"Maybe."

After that, Jasper went to work. He studied the instructions in silence for a few more minutes, then placed them to one side and started fitting parts together: quickly twisting, turning and manipulating screws and metal pieces with his long fingers. Before Violet knew it, the tree stand was whole. He set it on the floor, stood, and moved toward the tree.

"Where do you want this set up?" he asked.

"I can help you lift that."

He smiled. "You take care of your elbow. Where?"

"Maybe right in front of the window? Gram always displayed it there."

"She did indeed." He slid the stand a little closer to the window with his foot, grabbed and lifted the tree, then placed it in the stand. When he had it straightened, he looked at Violet. "Okay, now I need your good arm, just to hold the tree upright while I tighten the screws in the stand."

Laying her ice pack to the side, Violet stood and took over the job of holding the tree. While Jasper was bent down, he exhaled a muffled yawn.

"You alright?" Violet asked.

"Mmhm. It's just, I think I've moved around more today than I have in over a decade... as a human, anyway. I'm much more active when I'm a rat."

Violet shook her head. "You cater to your mouse form, don't you? You even eat like a mouse—hardly any real meals."

"If I eat like a human, have a giant meal and then shrink down later, it makes things more awful in that form, so I just snack all day. I don't drink alcohol either. I had to learn that lesson the hard way."

"Yikes, that makes sense, I guess."

Jasper stood, dusting off his hands against his trousers. "I'll sleep well tomorrow. Probably all day? If Freddie comes by, let him know I'm fine."

"I don't plan on speaking to Freddie until this party thing, if I can help it. Maybe not even then. Jas, why wait until tomorrow morning to sleep when you're tired now? Just find a safe spot in the house to sleep in your mouse form."

"No, I feel too anxious about it. It's alright, I'm used to this—and December is my month off from writing, so I can sleep all day tomorrow and go right back to being a rat at night."

"When will you eat?"

"I'll put an apple out for myself. Sunflower seeds. Easy things."

Violet nodded. There was no use arguing with him. He was set in his fifteen-year routine. Trying to convince him to do otherwise was a losing battle.

"Should I cut the twine off?" he asked. "Can we start decorating it?"

"If you're not too tired?"

Jasper looked up at the wall clock, which drew Violet's attention to it as well. 3:02 p.m.

"I'm fine," he said. "I should leave at about four thirty, though, to make sure I'm back home by five. Is that okay?"

"Of course. I'm happy to have your help and company, especially given this sudden elbow injury."

"At least you don't fall out of trees anymore... Or have a concussion—"

"Alright, alright. The boxes with the tree decorations are on the back porch stacked in the corner. I'll show you."

Violet walked toward the kitchen with Jasper chuckling beside her. "Gloria told me you twisted your ankle playing soccer in high school. Twice."

"Did she, now?"

"And that you jammed your pinky finger against the front door because you went too hard for the knob the night before you moved to the city."

"Jasper, is there a point to all this?"

"I don't know, I just think it's funny—you with your self-inflicted mishaps and me being cursed with literal witch magic. It's no wonder we get along."

"Yup. Clearly, we're meant to be."

"A match made in misfortune."

Violet stopped at the back door to the patio. She turned and faced Jasper, lifting her chin to look up into his eyes. "I don't like that."

"I was just joking... Mostly."

She looked him over before sticking her index finger out to poke him smack in his bellybutton. He doubled over and stepped away with a breathy laugh. Direct hit. Violet smirked, satisfied as she unlocked and pulled the back-patio door open. But her smile dropped, her heart sinking as she took in the utter mess of broken glass and an unhinged door.

"Oh no..."

"What is it?" Jasper asked.

Stepping onto the patio, the cold air sat stagnant around her. The beautiful pots of mint and Roman chamomile had been knocked over, the red-brown clay broken into large shards.

There was dirt everywhere, and when Violet looked over to the spot where her gram's red poppy chest should have been—that large, seemingly permanent fixture on the patio that had been hand-painted with love—it was empty. The chest was gone.

THIS TIME, Violet did call the police.

"This is so ridiculous," Rose exclaimed through the phone. "Who would do this? Are the police finished yet?"

Violet sighed as she sat against the couch. "No. They're taking pictures of the patio. I went ahead and told them that this is the second break-in—but I said nothing was stolen the first time."

"Have they mentioned anything about a string of burglaries throughout the village or something? Is this an isolated thing?"

"Seems like it," Violet confirmed. She closed her eyes, palm pressed to her face, trying to calm her nerves. "Rosie... Gram's poppy chest is a family heirloom. This is just..." She couldn't understand. There was nothing especially valuable in the chest. It held more sentimental meaning than anything else, so why on earth would someone take it?

Everything crashed down on Violet—Gram was gone. This would be her first Christmas without her, and now her home had been cruelly vandalized twice within the span of a month. Her safe space that she loved. Violet shook her head, depleted as silent tears rolled down her face.

"I know this sucks, Vi, but it's okay—and maybe they'll get it back?"

"Maybe." Violet's voice cracked. She took a deep breath but the tears wouldn't stop. "I feel like I'm making a mess of Gram's things. She left all this to me and I'm not even protecting it."

"It's just stuff, and you're doing a great job, alright? You wrapped up all her estate dealings within a month, you're working with the bakery lady to distribute and learn about the herbs. You're *painting* again. Gram would love all of that. We'll get past this."

Violet took a deep breath to let her sister's words sink in. Rose went on in her silence.

"Are you okay there alone? Should I drive up for the night to keep you company?"

"I think I'm alright. Actually, Jasper is here, talking with the police. I'm not alone."

"Wait, what? He's at *your* house right now? Like, he left his house? Did you call him over? I'm so confused."

This made Violet laugh, just a small huff. Which was a nice break from feeling miserable. "No. We went for a walk out to Poppy Bridge this morning. He was still with me when I realized someone had broken in."

"Wow, so... he left the house for you? To spend the day with you? Like a date? Are you two dating?"

Violet rolled her eyes. "Not *for* me. Just relax, Rosie, alright? Thank you for the offer, but you don't need to drive all the way here."

"Okay, okay. Is he staying the night with you? I don't want you alone, feeling sorry for yourself and missing Gram..."

"I—I don't think so. He needs to get back home."

"Well, let me know and I'll drive there. I was waiting for Jillian to come home but I can just text her. Keep me posted."

"Alright, I will." Violet hung up the phone and quickly rubbed her palm down her face to dry the tears. "Just a mini pity-party, folks, let's keep it moving." Violet rolled her shoulders. It would be okay and Rosie was right. Violet didn't want to keep emotionally crumbling this way. Or at least, when she did, she wanted her recovery process to be a little shorter each time.

The patio door off the kitchen shut and locked, and Violet turned her head. She expected to see two police officers, but only Jasper stood in the entryway. He sighed, dropping his shoulders.

"They have everything they need," he said, walking toward her. "They'll call with any updates. There were shoe prints in the dirt, so that could be helpful?"

"Thanks for going out there with them. I needed to talk to Rosie and let her know."

"Of course, Vi. I'm happy I could help. Are you okay?" He moved a little closer to Violet's position on the couch. She tried smiling up at him, but her effort was lackluster.

"I'm okay, it's just—oh shoot." Violet whipped her head around to the wall clock, her eyes wide. "Jasper, it's almost five, you're late getting home."

He ran his fingers up into the nest of his dark curls. "I—I do need to go, but… are you *really* okay? I'll start changing soon and I don't want… Is there anything I can do before I go? If there is, just tell me."

Violet shook her head, smiling. "You've already helped a lot. I'm okay, really. If I need company, Rosie said she'll drive up. Don't worry."

He glanced away and toward the empty hearth. "She lives two hours away. That's a long time to be by yourself after something like this…" He looked at her, his eyes filled with all kinds of emotions that Violet couldn't even begin to understand.

"You should go," she said calmly. "If you don't, I'll be worried that you didn't make it home, and I'll have nightmares about you running from owls and foxes all night."

He shook his head, his hand still gripping his hair and his eyes clenched shut. "Vi… I just—I wish…"

She reached down and took hold of his wrist, making him look at her. She gently pulled him toward the door. "You already told me you've only ever changed in your house, and that you wouldn't feel comfortable doing it anywhere else. I understand, and I'm fine."

They moved in silence as she guided him. The truth? Violet didn't want to be alone right now. Just having someone else present would distract her and help ease the deepening violation she felt. But she understood his situation—he was *cursed,* for goodness' sake.

When she opened the front door for him, she offered a small grin. "Alright, scurry home."

"That's not funny." He stepped outside and onto the porch, then turned to face her. "When I'm human again in the morning, I'll come back and help you clean… If that's okay?"

"Jasper, you're going to be exhausted. Don't worry—"

"I'll be fine. As soon as I'm normal again, I'll come back and we can finish the tree?"

Violet sighed, conceding. "Okay, I'll see you tomorrow."

Jasper watched her for a moment, nodding. He turned, his long legs moving him down the walkway, along the road and toward the woods that led to his home. Violet closed and locked the door, then went back into the sitting room. She plopped down onto the couch, lying on her stomach with her head resting against the seat cushions.

The house was totally silent and cold. As she breathed, she could hear the wall clock ticking away the seconds. She should probably salvage some firewood from the back porch and light a fire, but she didn't want to return to the scene of the crime. The gross destruction of her gram's personal space…Violet's personal space. Where she painted and breathed in chamomile and mint in the sunlight. Where she had cocoa with her sister and reminisced about their childhood days.

Thinking this way, focusing on it as she was, the sadness closed in on her again like a dark bubble, shrinking. The sphere enclosed her, smaller and smaller until warm tears gathered in her eyes yet again.

Tap-tap-tap. Violet jumped at the light knocking. She pulled herself upright, wiped her face, and went back to the front door.

Once there, she peeked through the small hole to see anxious gray eyes blinking back at her. She unlocked the door and pulled it open.

"I'm sorry... I'll be completely useless after I change, but... Do you want company? May I stay with you? I'll go outside to the greenhouse to transition, and if—if you just leave the back door cracked a little I can get back in when I'm done—"

Violet wrapped her fingers around his wrist to pull him back inside. When she closed the door, he went on, a weak smile on his face. "I know a rat in your house is pretty repulsive, but maybe it's better than nothing?"

"You're a mouse," she said, guiding him back to the sitting room. "And you're *not* going outside to change—"

"I have to. Violet, I don't want you to see—even *hear* anything with the change. It's really and truly horrific and I would *never* want... I wouldn't do that to you. I can't..." He shook his head, his eyes very serious. He swallowed. Violet could see his Adam's apple bob in his throat from the stress.

It occurred to her that this—Jasper's being here, changing somewhere outside his own home for the first time and showing his other self to her—was significant. He was pushing himself, spontaneously, and it was *not* easy for him. In fact, he was wound so tight right now that he reminded Violet of a champagne bottle, ready to pop if she jostled him even a little.

She reached down, taking hold of his other wrist and lifting her chin to look him in the eyes. "Listen, you can go in my bedroom to change. I'll stay out here—probably with a bottle of wine that you paid for and the fire going—and I won't hear or see anything. Leave the door cracked, and when you're ready, I'll be on the couch. Alright?"

He lifted one hand from hers, rubbing his palm across his forehead. "Okay... alright. I'm sorry this is... I don't know if I'm helping or making things worse, but I don't want you to feel alone right now. Don't be sad and alone, Vi."

Smiling, she held his one hand with both of hers. Violet opened her mouth to speak, but the tremor of his grip distracted her. His skin felt warm and tingly, almost like it was buzzing. "Why are you shaking?" she asked.

"This is how it starts. The spidery, itchy feeling, remember? That hasn't changed since I was nine."

"Does it hurt?"

"I'm used to it now. Don't worry about me. I can get the firewood for you before I... Are you sure it's okay for me to be in your room? I'm honestly okay with going outside—"

"*No*, Jasper. You're not going outside. And thank you for setting up the fire."

He nodded, slipping his hand from hers and quickly moving toward the kitchen, then out onto the patio. As she watched him go, she couldn't help but smile. It was a tired smile, but genuine. "Wine time," she said aloud to no one before sauntering to the wine rack just outside the kitchen door.

30

NOW

*V*iolet had thought that she was tired. She should have been exhausted after the long morning walk out to Poppy Bridge, wrestling with a giant soft pine tree (resulting in unexpected elbow bruising) and the emotional rollercoaster of being robbed yet again.

But an hour after Jasper had come back, lit a fire for her and then stealthily disappeared into her bedroom, she lay on the couch wide awake. She rested on her stomach once more, her arm dangling over the edge and her nearly empty wine glass just within reach.

How could one sleep when literal magic was occurring in their house? She'd promised Jasper she'd stay away—and he'd made her promise at least three times. But everything in her wanted to see and know. To witness what exactly was happening to him right now.

Even without seeing it, Violet could *feel* it. At first, she'd thought it was her imagination. But when the fine hairs on her arms began to stand upright, her skin tickling with some indiscernible frosty sensation, there was no denying it.

She could feel Jasper's change happening in the air—like a

dank, invisible fog rolling and pouring through the halls of the cottage. Malevolent... Heavy. Something in it made her shiver. Centuries old, an unfathomable power and intent. A strong emotion backed with the icy blister of a winter wind. Deep sorrow or pain.

She lay there, eyes wide. Waiting. The fire burned and danced, but she barely registered it. All she could do was stare, her body almost paralyzed.

After a full hour of this, the tension finally broke. It felt as if Violet had been snapped out of a trance. She blinked her eyes, the warmth of the room caressing her skin once more, bringing her back to earth and light and hope. She pushed herself up, just enough to grab her wine glass from the floor and bring it to her lips. "Good *grief.*" She tilted her head back and finished it off.

As she set her glass back down on the rug, she heard it. The softest little padding and squeaking sounds, almost like a whisper. She looked around from her lazy position—underneath the coffee table beside her, scanning the floor by the tree, in front of the fireplace and over by the kitchen. But nothing. Only the faint sounds.

Violet smirked, thoroughly amused. "Let me see you..."

She waited. Still nothing. Violet glanced around again, but got smart and leaned over the edge of the couch. Her thick, curly hair hit the floor as she hung upside down, ignoring the rush of blood to her head as she peeked underneath the sofa.

"Aha!" The little gray mouse with starburst whiskers. Just as she remembered him. He was frozen there, planted on all fours toward the back edge of the couch. Violet frowned. "Are you going to stay under there all night? You said you'd keep me company."

He sat upright on his haunches, his back curved and his tiny front feet pawing the air. Then he dropped back down. He moved sideways, not forward, then back to his original spot. Violet smiled helplessly as she watched him. *So much hesitation...*

She dropped her knuckles to the rug, curling her fingers in a gesture. "Jasper, come here, please. Before my head explodes."

That seemed to prompt him, because he scurried forward a few steps. Paused. Then a few more. Violet wiggled her fingers again to encourage him, waiting. When he was close, she stopped moving her hand and laid it as flat as possible. She'd never picked up any kind of rodent before, but she imagined grabbing him and squeezing would be a bad choice.

When his whiskers brushed against her fingertips, she chuckled. He placed one tiny, clammy front paw on her fingers —sniffing, looking and hesitating. When he finally placed both paws on board, Violet used her free hand to scoop and urge the back of him up so that he was cupped within her palms. Using her good elbow and upper body strength, she shifted herself to lay back onto the couch with a groan. Her head spun and tiny white lights zipped past her eyes. "Wow, that was a terrible idea... especially after wine."

Settling on her side, she rested her cupped palms on the couch, then opened her hands to deposit her fuzzy friend beside her. Her best friend. The boy with the big moon eyes... as a mouse. In her house. Cursed.

Violet laughed. "Jasper, this is utterly *insane*." He seemed anxious, rising onto his hind legs and crawling about as mice do. He didn't try to jump down, though, so Violet lay comfortably, resting her head on a throw pillow. The need to sleep fell heavy on her consciousness like a thick comforter.

Her eyelids drooped, her breathing deep and even. But she lazily flickered her eyes open when she felt the soft brush of whiskers against her nose. Drowsy, she started. "Are you hungry? We haven't even eaten all day... and what about a litter box or something? I didn't ask. I'll be honest, Jas, I won't be happy with you if I find mouse droppings in between my couch cushions tomorrow."

And that was the last thing she remembered.

∽

THE NEXT MORNING, Violet stretched her body and breathed in deep as she twisted against the couch. A rich smell floated in the air, and she felt warm and rested. She opened her eyes at the sensation of her face being held within someone's palms. When her gaze adjusted to the shadowed silhouette hovering over her, she grinned. "Oh, hi. He's human again." She closed her eyes. "Sorry I didn't feed you."

Now, something came to rest in the middle of her forehead. Frowning, she opened her eyes to see Jasper's finger there, poking her, his face unamused.

"First of all, you're hungover. It's already eleven o'clock. Second, I would *never* poop on your couch."

Violet burst into a fit of laughter, the unexpected kind that grips a person in totality. She spoke through her delight. "You remembered that?"

"I remember everything perfectly clear—I don't need a litter box. I'm not a cat."

His pride made Violet laugh harder. She reached up and removed his hand from her forehead. Clasping it within hers, she rested their hands against her upper chest, still grinning. "Sorry, sorry. Did you sleep at all?"

"Yes, I did," he said, his expression softening as he watched her.

"Well, that's good, right?" She brought his hand up, nuzzling her face against his palm. "At least I'm not a completely terrible hostess? Even though I drank a big glass of wine, passed out on the couch and didn't offer you any food." She breathed in. His hand was warm and surprisingly smelled like basil and rosemary. And butter?

"Have you been cooking? Why does your hand smell like something I want to eat?" He slipped his hand from within hers, still staring at her and looking displeased about something. "Is everything alright?" she asked.

He slid off the couch to sit on the floor beneath her, his back pressed against the edge of the cushions. "Yes, I baked a frittata. It should be ready in fifteen minutes."

"You can cook?"

"A few things. I used to cook for Dad when he came to visit me. He worked so hard and drove a long way to check on me. Learning to cook a few nice meals was the least I could do, even if I don't eat those things myself."

"That's really thoughtful of you. You were a good son."

"I don't think I was. But he was stuck with me, wasn't he? Violet, why aren't you more freaked out about this?"

"About... your curse?"

"*Yes,*" he said, turning his head and looking into her eyes. "I'm cursed and I shapeshift and you act like it's not a big deal, when none of this is normal. And even last night... I don't understand why you're so nonchalant about me. I—I'm a freak and it's disgusting and scary. I can't understand your thinking."

"Okay, alright." Violet pushed herself upright to sit straighter. She folded her legs underneath the thick quilt that had somehow materialized over her body. When she was settled, she took a deep breath. "You use that word a lot to describe yourself, Jasper. 'Disgusting.'"

"Because that's what I am."

Violet paused, pursing her lips. "Can we talk about your mother?" She watched as he sat unmoving and with his gaze fixed forward.

"I don't blame my mother," he said. "I don't think she's a bad person."

"Do you think she treated you well?"

"No... I know she didn't. But I believe her reaction to me was valid. Can you imagine?" he asked, turning to look up at her again.

"Her only child starts having strange symptoms that no doctor can explain. She's worried and scared—hoping things get better. Then out of nowhere he mutates and breaks down into an animal. Wouldn't that be like the bottom dropping out? The absolute worst result—realizing this *thing* is what she gave birth to... Who wouldn't react poorly to that? It's terrifying and unimaginable."

"But your dad didn't react that way," Violet reasoned. "So why do you adopt and repeat your mother's rhetoric, but not your father's?"

"Dad took care of me because he had to—and because he felt bad."

"He loved you," Violet added.

"I know that," Jasper said. "But he was stuck with me. And there was no one else. They couldn't just let me die. Someone *had* to take care of me."

Violet folded her arms and sighed, her heart heavy in her chest. "I don't know, Jasper. I think you're focusing on the wrong thing."

"But you don't have to do this," he said. "You don't have to be around me and see this. You could be doing anything, Violet. I don't understand *why*."

"Yes, you do. I already told you why. But you get all frazzled and upset when I say it." She raised one eyebrow, waiting for his response.

He turned his head away and toward the hearth, his shoulders rising and falling in a still moment. "Violet, I love you, too... Ever since we were six years old and we played in the sandbox together, I've loved you. But I feel *guilty* and ashamed. Who am I to love you? This cursed, mutant person who can't offer you anything. I can't even properly sit with you after your house has been broken into. I just... I feel like my love is useless to you."

For once, Violet didn't have any words. Well, she had them—lots of them. She could easily counter his insecurities, try to reassure him and give him some idea of how *not* useless his love was. How his kindness and thoughtfulness always warmed her heart, or how even when they were apart, he was still giving her joy through his books—taking her on thrilling adventures to foreign countries, sweeping landscapes and dense cities through the eyes of brave, shrewd heroines.

But listening to him, to this... she didn't think any of her words would truly reach him. Words weren't what Jasper needed. He had words and he knew them well. And anything she said at this moment would be like trying to put a bandage on an infected organ deep inside him. So she sat without saying a word, her heart in her throat.

Eventually, he looked up at her. "Vi? Are you listening?"

She opened her mouth to speak, but she blinked and tears came cascading down. Quietly, she reached over and grabbed a tissue from the small end table. She sniffed, her voice muffled and stuffy. "Why did you love me starting with the sandbox? What did I do?"

"You let me have the purple cup, and I thought 'Ah, I love her,' and it just kind of spiraled from there."

The laughter bubbled from up from deep inside Violet, and she let it overtake her, sitting back and losing her breath to it. Jasper laughed, too, the sound filling the quiet room filtered in silvery, overcast sunlight. They sat comfortably in the stillness after that, catching their breath. When Violet looked over, she realized that the twine had been cut from the soft pine tree. It stood full and majestic, rich in green and shadows just beside the window. The boxes of Gram's ornaments were neatly stacked by the fireplace, too.

"You've been busy this morning," Violet said. In a cautious movement, she crawled her hand toward Jasper, eyeing his neck and shoulders set above the couch cushions. She lifted her hand, then used one finger to caress the gentle curve at the back of his neck, ever so lightly. When he didn't flinch or shift away, she flipped her hand and grazed his skin with the backs of her fingers, following the natural symmetry of his upper spine.

"Breakfast should almost be ready," he said, matching her quiet. "After you eat, should we decorate the tree?"

"Will you eat with me? Just a little? I have some macadamia nuts and dried cherries in the pantry. There's havarti in the fridge, too."

"I can. That would be nice."

"Perfect."

They should have moved then, but neither of them did. Violet sat under the quilt, happily brushing her fingers up and down the delicate space of his spine—just underneath his thick hairline. He didn't object. Eventually, he even closed his eyes.

31

TWO WEEKS LATER

[Janet: Is everything ready for the dinner tomorrow night?]

*V*iolet scowled. *Everything like what? We show up, we eat. The end.* She typed out a message.

[Yes, I called the restaurant yesterday to reconfirm our reservation.]

[Janet: And that's it?]

[Yes. Unless you had something else in mind?]

The moment Violet hit send, she realized the mistake she'd made.

[Janet: Should we do gift baskets? What about a raffle? Could we put that together before tomorrow night? You can go and buy gift cards.]

"Ugh."

"What?" Jasper looked up from his book, worry coloring his face.

Violet dropped her hands and her phone at her side. "We've been planning this holiday party for the staff for three weeks, and the day before it takes place, my boss wants to put together a raffle and gift basket."

Jasper tilted his head. "So... do the raffle and gift basket? You're not busy—"

"That's not the point. Why do I need to run around, executing their harebrained schemes at the last minute when I could have taken care of this weeks ago? And every time they do this, I deliver. So it just gives them more cause to spring things on me again later. Over and over... I get tired of being at their beck and call."

"Hm," Jasper considered. "You're inadvertently punished for doing good work. I read an article about that with teachers. You know, the rate of burnout for skilled, quality educators is very high—and fast. Administration loads them up with challenging students because they're 'good at handling the tough ones.' It's stressful, though, so then the teachers end up quitting and switching careers entirely. One former teacher that they inter-viewed is an investment banker now. She'd been a kindergarten teacher before."

"That's a big jump," Violet said. "Like your life was full of color, smiles, fruit snacks and paper crafts, then totally black-and-white. Drab."

"Speaking of color..." Jasper said, turning himself on the floor so that he sat facing Violet's row of finished canvases. The fully decorated tree shimmered at his side, bright baubles shining in the soft lighting of the room. "Are you going to try selling some of these?"

"Yup, Simone is setting up an account for me."

"She bought two, right?"

"Mmhm."

"What's the name of the account?"

Violet grinned. "Painted Poppies. I don't know, she thought it had a ring to it."

"I like it." He turned to look at her over his shoulder. "I think this is exciting—and long overdue. You're gifted at recreating light and color, and you've always had such a strong eye for detail—I remember you drew a picture of the schoolhouse when we were in second grade. You even included that butterfly wind chime in the music teacher's window. I was so amazed."

Her smile broadening, Violet decided to take a chance. "Well, thank you for the support and encouragement. What I really need is more practice with faces and portraits. It would be nice if I had someone to help me with that, too."

"Help you how?"

"To sit for me."

Jasper froze. "I... I could ask René for you?"

"You *know* I don't want René."

"Vi, why would you want me?"

"Why wouldn't I want you? Of course I want you." She narrowed her eyes. He turned his back to her again, but she could still see the flush of color creeping up his neck, settling in his cheek from her view of his profile.

"There are a million reasons why you shouldn't."

"But they only exist in *your* mind," Violet assured him. "Sit for me, please?"

He looked back over his shoulder. "Starting when?"

"Tomorrow morning? Since it's the weekend... Are you staying with me tonight?"

"I—this would be the third time this week."

"So? You sleep when you're here, right? I don't mind, Jas. I enjoy your company... and your little whiskers are so dang cute—"

"Don't do that."

Violet chuckled as Jasper rubbed his palms up and down his face, shaking his head.

"You used to have dark circles under your eyes. They're already gone. Just stay."

He straightened his back as he faced the light with his legs folded. His voice soft, he said, "Okay. Thank you."

Violet's phone buzzed beside her, so she automatically picked it up and looked at the screen.

[Karen: Is everything ready for tomorrow?]
[Karen: Where is this restaurant again?]

32

JUST A FEW DAYS LATER

"They say that most robberies are committed by someone close to the victim."

Violet lifted the soft charcoal from the damp canvas and used her fingertips to smudge the lines she'd made. This was a messy business, but she liked it that way: the art being manipulated by her literal hands—no pencil or brush to come between her and what she was creating. Something about it felt versatile, flexible, and she found herself excited by the depth of shadows coming through the piece. "Is that supposed to make me feel better or worse?" she asked.

"It's just information." Jasper shrugged, then reached up and scratched his head.

"What did I tell you about moving around?"

"I can't scratch?"

"I'm already letting you read, now you want to scratch, next you'll ask me if you can do jumping jacks."

Jasper laughed. "Trust me, I won't. But seriously, I'm trying to be helpful. It's been a month since the chest was stolen and the police are still dragging their feet."

"No, no—I haven't updated you. They told me they're

making inquiries and have a lead. It isn't solid yet, but they haven't given up. I really want Gram's stuff back."

"Of course you do... and that's great news." Jasper grinned, then cast his gaze back down toward his novel. His only condition in sitting for her was that he could read while she drew. So that's how Violet had been sketching him for the past week and as they sat on the patio: the golden rays of light falling over him as he read, his eyes downcast. The pose had an unexpected angelic quality that she was quite pleased with.

Violet traced the compressed charcoal against the canvas, finally outlining the shape of Jasper's form: the curve of his jaw, the lines of his head, neck and shoulders. Next, she'd add more detail to his features, flipping between smudging the canvas to create more realistic shadows, and using a fine-tipped charcoal pencil to develop the contours of his nose, eyes and mouth. She hadn't started filling in his dark, wild, carefree hair yet. She'd save the best for last.

Jasper read and Violet sketched. There were a lot of things she enjoyed about spending time with Jasper, among them the ease of their conversation, the kind warmth of his presence, and secretly, his very cute, furry other self, curled up against the slope of her forehead when he slept on her pillow at night (he wanted to burrow underneath the blanket where it was warmer and cozier for him, but she outlawed it, terrified she'd squish him in the middle of the night).

But perhaps the best moments were like this. Where neither of them needed to talk, and simply resting in the comfort of each other's presence was sufficient. No awkwardness, no demands on anyone's attention, no contrived conversation.

Throughout her life, the only other person Violet had ever achieved this with was her gram. Her father, being a highly sought-after medical surgeon, was never home. Even now and for the past ten years, he'd been living in Los Angeles as a celebrity surgeon. So on the rare occasions he was home, the conversation was forced—condensed to achieve some sort of mandatory familiarity as appropriate between a father and daughter.

Conversations with Rosie were good, but sometimes ended in a lecture. Violet should try to be more stable. Violet should take her career choices more seriously. Violet should be more open to dating so that she could find someone. Rosie had done all of those things—a successful lawyer with a house in the city and the perfect girlfriend. Why couldn't Violet?

She flicked her eyes up to her subject, considering. "Why do you think your parents only had you? Your family was prosperous, so you'd think your mom would have had more kids."

"It's a pattern." Jasper stared down at his book. "If you look back through our family history, there's been one boy born to the Laurent name per generation since the late 1800s. Never any girls. The timing coincides with the Magic Cleanse, so it's safe to assume it's part of the curse."

"So your father knew about the curse, then? Had he told you or your mother?"

Jasper closed his book and met Violet's eyes. "Yes, he knew about it. But he didn't tell us until after I changed—after he was sure. The curse is unpredictable. The last Laurent to have it was my great-grandfather. My grandfather witnessed it in person and was traumatized by it, so when my father was a child, he knew all about the curse because his dad was really paranoid and anxious. Almost maniacal.

"But Dad never showed any signs of turning, and he hated what it had done to his father—his obsessive, overbearing behavior. So when Dad had me, he told himself he'd never mention it so that we could all lead a normal, happy life. He said he thought maybe the curse had finally broken since it had skipped both him and his father. He was wrong, though... obviously."

Violet laid her sketchpad against her thighs, enthralled. "Do you know anything about the surrounding circumstances of the curse? Like who specifically cast it and why?"

Jasper shook his head. "Other than it being an Ainsworth, no. There was a lot going on back then. Textbooks falsely paint my family as a group of pioneering settlers who founded this town and made it better. They don't talk about the indigenous people who were already here—the ones who lived off the land and explicitly believed in its energy and wielding its powers. Some of them conformed to the new edicts imposed by my ancestors. But some fought hard and lost. I've given this a lot of thought in my solitude. They say an Ainsworth cursed my family as she burned, but I don't know. What if it's the Earth and magic itself cursing us for disregarding its people and ravaging the land?"

Violet huffed a heavy sigh. "I don't know, Jas, that's pretty deep stuff."

He smiled. "You started it."

"Alright, well, I'm finishing it. Did you go get your groceries yesterday?"

"Yes, I did."

"How was that?"

Leaning back in the wicker chair, Jasper folded his arms. "I went as soon as the store opened, so it wasn't bad. Freddie looked like he was going to lay an egg when he saw me."

Violet shook her head. "Did you talk to him?"

"I hadn't planned to, but he opened up a new lane for me as soon as I walked up so I didn't need to wait." Jasper frowned. "Why are you so worried about Freddie talking to me lately?"

"I'm not worried—I'm just... I don't know. Maybe I'm interested in his therapy progress? I want to make sure he's being nice to you."

"He was never mean to me. It was always *you* he had something against. He probably liked you, Vi. As soon as you came back, he was making comments about your hips."

Violet rolled her eyes, a confession on the tip of her tongue. But it wasn't her business to disclose.

"Anyway," Jasper went on. "I bought the stuff you told me to get for the party tomorrow. And some fruit for myself."

"Perfect. Are you nervous?"

"A little. I feel like a fraud. They have no idea what I really am."

"What you really are is wonderful, Jas. The curse has no bearing on your personality and character."

"But there's a major part of my existence that's gruesome. If people knew that... If they saw it, they wouldn't want to be around me."

The deep wound inside him was bleeding again, and it made Violet's chest and throat tighten.

"I think they'll be glad that you're there. *I'll* be happy. Simone is looking forward to meeting you, too." She was thinking that Freddie would be happy, too. But she didn't say it.

33

NOW

*S*imone arrived at the cottage early Sunday morning to help prep. She was impressed with the work Violet and Jasper had already done in decorating the tree, but she strung more lights around the doorways and the kitchen counter, giving the atmosphere an extra bit of sparkle.

"I decided to do the tarts since you said he liked those when you were kids, and also my seasonal orange muffins because, well, they're amazing?" Simone beamed, looking glamorous in a red jumpsuit with a plunging neckline. "I just need to stick them in the oven so they're fresh for after we eat brunch."

"That works for me," Violet said, putting on her oven mitt to remove the quiche she had baking. She felt excited. She couldn't remember the last time she'd hosted a gathering like this. The smell of warm food in the air, the twinkling lights and the soft Christmas music playing in the background swirled around her, making her heart light.

"You look exquisite in this dress. Violet on Violet—the color is so rich. It looks gorgeous against your pretty, toasty skin."

"Tee-hee, thank you." Violet scrunched her nose. She loved

this dress and it fit her perfectly: cinched at her waist, then flowing out in a loose skirt to accentuate her hourglass figure.

When the doorbell rang, Simone squeaked with excitement. "Who do you think is first?"

"Probably Jasper since I asked him to bring some stuff?" Having removed the quiche, Violet set her oven mitt aside and walked to the front with Simone close on her heels. When she reached the door, she peeked through the hole to see Jasper, holding a large paper bag by its handle down at his side. She smiled, immediately noting the slight difference in his appearance. Violet opened the door and looked him over, her grin broadening. "Why, hello."

"Good morning..."

He'd gotten his hair cut. Trimmed on the top and shorter on the sides. Jasper usually wore some kind of sweater that was full of fuzzy lint due to repeated washings (likely over the course of years). But today's sweater was lint-free and fit him perfectly. His coat and slacks were clean and neat as well. He didn't look fashionable, simply more like an active and productive member of society and less like a dusty writer who rarely left his house.

Once he was inside, she closed the door, turning to her guests. "Simone Bisset, this is Jasper Laurent. Jasper, Simone."

"Bom dia! Como está?"

Both Jasper and Violet started, blinking at Simone. Jasper quickly recovered, clearing his throat. "Bem, obrigado. E você?"

"Também estou bem, obrigada. Muito prazer."

"Prazer em conhecê-la."

Simone breathed a little squeal and looked at Violet. "He's too adorable. I already like him so much."

Violet blinked. "I didn't know you spoke Portuguese?"

"There are a lot of things you don't know about me." Simone lifted her shoulder and gave a wink before reaching down for Jasper's bag. "I'll take care of this. Can I get you a drink?"

"N-No thank you, but I appreciate it."

"Sure thing." She turned and made her way into the kitchen.

"*You* speak Portuguese?" Violet stared at Jasper.

"Apparently... once every fifteen years?"

"I had no clue." She faced him, reaching up and fluffing out the top of his curls. "Did you go into town to get your hair cut? Look at you..." She reached down, holding the hem of his sweater with her fingertips. "Is this new? It's so soft, and this *color*. Is it blue or black?"

Jasper grasped her wrists, pulling her hands from his sweater and holding them in between their bodies. "Vi, *please*. It would be nice if I didn't look like a lobster in front of your friend."

She beamed. "You do blush easily. It starts off kind of rosy and subtle, but then quickly escalates to fire-engine red."

"Thanks. That's really helpful." He lifted one hand from hers to scratch his head.

Looking at him, Violet felt warm all over, like she could easily lift to her toes and catch his mouth in a quick kiss. Just a soft little gesture to express her affection and delight at his presence. At his personal growth and how much he'd opened up in the past two and a half months.

Suddenly, he felt very... Not cursed. Not traumatized and hiding himself away—a mop of dark hair, a dreary chateau and a dusty sweater. He was still Jasper, but a little sharper around the edges. A little brighter and well rested.

He looked down at her, taking her in with his big gray eyes. "You look beautiful."

She beamed. She *wanted* to kiss him. But her gut told her "no" and made the butterflies settle down.

"Thanks," she said, taking a few steps backward with his hands still in hers. "I have some hot cocoa in lieu of alcohol. Would you like that?"

"I would." He smiled, allowing himself to be pulled forward. "That sounds delicious."

AFTER ALL THE guests had arrived and the food had been served and devoured, everyone settled down in the front sitting room.

The fireplace roared and the tall pine tree flickered and shone with lights and colorful baubles. Scents like rosemary and thyme, cinnamon sticks and orange floated through the warm air of the cottage.

Simone, Violet and René sat on Gram's old squishy couch, the former two with large, cinnamon-citrus muffins warmly buttered on small plates in their laps and the latter opting for a cup of Irish coffee. After a tense battle for the armchair (where technically Jasper had won), Freddie sat in the seat perpendicular to the couch while Jasper sat on the floor near the fireplace. He hadn't eaten much during lunch, but Jasper was *not* being shy about the homemade blackberry raspberry tart on his plate. Freddie had tea, but he barely drank, his eyes too busy darting over to Jasper every ten seconds.

"Well, I think the show ended perfectly," Simone said, pinching off a large chunk of muffin with her shiny red fingernails. "I like the ambiguity. It lets me derive my own interpretation of the story's ending and everything that happened."

"I don't," Freddie said, looking up at Simone. "It's frustrating. Just tell me how it ends. I need closure. Straightforward."

Simone popped another bite into her mouth, then covered her lips with her palm in a polite gesture. "The intent of the artist is that you establish your own closure."

Freddie shook his head. "I don't like it. It's a tease. I gave it two stars on the streaming site." His eyes flickered over to Jasper yet again before he lifted his teacup to take a sip.

René sat a little straighter against the back of the couch. "I rated it four stars. I think the storyline gave us enough clues to draw upon in establishing a firm ending. He died, didn't he? At the very end."

"*No.*" Simone's eyes widened. "That was a five-star show. And I don't think he died. I think he was just tired after the battle and laid down. Even the director said he was just tired in an interview—"

"I saw that interview," Violet chimed in. "I think that was a joke. He was being facetious. I gave it three stars. I didn't think it was great, but it definitely wasn't bad."

"I agree," René said.

"It was perfection, and he didn't die." Simone shook her head, resolute. "Why wouldn't the director just say so in the interview?"

"See?" Freddie frowned. "This is why the ending was stupid. Just say what it is so everyone is on the same dang page. I had to push myself to finish it... Should have just stopped watching."

"But that is the very nature of art, my dear young man— subjective and open to a myriad of interpretations." René glanced over toward Jasper on the floor. "You are awfully quiet, Monsieur Laurent. No thoughts on this topic? You were quiet at lunch, too."

"He's always quiet," Freddie said, his voice soft. "He was like this when we were kids... never talked to anyone except Violet."

Jasper blinked, looking around at everyone suddenly staring back at him. Irritation was rising in Violet's chest at Freddie's direct assault, but Jasper's voice kept her quiet.

"I don't watch television, so I don't know what you're talking about... These shows. It was the same when I was little— everyone was always talking about TV shows and movies, but my parents didn't even have a television in the house. I think my parents took me to the movies once?"

"Some kids at our school thought Jasper was stuck up, but really he was just interested in other things," Violet added.

Simone tilted her head. "Other things like what?"

"He liked those brain teasers..." Freddie said, staring into his teacup. "And birds. In second grade, we did projects on any subject we liked and he picked birds. He even folded some out of paper to show the class. I remember thinking it was cool..."

"Oh." Simone smiled. "Origami?"

Jasper nodded, returning her grin. "Yes. My father taught me how."

"I did origami when I was little, too," Simone said.

"Did you, now?" René sat forward, looking past Violet beside him and over at Simone, one eyebrow raised coolly. "I would love to hear more about that."

Simone cut her eyes away from him. "Right. Jasper, do you still like birds? Do you have a favorite feathered friend?"

Jasper placed his empty plate onto the floor just in front of his folded legs. "I do... Probably the red-crowned crane?"

"Japanese cranes?" René mused. "Iconic. I've seen them on nature specials."

"Yes," Jasper said. "That's right. But they migrate to Korea and China, too."

"Why that particular bird?" Simone asked.

Folding his hands in the gap between his legs, Jasper considered. "Well... they're beautiful. Snow white with the tips of their wing feathers dipped in pitch black, and they have a bright red circle on the top of their head. When they mate, they form bonds for life. They're territorial over their family and space, and both the male and female do the work of protecting and building the nest. The most fascinating part is that they sing and dance together—it's their way of expressing excitement and keeping their bond strong. When one pair within the flock starts singing, the other couples flute in chorus as well. I just think it sounds like a pretty nice life, doesn't it?"

Everyone sat quietly, the image of beautiful long-necked cranes dancing and singing practically floating before their eyes. Simone put her hand against her chest. "It does. It's very romantic."

"So the three of you grew up together, yes?" René asked,

leaning forward and setting his empty mug against the coffee table. "What was that like? Indulge us, please."

Violet flipped her head so that her dead gaze landed on Freddie. "Difficult."

Freddie drew back, gaping. "Well, hold on now, wait—"

"Freddie was Mr. Popular," Violet went on, "but he took special care in making my everyday life as miserable as possible."

"I apologized to you for that already," Freddie asserted. "I said I was sorry."

René grinned. "So... not exactly the Three Musketeers, I take it?"

Violet set her empty plate on the coffee table in a huff. "Absolutely not."

"It wasn't all bad for you." Freddie sat forward, his voice strained as he pointed across the room at Jasper. "*He* ignored everyone but you, and the two of you were inseparable—like you had your own special club that nobody else could join."

Jasper blinked. "I-I didn't ignore everyone—"

"You did," Freddie insisted. "You never really talked to or played with anyone until *Violet* showed up... You didn't even sign my cast when I broke my arm in primary school. Everyone in the class signed it but you. Even Ms. Chauncey and the principal signed it. It's like you didn't even care."

The air in the room stilled, the tension thick as everyone's eyes shifted between Freddie and Jasper. Violet swallowed, but it went down slowly, like she'd taken too big a bite of muffin and didn't have anything to wash it down with.

Jasper reached up, scratching the back of his head and looking down at the empty plate on the floor in front of him. "I'm sorry... I didn't realize."

"It-It's okay..." Freddie sat back, his hands gripping his tea cup a little too tightly, his fingers and face turning red. "We were kids, it's stupid. I don't know why I even brought it up. Sorry."

"On that note…" Violet stood, hoping to alleviate the painful awkwardness. She looked up and checked the wall clock: 3:27 p.m. They needed to start wrapping things up because Jasper's change was fast approaching. "I'm going to start cleaning the kitchen, but feel free to enjoy any last desserts and drinks."

"The airing of uncomfortable childhood grievances aside, this was fun," René said. "I will take care to avoid this topic going forward. I hope we can do this again, soon?"

"We'll see." Violet flashed a smile at René before walking out of the sitting room and into the kitchen. Once there, she heard René declare a little too loudly, "And maybe you and I can do this privately?" Which made Violet huff out a laugh and shake her head. He wasn't giving up without a fight.

She put her hands on her hips, looking at all the picked-over food set on the counter, the pile of dishes in the sink. "Where to start?" she said to herself.

"I'll do the dishes?"

She turned and Jasper walked past her, his empty tart plate in hand. "You set all this up. I'll help clean," he continued. Not one to argue, Violet went to the table and took the seat facing him. She exhaled a deep sigh of contentment.

"Did you enjoy this?" she asked. "Your actual birthday isn't until next weekend, but…" On the other side of the counter, Jasper already had the water running, dish soap and sponge in hand with his sweater sleeves rolled up. He kept his voice low.

"I did. Did you?"

"Yes. Honestly, this was just what I needed."

"Good." He nodded. "I'm glad. It's been so long since I've been around this many people… I didn't know what to say. Did I seem strange?" He looked down and focused on his task, scrubbing plates, rinsing them and placing them in the rack beside the sink.

"No. I think you were alright. I'm sorry we talked so much about TV and movies."

"It's fine. It's a safe conversational topic for a group of people who don't know each other particularly well. It's understandable."

When Freddie walked into the kitchen, he had a strange, determined look on his face that made Violet narrow her eyes. *What is he doing now?*

But then she cursed herself. This innate distrust of Freddie had guided her across all her interactions with him from childhood. Now, it seemed unfair, and it made her feel weirdly guilty, which she hated.

"I need to go take over a shift at the store," he said, watching Jasper. "Thanks for inviting me... This was real nice."

Is he talking to me? "Sure..." Violet said, confused by his misplaced eye contact. He walked forward, then around the corner of the counter to stand at Jasper's side.

"Hey, Jasper?"

Busy, Jasper scrubbed the pot in his grip. "Yeah?"

Freddie stood still, staring at his profile. When he didn't say anything, Jasper shut the water off and turned his face toward him, frowning in half confusion, half annoyance. "Yes? Is there something else I didn't—"

"No, I—" Freddie took a visible breath, his broad chest rising and falling underneath his sky-blue sweater. He ran his fingers across the top of his blonde head, scratching. "It's not that. I just... You—you're like Mama's chaussons aux pommes."

Violet sat with her eyebrow raised. *Why the heck is he talking about apple turnovers...* She met Jasper's nervous gaze as it flickered over to her. It was as if he needed to confirm the peculiarity of the statement. He looked at Freddie again, frowning. "What?"

Freddie gulped, his words pouring out and his fingers mussing his hair. "Like when she makes them fresh and pulls them out of the oven, and they're still warm and flaky when I take the first bite and that gooey apple filling hits my tongue and sends this tingly feeling all throughout my whole body, because they're my favorite, you know? You're like that. That— That's how I feel when I see you. Ever since we were kids…"

No one moved or said a word: the hasty confession hanging in the warm air of the kitchen. That is, until Jasper blinked and opened his mouth to speak.

"Um… I—"

Freddie leaned in, tilted his head, and kissed Jasper on the cheek with a loud smack. Jasper jumped, his eyes wide as he took a step back. It happened so quickly that Violet gasped from the shock of it.

"Sorry…" Freddie grinned, his face flushed. "But, thank you for listening. And happy early birthday. I'm glad you're leaving your house more. I think it's good." He nodded once, turned and moved toward the doorway.

As he passed Violet, he lifted his chin. "I did it in front of you so you don't think I'm trying to steal him from you or something. I just needed him to *know*…"

Violet swallowed, shock still paralyzing her mind. "What? I don't—J-Jasper doesn't belong to me."

Freddie raised his dark golden eyebrow. "Of course he does." And then he was gone.

Blinking, she met Jasper's wide-eyed stare. Neither of them said a word, and eventually, Jasper exhaled a breath, turned the water back on and continued washing dishes. His face dropped into a discouraged little scowl that made Violet's heart sink.

"Are you alright?" she asked. "Are you in shock?"

He shook his head. "Considering my private circumstance, very little shocks me."

She leaned forward, whispering. "Jas… was that your first kiss?"

"Does a kiss on the cheek count?"

"Well, kind of?"

"Then no. Second. Because René did the exact same thing to me on my birthday when I turned twenty-one."

"Oh gosh."

"We'd been working together two years? He came over with champagne and—consequently, that was also the day I learned I can't drink at all. Anyway, long story short, this kind of thing has happened to me before, so..." Jasper shrugged. "I don't care for it, though. These ambush kisses."

Violet bit the inside of her lip, wanting to console him but not knowing how. When the water shut off, Violet lifted her face to find him looking back at her.

"Is this normal?" he asked. "People just... kissing you out of the blue? A greeting is one thing, but people don't talk about it or ask first? They just go for it without even making sure it's okay?"

Sighing, Violet sat back and folded her arms. "Well, ideally there's some context or an established relationship. I wouldn't say your situations are normal, exactly..."

"Porn is the same way."

Violet choked on her spit. "Ex-Excuse me?"

"Porn."

"Yeah, I heard you. But how does this relate?"

"Because—well... I tried watching it before. It-It's online, you know? But it was always really aggressive. People just *went* for it without any discussion. It made me uncomfortable."

"You have a valid point," Violet said. "But sex doesn't have to be like that. It can be any way two people want it to be. Have you ever had sex with someone?"

"No. Just unprovoked kisses. Never on the mouth, though..."

Violet nodded awkwardly, unsure of where to take the conversation. She leaned with her elbows on the table and folded her arms in front of her, looking off toward the multi-color faery lights Simone had hung.

"You have?" Jasper asked quietly.

Violet met his gaze. "Have what?"

"Had sex…"

"Yes."

"And you enjoy it?"

"I do. I like sex, but I've learned that it's only good for me if I sincerely trust the person I'm with, because it's a very vulnerable thing. As an expression of love and conviction, it can be beautiful and freeing. It's our way of singing and dancing, like your pretty birds."

Jasper snorted. "That's not what it looks like on those porn sites—"

"Just forget about that. Don't ever look at that again."

Laughing, Jasper turned the water back on to continue his dish-washing. After a moment, he spoke, keeping his voice low. "I wonder if… René and Freddie's reaction to me has something to do with the curse?"

Violet's expression fell flat. "You think the curse makes beautiful men fall for you?"

"*No.*" Jasper frowned. "That's not—I mean the magic. Maybe something in the energy of it appeals to some people?"

She shook her head. "To answer your question, no, Jasper. I think you're an intelligent and intriguing person with beautiful eyes and a quiet disposition, and they sincerely find you attractive. *Of course* they do."

Jasper lifted a pot from the sink, avoiding her eyes as he set it in the rack. "Well… thank you."

"You're welcome."

Focusing on his task, he sighed. "They wouldn't, though. If they really knew what I was."

"I know what you are and I'm still friends with you."

"But you don't know the worst of it. If people knew, they wouldn't be anywhere near me."

Sitting straight, Violet watched him with her arms still

folded. *This* again. Always this. His mother and her cruel, emotionally abusive reaction toward him that he validated in his mind. He almost seemed to protect it, as if the pain of it were an important thing that he always needed to remember and reference. To keep himself in check in case he ever felt too free or too happy. The more Violet recognized it, she hated it.

She kept her gaze even, serious. "Show me the worst of it then. Let me see."

He froze. When he lifted his face, his expression was equally serious. "No."

"*I* have a date next weekend." René walked into the kitchen, cooing in his deep singsong voice. But he stopped dead, one eyebrow raised. "Am I interrupting something?"

34

NOW

*K*nowing Jasper's human time was winding down, Violet insisted to Simone that she and Jasper would handle the cleaning duties. It was a small battle, but thirty minutes later, she saw Simone and René out the front door with the promise that they would do this again very soon.

When Violet walked into the nearly spotless kitchen, Jasper was leaning with his sleeves still rolled up and his hands flat against the counter.

"Do you need to see and know *everything?*" he asked, distress in his eyes.

Violet took a few steps forward, stopping at the end of the kitchen table. "I don't know what that means."

"It means you know a lot already—more than anyone aside from my mother and father. You know I'm cursed, and you know the truth about my family history. You've seen me as a *rat*. Isn't that enough? I don't ask to see everything of you. I don't ask you if I can come in the bathroom when you pee."

Setting her shoulders, Violet took a breath. "Well, I think that's a little different because I'm not traumatized over peeing.

No one has ever emotionally abused me because of my peeing—"

"My mother didn't abuse me."

"Oh, she absolutely did."

"No, Violet—her reaction was natural. It was expected—"

"It wasn't, Jasper. She was wrong."

He shook his head, his eyes bewildered. "Y-You have no idea what it's like. How horrible it is."

"Then show me."

He ran his hand up into his hair, his chest heaving. "I won't. *Never.*"

"Why?"

"Because I'm not going to do that to you. I don't want you to be disturbed by that."

"But maybe I won't be?" Violet said, calm. "Can you trust me enough to try?"

His face twisted as he drew back, shaking his head in refusal. "This *isn't* about trust. Don't flip this into something it's not."

Sensing the rise in his temper, Violet held her palms up, conceding. "Okay, okay, I understand. I don't want you to feel pressured about this. I... If I see something that's hurting my friend—profoundly—and it keeps revealing itself in ways that makes my heart ache for you, I want to help, alright? But this doesn't need to be a fight, Jas. We're good. And if you want to watch me pee, if that's your thing, we can talk about it. I'm open."

"It's *not.*" He shook his head, his face softening and breaking into an incredulous smile despite himself. "I don't need that."

"I mean, I'm not completely opposed to it. That's all. I'm here for you."

"You're insane." He rubbed his palms against his face, the stress melting as he laughed.

"Are you shifting here and sleeping on my pillow tonight?

My forehead is cold now when you're not here. I never thought my forehead would feel lonely at night."

He dropped his hands from his face and shook his head. "No... I think I'll go home tonight. But I'll help you finish cleaning."

Violet walked over to meet him at the counter. Once there, she reached out with her hands, palms flipped up in between them. Jasper met her gesture, sliding his hands into hers and firmly clasping them together. She lifted her head to meet his eyes. "No pressure, okay? We're good."

He surprised her when he leaned down, gently resting his forehead against hers so that their noses brushed together. His face was so close that she could feel his breath against her lips when he spoke—the warmth of it laced with blackberry raspberry tart.

"Can... Can this be enough for you?"

"Can what be?" she asked, pulling away slightly from his warmth, ignoring the pulse of her heart in her throat.

"*Me*," he said, his eyes still closed. "Us. How we are now. I know we're not kids anymore. And I know... I can't give you everything you deserve. But I love you more than anything, and I'm selfish and ridiculous and—having you here, in my life again for these past few months, I don't know if I can go back to the way things were." He gripped her hands a little tighter.

She squeezed back, reassuring him. "Things won't ever go back to the way they were before. You're different now—you get your own groceries and you even went into town to get a haircut. People see you and they're welcoming you. Nobody is even asking about your being sick because you look healthier and brighter. I'm back home now, but even without me, you're growing and changing."

He stood straight, lifting one hand from hers to rub his palm down his face, exhaling a deep breath. Violet smiled. "I love you too, Jas. You *know* that. We'll always be friends. Always."

Staring blankly over the top of her head, he remained silent, a slight furrow in his brow. Violet narrowed her eyes, confused. "What is it?"

"So, you'll go off, find some guy and marry him... But we'll still be friends? I can sleep on your pillow at night sometimes and keep your forehead warm?"

Violet laughed openly, but when Jasper's face didn't budge at all, she pouted.

"Are you joking or being serious? I don't understand the intent behind this question."

"I'm being serious." He met her gaze, not laughing at all.

Still giggling, Violet shrugged. "Sheesh, Jasper, who knows? I can't say what the future holds. Let's not worry about hypothetical love triangles. We're really far off from that."

Jasper sighed, but he surprised her yet again when he pulled her hand, gently drawing her into the length of his body. He leaned down, wrapping his arms around her middle in a warm embrace, his face buried against the concave of her neck and loose hair. From head to toe, Violet's body flushed warm and tingly, overheated from the shock and delight. She lifted to her toes and placed her hands flat against his shoulders, trying to keep her breathing even.

"The last time we hugged, we were the same height," he said, his voice muffled against her neck and hair. He took a deep breath and spoke on an exhale. "It feels so different now."

"Yeah..." Violet said, sliding her palms across the line of his shoulders and wrapping her arms around him. He held her a little tighter in response and her heart skipped. Unexpectedly, she felt nervous and self-conscious, which was very unlike her.

"You smell the same though," he whispered.

Violet shut her eyes to the sparking sensation shooting through her belly like fireworks. "What... do I smell like?"

"Apple blossoms. Or chamomile. The scent is similar. You

smell like late summer to me, when the flowers in the orchard bloom."

Oh God...

She patted his back with her palms, the gesture something like hitting the dust out of a throw pillow. "You should go soon so you get home in time to shift." When he unwrapped her from his embrace, she breathed a sigh to relax the tension in her body. He stared down at her but she looked away.

"Am I allowed to change my mind?" he asked, the smile in his voice obvious. "Can I stay tonight, please?"

Truthfully, Violet would have preferred it if he'd gone home. She was already thinking about how she might need some *personal* time, on her own (maybe in the shower or in a hot bubble bath) after being all wound up by the declarations of love and tight hugs, blackberry sighs and sweet snuggling.

She thought herself an assertive woman, but not quite to the point where she could easily say, "No, go home so I can pleasure myself." So instead, she said, "Yes, you can stay."

THE FOLLOWING AFTERNOON, Violet opened the door to let Simone inside. She'd left her oversized muffin pan (her favorite one, apparently) and had insisted on coming back to get it despite Violet's offer to deliver it later in the week.

Simone beamed. "Hello, lovely. Yesterday turned out really well, yeah? We're like a bunch of misfits, but it was pretty cozy."

Violet nodded as Simone walked into the foyer. "Yes, yes, it was nice... Simone, I like sex."

Unaffected, Simone headed toward the kitchen, throwing one hand into the air. "Good for you, Violet. Be empowered— shout it from the rooftops."

"No..." Violet closed the door. "I mean, I know myself, and I *enjoy* a good, healthy orgasm. And I like physical intimacy and being naked and playful with the right person."

In the kitchen, Simone pulled her muffin pan from the drying rack, looking it over. "Okay... so go be naked and playful with the right somebody. What's the issue?"

"What if that right somebody doesn't like sex? Should I just... try to conform to that? But what if I don't want to? Obviously, relationships are not all about sex. They're *not*... but I still like it. I want it."

Finally, Simone met her gaze. "Are we talking about Jasper?"

"Maybe?"

"He is friggin' adorable. I want to put him in my pocket and carry him around—I mean, those eyes."

"I *can't* with his eyes right now. Let's not."

Simone leaned against the counter, her muffin pan gripped in her hands. "What the heck happened to you? You were all Buddhist monk and 'I love him fundamentally' a few weeks ago. What's flipped your switch? You sound like you're ready to dry hump him now."

"I probably would if he'd let me..." Violet took a deep breath. He'd only left an hour ago and he'd wanted to stay a second night—which was new. He stayed with her often now, but rarely consecutively. She'd sent him home, saying she needed to take care of some things. Well, technically, she did. And she had. The tension within her felt a little better, but it wasn't the release she really wanted.

"He's been prickly with me for weeks," Violet continued. "Everything was like an uphill battle. But suddenly, he's more relaxed and being all sweet and affectionate and it's just... causing a strong reaction in my lady parts. I thought they were dormant, honestly. At least covered in cobwebs."

"Have you tried talking to him about this?"

Violet shook her head. "No."

"Don't you think you should?"

"No."

"Why?"

"Jasper's situation is… complicated." Violet sighed. "He's already let me know nothing like that can ever happen, in his subtle way. He's not interested—and the last thing I would *ever* want is to make him feel pressured."

Simone shifted her stance, resting a hand on her hip. "If he's being a little more affectionate than he was before, maybe the snowball will continue to roll downhill? Just relax and take a cold shower. I think you'll be fine."

"But what if it isn't fine?"

"Then you'll need to talk to him, Vi. You two are obviously close. Just have a heart-to-heart and be honest about your physical attraction to him. If he doesn't reciprocate, then you'll both have to accept that and move forward accordingly."

Violet nodded, knowing Simone was right but still not wanting to broach the subject with Jasper. She was afraid that all their progress would blow up in her face. Scared of the "move forward accordingly" scenario and their relationship being strained. She shook it off. Enough about her problems. "Are you going on a date with René? When is this happening?"

"Against my better judgement, yes."

"Ah, don't be like that. That guy's got layers. He's not what he seems."

Simone raised her eyebrow. "What do you know that I don't?"

Violet clamped up. "Nothing."

"Smooth, Ainsworth. Real smooth."

"What made you change your mind?"

Simone sighed, breathing a little laugh. "Well… We've met before. It's very random."

"Say what?"

"Yeah, from a long time ago when I worked at Mère Macaron in the city."

"I didn't know you worked there. I love that bakery."

"I worked there for about a year and it was rough. It was a good experience but I was transitioning personally and the job was crazy demanding—anyway, it's a long story."

"I like long stories." Violet beamed. "When is the date?"

"Next weekend," Simone said, walking toward the front door. "When will my paintings be ready? I'm launching the account this week with the pictures I took from the party."

"Ah, well, I'm working on the second one starting today. I have this whole week off so I'll keep you posted?"

"I'm so excited," Simone sang. "Can you come to the bakery when the paintings are done? We can decide on the perfect place to hang them, rehash the date and you can help test a new spiced tea mix I'm making. Maybe before New Year's?"

"Sounds perfect."

Simone called out over her shoulder as she stood in the doorway. "And about Jasper—try masturbating?"

Violet pouted, folding her arms as she looked away. "I already did."

"Well, do it again! It's not like there's a limit." And then she closed the door behind her.

35

NOW

A week later, the door to Laurent House swung open before Violet had even made it up the walkway. Jasper was already in the doorway, backlit by warm yellow light as the heavy snow fell all around. When she got closer to the door, he was beaming.

"Hi."

"Hello and happy birthday!"

"Thank you—come in, come in."

Violet stepped inside and fluffed the damp from her hair with one hand. In the other, she held a small gift bag.

"I'll take your coat," he said, brimming with energy.

"You're awfully excited." Violet shrugged out of her coat. When she was free, she smoothed her sweater and lifted her chin. "It smells nice in here—fruity and cinnamony."

"It's the mulled wine. I'm making a test batch for tomorrow and it's almost ready. Can you taste it? I hope Rose and Jillian like it…"

"I'm sure they'll love it, and I'd be honored to have a taste." Violet had invited Jasper over to Gram's cottage for Christmas

Day celebrations. He'd happily accepted. "Why are you making something you can't have?" she asked.

"I can have a little, just not a full mug. My parents used to have this at Christmas when I was growing up—before the whole curse thing. It always made the house smell great and I couldn't wait until I was old enough to have a glass with them… That never happened, so I figured making it for you, Rose and Jillian presented a nice opportunity? It reminds me of happier times."

Violet sighed, nodding. Why shut down Christmas traditions over this curse? Why lay yet another heavy burden onto your son's shoulders? Wasn't being cursed enough?

"Happy times are here, Jas. Things are getting better. Are we sitting in the study?"

"We are."

Walking forward, Violet realized it'd been a while since she was here. Jasper had been visiting and staying at her house more and more, shrewdly opting for a good night of sleep and lively conversation. When she turned the corner to the study, she drew a breath in surprise. Tiny white lights and paper snowflakes were strung across the low ceiling, the latter slowly spinning in the stagnant air. The fireplace burned brightly, casting a soft glow and warm shadows everywhere she looked. Jasper had even set up a tree and decorated it with multicolor lights and silver baubles. The coffee table, usually piled high with books, magazines and used coffee cups, was clean and offered an array of beautiful charcuterie: crackers, meats, cheeses, nuts and dried fruit. Near the edge, a large bowl of perfectly plump red grapes glistened with drops of water.

"Oh my gosh…"

"Do you like it?" Jasper asked, standing at her side.

"This is amazing—it's beautiful. And so *clean*." Even Jasper's desk only held his computer, green banker's lamp and files. The thick goldenrod curtains were pulled back so that the cloudy afternoon sky and heavy snow drifts were visible.

Jasper grinned. "I can't take all the credit. René helped me— but it was my idea."

"It's so cozy and breathtaking, what a lovely surprise."

"Thank you for spending my birthday with me." He reached over, grasping her hand and entwining their fingers. "Are you hungry? These things are rat friendly but I thought you'd like them, too?" He stepped forward, pulling her to the couch. Violet chuckled.

"I think you're very healthy for a mouse, Jasper. You're like an upmarket, organic, locally sourced and non-GMO-eating mouse."

He laughed, sitting down and urging Violet to settle beside him. "I told you, it's better if I eat with the inner rat in mind. And lately I'm sleeping on your pillow and not running around all night anymore, so my metabolism is shifting."

"Mm, I was thinking my forehead blanket was starting to feel a little thicker."

Jasper dropped her hand and drew back, his face aghast. "I—"

"I'm just kidding." Violet laughed, reaching up and pinching his cheek. "I'm not fat-shaming your mouse body, relax."

He sat back, exhaling a huff and rubbing his forehead. "Why was I really offended?"

"Because you're a silly man." Violet reached over to pluck several grapes from the bunch. She popped one into her mouth and the burst of fresh, sweet juice made her sigh.

"I want to show you something." Jasper stood from the couch, abrupt in walking over to his desk. "Have you looked at your profile on social media for Painted Poppies?"

"No? Simone only launched it Wednesday."

He walked back with his laptop open in his hands and

plopped down just beside her, shoulder-to-shoulder, warm and easy. "Look…" Turning the screen toward her, Jasper explained, "She posted the four pieces in your living room, and you already have three hundred followers. And there are so many positive comments."

Violet almost choked on her grape. "What? How—so quickly?"

"You're talented, Vi. You've been drawing and painting casually since we were little, and you think it's no big deal. But you're a natural at this—like a hidden gem."

"Oh my goodness… This is crazy."

"It's real," he grinned. "You can make this work, if you want. I'll help you in any way I can."

Violet leaned and bumped his shoulder. "You sitting for me helps a lot."

"Yeah, that… when do I get to see it?"

"When it's ready."

"If you draw a big picture of a rat—"

"Jasper Oliver Laurent, I would never do that."

He stared at her, narrowing his eyes. Violet laughed. "I wouldn't. Not even to be funny. It *is* a good set-up for a joke though—"

"See…"

Violet reached down and grabbed the small bag she'd brought with her. "Anyway—enough showering me with surprises on *your* birthday. I got this for you."

"You didn't need to buy me anything." Setting his laptop aside, Jasper accepted the bag, examining. "Letting me get actual rest on your pillow is gift enough."

Violet reached for another grape, chuckling. "Soak that up while you can. My future husband might not be too keen on that."

"I don't find that funny." He pushed the thin paper aside,

then pulled his gift out. His big eyes grew even wider as he read the label on the box. "Oh wow—it's a Constantin…"

"I hope you don't have them already? One is the Hidden Corridor and the other is—"

"The Flower Maze." Jasper pulled the second box from the bag, turning it over in his hands. "It's like the one my father gave to me when I was little." He took a breath, his shoulders dropping. A distinct melancholy radiated from his posture as they sat in silence. Violet tensed. She hadn't meant to make him sad.

"Jas, I—I just thought it would be a fun gift, you know? Something from when we were kids. I don't mean to upset you."

"No, I'm not upset." He shook his head, turning and looking at her with a gentle smile. "I'm just… very grateful. For you. For this time together." Jasper searched her face, his gray eyes sincere in the twinkling light. Violet's heart pulsed, her body warming up again without her permission. She leaned forward to grab another grape.

"Well, that's good," she said, popping the fruit into her mouth and speaking around it. "Don't be sad on your birthday. I won't allow it." Smiling, she looked at him once more. He was still watching her, focused, as if searching for something. Neither of them spoke and it made Violet look away and squirm. Usually their silence was comfortable, amicable. This felt different.

"Should you check on the wine?"

"The *wine*." Jasper placed his gifts aside and stood. When he was gone, Violet sunk into the couch and exhaled, placing her palm against her forehead.

What the heck was that?

It had almost felt as if he was waiting for something. Or considering something? Violet shook her head, hoping that whatever it was, the odd moment had passed and was behind them. Hopefully she wasn't about to be fired for a fourth time…

When Jasper returned, his demeanor seemed to be reset to

normal. He smiled as he handed her a mug half-filled with dark red liquid—the rich cinnamon, honey and star anise swirled up with the steam and filled her senses.

"This smells divine."

"I hope it's good." He sat beside her, peeking into his own mug. He lifted it, grinning. "Cheers to your amazing talent and getting your art into the world."

"Cheers to *your birthday* and continued health and good nights of sleep."

After a quick tap of their mugs, Violet brought her drink to her nose first, inhaling deeply before taking a full sip. Warm and divine, she could taste the subtle hints of orange and the heady essence of brandy. She sighed. "Mm... This is wonderful, Jas."

"You like it?"

"I love it. You know, if you ever tire of writing—which I hope you never do—you could have a prosperous career in culinary arts. The frittata you made that one time was also scrumptious."

Jasper shrugged. "I'm just following recipes. I'm not special."

"Some people can't even manage that. Even more, some people don't bother to try. I dated a guy who told me he'd never even boiled water. Everything he ate was either restaurant takeout or from the freezer section at the grocery store."

"Was this person a teenager?"

Violet laughed. "No, this was when I was... twenty-two? I think he was twenty-six. He bragged about it and thought it was funny, actually. He only ate home-cooked food at his parents' house on Sundays—family tradition. His mom demanded it. He'd always tell me, 'I'll eat better when I'm married,' which totally rubbed me the wrong way."

Jasper drew back, frowning. "That's a pretty bold insinuation. What if his spouse can't cook very well?"

"Oh, he told me he'd make sure she could. He didn't say it

directly, but in his mind, feeding him was *her* duty, you know? Cooking was not, quote, 'the man's job.'"

"That's so weird, Vi—why were you dating this person?"

"I didn't date him for very long after that conversation. Unfortunately, he wasn't the first person I'd dated with chauvinistic expectations. That whole 'I'm a manly man' rhetoric, you know?"

"Mm." Jasper nodded. "Patriarchy."

"Exactly. Grumble grumble—go make me a sandwich and wash my clothes. Stuff like that." Violet chuckled, but there was an awkward pause as Jasper stared down at the coffee table. Violet leaned forward to catch his gaze. "Is something wrong?"

He blinked, serious as he looked up at her with his light eyes. "Are... those the kinds of guys you like?"

She shook her head, making her curls bounce. "Not at all."

"Then why did you date them?"

Violet sat back against the couch, making herself comfortable. "Well, growing up... it's like I was taught that relationships were supposed to be a certain way—Gram didn't teach me that, specifically. It was in the messages all around me. In TV shows or movies I watched. Books I read. But then, as I got older and tried to date—tried to conform to these set rules and expectations, it felt all wrong for me. I felt stifled and miserable being with those guys. It took me some time to realize that."

Jasper nodded, watching her and listening intently. "So, what kind of relationship do you want?"

Violet stifled a smile as she looked up toward the ceiling in contemplation. "Hmm, ideally, a relationship where I can just be myself—where I'm not constantly playing sidekick to someone else's much more important life story. A partnership, and we're *both* the main characters. And we can enjoy life and respect each other. Openly learning and growing together."

Jasper lifted his hand, his face scrunched as he mussed the

top of his hair. "Is that so difficult to find, Vi? Mutual respect and openness?"

She huffed, one eyebrow raised. "You'd be surprised. You've been stuck inside so you don't really know. But trust me, it's rough out there."

"I've been thinking about that lately," he said, dropping his hand and looking toward the window, the heavy snowflakes cascading down. "There are so many things I've never done. Never tried..." He turned, meeting Violet's eyes. "I've never been swimming or seen the ocean. I've never been to an amusement park or a coffee shop. I've never danced!"

"Some of those are easily remedied. I wouldn't combine the 'swimming' and 'seeing the ocean' events on the first time out, though. Please do those separately."

Chuckling, Jasper stood and walked to the tall bookshelves lining the walls behind them. For the first time, Violet noticed a small radio there—an old-timey-looking thing with silver dials and knobs. He pressed a button and it glowed to life. A man's voice rang out, hastily announcing that now was the perfect time to refinance your mortgage.

After some tinkering, the slow melody of a luscious Christmas song filled the space. The smooth voice, warm fireplace, glittery lights and slowly rotating snowflakes hanging from the ceiling made Violet feel as if she were in a movie scene. It was all too magical and didn't feel like her real life anymore. She watched Jasper, her pulse thumping as he turned and smiled.

"Will you dance with me? I don't know how to dance, but... can we try?"

Violet stood, nodding and meeting him behind the couch. Once she was in front of him, they just stood there, awkwardly. Jasper scratched the back of his head, a strained smile on his lips. "So..."

She reached out and grabbed his hands, placing them on her

waist before lifting her hands and resting them against his shoulders. "Let's keep it simple. We'll move side to side and keep up with the rhythm. Try not to step on my feet?"

"That doesn't sound too hard." He smiled, shifting to the side. Violet matched his movement. Surprisingly, he kept the beat as the song stretched on. And he didn't step on her toes. Not even once.

"I know you said there's no chance," Violet began, "but let's pretend. If your curse broke, what's the first thing you'd do?"

He looked over her head, blankly staring at the bookshelves behind her. "Eat a really big meal."

"You've given this some thought?"

"I have. I miss eating the way I did when I was a kid. To my heart's and appetite's content. All the rich, complex things that Gloria made for us back then. I get so tired of eating the same foods—always snacking and picking at things. When you made that lasagna, it was really savory and comforting. I wanted to eat a lot more of it, but I got nervous. It's just not worth it later."

Violet nodded. She hadn't considered that he disliked his restricted diet. He seemed so accustomed to it, Violet had assumed he enjoyed eating that way. As they moved slowly to the rhythm, she smiled up at him—a weak attempt to stifle the sudden sadness in her heart. "What's next on the list?" she asked.

"Next, I... I would do everything in my power to show the person I love that they would be the main character in my life— that we would be main characters together. If she wanted me..."

Stopping, Violet stared into his face. She blinked. "But you would eat first?"

"I need my strength."

They both laughed, a fit of genuine amusement. Violet's breath caught when he slid his hands to the small of her back, bringing her in closer. "I can't prove myself to you on an empty stomach."

Violet lifted to her toes, wrapping her arms around his

shoulders and reveling in the solidity of him. In his clean scent, like warm clothes fresh from the dryer. "You don't need to prove yourself. You being you is enough, Jas. It always has been."

And she meant it. As they swayed to the luscious melody, underneath spinning paper snowflakes and shadowed by glimmering lights, Violet melted into his warmth and knew that she would accept him exactly as he was. Whatever that entailed.

36

NOW

"*Y*ou'll have to give me the recipe for this wine, Jasper." Jillian smiled brightly, pushing her golden hair back over her shoulders with her free hand. "It is absolutely delicious. My mother used to make wine like this when we would spend winters in Scotland for the holidays, but yours is superior."

Christmas Day. Early afternoon. Having expressed Jasper's time limitations with regard to his sickness (a strict medical regimen that required him to be back home by five o'clock), they'd had dinner together early.

The atmosphere of this gathering was different than Violet's pre-Christmas party. Instead of talk about popular television shows and movies, the conversation leaned more toward books, career aspirations and even simple economics. As such, Jasper had contributed much, and Violet had learned that her friend closely followed unemployment trends, had a strong dislike of poetry, but oddly, liked cats. The latter revelation had made Violet narrow her eyes at him from across the table.

"I can tell you the website," Jasper assured her, sitting on the end of the couch with a mug of hot cocoa. "It's not difficult to make."

Rose peeked into the sitting room. "I'm putting the food away so it's not sitting out—last call?"

"I'm fine," Violet said from beside Jasper, her own mug of cocoa cradled in her hands (different from Jasper's in that hers was spiked with spiced rum).

"Same," Jillian called.

"Jasper, you didn't eat much. Do you want to take some home with you?"

"Thank you for the offer—I'm alright. But I appreciate it. I don't typically have a large appetite."

Rose shrugged. "Suit yourself. I meant to say that you look a lot healthier and stronger compared with the last time I saw you. Whatever you're doing lately, it seems to be working?"

"Yes, I... Thank you," Jasper said, bringing his mug to his lips.

"You all reading actual books is so surprising to me—and *old* ones," Jillian said, sitting back in the armchair and cradling her third cup of mulled wine. "I do audiobooks because of all my travel, and I prefer autobiographies. I think it's important to know the stories of influential people so that I can emulate them. But I have never touched Classical Greek lit."

"Some of those books were required reading in high school and college, Jill," Violet said.

"Right, but who *actually* reads them? You just do a quick search of the Internet and find the summaries and reviews, yeah? Brilliant if there's a movie adaptation."

"Some are interesting though," Jasper interjected. "They're worth the actual read."

"Like which ones?" Jillian asked, lifting her chin. "Where should I start, then?"

Jasper considered, his dark brows drawn and his very straight nose scrunched. "Hm, I enjoyed *The Frogs* by Aristo-

260

phanes. It's a play about the politics of ancient Greece. It made me laugh out loud a few times."

Jillian nodded. "That doesn't sound too awful."

"Yeah, you definitely want to start off lighter," Violet added. "Avoid jumping into the pool with both feet and landing in something like Oedipus Rex."

"What's that?"

"A guy kills his father and ends up marrying his own mother."

"Ew."

"And the mom hangs herself and the husband-son gouges his eyes out after he realizes incest is not super great."

"Violet, what the heck are you talking about?" Rosie walked back into the room, frowning at her sister. Violet shrugged.

"Greek tragedies."

"That explains a little, but *why?*"

The doorbell rang, making everyone pause. Rosie looked to Violet. "You expecting someone today?"

"Nope. But you're already standing, so…"

Rose rolled her eyes. "This girl." She stalked out of the room and down the hallway. Everyone listened as she pulled the door open, greeted someone… Two someones. A quiet, muffled explanation of some sort, and then the floor squeaking underneath the weight of other people before the front door shut again. Rose turned the corner first, followed by a tall, scruffy man in a trench coat and a uniformed officer.

Violet stood, surprised at having police in her house… and on Christmas. "Detective Moreau, is everything alright?"

"Good afternoon, Ms. Ainsworth, and Happy Christmas. My apologies for disrupting this cozy gathering. I hate to put a damper on things, but I'm wondering if one of your guests might accompany me to the station for some questioning?"

Scanning, Violet eyed everyone in the room. She frowned. "Who?"

Jillian jumped up from the armchair with a jolt, making Violet start in surprise. It was as if someone had shot a pistol and yelled "On your mark, get set, go!" completely unbeknownst to her. Jillian ran through the kitchen, slamming the back door open with a loud bang, and then pushing through the second door of the sun porch.

"Jillian?" Rose called out, bewildered.

The detective gestured toward the kitchen. "Officer Caron, if you please." The officer nodded and took off through the house to follow her.

"Wh—what the heck is going on?" Rose demanded.

"We've been looking for—Jillian? Is that what you called her?"

"*Yes*," Rose exclaimed. "That's her name!"

"Actually, it isn't," the detective said. "She's a fraud. She reestablishes herself in different places, with different people, then slowly steals their identities or possessions... If she's the person we think she is, she's got a record a mile long in the UK, and you'd be her fifth, and hopefully final, victim."

They all stared at the detective as he brushed down the arm of one coat sleeve, then the other. At their silence, he looked up. "Is it possible to have a cup of tea?"

"*What?*" Rose exclaimed. "*A fraud?*"

"Are—are you saying Jillian is the one who robbed me?" Violet asked. "What did she do with all my stuff? With Gram's chest?"

He shrugged. "As of now, we have no clue what she does with the things she steals. Her parents reported her first, when she was a teenager. She stole her mother's identity and ran up a debt of fifty thousand pounds. She got smart after that, though, and went for smaller sums. Smaller amounts over longer stretches of time... How about that tea?"

"Oh my God." Rose shook her head, her eyes wild. Violet

walked over, wrapping her arms around her big sister and holding her tight.

"I—I can make some tea," Jasper said, standing up from the couch and walking toward the kitchen.

AN HOUR LATER, Violet sat beside her sister on the couch, holding her hand tightly. Rose's head was tilted back as she stared up at the low ceiling of the cottage. The soft clatter of porcelain made Violet turn her head. Jasper walked into the room once more, carrying a second tray of fresh tea. He bent down on the opposite side of the low oak table and placed the tray on the smooth surface.

Rose sighed. "I would have been happier with the gender-nonconforming brothel."

Violet looked up at Jasper holding the teapot over a cup, frozen with his face scrunched in confusion. Violet shook her head at him.

"How could she do this to me?" Rose whined, bringing her free hand up to her forehead. "We've been together almost two years. How did I not realize that the thefts started when I met her? Why did it take a detective to point that out to me? I just... I thought it was a coincidence. We're supposed to be getting *married*." Rose turned her head, meeting Violet's gaze with her glassy eyes. "She was supposed to be the one, Vi. How can someone claim to love you, but hide something so... so crazy and ugly about themselves. That's not love!"

"I know, Rosie, I'm so sorry." Violet squeezed her sister's hand. "What a mess."

"I had *no* idea—I mean, you and I had joked about it, right? When the detective asked me what her actual job was, I couldn't even properly explain. I've never met any of her co-workers or gone to any holiday parties or work events. Never met *any* friends of hers. Of course, everything is so clear now. God, I'm such an idiot."

Jasper stood, smiling in his gentle way. "All the food is put away in the kitchen... I think I should give you two privacy? Unless you need anything else?"

"Thanks for making another pot of tea, Jas. We're good. Get home safe."

He nodded. "I will... For what it's worth, Happy Christmas. Thank you for inviting me today."

"Thank you, Jasper." Rose forced a smile. "At least you can't say it was a boring day?"

He offered another crooked grin, then left the sitting room. After they heard the front door open and shut, they sat together in silence, the atmosphere littered with the pop and crackle of the fireplace, the low howl of the winter wind outside.

"When that officer dragged her back in here all wet and dirty from rolling around in the snow, it's like she was a different person. I didn't even recognize her anymore."

Violet nodded, recalling the pitiful image of an indignant Jillian bucking against the officer and demanding to be let go. Assuring him she hadn't done anything to deserve this treatment. "Innocent people don't run," the detective had said, bringing his long-awaited tea to his mouth.

Jillian's reappearance had been brief, only a minute or two before the officer urged her through the house, to the front door and out to the police car. In that time, she'd begged Rose to defend her. Or to call some lawyer friend who might be able to. The police had the wrong person and everyone was conspiring against her.

Rose shook her head. "She broke in here and stole your things. *Gram's* things. You know I'm not especially sentimental about this house and town, but to violate my sister and my family after losing someone important... How could she? I just don't understand."

"This is just who she is, Rosie. She preys on people for her own benefit—you always told me about her big, important meetings in exotic locations. All of it was lies. She's deluded."

"I always... I think I have it all together, and I've been doing everything perfectly, the way I'm supposed to, you know? I feel like an idiot. She stole my wallet the day we met and I've been fooled by her ever since."

They sat in silence once more, allowing the surprise, disappointment and hurt to settle over them. Just holding each other's hands and breathing through it.

Out of the blue, Rose chuckled, making Violet shift her gaze toward her. "What?"

"I had told you that Art was my first, but actually it was Anne."

Pausing, Violet searched her memory. "Anne... Prissy Anne with the fluffy white poodle?"

"Yes."

"Ugh. I thought she was so obnoxious. And I was what? Six?"

Rose smiled. "She was absolutely obnoxious—and demanding. But very pretty, so I dealt with it for a while. Until she started openly dating a boy from our class, but still wanted me to come over and 'hang out' because we were 'friends.' She'd always end up kissing me, so I eventually cut her off."

"Good for you. I hated her... and her little dog, too."

"Then there was Timothy in college."

"I don't remember him."

"Yes, you do," Rose assured her. "I brought him home for Christmas one year? He's the only person I've ever brought here —he hated straight people?"

"Ah, right. The barista you met at Coffee Thyme. He said that a lot... I think I blocked him out."

"He adored *you*. Thought you were the funniest person he'd ever met. Such a weirdo. He ended up being judgmental about so many things—books I liked to read, food I ate, my career choice… Oppressing me in all these sneaky, microaggressive ways that I didn't notice. But when we first met, in my twenty-two-year-old head, I was so excited to meet a guy who was bisexual, too. I thought we'd get married, have bisexual babies and help diversify the planet."

Violet laughed. "You're the weirdo."

"I know." Rose chuckled. "I was young."

They both took a breath before Violet looked at her sister once more. "Hey, Rosie?"

"Yes?"

"I think you might have terrible taste in romantic partners."

Rose laughed as she shook her head. "Seems like it, yeah? Yikes… Distract me, please. How's Painted Poppies?"

"Oh my gosh, I have eight hundred followers, and people are asking me if I have prints for sale. It's crazy."

"That's great, Vi." Rose sat up, her dark eyes wide. "So great… Please pursue this. I was wrong before—about staying the course. Quit that stupid job, focus on this."

"Well, we'll see. Let's not be too hasty."

"What's going on with you and Jasper? You two seem cozy?"

"We're the same as always." Violet shrugged. "Drinking way too much coffee and tea, taking long walks and complaining about the patriarchy."

Rose sat back in disbelief. "You talk about the patriarchy with Jasper?"

"I talk about everything with Jasper. He asked me if he could come over the other day and I told him no because I was crampy and bleeding to death and didn't feel like being bothered. He went to Simone's, bought me a lemon meringue tart and left it on the front porch with some bandages and a note that said, 'Maybe one of these will help?'"

"Oh my gosh, I can't. What a cutie… Much sweeter than stupid Coffee Thyme Timothy. If I got snappy with him the first thing he'd say was, 'Are you on your period or something?'"

"Ooh, that's grounds for a swift execution."

"Right?" Rose frowned. "That grated me. He would be weirdly distant when I was on, too. Grossed out like a child."

"Oh *geeze*. Like periods aren't a tangible, miserable thing that's part of our everyday lives—like you were a woman from a movie or TV show. Did he expect you to always have on matching underwear, too? Or to wake up with a full face of perfect makeup?"

Rose laughed. "Right? And to have instant, effortless orgasms... Tell Jasper to bring you tampons next time instead of bandages. The organic cotton ones."

Violet shook her head. "I am not telling him that."

"You don't think he'd do it?"

"No, he probably *would* and then I'd be even more of a mess over him than I already am. Nobody can compete with him as it is. I have to keep my standards mediocre, you know? A little on the low side. Realistic—for the guy who tells me I'm weird for wanting to go sketch in the woods in the dead of winter, or avoids me when I'm on my period."

Leaning over, Rose adjusted so that she could lay her head against Violet's thigh, curling up onto the couch in the fetal position. "Screw that guy, Vi. Let's not settle for jerks." When Rose was comfortable, she took a deep breath. A warm spot against Violet's leg made her look down. Rose was crying.

Violet sat with her sister—her always perfectly put-together, career-driven and strong-as-a-rock sister—and she let her cry in her lap. She didn't say a word. Just smoothed her hair and stared into the flickering fireplace.

37

NOW

With a few days left before the New Year, Simone's bakery, Le Petit Sweet, was still lit up with sparkling blue faery lights. They were strung all across the ceiling, hung in a scalloped fashion that reminded Violet of ocean waves. The glass case shone bright in the warm darkness, illuminated further by the soft yellow glow radiating from the entrance to the kitchen.

Simone was back there, bustling about and banging cabinets and dishes as Violet waited at a table. It was dark out: the shop closed for the day. The black iron street lamps outside the large windows shone bright white. A car or two passed by, the thrum of rubber on wet pavement muffled inside the warm shop. Violet inhaled, smiling at the distinct scents of nutmeg and cinnamon, buttercream and sugar floating through the air. She pulled her sweater even tighter around her body, the material long and beautifully patterned like a thick blanket.

She sighed. She loved this little town.

"Are you sure you don't need any help?" Violet called.

"No, ma'am." Simone walked through the door with a tray. Once she was at the table, she set it down and Violet helped her remove the two mugs, glasses of water and glossy iced cinnamon rolls. They looked perfectly soft and melty, so Violet swiped her finger across the top of her dessert and put it in her mouth. The rich, creamy icing was still warm.

After setting the tray on the counter, Simone sat down in the chair across from Violet, beaming. "Okay, this is the new tea I want you to try. I'm thinking of introducing it as the tea of the month in January. I'm calling it 'Roseberry.'"

Violet leaned over the teacup, bringing her face down and inhaling so that the steam left a little condensation on her nose. "Mm, it smells pretty. I can smell ginger... and basil? Did you use the things from Gram's pantry?"

"Ooh she's learning ya'll. Yes. It has dried elderberries, calendula flowers, basil leaves, rose petals and a little cinnamon and ginger root. I added some healthy elements since, you know, cold and flu season. I want it to be wintery and comforting. Make sure you add a little honey."

Violet did just that. When she took a sip, the flavors swirled against her taste buds and warmed her from head to toe. She shimmied her shoulders. "Simone, this is delicious. Like winter flowers in a teacup."

"Mission accomplished. I have some extra from the experimental batch that you can take with you, if you want. Share it with your cute friend with the gray eyes."

"Aw, thank you." Violet smiled, clasping her mug with both hands. "I'm so happy you moved here and opened this shop. It's like my dream—being good friends with the local baker. Being her guinea pig for incredible treats."

Simone laughed, pinching off a piece of cinnamon roll with her fingers. "I think most people want that, but with a local bar. Free liquor and all that."

"I do like my wine, but if you put a cupcake in front of me, it'll win every single time. So, tell me about when you worked at

Mère Macaron. You baited me with it a week or so ago but didn't finish the story. And how was your date with René?"

Holding a finger up, Simone finished chewing her generous bite of dessert, then lifted her glass of water and took a long pull before sighing. "I worked there a long time ago when I was fresh out of high school. Vi... I was a complete mess. I didn't want to sit for college exams, but my parents were pressuring me to go. I just wanted to bake and be around pâtissiers so I could learn and have my own shop one day, you know?"

"You could have gone to university to study culinary arts?"

"My parents didn't want that. My father wanted me to be a dentist, of all things. He owns a practice and wanted me to take over for him someday, but I just couldn't. If I had done what they wanted and walked that path, I knew I would be dead on the inside. A walking zombie."

Violet nodded, pulling off a piece of her own roll. "I understand completely."

"It was a guaranteed path for me, but I just couldn't, and it broke my dad's heart. I also decided to start transitioning during that time, so my head was just a mess. But I got a job at Mère Macaron, and the position started on the exact same day that I was supposed to sit for my exam. So I took that as a sign. It was fate."

"Obviously," Violet agreed. "So how was the job? Was it amazing?"

"Oh, Vi, it was hell. Amazing, but hell. I worked insane hours for very little pay. Up before dawn, then walking home in the dark again when the moon was high, only to get up a few hours later and start the whole process over.

"I was exhausted but learning so much and finally doing what I had dreamed of. I was *in it*—the smells and the flour dusted all over my apron, the powdered sugar and raw dough underneath my fingernails. I'll never forget that experience. It was life-giving at a time when I desperately needed something tangible to hold onto."

"How are things between your parents now, considering what you've achieved?"

Simone took a sip of her tea, then sighed. "My mother comes here once a month and has coffee with me. We talk and catch up. She's very supportive of all my life choices. Father is still bitter. When I opened the shop, he called me and told me congratulations. We talked a little then and he told me he loved me. But our relationship has been different—strained ever since I told him I wouldn't be taking over the dentist office. It makes me sad, but it is what it is."

Violet considered. "I think sometimes people have kids because they want them to be miniature versions of themselves. Almost like… extreme narcissism."

"This is absolutely the case with my father," Simone agreed. "My dad always wanted to play piano when he was growing up, but they couldn't afford it at that time. So guess who plays piano?"

"You?"

"Me. Whether I liked it or not, he made me learn. Guess who also played baseball all through middle school because Dad loves him some baseball?"

Violet shook her head. "Oh man…"

"I wanted to join the swim team in high school. Dad said, 'Nope, it's baseball for you, and you're good at it.' I was, but I wanted to try other things. Experiment, you know? Wasn't happening."

"Okay, so you worked at Mère Macaron, it was wonderful but awful… How does René play into that experience? Was he a customer?"

Simone clapped, a broad grin on her face. "No—well, not exactly? So when I would leave at night, sometimes this home-less guy would be sitting outside the back door to the shop. Not right up by the door in a creepy way, but off to the side a bit. I could tell he was trying to keep his distance and show me he didn't mean any harm. I figured he probably ransacked the trash after we closed for the day and threw food out.

"Well, I saw him there some nights and just thought, 'Why don't I set some things out for him?' So I put our day-old breads and sandwiches in a bag—sometimes something fresh if I could manage it—along with a cup of coffee just outside the back door so he could get it. I never saw him up close, but he looked young, like me, and I just felt bad. Hard times can fall on any of us."

Violet sat wide-eyed. "Oh my God. The homeless kid was René!"

Simone froze, her smile dropping. "Why are you spoiling the story?"

"Sorry."

Simone rolled her eyes, but with a smile. "Anyway, *yes*, it was René. He told me about it when we had the pre-Christmas party at your house, after you left and went in the kitchen with Jasper. I almost spit my muffin in his face, I was so surprised. He asked me to have dinner with him to say thank you. He said he was so disappointed in himself back then for the state he'd fallen into, but my leaving bags of bread, dessert and coffee for him outside the door gave him a little bit of hope. So I said yes to dinner."

Violet wrapped her arms around her body, hugging herself. "Ohh, I really like this story."

"Even though you spoiled it."

"Even though I spoiled it. And how was dinner?"

"It was... pretty amazing. We talked a lot—comfortable conversation. Easy. At one point, he reached across the table and held my hands. He looked me in the eyes and sincerely thanked me for showing him kindness and called me beautiful. It was wonderful... and a little scary."

"Why scary?"

Simone sighed, looking down at her fork as she slowly twirled it with her fingers. "I'm comfortable alone. I'm content and I've made that decision. But then this tall, ridiculously good-looking man comes along and I don't know. I don't want... I don't want my peace to be disrupted by hope and then yet another letdown."

"Aw, Simone—"

"I know it sounds depressing, but it's honestly how I feel. He asked me to dinner again."

"What did you say?"

"I told him yes because I felt so swept up in the moment and conversation and candlelight. But now that I have a clear head, I'm thinking of cancelling."

Violet reached across the table and wrapped her fingers around Simone's wrist. When their eyes met, Violet said, "Don't cancel. Go and enjoy. Let yourself enjoy."

Simone frowned. "If I let myself enjoy now, what happens later when I'm in pain? What if I don't want to go through that?"

"Maybe you won't have to? And if you do, I'll be with you. We'll go through it together and I'll hold you in the palms of my hands like a baby bird."

Simone laughed. "I don't think I'll fit in the palms of your hands."

"Then in my arms." Violet stretched her arms out, declaring, "I'll wrap you up tight and we can curse the day he was born. Well, not literally..."

"Alright, alright." Simone smiled. "I do like the sound of that. You're on."

38

NOW

*T*he afternoon of New Year's Eve spent with Jasper was shaping up to be like any other day with Jasper: quirky conversation littered with warm chuckles, hot liquids and harmless snuggles. Earlier, he had sat for his portrait and read quietly while Violet sketched. It was coming along nicely, she thought, but still needed a lot of work.

The eyes. Capturing the bright innocence laced with sharp intellect—the quiet mystery and depth of pain and solitude. A curse fighting against small sparks of hope... It was difficult to render. Maybe impossible within the confines of a flat, black-and-white sketch. She needed dimension, depth and shadows. *Something* to bring her a little closer to what she wanted to express.

"The detective called me yesterday," Violet said, sitting tight against Jasper's side on the couch, her legs tucked beneath her as she rested on her hip.

"Did they find your stuff?"

"No," she said, taking a breath. "He thinks the chest and everything is gone. Jillian and some accomplice she was working with pawned it all, and they can't find Gram's chest. It's really hurtful, you know?"

"I'm so sorry, Vi. Why would they even steal an old chest? I don't understand."

"Well, it was an antique pine chest from the 1800s. I painted all over it when I was a kid, but I'm sure they got a good amount of money for it. Jillian keeps using her phone calls to reach out to Rosie. She asked her to find a good lawyer and is promising that she had nothing to do with this and it's all a big mistake."

"Is it?"

"No. She's just lying. The detective sent us her mug shot from the UK from when she was seventeen, and the friend she ratted out confessed to everything and is hoping to get some kind of plea deal. They're basically blaming each other. It's all so awful."

Jasper leaned down, resting his cheek against Violet's hair. The small gesture made her heart skip despite the melancholy over her gram's lost items: the chest, Ginger's journal and books. Little pieces of her family had been stolen and dispersed into the world without her permission and she hated it.

"I have something to tell you," Jasper said. "Something good, I think."

"I could use some good news. Do you now also change into laundry detergent? That would be handy since I'm out and need to do a load."

Jasper laughed. "No. I—I started seeing a therapist last week."

Violet blinked, sitting straight. "Oh wow. What made you decide to talk to someone?"

"Ever since you said Freddie started seeing someone, I don't know... The seed was planted in my head? Then all that awful stuff with Jillian last week. It just felt like a good time to start. We—" Jasper lifted his hand, threading his long fingers into his dark hair and making a mess of his trimmed but still wonder-fully floppy curls. "We talk a lot about my mom... and how she treated me. How she still doesn't contact me or interact with me."

"I think that's good, Jas. Talking to someone—wait. Did you tell the therapist about the curse?"

"Of course not."

"What did you tell her?"

"I just told her it's a very private matter and I don't want to disclose the details. I think she's making some assumptions though. She doesn't say anything directly but it's obvious she's decided something in her head."

"Hm, that's awkward."

"It's fine. For me, the truth is much worse than anything she could be imagining."

Violet shook her head, but smiled. "I'm proud of you."

He snickered. "Why?"

"You're doing all these things now. You buy your own groceries and go into town regularly. You're seeing a therapist and I noticed you even have painters refinishing the exterior of your house and fixing the shutters."

"I shouldn't have let things at the house get so bad like that anyway. In retrospect I'm pretty embarrassed about it."

"But you're living your life as a *human* now. You're changing your perspective and it's amazing to witness."

"I just... Maybe I needed someone to tell me I was allowed to do this? That it was okay to try?"

Like always, Violet's affection for him bubbled up in her chest. She reached over and grabbed his hand, lacing their fingers as she smiled. "It's more than okay."

He squeezed her hand, staring forward with reddish-orange shadows dancing across his face from the fire. "I wasn't allowed to go anywhere or do anything after I changed that first time. My mom was hysterical about me staying inside. I remember her screaming at my dad that nobody could ever know—that I was a 'disgusting monster' and it was like she had lost her child. She told him she felt like she didn't have a son anymore. That it would have been better if I'd died. So I just... I figured she was right and always stayed hidden. I tried to, anyway."

The knot in Violet's throat made it difficult to breathe. When she managed to inhale, tears streamed from her eyes. She reached her free hand up to wipe them away and Jasper leaned forward.

"I'm sorry, Vi—I shouldn't be dumping this on you. Especially not now with everything—"

"No, I—" She breathed again, trying to ease the pain in her chest. "I can't believe someone made you feel like that for so long. It hurts my heart and I had no idea what was happening to you. No clue at all." She looked up, meeting his eyes. "Your mother was wrong, Jas. Very, very wrong."

"I... Well, I'm learning as much. My therapist—her name is Maria—says it'll take time, and the things my mother said and did can't ever be erased. But... I can adopt new truths. I want to accept them and focus on those things. The things I feel and see around me now instead of focusing on the things of the past. Like you sitting next to me and holding my hand. This is something here, now, that I want to focus on. It's incredible to me."

Violet laid her head on his shoulder. "Nah, this is basic best friend stuff. Always and forever." Violet closed her eyes, but when Jasper didn't respond, she lifted her head and looked at him. "Hello?"

"Yes?"

"You didn't say anything."

"Wh-What am I supposed to say?"

Violet sat up further, frowning but amused. "I don't know, something equally childish like, 'Yeah, best friends for life.'"

"Yeah, best friends for life..."

They paused, staring at each other before Violet laughed and shook her head. *"Boooo."* She laid her head against his shoulder again, closing her eyes and smiling. "Next time with a little more enthusiasm, please."

"I love being your best friend, but..."

"But?"

Jasper took a breath. She could feel the subtle rise and fall of it as she relaxed against his shoulders. "After we had the brunch party at your house and Freddie kissed me, you said... You told me, 'Of course they find you attractive.' Do you remember?"

"Yes."

"So, does that mean... that you find me attractive?"

Opening her eyes, Violet sat up again and looked at him. His skin was flushed crimson in the firelight, his slate eyes darting between her and the hearth. He shook his head. *"No—*forget it. It's a stupid question and I—I'm being ridiculous—"

Violet lifted her fingers and pressed the tips to his mouth. When he was silent, she looked him in the eyes. "Yes, Jasper, I find you *very* attractive. Of course I do."

A moment's pause, dancing shadows and heat radiating both inside and outside of Violet's body. Jasper took hold of her wrist and brought her hand up to cover his face with it. Pressing her palm against the smooth contours of his nose and mouth, he closed his eyes.

With her hand awkwardly shielding his face, Violet remained still, her voice soft. "Are you attracted to me?"

His eyes still closed, Jasper's lips moved against her palm, the sensation tickling her skin. "Do you also remember when you accused authors of creating shallow, svelte and big-breasted chicks from their man fantasies?"

Violet held back a laugh at the absurd reference. "Um, yeah..."

He slid her hand down a little, opening his eyes and watching her. "I've never thought about those kinds of women —because it's *always* been you. You're my fantasy, Violet."

He smiled, melting Violet's insides into something like sparkly goop. Never one without words, Violet found herself speechless.

Jasper wrapped his hand around her fingers, clasping them and bringing her knuckles to his mouth once more. His lips were soft, brushing her skin as he spoke quietly. "I always want to be your best friend. But I want... I wish I could be more than that."

She could hardly breathe from the tension of everything swelling in her heart. Couldn't look away from his lovely, pale gaze staring back at her in the dim light. It was as if everything else had faded into the background and become muted. There was only Jasper and only this moment.

"You can be," she said.

"I'm cursed."

"So? That doesn't matter to me."

"It matters to me."

"I don't get a say in this? You tell me you love me, that I'm your fantasy and that you want to be more than my friend—but what am I supposed to do with all of that, Jasper? Do you expect me to sit here and not feel anything?"

"No, I-I don't know—"

"You tell me these things and then there's a hard stop. Like a door being slammed in my face over and over. You wriggle your finger and tell me to come closer and then you shut it closed again."

"I'm *sorry*. I'm not—" He stood with a jolt, raking his hands through his hair and pacing the floor. Standing by the hearth with his fingers still tangled against his scalp, his chest heaved. The background came to life once more with the fireplace burning. A dove cooing somewhere beyond the picture window.

"I don't know what you want from me." Violet turned her

head, gazing through the glass and up toward the stormy skyline filled with the puffy bluish-gray clouds.

"I want everything," he said. "And nothing. I want to live my life with you. Trying everything there is to try and doing everything. But I'm disgust—I'm... I'm cursed, and I want you to go as far away from me as possible and live the life you deserve with someone who can truly make you happy."

"I don't need someone to make me happy, Jas. I need someone who can sympathize and listen when I complain about toxic masculinity and my period. I need someone who walks through the forest with me in the middle of winter to sketch an old bridge. I need someone who encourages me when I have doubts in myself. It's not about you making me happy. I can make myself happy. Simone's lemon meringue makes me happy. It's about you *seeing* me—truly accepting who I am and loving me for it. That's what I need, Jasper, and you give me that. A thousand times over."

He stared at her in silence for a long moment before finally dropping his hands from his hair. His shoulders slowly rose and fell, eyes downcast. "Then... you have to see everything. All of it."

"Show me."

"You'll change your mind."

"I won't."

Jasper exhaled a heavy sigh. "Not today. I'm not ready."

"Not today," Violet confirmed. "I'll wait."

He shook his head and closed his eyes, tears running down his cheeks. "I'm *terrified*, Vi. You have no idea how awful—"

Violet stood and met him in front of the hearth, placing her hands at his waist as she looked up into his eyes. "If you don't want to show me, you don't have to. This is *your* self-imposed condition."

"Because I don't—If you choose me, then I don't want to

hide anything from you. I don't want to hide this. You need to know what you're choosing."

"I'm choosing you. Whatever that entails. Everything."

The declaration was bold, and Violet stared up into his face, wanting to emphasize her conviction. To make him understand. In truth, she was nervous. Of course she was. Magic being real was still a new concept in her mind—let alone very dark and malevolent magic. She had no idea what she was truly in for, but whatever it was, she would deal with it. She'd push through because on the other side of it was her best friend, sitting isolated and afraid. Violet didn't want that for him anymore. He'd handled it alone for long enough.

Exhaling, he leaned down, wrapping his arms around her shoulders and hugging her tightly. Violet snaked her arms around his waist, nestling into his lean frame and warmth.

"I feel like I keep crying in front of you," he said, voice muffled from his face being pressed into her hair. "I guess... I'm the opposite of a 'manly man.'"

Violet shook her head within his embrace. "That's stupid. You're a person and people can cry. And I'll cry with you. Always."

A COUPLE DAYS LATER, Violet was sitting in the living room, trying to figure out her pricing for portraits, prints and other art requests when someone knocked at the cottage door. She stood, running numbers in her mind as she walked toward the front of the house.

Since Simone had set up her profile, requests for print orders or personal commissions had been pouring in. It amazed her: that people would deeply value something that came naturally to her. Something wonderful that she enjoyed. She wasn't sure, but it seemed as if she could make a true career from this if she took it more seriously. So she was starting to do just that, and getting her rates in order. She still had so much research to do.

She lifted to her toes and looked out the peephole, then frowned.

"Violet Ainsworth, please open the door," Freddie called. "I saw a shadow pass over the peephole so I know you're standing there."

"Oh my God, what a creep," Violet mumbled, unlocking the door and reluctantly dragging it open. "What?" she scowled.

"Why are you still mad at me? I thought we were over this? You invited me to the Christmas party and everything."

"*Simone* invited you. And no, I'm still not thrilled to see you on my doorstep. What is it?"

She hadn't noticed, but Freddie had been holding one hand behind his back. When he brought it around, he held a little turquoise bag that was synonymous with Le Petit Sweet. "I asked Simone what you like and she—I should say 'she,' right?"

"Yes, absolutely."

"She suggested I bring this for you. It's a strawberry lemon tart. She's experimenting. There are two?"

Violet frowned, thinking she needed to have a stern talk with her friend. Without speaking, she pulled the door open and stepped aside.

"Thank you." Freddie grinned. "I don't dislike you, Violet. I told you what my problem was, but I just want to move past it."

"Okay, fine, but I don't get why *I* need to be involved in this."

"Because I wanna get to know you." Freddie moved into the doorway of the kitchen and paused. "Can you show me where the plates are? Maybe we can have tea?"

"Just go sit down and I'll do it." She walked past him, snatching the bag from his grip and going to set up the tea as she grumbled some more.

When they were eating and comfortable in the sitting room,

Freddie's voice was soft in breaking the awkward silence. "You know... I've never left this town."

"You've gone into the city at least, haven't you?"

"Yeah, but only a few times to get supplies for the store. I've never gone there to like, hang out or have dinner. Wander around. Sometimes I feel like I'll just live my whole life and die in this town."

"Well, that's sad." Violet took a bite of her tart. Her eyes widened at the sweet yet zesty flavor. Simone was truly a brilliant pâtissier.

"When you left the village and went off to college, I envied you again. I always knew I'd take over the grocery store for Dad, so there was no real need for me to go away to some fancy school. Dad said he'd teach me anything I needed to know about the business. Then Dad got sick. Mama spent all her time looking after him and I had to run everything with the store. You got to leave—Gloria told me you even went to another country?"

"Yeah, Spain and Greece."

"That's amazing. I wish I could do that... Simone, too. You know what I like about her?"

"What?"

"She seems so free. She's just being herself. Happy. She has this business that she made all by herself that she obviously loves. The two of you have a totally different atmosphere around you—like a halo. Even though you live in this little town just like me, you've experienced life. Seen some of what the world has to offer." He sighed heavily, then took another bite of his own tart.

"I know you have the business, but can't you take a vacation? Just for a long weekend or something?"

"I don't have anyone who can run things as well as I can. I'm training Lawrence—he's a new transplant to the village. But he's not quite there yet. Plus, Mama isn't getting any younger, so I worry. What if she fell down in the house the one week I was gone? I would feel so guilty if something happened to her. I'm all she has."

Violet set her plate down, along with her guard. She took a deep breath. "You can't live your life for other people, Freddie. I'm not saying you should be a selfish jerk, but it's okay to take some time for yourself occasionally. It's healthy."

"My therapist says the same thing. I would love to travel somewhere for a week or two... just to experience different things and people. You know I haven't... I've never been attracted to another man aside from Jasper. I don't know what it is about him, but just *seeing* him really gets me—"

"Alright, let's not."

Freddie laughed, sitting back and running his hand through his thick blonde hair. "Fine. But I don't know—maybe I *would* be attracted to another guy if I ever left this dang town. I'd like to know that about myself. Or at least try. Gosh... My mama would probably have a heart-attack if she knew I was thinking like this. I think about it, though. A lot..."

"You need to take a sabbatical."

"What's that?"

"A break. A vacation from your life in this small town. Look, get Lawrence or whoever trained enough to properly look after the store, then between the three of us—me, Jasper and Simone—we can check on your mom. She's a sweet lady despite this thing she gave birth to, so I don't mind." Violet folded her arms, pouting and already half regretting offering to do something nice for Freddie. Why should she? She didn't owe him anything. And now he'd barged into her house and dumped his problems on her... At least he'd brought delicious tarts.

He sat across from her, staring with a Chris-like smile on his face. White teeth shining and a sparkle in his stupid blue eyes. "You would do that for me?"

Violet turned her head away. "I don't know. Maybe... Maybe not."

Freddie huffed in a clipped laugh. "You called me 'Mr. Popularity' before... Honestly? It always seemed empty to me. All our classmates fawning over me—laughing at the stupid stuff I did. It wasn't anything like what you had with Jasper. It wasn't *genuine*. And I don't even talk to any of those people anymore... Not really."

With her arms still folded, Violet bit the inside of her lip. Freddie went on in her silence.

"I'm so sorry I was mean to you growing up, Violet Ainsworth. That was really dumb of me. Can you please stop hating me?"

"You're pouring it on a bit thick here. Just give it a rest. I don't hate you."

"That's a start." He sat forward, taking another bite of tart. "I'd like to be invited to the wedding."

Violet balked. "Whose wedding?"

"Yours and Jasper's. I wanna be there when you marry my 'unrequited childhood crush.' My therapist calls Jasper that. She says it'll be good for me to finally see him happy. She thinks part of my 'affection' for him is that I'm always worried about his well-being since he disappeared so abruptly from my life. As a kid, it was a kind of traumatic event for me and I didn't even know it."

"Well, you're not alone there..."

"So, if you marry him and I see him smiling and peaceful, she says I'll finally be able to let go and not worry anymore."

"Freddie, just—relax, okay? Nobody is marrying anyone—"

"Why? He's been in love with you since we were kids. You're back here for good and you love him, right? What's the problem?"

"I—" Violet opened her mouth, then closed it, heat rushing to her cheeks. She might not hate Freddie anymore but she was a long way off from having heart-to-hearts with him about her private relationship with Jasper. "First of all, you need to mind your own business. Second, that's enough for today. Thank you for the tart. It was delicious."

He grinned. "Are you telling me to get out?"

She mimicked his smile. "As politely as I can manage."

39

FEBRUARY

"*I* can't tell you how much it makes my heart smile to have you both in my little café." Simone grinned, standing over their table. "You're looking radiant and well-rested, Mr. Jasper."

"Right?" Violet chimed in, pulling her chair closer to the bistro table. "It seems like his eyes are even brighter."

"Ah—please…" Jasper shook his head, skin flushed.

"Oh, we're embarrassing him. He looks like my Roseberry tea."

"Jas," Violet leaned in, "you have to try it. I told you about it, remember? It doesn't have any peppermint, so you should be good?"

He nodded. "Sure, okay."

Violet lifted her fingers. "Two cups, please—and I'll have a croissant."

"Anything else for you, Jasper?" Simone asked, batting her eyes. "I might have made a fresh fruit tart last night that I would be willing to cut into, just for you."

"You indulge me." He smiled.

"I'm happy to. I'll be right back."

As Simone walked off, Violet folded her arms against the table and cast her gaze out the floor-to-ceiling picture window at their side. The clouds were thick and billowing in every hue of gray—pewter and slate, ash and dark shadow. Something in it felt romantic to Violet's mind—images of a stone castle perched on a jagged mountainside, the dark ocean tumultuous and swirling underneath the cliff's edge.

Their view was nothing like that, but she could imagine it. Some faraway place she'd love to visit and sketch, then paint with a rich blue, gray and black palette.

She and Jasper were together at a café. Finally outside the house (and not in the woods). Violet peeked at her companion and found him staring off into the distance as well. A quiet worry or maybe even uncertainty rested in his soft expression. He looked healthier than ever—since the first time she'd been reunited with him as an adult. He wasn't dusty anymore. No dark circles under his eyes or a mild strain in his brow.

Even so, something wasn't right. Violet cleared her throat. "Thank you for coming here with me," she said.

"Thank you for inviting me. Simone's shop is beautiful. It smells like heaven."

"It's an excellent 'first café' experience. It honestly doesn't get much better than this... I have something to tell you."

"What is it?"

Violet smoothed her thick hair back, lifting her chin. "I quit my full-time job."

Jasper's eyes went wide. "You did it."

"I did."

"When?"

"Yesterday. I did all the math like I told you I was going to, and combined with my savings and the orders I have coming in for the artwork, it works out. Jasper, I'm free! I'm going to pursue this with everything I've got."

"You already have twice as many orders as you did in

January. It's only going to get better and better. Soon you'll need to hire someone to help manage the back-end stuff."

"That sounds wild. Unfathomable."

"It's inevitable, Vi. You're brilliant—talented and creative. You… You truly deserve everything good that the world has to offer. Congratulations."

She reached her hand across the table, palm flipped up. "Thank you," she said, waiting. He hesitated, but met her gesture, sliding his palm into hers and warmly clasping their hands together. He was smiling, but it was off and didn't reach his eyes. Violet frowned. "What is it?"

"What is what?"

"You've been off ever since New Year's. It's like you're too quiet sometimes—"

"I'm talking right now." He grinned, still not fooling anyone.

"Jasper, just talk to me—"

"We're celebrating today. Celebrating you and this bold, incredible path that you're on. You're taking control of your life the way you always wanted—the same way that Gloria did. Can we focus on that? Please?"

Simone reappeared, setting their teacups, accoutrements and a beautiful little teapot covered in an intricate floral design down onto the table before sweeping away to answer another customer's beckoning call. Jasper picked up the pot, filling her cup before his own.

"Is your departure from the city job effective immediately?" he asked. "Or did you give them notice?"

He set the teapot down. When she didn't respond, he looked up. "Vi?"

"Are you going to disappear again?"

"What?"

"Just disappear. I'll go to your house one day and it'll be empty. You'll have packed everything in secret and left without telling me, because you think that would be best for me—because you think I'd be better off without you."

"Wh—where is this coming from?"

"Answer me."

They sat frozen with Jasper staring. Slowly, he shook his head. "I'm not... I wouldn't do that to you. I would never do that."

Violet sat back, exhaling to release the stiff tension in her shoulders, swallowing hard against the lump in her throat and lifting her palms to her face. The image kept plaguing her psyche. Laurent House empty and Jasper gone without a trace. Her heart broken a second time. Maybe forever. Unsalvageable.

"Hey."

She lifted her head to see Jasper reaching his arms across the table, leaning forward with both palms open and careful to avoid the tea setting in the center. Sighing, Violet placed her hands within his. He lifted one to his mouth, his lips resting against her knuckles and his eyes closed. He whispered. "I wouldn't do that."

"Even though you think I'd be better off without you?"

"I *know* you would."

Violet shook her head, blinking back tears. "You're so wrong."

He opened his eyes, but his stare was vacant—expressionless as he avoided her face. "I'll... I'll show you."

"When?"

"Tonight."

"I'm ready."

Now, his haunting steel irises flicked up to meet hers. He didn't speak, but shook his head, then placed the softest kiss against her hand. The gesture was so innocent, so subtle, but it made Violet's breath catch. Made everything beneath her navel flicker warm with sudden life and spark.

"Sorry, lovebirds, things got unexpectedly busy."

With Simone standing over them, Jasper sat back, smooth in placing Violet's hand on the table and focusing on the desserts being set in front of them.

"Is everything alright?" Simone asked.

Violet looked up at her friend, and realizing the bewildered state of her own expression, she took a breath. 'Yeah, everything is fine…" She looked over at Jasper once more. He took a bite of his tart, but he didn't say anything at all, and he didn't look at either of them.

THAT DAY, the minutes ticked by, slowly turning into hours. Time, that fuzzy and shifty thing, dripped slow like molasses: thick and messy as the seconds stretched on.

Jasper hardly said anything the rest of the afternoon and seemed to be in his own head. In his own world. Whenever Violet initiated conversation, his responses came short, concise or not at all. She'd asked him if he'd feel more comfortable showing her his transition in his own house, but his response was explicit.

"No. Not there."

Violet had nodded in compliance, and so they sat—silent together on her gram's couch and cast in dim light from the setting sun. Violet had lit the fireplace, so it was warm despite the frosty hush between them. She peeked over at her friend sitting at the opposite end of the couch. He stared forward, his shoulders gently rising and falling with concentrated breaths.

"I wish I could read your mind," she said.

He stayed perfectly still with his hands clasped neatly in his lap. He didn't meet her eyes. "I just… want you to know that these past four and a half months with you have been the happiest in my adult life. And much more than anything I ever could have imagined for myself, given my circumstance. Thank you, for that."

She shifted her body, turning so that she faced him. "You're welcome, but we're not finished. It isn't over."

Jasper took a very deep breath, closing his eyes as he slowly exhaled. At that moment, the atmosphere of the room shifted in a familiar way. In the same way it always did when Jasper stayed over. He typically hid himself in Violet's room, but the magic in the curse, the dark, vindictive power of it seeped out —crawling and rolling like a stampede of invisible spiders clambering over each other and conquering everything in their path.

The force and pull of it felt even stronger with him beside her. She looked up at the wall clock: 5:00 p.m. exactly. The time he always vanished from her sight as a man and eventually returned as a mouse. He didn't vanish this time. Only breathed deeply. Eyes closed. She waited in the silence.

5:12 p.m. "Jas?"

Another deep breath, the cold tingles of malevolent magic radiating from him and making her shiver. He turned to look at her, and his eyes were completely blacked out—no whites at all. The beautiful, glassy heather-gray was gone and replaced with dark, inky pools. Her shoulders tensed from the eerie shock of it, but then he offered a weak smile.

"It's time," he said, getting up from the couch. "Can we go in your room? I prefer smaller spaces. Plus you've got this giant window out here."

"Sure." Violet nodded, shaky as she stood. Jasper walked ahead of her toward the hall, but she quickly matched his stride. Just beside him, she grasped his hand. He started, jerking slightly, but he didn't pull away as she clasped their hands tighter. To her astonishment, his skin felt a little... fuzzy.

Inside the room, Violet moved to sit on the edge of her bed, pulling Jasper to sit beside her, but he disconnected their hands.

She blinked up at him standing over her. He glanced away, avoiding looking at her face with his black eyes.

"It's better if I'm naked when I transition."

Violet blinked. "Wh-What?"

"I get tangled up if I wear clothes and it just makes everything worse." He lifted the hem of his sweater as he spoke, yanking it up over his long torso and pulling it over his head. He tossed it onto the ottoman at the end of Violet's bed, then started unbuttoning his dress shirt.

"Oh... okay." Violet swallowed hard. She wasn't prepared to see him transition *and* completely naked. Not that she was truly prepared for whatever was about to happen, anyway. Her pulse raced, her throat dry, the magic hovering and making her skin prickly and cold.

Jasper removed his dress shirt and flickered his black eyes over to her, smirking. "This is the part when you usually insert a joke to lighten the mood."

"I don't think anything is funny at the moment."

"Mm." He nodded, unfastening his belt.

"But... You could have *warned* me."

"About?"

"I didn't know your eyes would turn black like this."

"Does it matter?" He snaked the belt through the loops, tossing it aside and unbuttoning his pants.

"I—well... Not really, I guess. But still, *communication*. Just a little, please? You've barely said anything since lunch."

"I can talk now?" he said, tossing his pants aside. Violet bit her bottom lip, rebuking the warm blush traveling up from her nether regions and revealing itself in her cheeks.

"You should have told me earlier and before you were standing in front of me in your underwear."

Jasper looked down at his long, lanky body, his fitted black boxer briefs. He shrugged. "In about thirty minutes, my being naked will be the least of your worries."

"Okay, so instead of being snarky and vague, tell me what's about to happen, please."

"I told you before," he said, walking over to plop down on the bed beside her. "My body is going to contort and shrink down. It's a hideous process and it takes about an hour—the last thirty minutes are the worst and fastest. But it's already started, see?" He held his arm out, urging Violet to investigate. She rubbed her palm across his forearm, amazed at the soft layer of gray fuzz already shadowed against his skin.

"It'll look painful—and I am in pain. It hurts a lot. But I'm used to it and I won't scream or anything, so you don't need to worry about me."

Violet lifted her hand, cupping his cheek with her palm and making him meet her eyes. "Telling me not to worry about you is pointless. *Of course* I'm going to worry." She stared into his very dark eyes and in a rare occurrence, he didn't look away. She couldn't tell exactly, but it almost seemed as if his eyes had flickered down to her mouth. The moment passed, though, and he pulled away. Jasper scooted down, sitting on the floor with his back against the mattress and bedframe. He maneuvered his briefs off and down his long legs as he spoke.

"It's also easier if I'm already on the floor... Violet, if at any time this is too much, I won't be offended if you look away or leave altogether—"

"I'm not going anywhere."

He paused, then brought his knees up to his chest as he tossed his underwear aside. "But it's okay if you do. You don't have anything to prove."

"It feels like I have everything to prove."

That his mother was wrong. That he was not disgusting or a monster—that he was someone worthy of love and a fulfilling life.

With all of these things, Jasper would have to decide within himself whether or not they were acceptable truths. She couldn't force the truth on him. She could only show it to him and hope that he embraced it. That he'd finally let go and try to live his life the way he truly desired—whatever that entailed.

With Jasper sitting below her, Violet reached out, sliding and tangling her fingers into the thick of his wild hair. The warm, dark luster and unruliness of it called to her—the wayward strands of gray despite his young, twenty-five years on the earth. She was surprised when he didn't refuse her. Didn't pull away from her touch.

Shivering, she took a deep breath, the hum of magic still bristling against her skin. It felt even colder now. Heavier. She looked down, watching Jasper as he sat perfectly still below her. "Once you're in mouse form, I'll cut up some strawberries and set them out with some almonds if—" Violet gasped, hand frozen in midair. The bone of Jasper's shoulder blade jutted out and moved as if someone… something was underneath his skin and trying to press its way to the surface of his flesh. The action made Jasper lurch forward, hunching away from her grasp.

Violet swallowed and glanced over at the clock on her bedside table: 5:38 p.m. She gripped the edge of the mattress. Human bones… They should *not* move like that. Not ever.

40

NOW

Oh God...
Violet flopped down onto the bed, sitting with a hand over her mouth and tears running down her cheeks. Jasper had called the change horrific. Disgusting. Something he desperately wanted to shield her from, worried that it might traumatize her.

She hadn't understood any of it before, but she did now. Every apprehension. Every doubt and fear—the root of all the insecurities and forebodings twisted deep within him were validated before her eyes.

Violet stared helplessly as bones cracked and snapped, contorted and shifted in unimaginable ways—in ways considered impossible for any biological creature documented by humanity. Then there were pauses. Halting moments where Jasper's distorted body became still: the confusing, fleshy bulk of him pulsing with shallow, labored breaths before another dramatic shift of bones and joints made him tumble over. His skin stretched, then shrunk down little by little, shriveling and changing the sparse hairs into a coating of gray fur.

She wanted to scream. She wanted to run away and free

herself from the heavy weight of the cold, dark energy surrounding and suffocating her—squeezing as if intentionally wrapping her up in a malevolent embrace. Urging her to flee from its power and from the knotted-up creature it controlled: this cursed thing in the middle of her bedroom floor that served as its vessel and origin.

But Violet didn't move. Despite the weight and bitterness of the atmosphere, the strength of its compulsion, she didn't leave. Because it wasn't a thing or a creature in front of her. It was her best friend. It was as if the curse wanted her to forget that fact— that nothing she knew about Jasper before this moment had been true. *This* was the truth now. This ugliness. This repulsiveness and confusion. "*Isn't it disgusting?*" it whispered in a nasty voice, like a putrid mist floating through the air. "*Go... Get as far away from him as possible.*"

She stayed. She cried. And in some moments, when there was a big shift and the cracking of his bones made it too gruesome to watch, she shut her eyes tight. When she did, she focused her mind, blocking out the voice and repeating a single thought over and over. *This is Jasper and I love him. I love him...*

What felt like hours had only been thirty minutes. Violet opened her eyes, realizing she'd taken shelter within her own mind. Concealing herself from being swallowed up by the dark magic and lies swirling around her like thick snakes. But there was no Jasper. The floor was empty.

"Jas?" she said, her voice quiet and shaky. She wiped her face with her palms and her nose was all stuffy from crying. Nothing. No little gray mouse appeared.

The bedroom door was closed. She'd pulled it shut when she'd walked in behind him, and the door sweep underneath was too tight for him to have crawled through. Feeling nauseous, she slid off the bed, her knees hitting the floor.

"Jasper?" Bending, she peeked under the bed first. Nothing. Turning her head toward the nightstand proved fruitless as well. Violet crawled forward a little so she could look underneath the large oak dresser. It was dark because the space was so narrow, but he was there, crouched against the wall with his back turned.

"Hey…" She sniffed. Her voice sounded all wrong with her nose clogged. Her throat was painfully dry and her temples throbbed. "Why are you under there? You can come out."

He didn't move. If anything, he curled his tiny body up tighter so he looked like a gray dust ball. "Jasper?" Still nothing.

Sighing, she stood. Drained and tired, she opened the door and headed to the kitchen. Her brain felt like mush and her heart ached. Every day he went through that. For *fifteen years*. Every, single, day. And for some of it, he was alone. His father gone and his mother repulsed by him. Seduced by the magic's compulsion and openly hating him.

When Violet stood in the kitchen, the tears fell yet again. She cried at the images burned behind her eyelids like a light that had shone too brightly. Her heart ached for his pain and torture. For the stark loneliness of it all. This burden that he'd carried by himself.

She took strawberries out and rinsed them, got a handful of almonds and put everything on a small plate. It felt as if she would never breathe through her nose again by the time she wandered back toward her bedroom, her face dry and stiff from the repeated cycle of teardrops and frantic wiping.

To her dismay, the door was open. She'd forgotten to close it behind her when she'd left. Moving swiftly, she walked inside, set the plate down first, then rested on her knees and bent to look underneath the dresser again. Thankfully, he was still there, crouched with his fuzzy ball of a body heaving. Sleeping.

Exhausted, Violet lay on her side, watching him and settling down on the thick throw rug. She closed her eyes. Sleeping on the floor wasn't ideal, but standing up and getting in bed felt like one more challenge she was simply not willing to rise to. She'd hit her limit for the day.

IN THE MORNING, Violet woke up to an arm that felt like dead weight, and a soft creaking at her feet. Startled, she opened her eyes and lifted her head. Jasper was standing by the ottoman, all long legs and naked body as he pulled his briefs up over his narrow hips.

"Hey, you."

He froze. Expressive gray eyes locked on hers in a weighted moment before he reached down and started separating his rumpled clothes. He didn't speak.

"What are you doing?" she asked, sitting upright and groaning, rolling her shoulder and rubbing her arm to help circulate the blood.

"Getting dressed."

"Where are you going?"

"Home."

"Why?"

He avoided her gaze while he pulled his pants from the pile. "Because that's where I live. I tried not to wake you."

Violet watched him move in silence. His eyes—usually soft and transparent with emotion after their continued time together—were hard and unfeeling. His demeanor was completely rigid. It was as if every internal and external wall he possessed had been drawn up to protect himself and shut her out. Everything they'd worked up to and shared together was dissolving right before her eyes, as if they were strangers again. Back at square one.

Violet stood in a panic, her chest tight. "Are you upset with me?"

He paused, finally looking at her once more. "No... Why would I be upset with you?"

"I don't know." Violet took a breath, self-consciously pushing her frizzy hair back from her face. "You're being cold to me. And you hid underneath the dresser all night and you didn't eat. You didn't come to me when I called you. Could you hear me? Is... Is your head getting foggy again when you change? You told me last week that your 'rat brain' is like nonexistent now."

Swallowing hard, she glanced over at the untouched plate of strawberries and almonds. He'd told her that things were "crystal clear" now when he changed into a mouse—that aside from not being able to speak, his mind and awareness were just as sharp as when he was human. Had something changed?

Jasper dropped his pants on the ottoman and rubbed his palms against his face, his voice muffled. "You've seen me. What I am. And what happens to me."

"Yes."

He inhaled, then exhaled a heavy breath as he stared down at his clothes. "And you don't hate me? You're not afraid... or disgusted?"

Violet stepped toward him, never taking her eyes from his face, but nervous as she reached to touch his hand. "I don't. I'm not." She slid her fingers against his palm, half afraid he'd snatch away from her touch. He didn't. But when she wrapped her hand around his, he didn't reciprocate.

It was only a few seconds, but it felt like forever as she waited with her heart in her throat. He glanced down, looking into her face with a softened gaze. His voice registered so quietly, even in the silence. "Why?"

Violet smiled. "Because I love you. And you're too cute to hate." He glanced away again, pulling one hand up to his face, but finally reciprocating and squeezing her hand with the other.

Relieved, Violet stepped toward the bed, pulling him with her as she climbed on top. He let her drag him along until they were both lying down against the soft comforter. She leaned on her side, wrapping her arms around his naked shoulders and holding him tight, nuzzling her face into his dark, messy hair.

It took a minute, but slowly, he snaked his arms around her waist, pulling her even closer. "I'm sorry that I made you cry so much. I hate that."

"I've cried over less," Violet assured him. "I bit my tongue the other day and cried for at least five minutes." She breathed in against the silky fluff atop his head. He smelled like something warm and earthy and alive: like the greenest plant that thrived in the sunlight. She could never put her finger on it, but she loved it. Jasper's smell.

"Dad cried a lot too when he sat with me," he said, holding her a little tighter. "I don't want to make you suffer."

"It's not *you*—it's the curse. You take so much ownership of it, like you conjured it up yourself. It's not something you created. What we feel isn't because of you. It's because of what this awful thing does to you. How it terrorizes someone that we love so much, and we're powerless. All we can do is sit and watch you suffer."

"I'm used to it."

"That doesn't make it better." Feeling him long and warm and wrapped in her arms within her bed made Violet smile. "You just took off all your clothes and started strutting around in front of me in your little black briefs. You're sexy, Jasper—all legs."

He pushed away from her, breaking free of their embrace. "I —I am *not*—that word has nothing to do with me... I did not strut." He sat staring at her, mouth twisted in a frown and his face beet red.

Violet batted her eyes, peeking up at him from her pillow. "Sweet *and* sexy."

"Th-That's not—" He stood quickly, moving to the ottoman and sitting down in a huff. He threaded his arms through his dress shirt first, then focused on the buttons. "Clearly the curse has done something weird to your head. It's probably like being exposed to a dangerous chemical. Maybe I'm radioactive and I don't know it."

Sitting up, Violet crawled toward the end of the bed. When she reached him, he was pulling his sweater over his head. He finished, fretting and fixing the hem as Violet rested her chin against his shoulder. "There's nothing wrong with my head. I've always felt this way about you. I've just never had the pleasure of seeing you naked before."

He groaned and raked his hand through his hair, the beet-red blotches across his neck and face relentless. Violet leaned forward, sliding her arms underneath his to hug him from behind, holding him close. "Why are you being so fussy? Are you really going home?"

She felt him inhale deeply and breathe out, chest rising and falling underneath her palms, calming himself. "I don't have to. If you want me here."

"I do."

"And you... You're really okay? We're alright?"

"Yes."

Lowering his head, he closed his eyes. Violet leaned into his back, pulling him even closer. "Will you make a frittata, please? I have basil, tomatoes and mushrooms in the fridge. I've been trying to duplicate what you did that one time, but I can't. You just make it better. I can mix up a smoothie with spinach, oat milk and strawberries for you? I think I have frozen peaches, too, if you prefer those?"

When he nodded, a tear ran down his cheek. But he reached up, swift in wiping his face with his fingers. "Sure."

THE DAYLIGHT WAS PARTICULARLY soft and gray because of the cloudy sky. Something in it felt calming to Violet. Soothing to her mind and nerves like a warm cup of coffee or fresh towels from a dryer. They had cooked together in the kitchen, peaceably, unhurried in their movements. Talking, but not too much. It wasn't so quiet that it became awkward, but the weight of the magic and their shared experience sat invisible between them— over them like a thick and darkly shimmering veil.

Where do we go from here?

Violet didn't know. She knew what she wanted and what she hoped for: just a little bit more. Nothing too crazy. She wasn't expecting him to suddenly overcome his trauma—for the curse to be broken, and everything between them easy and simple.

But maybe *something*. A little glimpse into his mind, or a sign of what would become of them. Would they just be this way forever? Best friends snuggling and cuddling on the couch? Completely fulfilled with emotional intimacy and mental stimulation, but never physical? Knowing each other's minds and hearts, but their bodies off-limits?

Well... so be it.

There was no one like Jasper. No one. And as Simone had lovingly reminded her, she was never limited in the things she could do by herself.

In the afternoon, they sat on the sun porch (despite the distinct lack of sun). Violet was nearly done with Jasper's portrait and had promised him that this was the final sitting. She focused on her canvas, in her element and feeling a bit like she did when she was a child—her hair piled up in a haphazard bun, charcoal smudges on her fingers and pants.

Jasper sat across from her in a wicker chair, silent. Usually his eyes were downcast and zeroed in on whatever book he had in his hands. Today, though, every time Violet looked up, his eyes were on hers. Searching. With disbelief? Confusion? She couldn't know. Whatever it was, she decided to let him sort it out on his own.

"This book you're reading must not be very good," she said eventually, grinning as she worked.

He looked down at the thick hardcover in his lap. "It's fine... Why do you say that?"

She chuckled. "Because you keep staring at *me*. Either this book is boring or I'm suddenly more interesting."

"You are always more interesting. The most interesting." He took a breath and then plastered his palm to his forehead. His creamy skin shifted to rosy pink. Violet stopped and set her messy hands in her lap with her palms up.

"Jas, what is it? Whatever it is, just say it, okay? You can talk to me—*always*."

He dropped his hand from his forehead, meeting her eyes. He didn't say anything, but put his book aside and stood. Violet was surprised when he hovered over her, then knelt down in front of her as she sat on the bench with one leg tucked underneath her body, the other hanging over the edge. She blinked, looking down into his flushed face. "What's wrong?"

Resting with his hands on either side of her hips, he gripped the soft cushion in his fists and stared at her knees. "Would... Violet, would you kiss me?" He lifted his head, but then flicked his eyes away. Shoulders tense.

Violet bit her bottom lip, thinking she absolutely would. *Absolutely.* But she smirked, her cheeky sense of humor getting the better of her. "I would," she said, looking down at him, "but I'm not sure I can compete with René and Fre—"

In a flash, Jasper lifted and caught her mouth in a quick kiss, but he caught Violet's forehead, too. The throb of their skulls clashing overshadowed any delight from the first glorious moment of their lips touching. Violet sat straight, groaning and lifting the back of her hand to the tender spot between her eyebrows. "Ah—*God,* Jas—"

"Sorry! But don't make jokes right now—"

"Okay, but you don't need to headbutt me."

"I don't know what I'm doing. Tell me what to *do*."

"J-Just calm down." Violet rolled her shoulders. "Everybody calm down and take a breath." As she exhaled, Jasper dropped his head, lying against her thigh and rubbing his face there, mumbling.

"Humiliating… so stupid."

"No, no no. None of that. Just, ah…" She grabbed the damp towel she kept nearby while she worked, except it was almost dry. Still, she wiped her hands as best she could, her fingers dark and messy with charcoal.

He turned his head to the side as he lay in her lap, blinking up at the canvas beside them. He sat straighter, taking in his portrait for the first time. She hadn't allowed him to see it until it was ready, but it was nearly there now.

"Is this supposed to be me?" he asked.

"Um, yeah."

"This is how I look to you?"

"This is how you look, period, Jas. Even Simone saw it the other day and said it perfectly resembles you. This is my first serious attempt at painting a portrait in charcoal. Not to toot my own horn, but… Toot toot."

He shook his head as he stared at the canvas, as if refuting the painting and the truth of it: the straight nose and narrow jawline, the haunting depth of his stormy eyes and the complex emotion in his expression. Darkness and light. Despair and hope.

"Can you look at me, please?"

Miraculously, he did. Turning his head and meeting her eyes. She smiled. "About kissing. You've got the baseline objective, just… a little softer and slower. That's all."

"Okay…"

She leaned down until their noses brushed, then tilted her

head just a bit as she whispered. "Part your lips, but only enough to take a breath, not wide."

He did. But instead of breathing in, he exhaled, the heat of it interwoven with the scent of the second strawberry smoothie he'd had a little earlier. She pressed into him once, firmly, parting her lips as she did so: a gentle push of their mouths meeting and colliding. Violet pulled away slightly, her voice low. "How's that?"

Subtly, he slid his tongue across his bottom lip before pulling it in to bite, as if he were tasting and thoroughly considering all the evidence before answering. He'd kept his gray eyes open, and now they flickered back and forth between her eyes and mouth. "Good..."

Violet leaned down, keeping her dirty hands in her lap but tilting her head once more. This time, she moved against his mouth, slow and careful, as if she were tasting something that she knew she'd love and want to devour, but needed to savor. Something extraordinary that should be cherished.

She felt Jasper lift his chin and stretch, his instincts kicking in, mimicking her movement and sighing in the kiss. Violet's heart beat even harder, working overtime to keep up with the sheer delight of the moment. His palms unclenched at her sides and found their way into her own hands within her lap. Despite their grimy state, she opened to him, clasping their hands together as their mouths explored, gentle and sweet. Cautious but intentional.

She'd expected Jasper to show some sign of wanting to stop —of having enough. When he didn't, Violet pulled up first. She was thinking that shoving her tongue in his mouth might be a bit much, so she should probably quit while she was ahead. But the naked disappointment in his face when she sat straighter made her question that decision.

Violet smiled. Her blood rushed through her body as if it were carbonated. "You don't hate this, I take it?"

Jasper smiled, dropping his shoulders and sighing heavily. He wilted, leaning forward and laying his head in her lap again. Violet blinked, grinning and confused. "Are you okay?"

"All I could think about was how I had never kissed you."

"What? When?"

"Yesterday," he breathed, "*all day*. I've been wanting to kiss you since I was eight years old. But I... I knew if I showed you what I am, I wouldn't ever be able to and I was really stressed about it. That you'd find me repulsive and everything would be over. I wanted to kiss you yesterday—I wanted to kiss you on my *birthday*, or for you to kiss me, but I didn't know what to say." He held her hands even tighter as the words spilled out in a rush. Frenzied and relieved.

"Hm, I thought you were acting strange on your birthday."

He whipped up, dark brows furrowed. "Why didn't you kiss me? That's what people do to me on my birthday—they kiss me."

"First of all, I'm not 'people.' Second, you had just complained to me about 'ambush kisses' the week before. Why would I do that?"

"Because it's different with you, obviously. I want to kiss *you*. I want to do everything with you."

Violet raised her eyebrow. "Everything?"

Realizing what he'd said, Jasper blinked before shifting his eyes away. "Well... I... I don't know what I'm doing with anything, so I should probably not—"

"It isn't about 'knowing what you're doing,' Jas. It's about discovering things together and learning about each other. Trying new things when we're ready. The more we practice, the better we'll get."

"So..." He grinned, surprising Violet when he stood. He leaned over her with his palms resting on either side of her body so that she had to lift her face to look into his eyes. "The more I kiss you, the better I'll get?"

"Inevitably, yes..." Violet swallowed, dumbfounded by the playful glint in his steel eyes. The joy and warmth radiating from his skin and seeping into her like osmosis. Her entire body tingled from the thrill of his conviction. His sudden assuredness.

Who is this person?

"I really, *really* want to kiss you, Vi. Frequently."

"Regularly?"

"Habitually. Can I? Is that okay?" He tilted his head as he leaned into her. A quick study: clever man that he was. When their noses brushed so softly, Violet closed her eyes, feeling as if she might lose her breath and float away.

"Yes," she sighed. He parted his lips and pressed into her. Practicing to his heart's content.

41

LATER ON

*T*raditionally, March was always the most difficult month for Violet. Nature was beginning to thaw and shed its winter coat, but not enough to produce anything interesting or substantial. The village was cold and gray and wet, stuck within a kind of purgatory—lacking the magic and wonder of winter and without the exuberance and genesis of spring.

Thankfully, though, she had plenty to keep her mind occupied.

The door to Laurent House swung open as she moved down the cobblestone path. Jasper stood in the door, beaming. "Did you call the woman from the museum back? What did she say?"

"One thing at a time, please." Violet scrunched her nose, walking up onto the small porch. Jasper stepped aside to allow her to cross the threshold, but he didn't let her pass. He shifted into her, threading his long fingers into her hair and cradling the back of her head to pull her in close.

"Hi," he whispered, his breath warm against her mouth. Violet didn't even bother answering and instead closed her eyes and parted her lips. He kissed her like he always did now: insatiable and luscious. Slow and absorbed—like someone taking a bite out of a new confectionary and trying to discern every ingredient and spice gracing their tongue. Brown sugar and cinnamon, or ground ginger and nutmeg with a hint of caramel. Jasper kissed her, discerning her every flavor and sliding his tongue inside to learn and know every element of her.

This tongue business would be Violet's downfall. After the first time they'd done it, there had been no turning back. Every kiss from Jasper was all-consuming. Violet could only breathe through it and keep herself calm.

After just one month, he was kissing her with the expertise of someone who had been doing it their entire life. Kissing *her*, in particular. Uniquely. He paid such close attention to her every response, knowing exactly how much pressure to apply, how to shift his head or when to pull back and tease her... When he should dive in and give her everything he had.

Still holding her captive, Jasper lifted from the kiss, staring and grinning. "You taste like coffee and raspberries. Did you just leave Simone's?"

"You are not allowed to track my whereabouts based on the way I taste."

"Is that weird?"

"A little, yeah."

They laughed. He reached down and grabbed her hand, pushing the door closed with his free one before pulling her toward the kitchen. "I'm part rat so tastes and smells are important. Tell me what happened."

"Yes, I called the museum back, and they want me to come in for a meeting. They asked me to bring a portfolio of my art. Jas, I have to make a portfolio of my art."

"They want you to have a showing, I just know it. It's happening. And René told me that Simone's feature in that big foodie magazine has been pushed up a month because they're so excited. You two are incredible. Unstoppable. When is the meeting?"

The kitchen was warm and filled with even more smells for her senses to delight in. Something creamy and earthy with rosemary. Oregano? "In two weeks. I'm still shocked by all of it —like I can't process it yet. The requests for prints just keep flooding in, and Simone's bakery is getting so crowded lately. She's needed to hire two staff members already... What did you make?"

"Potato soup. Do you feel comfortable establishing your portfolio within two weeks?"

Violet leaned toward the stove and lifted the glass lid from the large copper pot. Steam swirled, filling her nostrils with creamy, herby potato goodness. "I feel good about it. I already have a lot of new examples I can take. I just need to figure out how to present them. I'm sure there's a much more efficient and professional way rather than carrying a bunch of canvases downtown. I have to do some research."

"I'll look into it, too, and let you know what I find. René is trying to figure out how he can plug Simone's bakery at his next speaking engagement." Jasper shook his head. "She doesn't even need it. But he keeps telling me she's his 'guardian angel' and he wants to help her however he can."

Violet chuckled, replacing the lid and reaching for the teapot. "I adore René and his flair for the dramatic. He is just head over heels."

She paused when Jasper stepped even closer into her side, making her look up at his sweet smile and bright eyes.

"I know exactly how he feels..." He bent, brushing their mouths together slowly, but instead of kissing her further, he dipped his head into the curve of her neck and pressed his lips against her skin. Violet hunched her shoulder and placed a hand against his chest, gently pushing him.

"Ah, *enough*, Jas."

He pulled up, pouting. "But you like it when I do that. You get all squirmy and you giggle."

"I—I know, but…" Violet inhaled a breath, her face flushed. "Listen. I'm going to make tea, you're going to get the bowls and soup ready and then we're going to sit and have lunch, okay?"

"Okay… Did I do something wrong?" He frowned, a familiar shade of doubt coloring his eyes. The signs of his inner turmoil bubbling to the surface.

"No. You're a sexy, long-legged and sneaky fox of a man, and I just need you to stop nipping at me for ten minutes."

Jasper stared, blinking with his lips pursed. "I…"

"You heard me." Violet smiled.

Hesitating, he walked to the cabinet to get bowls. He turned, looking over his shoulder. "I'm not—"

"You *are*. That's your problem, sexy fox-man. You have zero awareness of your own power and attractiveness. In your head, I'm 'letting' you kiss me as some kind of favor. Because I'm nice or something. But it's not like that *at all*, Jasper. This isn't one-sided, and you're not thinking about the deeper impact you might be having on me. Not really."

He stood still at the island counter, watching her. Hopefully listening. When he didn't say anything, Violet added, "Just… try to let that sink in, alright? I'll meet you in the study."

They were quiet as they worked on their respective tasks, but once Jasper had the bowls and utensils loaded onto a tray, he walked away from the counter. When he passed through the door, she heard him grumble loudly.

"I'm a *rat*. Not a fox."

Violet rolled her eyes.

∼

MUCH LATER, when the two sat comfortably in the study on the sofa (a healthy distance apart and their bellies full of warm soup and tea), Violet looked over at Jasper.

"What would happen if you and René wanted to end your arrangement? How would that work?"

Jasper folded his arms. "We've talked about it—since he wants to pursue acting in the future. We decided that he could keep the author name and celebrity, and I'll just start my writing career over when I'm ready."

"What?" Violet sat up straighter, her legs tucked underneath her body. "Are you serious? But what about all the hard work you've put into your pen name? All those incredible books—the awards and recognition."

Jasper shrugged. "None of that matters. Behind the scenes, I'll still keep all my royalties from the books so I can sustain myself. I started writing as a way to stay sane when I was alone for all those years—day in and day out in this big, silent house. It was an escape for me, and I enjoy researching and learning about places and things. Of course, I needed the money, too. I wanted to help take some of the financial burden off of my dad. None of that other stuff matters."

Nodding, Violet sighed. "That makes sense, but... René is fine with pretending to be a brilliant writer? He's going to keep up the lie?"

"Not exactly. When I've got a new series ready, he'll reveal me as his ghost writer. His popularity might take a small hit for that, but we've both calculated that the revelation will blow over after some time—especially since René is genuinely talented in his own ways. He has a unique... *something* about him. I think he'll be fine."

"I agree with that. He definitely does. Are you working on a new series now? Can I read it?"

"I'm not." Jasper chuckled. "Nothing serious, anyway. I have a project outlined and some ideas... Someone important once told me that I should try adding more romance elements, but I'm not ready. I have a lot on my mind and there's still so much I don't know."

She smiled. "Anything you want to talk about?"

He huffed out a breath. "Yeah. Can… Can we talk about sex?"

"Yes."

Jasper unfolded one arm and rubbed his palm against his forehead. "You answered me too quickly."

Violet laughed. "You told me before that you don't want to have sex."

"It's not that I don't *want* to. It's more so… I can't. Or, I shouldn't. I have to be the last person with this curse, Violet. I don't want there to be any chance of my bringing another person into this world and they have to deal with this for another generation. Does that make sense? I would never forgive myself for burdening someone that way. Can you imagine?" He turned, sincerity in his eyes.

"I understand. But Jasper, people can have sex in all different kinds of ways. It doesn't *have* to be someone sticking something inside someone else. And even if that's the case, there are contraceptives."

"But those aren't a guarantee."

"You're right. And so, there are other things we could do."

"Like what?"

"Well…" Violet shifted, crawling across the couch to meet him. His giant eyes grew even wider when she pressed her fingertips to his chest and urged him to lie on his back. He hesitated, but slowly fell backward. She climbed up and straddled his hips, then leaned over him with one hand resting beside his head. "We explore. We take some time and focus on each other, discovering what feels good—how we can give and share in each other's pleasure."

Violet moved her free hand underneath the hem of Jasper's sweater. When she reached his warm flesh, she slid her palm up his naked belly. He sucked in a breath, his stomach clenching beneath her fingertips.

She grinned. "For instance, I already know that your tummy is very sensitive, and you already know that I like it when you kiss my neck. So we do those things to each other, but we also go further, little by little, and learn more." She slid her fingers down the center of his stomach and he writhed underneath her, gasping and closing his eyes. Violet settled harder against him, gloriously feeling his body respond to her for the first time. Without question.

She shifted her hips, reveling in the undeniable firmness of him as she leaned down closer to his rosy face and parted lips. Violet kept her hand on his belly between them, slowly dragging it up and down. "And we communicate," she whispered. "We don't need to pretend like we're experts who know everything there is to know about sex. We talk to each other. Does this feel good to you?" She slid her knuckles below his navel, teasing him at the waist of his slacks.

He opened his eyes, breathing labored. "Mm—yes, but... Are-Are you enjoying this?"

"I am."

"Vi, I'm sorry if I'm not thinking about you enough... I feel like I never stop thinking about you—like I've been thinking about you since the day I met you."

She leaned down, catching his open mouth and stealing a delectable kiss. He breathed a quiet little moan when her tongue met his. She smiled when she pulled away. "That's not what I meant. What I want, is for you to internalize that you are attractive. You are sexy and you excite me. When you touch and kiss me, it makes me want you even more than I already do."

He closed his eyes again, grinning. "That... sounds so bizarre to me—"

"Do you think *I'm* bizarre?"

His eyes flashed open. "No. I would never. I just—I don't see myself that way... As someone capable of making another person feel that way. What am I even doing?"

Violet pulled her hand from between their bodies, flattening herself against his chest, warm and tight. "You're being you and it's enough. Like it's always been. Always will be. I want you naked and in bed, Jasper. Can we do that? Will you play with me?"

He surprised Violet when he lifted his head and pressed a soft kiss to her lips. "Yes," he said. "I want to. I will, but... I have a question."

"Yes?"

"Do you want children? Is that important to you?"

Violet shrugged. "Meh. I was not one of those little girls that grew up fantasizing about having babies someday. That topic is a non-issue, my sweet friend."

Jasper frowned as if something distasteful hit his palate. "Another question. If I'm going to be naked and in bed with you, can I be more than your friend?"

Violet bit her lip, grinning. "Mmhm. What do you want to be?"

He relaxed underneath her, shifting his eyes to the side. "I want... to be the only one. If I can, I want to help and give you whatever you need."

"I won't depend on you for everything, Jas. That's not who I am, and I don't think it's healthy at all."

"I know. But... I want to always be there, and for us to walk through life together—trying things, like you said. And I want to support you the way you've helped me."

She leaned down, her heart warm as she kissed his nose, then his cheek. "Jasper Oliver Laurent, are you telling me that I need to put a ring on your finger before I'm allowed to devour your naked body?"

He snorted in a laugh. "*No*, but, good God... You keep moving your hips against me and I can't focus—"

"You want to be my partner." Violet lifted, facing him and keeping her hips still.

"Yes." He swallowed, his throat bobbing. "And I don't want you to joke anymore about your future husband letting me sleep on your pillow."

Violet giggled, snuggling down to kiss his jawline. "Aw, I think that's funny—"

"It's not. I love most of your jokes, but not that one. And please don't bring up René or Freddie kissing me anymore, either. That's also not funny. I'm not angry with them, but I don't like that they thought it was okay to just do that to me. That I didn't have a say—and I've never had *any* kind of intimate relationship with either of them. I ended up talking to my therapist about those situations because I couldn't figure out if I had done something to encourage them."

Sensing the shift in his mood, Violet crawled back and off of him, sitting up on her knees. He pushed up as well, then reached and grabbed one of her hands.

"We've been casual in spending time together these past several months, just going with the flow... But I have been scared to death, Violet. I've been in love with you since I was six years old. You being back in my life has been an emotional rollercoaster—wonderful and terrifying, incredible but stressful to the point where some days I thought I would throw up or have a heart attack. I *really* want you. You have no idea how much I've always wanted you and thought about you. And I don't want to just play together naked, or have lunch sometimes or drink tea occasionally. I want everything."

He took a breath, running his free hand into his hair before looking up at her once more. "You... You accept me, like this. The way I am... Right?"

"Of course."

"So, I want us to make it clear. That we're together—not just best friends, but more. Partners. Without making jokes or just haphazardly wandering along. We're choosing each other, on purpose. I... I need to know that."

Violet swallowed, her shoulders stiff. She dropped them and took a breath. "I want you too, Jasper. On purpose. I choose you."

"Okay... I love you, Violet."

"I love you, too."

He lifted his hands to cup her face, then pulled her into a kiss—urging her to open and fall into his rhythm and intent. Slow and deep. It was as if he longed to seal the words and assurances spoken between them. When he finally pulled away, Violet's heart was so warm and full, it felt as if it might burst.

Jasper grinned. "If... you still want me naked in bed, I'm ready now."

"Can I make a joke?"

"Yes..."

Violet chuckled. "It genuinely feels like I had to pseudo marry you before I could have you."

"It's not like that." He stood from the couch, pulling her up and gripping her hand as he walked toward the doors of the study. "I just need to know that I can *breathe*. Spending all this time with you... It's something I've always wanted, but I keep waiting for the bottom to drop out from underneath me again and I can't... I've been trying to act calm, but I need to know that I'm finally standing on solid ground."

"You don't ever need to act. We're solid... I might joke a lot, but I've always been serious about you, sexy fox-man."

Jasper laughed, pulling her up the stairs. "I am *not* a fox."

"I bet you were in a past life. Foxy, long-legged—"

"Vi, enough."

"Nope. I'm going to keep saying it until you *get* it. Until it sinks in."

He stopped on the stairs and turned to face her. Dead serious. "I get it. I believe you."

They stood looking at each other in silence until Violet moved swiftly and poked him in the stomach, making him laugh and double over.

"Liar." She walked up ahead, pulling him forward. "That's alright, because about fifteen minutes from now, you're going to be so out of your mind, you won't be able to say a word."

42

AND LATER STILL

*T*he wind whipped Violet's raincoat and deep maroon dress as she dashed from her car, through the parking lot and toward the large glass doors of the Libellule Heritage Art Museum. Rain pelted her upside her face. Rude. She squealed as she ran past a stunning bloom of bright tulips all along the front—like happy sunbursts of deep pink, yellow and red despite the gray gloom of April showers.

Inside, she caught her breath and briefly took in the lovely space. This museum was small, but unlike the local library, it had been remodeled and updated with a creamy marble floor, glass walls separating each gallery and a bright, hand-blown glass sculpture hanging from the ceiling. It was stunning—like a burst of color and chaos. Loops and swirls interwoven and reflecting against the skylights.

She stepped up to the woman behind the front desk, gave her name, and was escorted down a narrow hallway and into a cozy conference room.

"Would you like some water? Tea?" the redhead asked, smiling.

"Earl Grey would be wonderful," Violet said, setting her bags down in a chair at the large table. Everything was so modern and bright. Even the outer wall of the conference room was glass: showcasing a small garden atrium full of green, leafy plants and a stone fountain, all covered in fresh rainwater from the day's weather.

"Of course," the woman said. "I'll be right back. I must tell you, the director is very excited about you. She saw your paintings hanging in Le Petit Sweet and was awestruck. We can't believe you're local. Where have you been hiding?"

Violet laughed, flattered but awkward. She still wasn't used to these compliments—people fussing over her work. "I don't know... within myself, maybe?" She shrugged. It was the truth.

"Well, we're so glad you're here. She'll be with you in a few moments and I'll be right back with the tea."

Once the woman was gone, Violet pulled her tablet from her bag, set it on the table and then fluffed out her hair before sitting down. She was nervous and excited and had no idea what to expect. How was she here? In this stunning museum, having a meeting with the director about an art exhibition. For *her* art. It was baffling.

In the end, Jasper had helped her put together a clean-looking website full of her artwork. There were multiple sections with clickable links in the menu: watercolor on canvas, acrylic, gouache and charcoal. Landscapes, still-life and portraits. He'd set up a website for himself at the very start of his book business, but Violet was completely useless in this area. Between the two of them, they'd made a stunning online portfolio that helped showcase Violet's work, with the option to expand upon it later when needed.

She took a deep breath and exhaled, staring at the rain falling within the green atrium in front of her. Five months ago, she'd felt bewildered. Hating her job, distraught at the loss of Gloria and painfully, perpetually confused over the disappearance of her childhood friend. Even though the gaping hole in her chest was still there (she didn't think it would ever go away), she felt a strange peace within it and around it. A loving warmth, even.

Somehow, miraculously, she was living the life she wanted. And wasn't that what her gram had told her to do? Something in that comforted Violet, knowing that Gloria would be proud of her—that she'd approve of all of this and was maybe even cheering her on from somewhere Violet couldn't see, but could definitely feel.

She was doing it now: charging forward and living her own colorful life.

Violet stood when a woman in a fashionable and creamy taupe dress sauntered into the conference room, wrangling two cups of tea as she entered. Violet hurried around the table to meet her, helping by taking one off her hands. They smiled and exchanged warm greetings, then sat with their tea. Even though they had been strangers before this meeting, within a few moments, they were talking and laughing as if they were very old friends.

LATER THAT AFTERNOON, when Violet unlocked the door to the cottage, a wash of warm, savory air greeted her. She beamed, closing the door and shimmying out of her black-and-white chevron rain jacket. "Jas?"

"Kitchen!"

She moved quickly, feeling as if her feet had sprouted wings and she had ascended from walking to floating. In the kitchen, Jasper was busy at the counter, but he turned when she entered, smiling brightly. "How did it go?"

She walked past the table to meet him, her heart thumping in her chest at the warmth and smells and his presence. He'd gotten his hair cut again and he looked neat and clean in a patterned gray sweater. "I didn't know you'd be here," she said.

"That's the key element of a surprise." He leaned down as she stepped into him, clenching his sweater in her fists and lifting to her toes to reach his mouth.

"You cooked for me..." she whispered against his lips. "You know my favorite thing is walking into a house and smelling food already cooked."

"I know. You look beautiful."

She batted her eyes. "Thank you."

He pressed into her—a good, firm kiss—before raising his head. "Tell me how it went at the gallery. What did the director say?"

Violet stepped back and leaned against the counter, placing her palms atop the surface and lifting her chin. "*I* have an art exhibition scheduled for August."

"That's incredible. I *knew* it." He threaded his arms tightly around her waist. She hugged his shoulders, squeezing him and loving him for being here at this moment. To help her celebrate this unbelievable opportunity.

Jasper rested his forehead against hers and she smiled at the clean earthy scent of him. Like rain and sandalwood. "Five months ago, you didn't even know what you wanted to do. Look at you now, Vi. You're an artist."

She rubbed her nose against him, scrunching her face. "I'm an artist."

"Will you create new pieces for the exhibition? Or use the ones you already have? You're going to need to hire an assistant to manage your online sales—officially."

"Bah. I don't want to think about that right now..." She grabbed his wrist at her waist and guided it down slowly along the curve of her hip, brushing the silky material of her dress. "I'm on this high and what I really want is for the foxy man standing in my kitchen to use his long, beautiful, writer-chef fingers to do something dirty to me…" Violet guided his hand even lower until he grazed the skin of her naked thigh.

Jasper huffed in a quiet laugh, his cheeks shifting to the familiar rosy color. "I… Well, now's not a good time, Vi."

Violet pouted, lacing their fingers together at her side. Sex with Jasper… Turns out, it wasn't like sex at all. It felt like something more—an adventure. An exploration. Like when they were young and the summer sun was high and streaming through the deep green of the forest canopy. Rays of light showered them as they ran against the warm breeze and through shadows, finding new bugs or butterflies, hidden alcoves or new pathways.

Except now, the escapades involved bare skin and long limbs: fingertips and lips sliding against delicate curves and bumps, deep breaths and soft, thoughtful touches. Hands clasped, eyes locked as their bodies stretched, pressed and entwined together. And talking—honestly, comfortably, like always.

It was really something, sex with Jasper. Not like any sex Violet had ever known. Graceful and cautious. Superior.

She pressed into him a little, lifting her chin and holding his hand tighter. "Feels like a good time to me…"

"I—I was thinking about something and I wanted to tell you."

"Yes?"

He exhaled, leaning into her and resting his chin atop her head. "When I was in the attic, I thought about you all the time. Especially in the early days. You being my friend… Those memories of us playing together in the poppy field or the forest, they were all I had to hold on to. The only happy things in my life that remained unmarred. I don't know if I could have survived the agony without that. Thinking about you and maybe seeing you again someday… It helped me to push through."

Violet lifted her arms, wrapping them around his waist to pull him even closer. It hurt to know he was suffering as he was. She'd known something was wrong, but she'd had no idea. She couldn't have imagined the truth of his circumstance.

He dipped his head and kissed between her eyebrows. "We were apart, but you helped me survive, Violet. You made me want to live."

Violet leaned her forehead into the soft fabric at his chest, feeling it rise and fall in a deep breath.

"For me," he said, "these things—being with you, touching you and cooking for you—I imagined it. I fantasized about it over and over, but I never thought I would actually get here. It doesn't seem real to me. My mother taught me that it was impossible for someone to love me like this... That I was repulsive. And I agreed with her. I thought she was right."

"Do you still feel that way?" Violet asked, sniffling with her ear pressed against his chest. Holding him tight.

"No. Now I understand that her reaction to me was harmful. Growing up, I only thought about how terrible I made her feel. I had ruined my mom's life. It was all my fault... I never once considered that the way she treated *me* was wrong."

The doorbell rang and Violet lifted her head from his chest. "Are we having company?" She looked up at him, and Jasper bent and kissed her mouth. He smiled.

"Surprise. Can you go answer it and I'll get everything finished?"

Nodding and wiping her eyes with her fingers, Violet walked out of the kitchen. She sighed, thinking the minute their company was gone, she'd drag him to the bedroom and make sure he understood just how real their relationship was, and how deeply loved he could be.

When Violet swung the front door open, she was delighted to see Simone and René standing on the other side, their hands clasped as they frantically whispered.

"Why, hello, beautiful people." Violet grinned. Simone let go of René's hand and stepped into her for a warm hug.

"Congratulations, gorgeous—I'm so proud of you."

Violet embraced her, confused. "Um, how did you know I got the exhibit? I *just* told Jasper. Nobody else."

"Perhaps you would not have greeted us with such... exuberance?" René grinned, stepping through the doorframe and removing his hand from behind his back to reveal a giant bouquet of white lilies.

When Simone released her from the hug, Violet accepted the glorious offering. "Oh gosh, these are beautiful."

René smiled. "Lilies are a classic symbol of new beginnings and happiness."

"What would you have done if I hadn't gotten the exhibition?"

René frowned. "Lilies are a classic symbol of peace and awakening after a storm in life."

Simone giggled, resting her hand against her chest. "I asked him the same question and he did that to me—I must have laughed for fifteen minutes straight."

"Yeah, you two are real cute." Violet stepped aside. "Come in, come in. I don't know what Jasper made, but it smells like heaven. Have things calmed down at the bakery at all? Since that magazine article published last week, there've been so many new people from the city showing up to—"

Violet was about to close the door, but a familiar red truck pulled up and parked on the opposite side of the street. Despite herself, she groaned. "Who the heck invited Freddie?"

"Me," Simone chirped from behind. "He asked me if you got the exhibit when he came in for his regular coffee the other day and I told him about this surprise gathering to celebrate."

Turning, Violet stared at her friend, her mouth agape and no words. Simone frowned. "Violet, he just seems lonely, alright? He was so happy to be included. Will you cut him a break?"

Violet shook her head. "No." When she turned back to the door, Freddie was bounding up the walkway in his usual brown leather jacket, but he was carrying a bright bouquet of sunflowers in his hand. When he reached the porch, he grinned.

"Congratulations?" He held the flowers out, one dark golden eyebrow quirked up in hesitation.

Exhaling a breath, Violet stepped aside. "Yes, thank you. Please come in."

"I don't know anything about art, really." He walked inside, happy as a clam. "But I'm excited to see what you do. It sounds really fancy."

Before she could force another polite response, a large, unfamiliar van pulled up just outside the house. Whoever was inside beeped the horn multiple times. Violet set both bouquets on the entryway table and stepped outside. Simone, René and Freddie followed her and soon, Jasper was there, too.

The door to the driver side opened. When her sister hopped out of the vehicle, Violet's jaw dropped. She walked down the path and past the thick hedge of purple hydrangeas lining the front area of the cottage. Thankfully, the rain was only misty now, the sun fighting and peeking its way through the cloud cover overhead. "Rosie? What on earth?"

Her sister walked up the path and wrapped Violet up in a tight hug. "Hi sweetie. Congratulations on the exhibit. Jasper texted me."

"Thank you—what is this van?"

"I brought you something. My lying, manipulative, imposter of an ex-girlfriend finally fessed up to some things." She leaned past Violet, looking at everyone on the porch. "Hey, people, can you help?" Rose turned and walked back down the path toward the van. Violet followed.

When they were all gathered at the back, Rose pulled the double doors open in a grand gesture. "Ta-da! It's Gram's chest.

Ginger's grimoire and most of the other creepy witchy things that were inside are missing, but the police are still tracking."

"Wicca isn't 'creepy,'" Simone said, lips pursed. "It's just misunderstood." Rose looked at her, scanning her from head to toe and then looking away, not saying a word.

Violet leaned into the van, running her fingers across the familiar surface, quietly taking in all the details she'd painted when she was so small. She felt disappointed about the absence her great-grandmother's journal, but on the whole, her heart swelled, like she'd never seen anything more beautiful.

Rosie hopped into the van, oddly chipper for someone who'd recently had their heart broken. "Between the six of us, we can get this on the back porch, you think?"

Jasper sighed, folding his arms. "We can hire people for things like this?"

Rose slapped the top of the box with her hand. "Nah, we can handle it. We got this."

"Yeah," Freddie nodded. "I think we can do this."

Everyone else groaned, but Simone walked back toward the house. "I'll be the door holder."

43

NOW

They'd handled it, somehow, working together to get the large chest to the back of the cottage and onto the sun porch (and without any injuries on Violet's behalf).

Throughout dinner, they'd all talked and laughed comfortably, excited about all the new business the town was getting because of Simone's big magazine article. Quietly, though, Violet noticed her sister losing steam and slowly retreating into herself.

Freddie left first, needing to get back to the store to check on things. Shortly after, Violet walked René and Simone to the door as well. Halfway there, though, Simone turned and stomped back toward the kitchen.

"Oh shoot, I left my shawl on my chair."

Violet smiled as her friend turned and sauntered back down the hall.

"Jasper seems to be very well these days," René said coolly as they continued walking toward the foyer.

Violet looked up at him. "You told me that you know what's wrong with Jasper."

"I did."

"I know now, too."

"An excellent development."

He stared at her with his infinite brown eyes, his expression suddenly like a gentle mask: pleasant but unreadable. She narrowed her eyes. "How do you know, René? If Jasper didn't tell you, how *can* you know?"

Neither of them moved as Violet waited. The moment felt frozen, weighted, before he finally spoke—his smooth voice without its usual playfulness and inflection.

"Knowing comes with age, Violet Ainsworth. And I know many things."

"Alright, I'm ready now." Simone strolled into the foyer, her bright yellow shawl neatly wrapped around her shoulders.

Violet blinked, pushing through her confusion at René's very odd statement and seeing her guests off with warm goodbyes. *Such a strange man...* When she walked back into the sitting room, only Jasper was standing there. She tilted her head. "Where's Rosie?"

"Well, she was pretty intoxicated after we ate, so she went back to your bedroom to lay down—but not before telling me she's really happy that you and I are finally together, and also that I remind her of a rabbit?"

"Oh geez, this day has just been wild." Violet met him in the center of the room. "Well, looks like you can't shift here tonight like we planned. Sister duty calls."

"That's fine, but... look at the clock, Violet."

She blinked, then did as told. "Seven eighteen." Violet paused, her eyes wide. "Oh my God—I totally lost track of time. Jas, are you okay? What's happening?"

"I don't know."

"You're... You haven't changed—is the curse broken?"

"No. I still feel the tremors, but... This happened yesterday, too. The process started an hour and a half late..."

"Wait—why are you just now telling me this?"

He ran his fingers up through his dark hair. "You were busy prepping for the museum meeting, and that was the first time something like that had ever happened to me. I didn't know if it was a fluke or not. All my life, the time of my changing has always shifted earlier and gotten longer. *Never* the opposite."

Violet reached up and grasped his wrists, pulling his hands from his hair and clasping them in her own. "How do you feel about this? How are we feeling?"

He took a shaky breath. "Honestly? I'm afraid. I don't know what this means, and I don't want to get my hopes up."

She squeezed his palms. "I think this is good? Obviously, I don't know for sure. But Jas, you've changed *so much* in the past six months. Back in October, everything about you was focused and centered around your mouse life. You catered to that part of yourself, exclusively. But now you're focusing on being human. It *has* to be a good sign."

Sighing, he lifted a hand and rubbed his forehead. "I hope so... Or, maybe you have some powers and they're slowly breaking the curse down?"

She shook her head. "No, it's not me. It's you and your choices. I was hoping it would be me, and I could kiss you and break it like in the movies. But I've kissed you countless times and across every inch of you at this point, but still, nothing."

"I wouldn't say nothing." Jasper grinned. "Those kisses are unquestionably *something*."

They laughed. Jasper closed his eyes and sighed. When he opened them, his eyeballs were blacked out.

"You have mouse eyes."

"I'm leaving."

"Take Gram's car."

"I haven't officially gotten my license in the mail yet."

"True, but you know how to drive and I'll be worried that you got stuck halfway in the woods. Please?"

He nodded. "Alright. Keys?"

"By the front door on the little mirror hanger thing. Call me when you get home." She wrapped her hands behind his neck, urging him down and into a healthy kiss. A few weeks earlier, Jasper had been anxious about Violet touching him when he was close to transitioning—pulling away or startled when she reached for him. Already, he was more open. Constantly changing and growing.

Violet had meant for it to be a quick peck, but the kiss carried on. Intensifying with a silent need building and bubbling between their hearts and bodies. Jasper lifted, but Violet kept him close, brushing her forehead and nose with his.

He whispered. "I need to go."

"I know, I know. But I think Rosie will probably want to stay the weekend. I'll come over Monday?"

"That's fine. I'll be home."

"I'll spend the day with you. And sleepover?"

"Also fine."

"And... you can do things to me with your fingers since we didn't have time earlier—"

"Goodnight, Vi." He laughed and pressed another swift kiss to her mouth before easing himself from her grip. She stood, huffing out a sigh.

"Goodnight, foxy."

Just before leaving the sitting room, he turned, throwing a little smirk over his shoulder that probably wasn't intended to read as devilish and charming, but definitely was. That was one of Violet's favorite things about him—that in some moments, he'd surprise her and unintentionally ooze roguish sex appeal. This delicious side of him seemed to grow as he became more confident in their established situation.

It was perfect. And it was driving her crazy.

She rolled her shoulders and shook her head to clear it. First, cold shower. Second, cuddling with her sad big sister.

To Violet's surprise, Rosie got up early the next morning (in her grumpy and hungover but sobered state) and drove back to the city. She'd only rented the van for one day and had no interest in paying extra fees to keep it the whole weekend.

Violet dressed, packed up her sketch pad and pencils, then decided to walk the forest path to Laurent House. The rain and heavy clouds from the previous day had cleared, leaving everything along the wood-chip trail glimmering and fresh with dew drops. She looked up as she walked, smiling into the sunlight peeking through the trees. Birds sang and bees zipped all around, everything moving and breathing in a joyful spring chorus of new life and freedom.

When she reached Laurent House, the soft shade of the yellow stucco made Violet grin. The color radiated in the warm light with vivid green ivy leaves trickling and weaving down the beautiful new paint job. The gate squeaked loudly as she entered, then pushed it shut. She walked up the path, pulling her key from her dress pocket.

When she was on the porch, the wild growth of daisies shuddered at her side. She paused, hesitating. But a moment later, the black cat with white paws bounded out onto the patchy grass, chasing a butterfly and narrowly missing its capture. Violet shook her head, but the cat sauntered over, rubbing his fuzzy body against her shins as she unlocked the front door.

"Good morning. I'll put something out for you later." The cat meowed in response, then hopped off the porch as Violet pushed the door open.

Inside, the house was silent. Everything was cool and calm as usual—the old, faded, ornate burgundy rug. The dark coatrack in the corner and the happy family portraits on the wall. She closed the door softly behind her, noting the morning sunlight flooding in from the windows of the study and living room on either side of her, the curtains drawn back wide. Welcoming.

"It's me," she said, walking past the study and up the narrow flight of stairs leading to the second floor. The hardwood squeaked and moaned loudly as she climbed. If Jasper had been asleep, surely he was awake by now.

Violet reached his bedroom at the top of the stairs and pushed the door open. More bright sunlight flooded the sparse room. Her first instinct was to look at the floor, but she didn't need to, because Jasper was lying in bed on his back, half-tangled in his stark-white bedsheets. When she walked forward, he rolled, shifting onto his side and watching her approach. His hair was a mess and his eyelids heavy. "Hey."

"Good morning." Violet set her bag down on his bedside table before sitting on the edge of the mattress.

"What happened to Rosie?" he asked, then took a deep breath, his naked chest rising and falling, the length of his side and hip exposed as he rested comfortably.

"She needed to return the van. Can we talk about the fact that you're not a mouse right now?" Violet lifted her wrist to check her watch: 7:01 a.m. "How long have you been like this?"

He tumbled onto his back, the bunched sheets just barely covering him as he drew one knee up, rubbing his palms against his face and up into his hair. "I changed back an hour ago. And I didn't fully transition yesterday evening until eight fifteen. That's ten hours total. *Not* twelve like usual."

Violet swallowed hard as she brought her hand to her chest. "Jas…"

He dropped his hands and took another deep breath as he stared up at the ceiling. "I don't know, Vi. It's weird."

"It's *good*," she said, reaching and entwining their fingers at his side. "It's wonderful."

He turned his head against the pillow, meeting her gaze and

bringing their hands up to rest against his abdomen. "Do you want breakfast?"

Violet shook her head. "You don't have to. I'll just make myself some tea. Do you want a smoothie?"

He grinned. "Yes, please."

"I was thinking... Maybe I'll try making Gram's cannelés later today. She left me the recipe, but I don't want to eat them alone."

"You won't. I'll make sure I have room for those." Closing his eyes, he breathed out in a heavy sigh. The time had been shorter, but mornings were always hard on Jasper. Shifting back into a human left him disoriented for a little while and he needed time to get his bearings.

While she sat, he absently rubbed his thumb against the back of her hand with his eyes still closed. The light streaming in gave his bare skin a healthy glow, and the house around them was so still that Violet could hear the birds singing outside. She glanced out the window at the pristine blue sky.

"I'm glad you got Gloria's chest back," Jasper said, his slate-colored eyes a little more alert. "I had no idea Rosie was going to surprise you like that."

"Yeah," Violet said, squeezing his hand. "That chest is like a piece of Gram, you know? I feel so relieved having it back in the house. When it was stolen, I felt like I let her down."

Jasper shook his head against the pillow. "Gloria would never think that. She bragged about you all the time."

"Really?"

He smiled, still stroking the top of her hand with his thumb as their clasped palms rested atop his belly. "Mmhm. Always. And look at you now. She'd be beside herself."

The vacant space in Violet's chest warmed. Lately, it did this. It was still very present, of course. But perhaps, just a little lighter. A little less raw, knowing she was now embodying

Gloria's ethos on life. That she had sincerely listened to and applied her gram's advice.

About everything.

Violet squeezed his hand tighter—the warmth of his bare skin sending tingles up her arm. "I took a good look at the chest last night. It needs quite a bit of retouching because it's pretty scratched up."

He frowned. "That's not good."

"I don't mind." Violet grinned. "I'll just re-paint it—give the poppies a new coat of red, and maybe add a small-scale version of the slate bridge?"

His expression softened as he returned her smile. "Sounds perfect."

She was also thinking of adding a little gray mouse with starburst whiskers somewhere within the scenery, but she kept that bit to herself.

~

The End

ALSO BY KARLA NIKOLE

Lore & Lust: A Queer Vampire Romance

Lore & Lust Book Two: The Vanishing

Lore & Lust Book Three: The Awakening (Coming October 1st)

~

ACKNOWLEDGMENTS

It takes a small village of lovely and professional people to put a book together, so I'd like to give my special thanks to Lily Uivel for creating this beautiful cover; Nia Quinn and Jericho Tadeo for their editing prowess; Lindsay Taylor for being the best beta reader there ever was; Maia, Megan, Madeline, Juli, Heather and Towanna for all your incredible love, support and friendship; and last but certainly not least, Roy and Ann for always supporting me in my goals and dreams (I love and appreciate you more than I can even say).

Love, Magic and Misfortune is close to my heart and is filled with very personal experiences (although I do not know any boys who shape shift into mice or any other animals... I wish I did). Living in the fullness of who we are meant to be and having the freedom, time and opportunity to explore ourselves should be, in my opinion, a given. An obvious fundamental allowance as human beings. But there are so many elements (financial burdens, the pressure of societal expectations and gender roles, family obligations, trauma and on and on) that hinder us.

Like the characters in Love, Magic and Misfortune, my hope is that more people would have the opportunity to explore and learn their true selves. To find the art, talent and love within themselves, and then share it with the rest of the world, because we desperately need it.

ABOUT THE AUTHOR

Karla Nikole is a writer and explorer. She loves cultures, travel, food, music and discovering all the incredible things this world has to offer. She has lived in Japan, South Korea and Prague. Karla has also traveled to other European countries and dreams of one day settling in Italy where she can write and publish all the quirky romance stories in her heart.

instagram.com/karlanikolepublishing

CPSIA information can be obtained
at www.ICGtesting.com
Printed in the USA
FSHW010109111021
85375FS